World Enough (And Time)

By Edmund Jorgensen

Speculation

Other Copenhagens (And Other Stories)

World Enough (And Time)

by Edmund Jorgensen

Inkwell & Often

Inkwell & Often

Cover art by Jeff Ward (stungeonstudios.com)
Cover design by Moira Racich (moiraracich.com)

ISBN: 0-9847492-3-3
ISBN 13: 978-0-9847492-3-2

For my dad

Contents

1

A State of Imminent Default

Friday (9 days until arrival)

"**F**ERRETS?" said Jeremiah Brown. "I don't remember Uncle Leo particularly *liking* ferrets."

"People change in 20 years, Mr. Brown," said Mr. Grubel.

"Uncle Leo hardly changed his socks. Besides, can you even maltreat a ferret?"

Mr. Grubel pushed his lensless silver glasses further up the bridge of his nose. His hypermodern silver suit shimmered as he squared his shoulders.

"You can maltreat anything," he said.

"I'm just saying, it sounds larky."

"There is nothing larky about your situation, Mr. Brown. Your uncle has altered his will, leaving the entirety of his estate to a home for maltreated ferrets. You are no longer in a position to honor the financial arrangements you made to purchase passage on this ship—a passage you have nearly completed. You are in a state of imminent default."

"Look," said Jeremiah, "I have no intention of defaulting, imminently or otherwise. The instant we get back, I'll go see Uncle Leo and straighten things out."

"That might prove difficult."

"Uncle Leo loves me like the son he never had—or particularly wanted. But he's always made sure I'm provided for, and the minute he sees my face the ferrets will be out of the picture."

"Your Uncle Leopold has been dead for the better part of two years Earth time."

Jeremiah blanched.

"Don't play the naive, shocked nephew, Mr. Brown. Wasn't that the point of your booking a relativistic cruise in the first place? To accelerate your inheritance?"

"Yes, it's just—poor old Uncle Leo. His ticker finally gave out?"

"Mr. Brown."

"He wasn't a bad man," said Jeremiah. "He was even a good man, in his way. He looked after me the best he knew how, when no one else would do it. Did he go peacefully, at least?"

"Mr. Brown! You can mourn your uncle on your own time. Right now you would do well to focus on the situation at hand. You are in a state of *imminent default.*"

"Would you stop saying those words? As soon as we dock I'll talk to Appleton, and he'll get you your credit."

"Appleton?" said Mr. Grubel, with sudden interest. "Who is Appleton? Another relative of means I somehow missed?" He began tapping at the surface of his desk, where a recessed screen was angled away from Jeremiah's line of sight.

"Appleton is my lawyer."

"Ah, your *lawyer.*" Grubel's interest faded. He continued tapping away at the screen, but with the depressive air of due diligence.

" 'Lawyer' only scratches the surface," said Jeremiah, hoping to recapture some of Mr. Grubel's enthusiasm, which seemed key to forestalling any more of this *imminent default* talk. "Lawyer, advisor, agent, general role model and day-saver. The Jeeves to my Bertie. Well, if Jeeves were an ex-special-forces Samoan with an ivy league law degree and arms like 100-year-old tree trunks. Oh, and gay as the day is long."

"I'm sorry?" said Mr. Grubel, looking up.

"What?"

"What did you say about long days?"

"As gay as the day is long?"

"Mr. Brown, your sexual preferences have no bearing here."

"No, I'm saying that my *lawyer,* Appleton—"

"Threatening me with some frivolous discrimination suit will get you nowhere. This matter concerns a contract, pure and simple—a contract in which you agree to compensate Golden Worldlines for the passage you have enjoyed for the last two years. A contract which spells out consequences for your imminent default."

"I'm just saying I'll wave my lawyer to ask about contesting the will, and maybe we can postpone all this talk about 'imminent default' for 24 hours or so."

"By all means, you should wave him immediately—the Quantum Caterpillar field is weak enough now that waves can be sent and received. But you won't have a reply within 24 hours."

"Even with the time dilation?"

"We are at roughly five percent of the speed of light and slowing rapidly, Mr. Brown. The time dilation is negligible. Have you received a copy of the pamphlet?"

Before Jeremiah could respond, Mr. Grubel took a pamphlet from a drawer and set it on his desk in front of Jeremiah. It was perhaps the 100th copy of "Golden Worldlines, Special Relativity, and You" that Jeremiah had seen over the last two years. Every member of the staff carried a few copies at all times, and they had been trained—and trained well—to whip one out the moment a passenger betrayed the slightest doubt about the subtleties of relativistic travel. Jeremiah had not opened one of these pamphlets once in two years, and even in such dire straits as he found himself he did not intend to start now.

"I guess I'd better get moving and wave Appleton as soon as possible," said Jeremiah. It did not seem strictly necessary to clarify that by *as soon as possible* Jeremiah meant *immediately after breakfast,* which he had been on his way to enjoy when Grubel called him over the PA to the Financial Office. "If there's nothing else?"

"It says in your file that you earned a living by playing the banjo?"

"Not always a full, complete, entire living. Uncle Leo did subsidize my musical career a bit here and there."

Mr. Grubel established eye contact.

"Well, pretty substantially at times," Jeremiah added after a few seconds.

Mr. Grubel maintained eye contact.

"Look," said Jeremiah, "basically he paid for everything, all right? Is that what you want to hear? Food, housing, clothes. Everything."

Mr. Grubel looked down and resumed typing.

"What about your education?" he asked.

"He paid for that too."

"I don't care who paid for it. Your file lists your degree as 'demomusicology.' Is that something related to medicine? The medical staff is always underwater, particularly this late in the cruise."

"Not exactly," said Jeremiah. "It's the study of folk music. My dissertation was entitled *Through the Hobo Jungle: Freighthopping as Self-...*"

"Computer skills?"

"*...Discovery.*' No, computers and I don't really get along. But Mr. Grubel, why are we wasting time with my personal history when I could be waving Appleton right now?"

Mr. Grubel stopped tapping at the recessed screen and looked up again.

"In other words, Mr. Brown, you have no relevant experience or training whatsoever."

"Well, that's a matter of opinion, isn't it? I mean— relevant to *what* is really the question."

"To the day-to-day operations of the Einstein IV."

"Ah," said Jeremiah. "Then—no."

"I'm assigning you to the Department of Guest Services, Event Planning, and General Clerical. You'll report to Alfred Reynolds."

Grubel picked up a microphone from behind his desk and switched it on.

"Reynolds to the Financial Office," he said. The words echoed in the hall outside.

"What do you mean 'report to' Alfred Reynolds?" said Jeremiah. "What exactly will I be reporting to him?"

"It's spelled out quite clearly in your contract, Mr. Brown."

Mr. Grubel gestured vaguely behind him, and in response glowing letters appeared on the wall there: a contract, with Jeremiah's electronic signature highlighted.

"Section 14.2.1.1, 'Remedies and Recourse for Imminent Default.' " The contract scrolled to the aforementioned section and stopped. "You're welcome to review it at your convenience, but I'll summarize: if you can't pay, you work."

"But that's crazy! It's not like doing dishes to work off a meal in a restaurant. We're talking tens of millions of credits. In my whole life I couldn't work that off!"

"Don't I know it, Mr. Brown. Unfortunately—"

Mr. Grubel reclined in his chair and waved the contract away.

"—and I cannot express to you how much this frosts my muffin—the terms of your contract only allow me to impress duties upon you for the remainder of your passage."

"Oh," said Jeremiah, "so that means—nine days?"

"*Ten* days, Mr. Brown, including the day we dock at the space elevator."

That would be a full week and three days longer than any other job Jeremiah had ever held, but given the gravity of the situation, he considered that he had gotten off rather lightly.

"And lest you think you've gotten off lightly," said Mr. Grubel, whose talents apparently extended to telepathy, "your contract provides for the passengers of this ship to review your performance at the cruise's end. If you do not score an average of at least 'Satisfied' on those reviews—or if you receive even a *single* score of 'Highly Dissatisfied'—then we'll be seeing each other again."

"In court?" Jeremiah had never thought he'd imbue those two words with such hope.

"No, Mr. Brown: here. Right back here on the Einstein IV, where you will be obligated to work additional 2/20 tours until you achieve reviews of sufficient quality."

"Oh," said Jeremiah, "so instead of ten days that would mean at least—"

"Two years. Two years ship time, that is, and 20 Earth time. And believe me, I will personally make sure those are the longest two years of your life."

"I believe you," Jeremiah said.

"I know you don't like me, Mr. Brown."

"Oh," said Jeremiah, "well—"

"No doubt you think I'm just a pencil pusher. But pencils don't push themselves. Someone needs to maintain order.

On this ship, I am that someone, and if you attempt to get around the rules—or me—you will fail, and you will regret it. Believe me, you *will* regret it. Reynolds," Mr. Grubel said, before Jeremiah could profess his continued belief, "there you are. I'm sure you know Jeremiah."

Jeremiah turned around. Standing in the doorway was a man, perhaps 65 years of age, with white hair and an impressive white mustache. Unlike Grubel's, his glasses had thick lenses, and he was wearing two pairs—one on his nose, and one propped upon his head. Only his turquoise blue sweater fought against the impression that he was responding not to Grubel's summons but to a casting call seeking the definitive Geppetto for the 24th Century. With a toss of his head, a wiggle of his nose, and impressively little involvement from his hands, Reynolds transposed the two pairs of glasses and studied Jeremiah through the second. Jeremiah had the impression he had seen the man here and there around the ship, but he could not place him. Evidently the feeling was mutual.

"I can't place him," said Reynolds. "Stowaway?"

"An imminent defaulter," said Grubel. "He'll be assisting you for the duration of the cruise. Jeremiah, you will take direction from Reynolds. That's all."

"Pleased to be working with you, Jeremiah," Reynolds said, extending his hand. He had long, beautiful fingers, like a watchmaker's, and a firm handshake. "The office opens at nine, so we'd best get a move on." In preparation for which travel he did the trick shot with his glasses again.

Jeremiah looked at Grubel, who had already started tapping away at other matters on his desk, and for a moment he considered not going quietly. He could protest that he wouldn't sit still for such treatment, and even stand up and move around a bit, to underscore the point about not sitting still. He could demand names of managers and their managers above them, and threaten to write a strongly worded wave to every name on that list. What would Grubel do then? After all, he wasn't going to wrangle Jeremiah to the ground.

No, Jeremiah realized in a flash—what Grubel would do then was call over to the Security Office and outsource the wrangling to The Specimen. Jeremiah had seen the look in The Specimen's eyes as he stood in the corner, providing nominal security at dances and other social events, and it was not the look of a man who enjoyed hearing all sides of a story or giving the little guy a fair shake or even a head start.

Jeremiah stood up to go with Reynolds.

"Jeremiah?" said Grubel, his eyes still down on his desk.

"Yes?"

"Don't forget your pamphlet." He pointed to it on the desk.

Jeremiah picked up the pamphlet.

"And Jeremiah? I *will* be watching you."

WORLD ENOUGH (AND TIME)

2

Now Serving Number

Still Friday (9 days until arrival)

"**N**OT much to the job, really," said Reynolds as he led Jeremiah back through the unfamiliar service corridors. They followed a more efficient path than the one Jeremiah had picked out by trial and error while looking for the Financial Office. "Follow the three rules and you'll be fine. Rule one: every guest takes a ticket. Rule two: start every interaction with 'Hello Mr. or Mrs. So-and-so, how may I help you today?' Never call the guests by their first names. Rule 3: end every interaction with 'Thank you for visiting the Guest Services Desk, have a Golden Worldlines day.' "

"That all seems pretty straightforward," said Jeremiah. A door hissed open and they were back in the passenger section of the ship, the bare metallic walls of the service corridor giving way to holo-portals on which played morning reels of misty forests and sunrises over white beaches.

"Extremely straightforward. Oh, and make sure you keep the dish of mints on the desk full. Some of the guests go crazy for those mints. There are whole bags of them in the cabinet."

"Mints in the cabinet, all right."

"That's about it," said Mr. Reynolds. "Here we are."

The door in front of them was, like the door to the Financial Office, one of the old-fashioned wooden doors that the designers of the Einstein IV had sprinkled throughout the ship to add a romantic, if inconsistent, 21st-century touch. Jeremiah must have walked by this door a hundred times in the last two years, coming from the library or heading to the pool room, and yet he had never registered the tasteful gilded letters above that spelled out "Guest Services and Event Planning (9–12 and 1–5, 7 days)"—presumably because in his days as a guest he had never itched to plan an event or felt the lack of any services beyond the plethora already being provided to him.

"I'll be back to look in on you at lunchtime," said Mr. Reynolds, handing Jeremiah the key.

"Aren't you coming in?"

"Oh, no. I have some important business to attend to."

"But I don't know what I'm doing," said Jeremiah.

"Event planning is the hard part. Now that the Valentine's Day Dance is over, and there are no more events to plan, it's just guest services. Manning the desk is a one-man job."

"But what if the one man doesn't know how to do it?"

"You remember the three rules, don't you?" Reynolds asked. "All guests take a?"

"Ticket?" said Jeremiah.

"Good! And you start each interaction with?"

"Hello Mr. or Mrs. or Ms. So-and-so, how may I help you today?"

"Very nice. And what kind of day do you wish them when you're done?"

"A good day?" said Jeremiah. "Great? Amazing? Larky?"

"A Golden…"

"Worldlines Day!" Jeremiah said, unaccountably pleased with himself.

"You're a natural. Follow the three rules and keep the mints stocked, and you'll do fine. Any last minute questions?" He tugged at one end of his mustache, as if grave and urgent responsibilities were pulling from the other end, and this counterbalance was necessary to forestall his departure.

"Just one," said Jeremiah. "What do I do between asking the guests how I can help them and telling them to have a Golden Worldlines day?"

"Oh, that's the easy part: follow the playbook. That's the three-ring binder in the top drawer of the desk. You look up the problem and you find the solution and you follow the steps that will be very clearly laid out for you. Nothing could be simpler. Ah, look—here's the day's first customer—a chance for you to dive right in. Good morning, Mr. Porter."

Damon Porter had arrived in his usual dress, meaning he could have been confused for James Bond headed to the senior prom. He had also arrived in his usual state, meaning he was twitching and frowning and looking over his shoulder, as if he had come into accidental possession of state secrets, did not know who he could trust, and had just left a café where he had tried to drown these anxieties in twelve to fifteen double espressos. Unusually for him, on the other hand, he was carrying something wrapped up in a towel, the edges of which fluttered in the air at the same rate as his essential caffeinated tremor.

"Alfred, thank goodness. I know the office doesn't open officially for another two minutes, but I need your help. Jeremiah, do you mind if I jump the line and go first? This is bad," said Mr. Porter, offering up the towel-wrapped bundle as evidence of the situation's badness. "Very, very bad. By the way, Jeremiah, did you know they were calling you to the Financial Office?"

"Actually, Mr. Porter," Reynolds said, "I'm just on my way out. But Jeremiah is working in the office now. He'll sort you out."

"Jeremiah?" said Mr. Porter. He did not seem to be asking a question of Jeremiah, but rather the broader "Question of Jeremiah," and he did not appear optimistic about the answer—the towel's range of motion widened by a few millimeters.

"But I don't know what I'm doing," Jeremiah reminded Reynolds, under his breath.

"I have every confidence in you," said Reynolds to Jeremiah. He smiled broadly, more in Mr. Porter's direction than Jeremiah's, and leaned in close to Jeremiah's ear. "And so must our guests," he whispered, "if they are to be *satisfied* with your service."

Reynolds retreated and gave Jeremiah a significant look and a subtle toss of his head towards the dubious Mr. Porter. Jeremiah would not have described the look on Mr. Porter's face as "satisfied," and he could imagine several plausible futures where a continued lack of belief in Jeremiah's abilities could translate into Mr. Porter's full and unequivocal dissatisfaction. So he smiled as broadly as he was able and unlocked the door.

"After you, Mr. Porter," Jeremiah said. "Let's have a look at what's under that towel." Despite his deep misgivings, Jeremiah flattered himself that Reynolds himself could not have delivered the line more naturally. Nor could a dermatologist, for that matter. Or a director of adult waves. Luckily Mr. Porter still appeared too preoccupied with questions of Jeremiah's competence to pick up on any such untoward resonances.

Mr. Porter entered the office, alternating suspicious looks at Jeremiah with wistful gazes towards Reynolds, who meanwhile gave free rein to the pressing appointments pulling the other end of his mustache and took his cheery leave. Sensing Mr. Porter's movement, the lights of the office came up. Jeremiah followed and shut the door.

The Office of Guest Services and Event Planning was decorated in the same stew of 20th- and 21st-century styles as all the guest areas of the Einstein IV. In the back of the room a brass lantern, swinging in the climate-controlled breeze, cast its faux flicker through a curtain of colored beads, dappling the walls. Only the coffee and tea synthesizer was incongruously modern—it looked to have been recently repaired and not yet re-covered with a period-appropriate vending machine facade. Jeremiah saw Mr. Porter give the synthesizer a once over—no doubt considering a quick cuppa to steady his nerves—before deciding that he had not yet sunk so low into addiction as to accept synthed java.

"So you're Reynolds now?" Mr. Porter asked as he and Jeremiah walked to their respective sides of the desk.

In the interest of brevity, Jeremiah jumped past any legal or philosophical questions of function vs. identity. "Yes," he said.

"I see. So I should just—take a ticket?" Mr. Porter asked when Jeremiah had finished. "Like always?" The question seemed as much a test as a request for guidance.

"Just like always," said Jeremiah.

Watching Jeremiah carefully, as if he might be waved off at any moment, Mr. Porter reached to his left and took a ticket from the dispenser next to the desk. Immediately a button, positioned behind the desk where it was visible only to Jeremiah, began to blink red. Mostly sure that he was not summoning The Specimen from security or dropping the ship's shielding against lethal space debris, Jeremiah pushed it.

"*Now serving number,*" said a female robotic voice from hidden speakers. "**ONE**," finished a recorded male, in a tone that made it clear no nonsense would be brooked from numbers two or higher until the urgent matter of number one had been cleared up. And just like that, the first rule was in the books.

"Hello Mr. Porter," Jeremiah said, making short work of rule number two, "how may I help you today?" Everyone was sticking to their parts, and Jeremiah felt a meager swell of confidence.

"This is embarrassing," said Mr. Porter. "I was in the bath, playing the backgammon program—I have to beat Wendstrom at least once before we get home—and I dropped it into the water. Just for a second! I fished it right out and dried it off, but now it won't stop doing this." He unwrapped the towel to reveal a PED upon whose dark screen glowing white letters winked on and off endlessly, spelling out "12:00 A.M."

Jeremiah's meager confidence vanished in a puff. He knew exactly one thing about the Einstein IV's PEDs, which was that they seemed to have something against him personally. Back on the red leg of the journey his own had started reporting an occasional error of type 12, which had progressed naturally into an error of type 13 several times per day, then an error of type 14 every few minutes, and then—in a display of astonishingly hostile escalation—a fatal error of type 255 every time Jeremiah dared so much as touch the screen. Not realizing back then that he could have wrapped it in a towel and brought it to Reynolds at the Guest Services desk, Jeremiah had instead buried the PED at the back of his sock drawer, where he assumed it was still waiting for the day he reached back for the argyles he never wore so it could pounce on him with an error of even more impressive magnitude and severity. Jeremiah was about to suggest that Mr. Porter's best course of action might be to sprint down the hall and see if by any stretch he could still catch Reynolds—but then he remembered the playbook.

Jeremiah opened the drawer of the desk, and there

it was, precisely as Reynolds had promised: a black and battered binder. Gently, almost reverently, Jeremiah lifted the object from the drawer, feeling in its heft the romance, the antiquity, the sheer *physicality* of the thing. He had not even seen a three-ring binder since—well, he supposed since he had taken Lana antiquing in the stores of Detroit, which felt like a lifetime ago. The cover was original cardboard laminated with a vintage black plastic, which had faded in some areas to a dark gray and was coming apart at the edges. The metalwork of the binder itself—also apparently original—showed spots of green corrosion and others that looked like salt deposits. The paper of the pages, when Jeremiah swung the cover open, had yellowed over the years to a wise shade. Jeremiah truly felt that he held in his hands a tome, a collection of experience and tough lessons learned the hard way, all wrapped up as a gift for posterity—which was to say, a gift for Jeremiah himself.

After this powerful first impression Jeremiah could not doubt that he would find the answer he sought within, and there it was, right on the first page of the contents:

1. Personal Entertainment Devices
... D) Time / Date
... i) Blinking 12:00 A.M. p. 35-6

Jeremiah flipped to page 35 and skimmed the contents.

"Hand the beast over for just a moment, if you would," he said to Mr. Porter. "Let's see, up, up, down, down, left, right, left, right, B and finally: A."

The screen flickered once, twice, and then settled into a steady display of "9:08 a.m."

"It seems to be behaving just fine now," said Jeremiah. He handed the PED back before it had a chance to change its mind. "Is there anything else?"

Mr. Porter, awe-struck, shook his head. It seemed all he could do to take a mint from the bowl—which, Jeremiah noted in passing, could use some topping up.

"Then thank you for visiting the Guest Services Desk," Jeremiah said, "and have a Golden Worldlines day."

As Mr. Porter made his exit, the clock on the wall ticked over to 9:09. The dust had not even settled on the door before the morning's next customer came through it, holding another PED—this one uncovered.

"Now serving number ... **TWO.***"*

"This is embarrassing," said Mrs. Telluride, "but I can't get my Personally Entertaining Device to lower the volume. Also, did you know they were calling you to the Financial Office earlier? And where's Reynolds?"

"Now serving number ... **FOUR.***"*

"Jeremiah?" Mr. Morton said. "What are you doing here? Ah, yes? Well: bad luck for you. Anyway, this is embarrassing—it's stuck on mute."

"Now serving number ... **EIGHT.***"*

"I heard what happened in the Financial Office, Jeremiah. That sounds terrible. Anyway, I need to clear the viewing history on my PED before my wife sees this."

"Now serving number ... **FIFTEEN.***"*

"You know, I don't ever remember *choosing* Spanish subtitles on my PED to begin with."

"Now serving number ... **TWENTY-ONE.***"*

"You see? Green. Everything on the PED is green. Even the faces of the people are green. It's like every wave I watch is about Martians."

Customer number 25, also known as Mrs. Biltmore, was making her Highly Satisfied way out of the office when she nearly bumped into Alfred Reynolds, who, having averted collision, held the door for her.

"Thank you, Alfred," she said. "I was worried when it wasn't you behind the desk, but this nice young man fixed my PED so it plays at regular speed again. Now I don't have to worry about having a heart attack every time I put on my Senior Exercise Program."

"You look like a natural there behind the desk," Reynolds said to Jeremiah after Mrs. Biltmore had gone. "To the manner born. And 25 tickets already! How did the first morning go?"

"Nothing I couldn't handle," said Jeremiah, trying not to sound too nonchalant.

"Good, good. How are the mints holding up?"

"I've refilled the dish twice."

"Like I said, a natural." Pressing matters had already started tugging at Reynolds's mustache again, and he responded in kind. "I'm off, then. I'll check in on you again at five o'clock."

"Oh," said Jeremiah. "Do you have to run? I thought maybe we could talk shop for a few minutes."

"Knock knock!" shouted someone from the hall, without actually knocking.

Before either Reynolds or Jeremiah could answer, a head poked through the door. It was a perfectly round head, like the head of a snowman, topped with an inch of fluffy white hair. It was unfortunate that the Powers that Be had plopped such a head on top of a man as nice as Clarence Drinkwater in the first place—but it was downright tragic that afterwards they had not found it in their hearts to endow him with a nose that bore less resemblance to a carrot.

"Hello Alfred," said Mr. Drinkwater, still keeping his body in the hall. "Hello Jeremiah—they told me you were working here now. I've actually come to ask for your help with something. Did I catch you in time? I can come back after lunch if I'm too late."

Reynolds looked at Jeremiah, who looked at the clock, which now read 12:01. For a moment Jeremiah hesitated—he had already missed breakfast in the line of duty, and he was hungry. But then he thought he saw a glimmer of nascent respect in Reynolds's eyes, and in response a swell of pride rose in Jeremiah's chest. Not only was this "working for a living" thing not nearly as bad as folks had made it out to

16

be, but he was going to seize this opportunity to go above and beyond. And besides, with the playbook at his side, how long could it take to straighten out one more misbehaving PED?

"Of course not, Mr. Drinkwater," Jeremiah said. "Please come in. Take a number and a seat."

Mr. Drinkwater waddled in, puffing slightly as he coordinated his big round belly and expansive hips and thighs, the motions of which were rendered semi-independent by his narrowish waist. This neck-down resemblance to two stacked spheres of increasing size did not do much to mitigate his unfortunate resonance with all things snowman, and Jeremiah reflected that perhaps Mr. Drinkwater had not done himself a great service earlier that morning by choosing to accessorize his usual costume with a turquoise wool scarf.

Jeremiah was not the only one to notice the scarf: Reynolds did too, and seemed suddenly uncomfortable about the similarity, in material and style, that it bore to his turquoise blue wool sweater—which sweater, when Mr. Drinkwater saw it, appeared to kindle the very same awkwardness in him.

"Cold on the ship these days," Mr. Drinkwater said, half acknowledging his scarf.

"Isn't it?" said Reynolds, admitting the existence of his sweater in the same fraction. "The climate is on the fritz—they say they won't have it fixed before we dock. Well, Jeremiah seems to have things well in hand, and I have some errands to run, so I'll leave you to it."

As Reynolds did so, Jeremiah could not help but notice that Mr. Drinkwater was not carrying a PED, or even a PED-shaped bundle wrapped in a towel. In fact he was not carrying anything, which made Jeremiah nervous. He touched the playbook like a talisman.

"This is actually more of a personal matter," said Mr. Drinkwater, "but should I still take a ticket? Pad the numbers a bit?"

"Sure," said Jeremiah, all nerves vanishing. Mr. Drinkwater's visit was not a brewing failure, and not even another notch on the PED repairman belt—this was a windfall, a personal visit for which Jeremiah would earn professional credit.

"*Now serving number ... **TWENTY-SIX**.*"

"Hello Mr. Drinkwater," Jeremiah said. "How may I help you today? Personally, I mean?"

"I've been trying to find a way to talk to you for a while, but it seems whenever we cross paths in the dining room, Mrs. Abdurov is within earshot."

At the mention of Mrs. Abdurov, Jeremiah's nerves reasserted themselves ever so slightly, but he shrugged them off.

"I suppose it's obvious," continued Mr. Drinkwater, "so I might as well just come out with it. I'm in love with Mrs. Abdurov, and I want you to teach me the secrets of seduction."

Jeremiah had always considered himself a firm believer in the principle of "to each his own"—especially where matters of the heart were concerned. But Mr. Drinkwater's revelation tested the firmness of Jeremiah's conviction.

Lyuba Abdurov was an impressive lady, and no doubt about it—but an F5 tornado ripping through the Southwest's oldest continuously operating cactus farm would have been just as impressive, about as sentimental, and almost as prickly. So how was it that someone like Mr. Drinkwater had fallen in love with her? Had he seen some softer side, revealed only in private? Detected some romantic streak hidden behind the whirlwind? Or was this merely a case of attraction between opposites so extreme that Guinness required immediate notification?

But as much as Jeremiah would have taken a friendly and anthropological interest in digging into these questions, there was another matter to attend to first—less an exploration of the deep mysteries of the human heart, and more a pressing practical problem.

"But Mr. Drinkwater," Jeremiah said, "I don't know the secrets of seduction."

"Don't be modest, Jeremiah. All the ladies are in love with you—even Mrs. Abdurov pays you a lot of attention."

"Maybe they see me as a kind of son figure—or grandson figure—but that's just a question of age. Seduction has nothing to do with it."

"And then there's that waitress, Katherine. She's always flirting with you."

"Oh," said Jeremiah, blushing a bit, "every now and again, perhaps. Against her better judgment."

"You have to help me, Jeremiah," said Mr. Drinkwater. "If I can't win Mrs. Abdurov's heart, my own won't go on beating. Surely you can think of something?"

"Well," asked Jeremiah, wracking his brain, "have you tried just talking to her?"

"Yes, but it seems to make her angry."

"Do you have any shared interests?"

Mr. Drinkwater thought for a moment and brightened.

"We both like seafood."

"Why don't you invite her for a seafood dinner when we're back on Earth?"

"No," said Mr. Drinkwater. "That's too late. I have to win her heart before we dock."

"What's the rush?"

"Do you know why Mrs. Abdurov is on the E4?" Mr. Drinkwater asked.

"Hmm," said Jeremiah. He knew quite well, of course, that Mrs. Abdurov was one of the majority—the poor souls who were on the cruise to give medical science an extra eighteen years to catch up with their rare and degenerative diseases—but the Golden Unwritten Rule of the E4 was that all passengers pretend mutual ignorance concerning the misfortunes that had driven them there. As far as Polite Ship Society was concerned, an interstellar round trip at relativistic speeds was something one undertook for the larkiest of reasons, and if one possessed any knowledge to the contrary regarding one's shipmates, one had best keep it to oneself. Jeremiah was even less sure about the etiquette of admitting such knowledge in his new circumstances as, technically, the help.

"Of course you do," said Mr. Drinkwater. "Everyone knows. Well, she promised her granddaughter Clara—who was eight years old when we left Earth—that she'd live to dance at her wedding, and now it seems her granddaughter has met a nice Russian man and they're going to be married, so Mrs. Abdurov will be heading straight to Moscow when we dock. I have to go with her, Jeremiah. I have to be the man to dance with her at that wedding—which means she has to be in love with me by the time we arrive on Earth."

"Then I guess we don't have much time," said Jeremiah. "Let's see, I remember seeing a wave once that said people fell in love in three different ways. Some wanted to be romanced, some entranced, and some impressed. I'm thinking Mrs. Abdurov is more of the 'impress me' type."

"That's terrible news," Mr. Drinkwater said. "How can *I* impress a woman like *that*?"

"Mr. Drinkwater, don't sell yourself short! Does Mrs. Abdurov know about your literary success?"

"If she doesn't, she's not going to hear it from me," said Mr. Drinkwater. "I don't want her to know I *made* my credit. You know what they say, Jeremiah: credit makes credit, people make people. Anyway, I came on the E4 to get away from all that."

"I thought you came on the E4 to extend your copyright. Sorry," Jeremiah added, realizing that his toes had once again crossed the line of propriety laid down by the Golden Unwritten Rule, "I don't mean to pry."

"What in the all-fire H-E-C-K do I care about my copyright?" Mr. Drinkwater said. Jeremiah was familiar with his verbal tic of spelling out even the lightest curse—a consequence, he supposed, of a life surrounded by the young, impressionable ears of his fans. "What use will I have for royalties when I've been stone cold dead for a century? It's my publishers who want the copyright extended. So we cut a deal: I came on this cruise, giving them an extra eighteen years before my work became public domain."

"But what did you get in return?"

"I got out seven books early, is what I got! I got away from that S-T-U-P-I-D little penguin and his so-called 'adventures.' My heart was never really in children's literature in the first place, Jeremiah—I wanted to do art that was edgier, not so D-A-R-N safe."

"All right," said Jeremiah, "we'll have to find something else to impress Mrs. Abdurov. What was that edgier art you wanted to try?"

Mr. Drinkwater chewed his lower lip. He looked both eager and abashed, as if he had taken a coin representing his fear on one side and his desire on the other, flipped it, and seen it land perched on its edge.

"Mime," he whispered finally.

"Sorry," said Jeremiah, "did you just—did you say 'mime'?"

"Yes."

"Like the clowns with the white paint who do the whole 'oh no, I'm trapped in a box' act?"

Mr. Drinkwater smiled indulgently.

"You could call that mime," he said, "in the same way you could call a Budbusch a beer, or a McSynthy's a hamburger. Mime is an ancient and beautiful art form. I wanted to turn professional, you know, as a young man—my parents insisted I go into something safer."

"Like what?" asked Jeremiah.

"Children's literature, of course. But I still wonder to this day whether I could have made it as a professional mime."

Mr. Drinkwater shook his head and pursed his lips, as if he could taste the past on them, and it was not sweet. Jeremiah did not enjoy seeing such a kind man so disappointed—a man whose work had brought happiness not just to Jeremiah but to so many other children as well.

"Well *I* for one am sure you could have been a professional mime," said Jeremiah. "Anyone would know it just by looking at you. The way you move, the way you sit, the way you hold yourself. Everything about it says 'this man is a very talented mime.' "

Mr. Drinkwater brightened.

"Thank you," he said. "Thank you, Jeremiah. You know, I think you're right: if we're going to impress Mrs. Abdurov, mime is how we're going to do it."

"Well," said Jeremiah. "I didn't quite mean—that is, mime isn't the easiest way to impress someone on your average occasion. It's not really the sort of thing you can just break out in the middle of breakfast or cocktails, is it? You need to find the right atmosphere—a social context, you could say, more conducive to miming."

"That's it!" cried Mr. Drinkwater, leaping from his chair. "Jeremiah, you're a genius!"

"Thank you, Mr. Drinkwater. And thank you," Jeremiah said optimistically, "for visiting the Guest Services Desk. Have a Golden Worldlines day."

"I need a *platform* to showcase my mime!" Mr. Drinkwater continued. "Somewhere I can stand out from the pack of preening suitors! Somewhere that it's not just socially *acceptable* to display one's talent, but *expected*. I need a *talent show*!"

"A talent show it is, then," said Jeremiah. "And now, if you don't mind, I'll head to a slightly belated lunch."

"You should," said Mr. Drinkwater. "You go on and get some lunch, Jeremiah. Enjoy it. Savor it. You've earned it, by G-O-D."

He shook Jeremiah's hand as the latter stood up, and kept shaking it as they walked out of the office side-by-side, like two politicians creating some awkward b-roll waves at the conclusion of all-night peace talks that had gone better than expected.

"Mr. Drinkwater?" said Jeremiah when they reached the hall, still shaking hands.

"Yes?"

"I have to lock the door."

"Ah, of course you do!" said Mr. Drinkwater, releasing Jeremiah's hand at last. "So will you announce tomorrow? We have less than two weeks left on the cruise!"

"Announce what?" asked Jeremiah.

"The talent show!" said Mr. Drinkwater.

"Oh," Jeremiah said, "events like that aren't really my forte. I thought that you'd be handling more of the announcing and organizing and various—Mr. Drinkwater, why do you keep pointing above the door?"

"What does it say there, Jeremiah? Right where I'm pointing?"

"Office of Guest Services?" said Jeremiah.

"And?"

Jeremiah's heart sank.

"Event Planning."

"Enjoy your lunch," said Mr. Drinkwater, grabbing Jeremiah's hand for one more pump. "By G-O-D, enjoy every morsel."

3

Civil Rights, Sharp Lefts

Still Friday (9 days until arrival)

DESPITE this rough end to the morning shift, Jeremiah felt a bit better as he hurried to the dining room. The holo-portals were showing fields of sunflowers as far as the eye could see, their faces turned upward to catch the noon rays, rustling in the digital breeze. As he passed the library, Jeremiah thought for perhaps the 1000th time that he should really get back to reading a bit more. When he cut through the billiards room, Jeremiah imagined with pleasure how much more relaxing tonight's friendly game and brandy with the Chapins would be, with a day of hard labor behind it.

His arrival in the dining room did nothing to change his mood's upward trend. A general hush fell over the diners, and for a moment Jeremiah enjoyed the pleasant sensation of a minor celebrity strolling among a crowd that is still trying to figure out whether he just looks like himself or actually is.

"Jeremiah!" called Mrs. Chapin from across the dining room. She waved him over to the table where she and her husband were occupying two of the four seats.

"We saved your seat," she said, pointing out the one next to Mr. Chapin, where Jeremiah was accustomed to sit during lunch, and did so now. "And we waited to order—I told you he'd be here, Henry."

"Hello Jeremiah," said Mr. Chapin.

"Hello, Mr. Chapin."

Mr. Chapin wrinkled his nose.

"I think you mean Henry," he said.

"Apparently in my new situation I am to call you Mr. Chapin, or suffer dire consequences."

"We heard a bit about that, but you'll have to tell us more," said Mr. Chapin. "Perhaps after we order?"

"How can you think of food at a time like this?" said Mrs. Chapin. "Ordering lunch while Jeremiah can't even call us by our given names? And before Alastair arrives? Where could he be? He's never late for lunch. But I don't want to hear another mention of food until we've got the whole story. Now, Jeremiah: was it awful? Were you persecuted? Tell us everything," she said. "*Everything*."

"They can't do that to you," Mrs. Chapin pronounced, when Jeremiah had finished. "It's not like you could even make enough credit to pay your passage. You know what they say: credit makes credit, people make people."

In his narration of the morning's events, Jeremiah had attempted to balance the rich detail that Mrs. Chapin demanded with the quick summary for which Mr. Chapin's hungry eyes had pleaded—and with which Jeremiah, conscious of the brevity of his lunch hour and hollowness in his own stomach, sympathized.

"Yes, and if it's just a matter of credit," said Mr. Chapin, relieved that the fix was so simple, "we would happily—"

"No," Jeremiah said. "Thank you, but I couldn't possibly. It's just riding a desk and fixing the odd PED for ten days. I'll be done by five every night, just in time to tell you all the day's war stories over dinner and billiards. I'll soldier through. You know, perhaps we *should* order..."

"Soldier through?" Mrs. Chapin said. "This is indentured servitude! A violation of your civil rights. Wait, do we have civil rights out here?"

"I assume so," said Jeremiah.

"Which kind? British?"

"American, I would think."

"But we departed from London."

"But Golden Worldlines is an American company."

Mrs. Chapin frowned.

"I would prefer British civil rights," she said.

24

"Do you even know the difference?" Mr. Chapin asked.

"No, but I've had American civil rights my whole life. A little variety might be nice." She turned back to Jeremiah. "Anyway you're British, aren't you?"

"Detroit," Jeremiah said, "born and bred."

"Honestly Sara," said Mr. Chapin, "he doesn't even have the accent."

"Well, he has the air."

Jeremiah smiled. *This* was life aboard the Einstein IV— the Chapins bickering pleasantly about matters of no consequence, the sounds of silver- and glassware in the background, and the prospect of a good lunch. All was once more as it should be—the only minor nuisance being that Jeremiah had to keep checking the clock.

"The only Brit on this cruise is Roof, as you well know," Mr. Chapin was saying. "Where has he got to, anyway? I'm starving. Ah, speak of the handsome devil himself."

Upon this announcement, Mrs. Chapin made a discreet survey of her sixty-years-young beauty under the pretense of frowning at a spot in her soup spoon, flattening her blouse so that a bit more of her ruby necklace peeped out from the neckline.

"Crowded today," Alastair Roof observed.

"Only because you're later than usual," said Mr. Chapin.

"Yes," said Mr. Roof, "matters to attend to and all that. May I? Have you already ordered?"

"We waited," said Mr. Chapin. "I'll call Katherine over now."

Mr. Chapin waved over Jeremiah's shoulder while Mr. Roof began the 30-second process of sitting down without dulling a single one of the knife-creases in his clothing. As the Brit crossed his long legs, he admired the turquoise blue of a fine wool sock that peeked out from beneath his pant cuff. He smiled—though whether at the warmth of the socks or their rare incongruity with the rest of his costume, Jeremiah could not tell.

"I like your socks," said Jeremiah.

Mr. Roof frowned and hid his legs below the table.

"The climate control has been kept rather cold lately," he said. He looked relieved as Mr. Chapin began to cough, sparing him any further explanation.

25

Mr. Roof's relief faded as those first few dry hacks grew into a full-blown attack. Mr. Chapin turned his head to the side and waved away the water that his wife pressed on him, while Mr. Roof and Jeremiah found other things to study in the dining room—the chandelier, the period brasswork, the dance floor gleaming in the middle of the rich maroon carpet, unused since the Valentine's Day dance—as if neither had any inkling that Henry Chapin might have had anything worse than a tickle in his throat. But as the seconds became minutes, Mr. Roof and Jeremiah could no longer maintain the pretense of examining the decor. They exchanged a worried, questioning glance, while Mrs. Chapin abandoned the water angle and started whacking her husband on the back. Jeremiah was just about to summon help when Mr. Chapin recovered in one fell swoop and said, with only a trace of hoarseness, "Good afternoon, Katherine. I'll have the oyster tempura to start and then the venison, on the rarer side, hold the asparagus."

Jeremiah turned and looked over his shoulder, where Henry Chapin had directed these remarks, and indeed, there she was: Katherine, lovely and cheerful in her simple black slacks and white blouse, holding her notepad and pen at the ready (though Jeremiah had never seen her take a single note or mistake a single order).

"Would you like to sub in a different vegetable for the asparagus, Mr. Chapin?" she asked. "We've just thawed out some carrots, and there might be a few green beans left from last night."

"Vegetables aren't food, Katherine," said Mr. Chapin. "They're what food eats."

"Potato?"

"Give it up, dear," Mrs. Chapin said. "I've been trying to get him to eat vegetables since I was your age, and it's larky. Do you know, once at the Maplewood I tried hiding a pea under Hollandaise sauce while he was away from the table—a single pea under a whole blanket of the stuff—and he picked it out immediately when he came back. 'What's this?' he said, holding it towards me with his fork, just like that, dripping with Hollandaise. 'What's this?' "

"Did he?" said Mr. Roof in a tone of polite wonder, as if he had not heard this same story a significant fraction of the

2,100-plus meals they had shared during the previous 700-plus days. "Hollandaise sauce, you say?"

"Like the princess and the pea," Mrs. Chapin said, "only with Hollandaise."

"I think that's enough discussion of my dietary habits for one day," said Mr. Chapin, handing his menu across the table to Katherine. "What are you having, Sara my dear?"

"The chicken cacciatore sounds interesting," she said, "but I just don't think I can face chewing chicken right now. I do feel like the *flavor* of chicken, though. Could the chef cook the sauce with the chicken for a while and then remove it?"

"Are you congenitally unable to order from the menu?" her husband asked.

"I miss being able to cook for myself."

"You haven't cooked for yourself three times in the 40 years we've been married."

"I didn't say I missed *cooking*, I said I missed *being able* to cook. Sometimes," said Mrs. Chapin, handing her menu to Katherine, "you don't appreciate what you have until it's gone. And it's 43 years we've been married—next month it will be 44."

As the Chapins began a vigorous debate about how many years it was that they had been vigorously debating any and all such matters legally in the eyes of man and God, Katherine turned to Jeremiah.

"Mr. Brown?"

"I'd like the oysters and venison as well—and for the 100th time, for you to call me Jeremiah."

"We're still not allowed to call the guests by their first names, Mr. Brown."

"What if circumstances had changed?" asked Jeremiah.

"What do you mean?"

Jeremiah stole a glance at his fellow diners: Mr. and Mrs. Chapin were now arguing about whether the relativistic cruise they were on affected the counting of their anniversaries. Mr. Roof, whose judgment was occasionally being appealed to in the anniversary argument, was alternating polite but meaningless smiles at the Chapins with nervous, sidelong surveillance of the door. None of them were paying the slightest attention to Katherine and Jeremiah.

"Katherine," said Jeremiah, "do you remember how one night a good while ago, back in the red leg of the cruise, I dawdled a bit after everyone had finished dinner, and—after you and I had been chatting pleasantly for a while about this and that—I asked you a potentially embarrassing question?"

Katherine crossed her arms. Her left eyebrow, which was naturally higher than her right, lifted higher still. Jeremiah saw her perform the same survey of the Chapins' and Roof's attention as he had, and reach the same conclusion.

"Yes," she said.

"Do you remember what you said?" asked Jeremiah.

"That I don't have coffee with guests."

"So if I were to tell you that, due to imminent default on my ticket, I had been assigned to work in the Office of Guest Services with Alfred Reynolds—thereby making us co-workers—what would you say?"

"First, that I don't have coffee with co-workers. Second, I would ask you why, if you're not a ticketed passenger anymore, you were eating lunch in the guest dining room instead of the staff cafeteria."

She had a point. It was a good point, a strong point—a point that Jeremiah had not considered. It was also a point that he was eager to continue not considering as long as possible—which did not promise to be long, as Mr. Grubel had just entered the dining room. He had stopped right inside the door and was scanning the tables.

Jeremiah hid behind his menu, but too late—he had been spotted, and Grubel approached the table like a man on a mission.

"Jeremiah, thank goodness I found you!" said Grubel. "And Katherine, you're here too, excellent." He turned and addressed himself to the Chapins and Mr. Roof. "Good afternoon, I'm Benedict Grubel, Financial Officer on the Einstein IV. I'm sorry to interrupt your lunch, but I have some business with Jeremiah."

"I know who you are," said Mrs. Chapin. "You're the one who violated Jeremiah's civil rights."

"Technically, Mrs. Chapin, this far from Earth, Jeremiah doesn't have civil rights. He acknowledged as much in the contract he signed—as did you all."

"How do you know my name?" asked Mrs. Chapin.

"Mrs. Chapin, it is my business to know our guests—in certain aspects of their lives—better than they know themselves. If you have any further questions about civil rights— Jeremiah's or in general—I am happy to point you to the apropos sections of the contract. Or if you have the leisure, I encourage you to read it in its entirety—it's quite enlightening."

Mrs. Chapin worried the bejeweled end of her necklace between her thumb and index finger, as if it were a talisman against this horrifying suggestion.

"In the meantime," said Mr. Grubel, "Jeremiah, I owe you an apology: an important detail completely slipped my mind."

"All right," said Jeremiah, allowing himself the tiniest sprig of hope—perhaps there had been a misunderstanding. Perhaps everything *would* be all right after all, owing to this forgotten but important detail.

"Since you are no longer a guest of Golden Worldlines, it's inappropriate for you to utilize the guest dining facilities. Katherine can give you directions to the staff cafeteria."

"All right," said Jeremiah, more stoically.

"That goes for your sleeping arrangements as well— you'll have to move into staff quarters. Given your ..." Grubel looked at Mr. Roof and the Chapins, gauging their appetite for scandal. "...predilections, I won't put you in the men's wing. I won't have you turning your imminent default into a pleasure cruise."

"Mr. Grubel, I was talking about my lawyer, not—"

Grubel held up his hand.

"Not another word about lawsuits and lawyers, or I will personally make sure that your evaluations are the worst in the Einstein IV's history."

Jeremiah bit his lip.

"Unfortunately," Grubel continued, "there are no free quarters in the women's wing."

"All right," said Jeremiah again, now suspecting that it would not, in fact, be all right.

"Which is where you come in, Katherine," Grubel said.

"Sorry?" she said.

"You have one of the staff suites. Jeremiah will sleep on the sofa."

"No," Katherine said.

It did not seem that Mr. Grubel was used to hearing this word much, or that he was enjoying the novelty. The silver frames of his empty glasses bit into his cheeks as he squinted. If the frames had actually sported lenses, they would have been fogging up.

"What?"

"I'm not sharing my suite with this man."

Grubel put on his version of a sympathetic face.

"Rest assured, Jeremiah is not a man in that sense. It will be like your brother staying on your couch for a few days."

"I don't have a brother, and I'm not sharing my suite with anyone. I earned that suite through seniority."

"That suite you 'earned' belongs to Golden Worldlines," said Grubel. "If you want to keep it, I suggest you reconsider your tone."

"This is all a huge misunderstanding," said Jeremiah, standing up. "I'm not gay."

"Jeremiah, sit—"

"He just asked me out," Katherine said, pointing at Jeremiah, "for the second time."

"Katherine, calm—"

"I did," said Jeremiah. "It was totally inappropriate, and I did it because I'm totally not gay. Both times."

"You can't force me to let this man stay in—"

"Enough!"

Mr. Grubel slammed his fist on the table so hard that two legs briefly lost contact with the ground.

Mrs. Chapin gasped and clamped her hands over her necklace, as if looting and personal theft could be the only logical sequels to such a breakdown of the social contract. Mr. Chapin took her arm.

Mr. Moakley, who was sitting two tables away, put down his soup spoon, replaced his teeth, and put one hand on his walker, in case he might be required to step in.

"The situation is very simple," said Mr. Grubel, fixing his crooked glasses. "Jeremiah, unless you want to work another two years for Golden Worldlines, you will sleep where I tell you. Katherine, unless you *don't* want to work here any longer, you will accommodate whatever roommate I see fit to assign. After the office closes at five, Jeremiah, you will pack your belongings. And you, Katherine, will show him to his new room. Is that clear? Good. My apologies for interrupting your lunch," he said to the Chapins and Mr. Roof.

"I'm really, really sorry," Jeremiah said as soon as Grubel had gone. Katherine refused to meet his eyes, her cheeks scarlet and her arms akimbo.

"I was trying to tell him about my lawyer, and he just wasn't paying attention, and he thought that I—"

"Just stop talking to me." Katherine turned away from him and faced his table mates. "Your food will be right out," she said.

WORLD ENOUGH (AND TIME)

4

Winners and Losers and Which Are You?

LESS than an hour ago, when Jeremiah had found himself the organizer of a talent show in what amounted to an interstellar assisted living community—and its resident matchmaker besides—that had seemed but a temporary speed bump between a productive morning and pleasant lunch. Now, with his cabin forfeit, the dining room denied, and Katherine furious, Jeremiah felt his situation deteriorating sharply, and worried that his brief success with the PEDs that morning had been but a momentary and meaningless spike in a graph trending sharply down and to the right.

So it was with great relief that Jeremiah saw Bernie Wendstrom waiting outside the office door, frowning and clutching to his chest something swaddled in a towel.

"There you are," said Mr. Wendstrom. "Finally."

Jeremiah resisted the urge to point out the hours on the door, instead welcoming Mr. Wendstrom inside and guiding him through the opening ceremonies with the ticketing machine.

"This is a delicate and confidential situation," Mr. Wendstrom said. He nodded his head towards the towel-wrapped PED he still clutched, even while seated, and his comb-over flopped against his forehead like a fish whose years of frustrated thespian ambitions had at long last burst forth into a prolonged rendition of the death scene from *Romeo and Juliet*.

33

"Nothing to worry about. Guests come for help with theirs all the time," said Jeremiah.

"They do?"

"Absolutely. They're perplexing, infuriating, little devils, aren't they? Always doing this when you want them to do that."

Jeremiah had expected this remark to relax Mr. Wendstrom— to give him permission, as it were, to be defeated by his PED. But Mr. Wendstrom narrowed his eyes and clutched the towel even tighter. So Jeremiah tried a different tack.

"I got so frustrated with mine that I threw it in my sock drawer back on the red leg, and haven't taken it out since."

Mr. Wendstrom's concerns did not seem to be allayed— if anything, his suspicion was edging on horror now, and he seemed on the verge of standing up.

"Why don't you just throw it here on the desk," Jeremiah said desperately, "and we'll have a look?"

After a few seconds of consideration, Mr. Wendstrom put the package up on Jeremiah's desk, hesitating another beat before whisking the towel away.

"That's not a Personal Entertainment Device," Jeremiah said.

"Of course it's not," said Mr. Wendstrom.

"That's a—terrarium?"

"Of course it is."

"Let's start over," said Jeremiah. "What seems to be the problem?"

"As I was explaining to you quite clearly," Mr. Wendstrom said, "the problem is Carolus the Bold."

"I see," said Jeremiah, when it appeared that no more information was forthcoming. "And Carolus the Bold is?"

"An iguana. A southern blood-throated iguana. *My* southern blood-throated iguana. He's gone missing."

"And this was his terrarium?"

"Yes. And before you say anything," said Mr. Wendstrom, waving his finger at Jeremiah, who in fact had been at a loss for anything to say and appreciated the chance to ruminate a bit more, "I know that no animals are allowed on board, but I couldn't leave him. Iguanas are very social creatures, and Carolus in particular needs other people in his life. Besides, I couldn't let him die without having read *Penultimate Battle*

34

Royale and *Last Battle Royale*."

"Oh," Jeremiah said, dimly recalling from his days as a guest a number of conversations that at the time he had tried hard to immediately forget, "that series of books, right? Where the animals are kings and queens and whatnot?"

Mr. Wendstrom's face turned a raging shade of scarlet. His lips were slightly parted—he seemed to be actually, literally, biting his tongue.

"An anger management technique," he said when he was calm enough to replace his tongue to its normal place and regain the power of speech. "Jeremiah, *Princes of Alcance* is a 'series of books.' *The Kingkiller Chronicle* is a 'series of books.' *The Lord of the Rings* is a 'series of books.' *Crowns on Fire* is one of the highest achievements ever attained by the human species. Or it will be, if that damned Michael L. L. Gregory ever gets off his butt and finishes the last two books. Then all questions will finally be answered. We'll find out who killed Creon the Howlmaster, and what treasure lies in the Ark of Baneling, and most important of all," said Mr. Wendstrom, his eyes glowing, "who is Andwen Longtail's real father? I'm on this cruise so that Carolus and I could wait two years for those books instead of 20, Jeremiah. I couldn't deny Carolus the pleasure of discovering all those secrets with me."

"But you're not saying that Carolus the Bold—that is to say, he hasn't actually *read* the *Crowns on Fire* series?"

"Of course he hasn't, Jeremiah. He's an iguana."

"That's a relief. For a moment I thought you meant—"

"I read it *to* him."

"I see. Well, let's start with the basics: where and when did you see him last?"

"Between breakfast and lunch. I gave him a few treats— Aunt Mildred's Organic Iguana Treats—shouldn't you be writing this down?"

Jeremiah took a pad of paper and pen from the desk and jotted down the word "TREATS."

"Anyway," Mr. Wendstrom continued, "when I got back from lunch, the terrarium was empty and Carolus was gone. What else do you need to know?"

Jeremiah tried to remember what questions the police asked on the missing person procedurals that Lana had loved. He tapped his pen on the pad.

"Any enemies?" he asked.

"He's an iguana."

"I meant you."

"Of course *I* have enemies," Mr. Wendstrom said. "A man doesn't reach my position in life without enemies— especially not a man who actually *made* his credit. Do you know how much they hate that? It flies right in the face of every lazy thing they've ever learned. They'd rather just repeat 'credit makes credit, people make people,' over and over. I have compiled a long list of losers who hate me for upsetting their worldview, and who blame me for their own failures. I couldn't possibly name them all."

"All right then," said Jeremiah, "that ought to be enough to get started."

"What milestones should we set for you?"

"I'm not sure I understand," said Jeremiah, who was actually sure he didn't.

"Jeremiah, do you know how I made the credit I was just talking about?"

"Books, right? And waves? Self-help stuff?"

Mr. Wendstrom bit his tongue again, until this round of fury passed.

"I hate that term, Jeremiah. How can the self possibly need *help*, when the self is the *solution*?"

"I just—"

"There are only two kinds of people in the world, Jeremiah: winners and losers. Do you know which one you are? You're a loser. I'm not trying to insult you! Most people are losers at everything. Life, business, backgammon. That's where I come in: I turn losers into winners. And I'm good at it. Believe me—I'm very, very good."

"I believe you," Jeremiah said.

"Then believe that the long road from loser to winner is lined with *milestones*. Say you wanted to lose 30 pounds. Would we weigh you just twice, once at the beginning and once at the end? Of course not. We'd break your weight loss into smaller goals—five pounds, then ten, then fifteen—and weigh you every week against those *milestones*."

"That makes sense," said Jeremiah.

"So on your own journey from loser to winner, what will your milestones be?"

"I mean, it makes perfect sense with weight loss. But what milestones are involved in finding an iguana? Either I've found him or I haven't."

Wendstrom grunted and squinted his eyes.

"You're sharp, Jeremiah. Maybe there's more winner in you than I thought. Fine, no milestones—we'll do daily status reports." He stood up. "You'll need a place to put Carolus the Bold when you find him, so I'll leave the terrarium."

"How does this thing even open?" asked Jeremiah, turning it around in the vain search for a latch of some kind.

"Hand it over. There's nothing to it: first this, then this, and then like *this*."

The top of the terrarium popped off, as if spring-loaded, and clattered on the desk.

"It takes practice. Maybe," said Mr. Wendstrom almost wistfully, "that could have been one of your milestones."

After Mr. Wendstrom had taken his leave, and Jeremiah had stowed the terrarium safely behind the desk, he checked the clock. It was 1:21. Jeremiah synthed himself a coffee. He sat down in the antique office chair and sipped his coffee. It was 1:23. He fiddled with the height and reclining distance of the chair until further adjustment in any direction reduced his comfort. Jeremiah looked at the clock again: it was 1:26, and not a single new guest had required service. On the plus side, guests who didn't get service from Jeremiah couldn't review him negatively. On the minus side, he had just gone five minutes without entertainment or distraction—which was more than he had gone in two years—and he wasn't sure how much longer he could last.

He would have waved Appleton, but there was no terminal. He might have listened to music or watched something, but there was no PED. By 1:29 he was so desperate that he actually dug out the pamphlet Grubel had forced on him, and—after a few minutes of turning it over in his hands—began to read. In the process, Jeremiah discovered three things.

First, that he still didn't understand special relativity, even when it was explained to him with **important concepts** called out in **bold type.** He could parrot the fundamental tenets of faith involved: that as the Einstein IV accelerated to an appreciable fraction of the **speed of light**, those on board would experience **time dilation**, which was a fancy way of saying that the **passage of time** would **slow down** for them, and after a two-year journey among the stars they would arrive home to Earth to find that 20 years had passed there meanwhile. But—all due respect to Mr. Einstein, who had a reputation as something of a smarty-pants—Jeremiah could not wrap his mind around this **obvious absurdity**, or at some level even **believe it**, and he would not have been **completely shocked** to arrive back on Earth and discover that 20 years had not passed there, but only the **same two years** he had experienced, and that he and all the other passengers had been the **victims of an elaborate hoax** or at best **unwitting participants** in a **psychological experiment** mapping the bounds of gullibility.

Second, Jeremiah discovered that he did **not enjoy** having ideas presented to him with **important concepts** called out in **bold type**, which started to feel like **watching a wave** with a **personal assistant** standing by his side and **hitting him on the head** with a **foam noodle** every time something important happened on screen, so that he kept feeling the phantom noodle **smack against his noggin** even after the assistant had long since been **punched in the mouth** and **hauled away** to a session of **revenge water torture**.

Third and finally, that he should have signed up for the Golden Worldlines Rewards Program before departing on his cruise, as he would be at this very moment earning frequent-flyer light-seconds, which upon his return to Earth could be redeemed for valuable prizes—assuming, of course, that his imminent default did not invalidate his participation in the program.

After this thorough perusal of the pamphlet, which he estimated must have shaved at least a half hour off his sentence, Jeremiah checked the clock once more. It read 1:34, which was the strongest evidence for relativity that Jeremiah had seen yet.

When Reynolds arrived at the stroke of five for his evening check-in, Jeremiah practically pounced on him, pouring out the whole story as fast as he could give words to it: how between lunch and the close of business Jeremiah had somehow found himself responsible for a talent show, a mime's love life, and the tracking down of an AWOL iguana who was, to hear his owner tell it, the Socrates, Newton, and Einstein of iguanas all rolled into one, and apparently quite bold to boot.

"Sounds like a fine day," said Mr. Reynolds. "A fine first day. Apart from signing up to organize the talent show—that was a mistake. Event planning is the hard part of the job. But never mind, you'll manage."

"What am I supposed to do?" asked Jeremiah.

"Did you check the playbook?"

"Just for the PEDs," said Jeremiah.

He opened the three-ring binder slowly, with suspicion, as a volunteer from the audience might open a box at the urging of a magician.

"Always check the playbook first, Jeremiah. Take it to bed with you tonight and read the section called 'Event Planning.' You'll have that talent show up and running in no time."

"The talent show? That's the least of my worries. How do I get Mrs. Abdurov to fall in love with Mr. Drinkwater? How do I find Mr. Wendstrom's iguana? You're not telling me *that's* in the playbook?"

"Probably not," said Mr. Reynolds, "but it's worth a look. Ah, I almost forgot to tell you—make sure you reset the numbers on the ticket machine every night. We don't like the guests to have to count too high. After a certain age, people start getting nervous with numbers above 50."

"I can handle the ticket machine just fine, but what do I do about Mr. Drinkwater and Mr. Wendstrom?"

"You *do* get the odd problem now and then, working the service desk," said Mr. Reynolds. "But I wouldn't worry too much—you'll figure something out."

"How often is 'now and then'?"

"Oh, just occasionally and so on. The tough ones always seem to come in the afternoon. Now get some dinner and then some rest, Jeremiah. You've had a fine first day—a very fine first day."

WORLD ENOUGH (AND TIME)

5

End to the Longest Day

Still Friday (9 days until arrival)

A S Jeremiah followed Reynolds's directions to the cafeteria, he could hardly believe that these ugly corridors, underlit by fluorescent panels in the false ceiling and punctuated by heavy gray metal doors—these whole wings of the ship that dwarfed the guest areas—had existed all this time. During his days as a passenger Jeremiah would have deduced—had he been prompted to do so—that somewhere on board there must be laundry and cooking and plumbing taking place. But he had never been prompted, and he realized now that this omission was no accident: his entire experience as a Golden Worldlines passenger had been designed with great care to keep him from ever considering such mundane matters.

As he passed one of the heavy doors it hissed open, releasing the powerful smell of a chemical laundry, and a middle-aged Asian woman in white hurried past. Through another door, which had been propped open with a cinder-block, the scent of baking bread escaped. Inside, three men were shouting at each other in Spanish—the first word of anything except English and butchered dinner-table French that Jeremiah had heard in almost two years.

The ceiling of the cafeteria was even lower and falser than the ceiling in the hallway, and Jeremiah could feel the hum

41

of vast quantities of power moving through fat cables somewhere above—very little of which power seemed to have been
diverted into the cafeteria lights. The small circular tables
were arranged in a strict grid and bolted in place, as Jeremiah
discovered when he bumped into one while trying to make
space for a statuesque Canadian who went sprinting towards
the buffet to deliver a tray of synthed ham half his size.

So many people were talking at once, in so many different
languages, that it put Jeremiah in mind of a cocktail party at
the United Nations. Over here a group of Haitians seemed to
be arguing about soccer players who were likely long retired
back on Earth by now, pointing to the names on the jerseys
they wore as supporting evidence. Four Chinese ladies were
sneaking in a few hands of mahjong. Two tables of Latinos
in grease-stained aprons hooted and gestured to each other
across the room. And everywhere Canadians were hard at
work, their maple-leaf pins on their sleeves—three bussing
and wiping down tables as they were vacated, four serving at
the buffet line, one mopping up the evidence of some dining
misadventure. Jeremiah felt he had stepped through a magi-
cal portal and right back into Detroit.

He made his way through the line at the back of the cafeteria. The synthed ham looked tired but the synthed chicken
exhausted, so he asked the blond Canadian server for a slice
of ham.

"You're welcome," the Canadian said as he laid the ham
gently on Jeremiah's plate. "I'm sorry."

After augmenting the ham with a hunk of stony synthed
bread and some synthed purée of root vegetables that
smelled faintly of soap, Jeremiah emerged from the line
and saw Katherine sitting and eating alone at a table in the
corner. He walked over to her.

"Hello," he said, positioning himself discreetly beside an
empty chair.

Katherine pushed a keycard across the table.

"It's W24."

"I'm really sorry," said Jeremiah.   "If you'd let me
explain—"

"I'll leave a blanket on the sofa."

"Could I sit down and chat for a minute?"

"I prefer to eat alone," said Katherine, and continued doing so.

Jeremiah looked around for another place to sit. The cafeteria was filling up, but over in the opposite corner he saw a table with a few empty seats. He was about to start towards it when he realized it was a table of Canadian doctors.

They were not only Canadian doctors in the idiomatic sense of "highly skilled and specialized individuals, such as doctors, who are rendered borderline unemployable by vice of being Canadian," but in the literal sense of "highly skilled and specialized *doctors* who were rendered borderline unemployable by vice of being Canadian, complete with the mandated maple leaf pins on their white lab coats and ready apologies on their lips."

Jeremiah recognized one of them—the pretty blonde doctor who had treated him on his only visit to the infirmary, when he had confused a twisted ankle with imminent death. She happened to look up as he was looking over, and for a moment her attention caught on Jeremiah like a sweater drawn across a hook. But although Jeremiah considered himself highly tolerant in general, and had nothing against Canadians in particular—even having once had a friend who he suspected was a Canadian—and even though he did not particularly want to eat alone—he looked away quickly.

At that moment, a group of Indian men in gray jumpsuits happened to vacate a table a few steps from him, and Jeremiah sat down. He took a few bites of his ham, which tasted a bit off, tapped the igneous bread with his thumbnail, and sniffed the purée before deciding he wasn't that hungry. Maybe he'd go find somewhere to send Appleton a wave.

Once again he dared to approach Katherine, who had finished her food and started reading off an ancient PED in the meanwhile.

"Sorry to bug you," he said, "but could you tell me where I could send a wave?"

She did not even look up.

Jeremiah looked around for a friendlier source of information. The Canadian doctors were just as out of the question for advice as for companionship. At most other tables, conversations continued in languages he did not speak—or *mostly* in languages he did not speak.

Back on the folk music circuit in Detroit, Jeremiah

had spent a good amount of time loitering in bars and coffee houses before they opened and after they closed, where he had chatted with the kitchen and janitorial staff meanwhile. In the process, he had not only met his fair share of Canadians, but picked up a smattering of Spanish from the shift managers and chefs—enough, he thought modestly, to get around. He had not found many opportunities to exercise his Spanish on the Einstein IV, but he supposed it was like falling off a bike—you never really forgot how. So Jeremiah took a moment to compose himself—and his request—and then approached one of the raucous Latino tables. The moment had come for Jeremiah to employ his Spanish language skills.

"Horses," he said, *"you tell me where it is, the hellos for the proletariats?"*

All ten men crowded around the table exploded into laughter, and Jeremiah could just make out snatches of the ensuing Spanish flood: something about the workers of the world and a revolution, some inexplicable neighing, and then something—just possibly—about someone not speaking Spanish particularly well.

One of the men held out his hand and quieted the riot. He had dark smiling eyes set in a round open face. A deep scar ran from the left corner of his mouth across his cheek before making a sharp turn and stopping just short of his neck. This scar was only the most pronounced of several, but whatever disagreements with edged weapons the man had taken part in during his life, it did not seem to have blunted his good mood, and Jeremiah could not tell whether some of the lines in the corner of his eyes were records of brushes with knife-induced blindness or crow's feet from 30 years of smiling as broadly as he was now.

"Luis," the man said, holding out his hand.

"Jeremiah," said Jeremiah, allowing Luis to clasp his hand as if they were about to arm wrestle.

"My English is not good," Luis said. "But is better than your Spanish. Tell me other time what are you looking for. In English."

"Somewhere employees can send a wave."

Luis translated and the table sprang into action, describing to Jeremiah in a stew of English, Spanish, waving arms, and lines of watery ketchup smeared across a plank of syn-thed ham, how to find what he was looking for.

Appleton,

They broke the news about Uncle Leo today. He was a hel-luva guy in some ways and certainly more of a dad to me than my "real" dad and I hope he wasn't too disappointed in me as he left this vale of tears. Also that he didn't suffer.

Speaking of suffering, what's this about abject poverty? Hav-ing been impressed by the service here I now find myself impressed into it, with threats of more where that came from if I don't mea-sure up to some very exacting standards. Even if that somehow turns out all right there's the minor question of how I earn a liv-ing upon my return to a planet where the marketable skills I don't possess in the first place are 20 years out of date.

Is the will bulletproof? Are the ferrets triumphant and unas-sailable? Send me some happy news, tell me you've been working all angles and already have a fix or two in mind.

Also, how are you? How are Melvin and the twins, who must be—good lord—out of college by now? What do you bench these days?

Love to all,

Bullfrog

P.S. Apparently you won't get this right away, and I might not even get your reply before we get home (I still don't really un-derstand all that relativity stuff, even after reading this pamphlet they throw at us), but I'm sending it anyway.

P.P.S. If I get out of this alive I've decided to call my autobiog-raphy A Business of Ferrets. Like the term of venery—get it?

After bidding a sad farewell to his home of the last two years, Jeremiah rolled his trunk, both suitcases stacked on top, along the drab hallways of the service quarters until he found his way to W24. He passed his keycard, the door hissed open, and Jeremiah entered Katherine's—and now his—suite.

Suite was more a marketer's description than an archi-tect's. The nominal living room better resembled a small foyer where a displaced friend was stashing a pygmy sofa and a miniature end table, which had been field promoted to a de facto coffee table when it could not fit at either end of the sofa and had to go in front of it. Only two doors opened off the "living room"—one, which was open, led to the bathroom. Jeremiah presumed that the other was Katherine's bedroom—which was closed. There was no kitchen, kitchenette, dining room, family room, sunroom, breakfast nook, or any of those other rooms Jeremiah associated with the word *suite*.

On the walls Katherine had hung posters for three 21st century waves, two of which (*Wanderlust* and *Nowhere Fast*) Jeremiah recognized, and one of which (*The Truth about Ruth*) he did not. It made his chest ache a little both to discover that she might share his passion for early cinema, and that they were not currently on good enough terms that he could ask her where she had found such excellent reproductions.

Katherine was already holed up in her bedroom, from whence Jeremiah could hear muffled music playing. He tiptoed up to her door—which was of the old-fashioned swinging type, doorknob and all—and put his ear against it. The music was late 20th or early 21st century, with a strong backbeat and hook, but he didn't recognize the song. Jeremiah could still hear the music as he changed into his pajamas and stretched out on the scratchy sofa with the playbook. Around 9:30 the music stopped, but Katherine never came out.

Which was a shame, because Jeremiah would have enjoyed the opportunity to hear about her day and tell her about his, which—he realized—had been the longest, most infuriating, and most eventful of his life.

Sometime after midnight, Jeremiah dropped off to sleep under the gaze of the titular Ruth, the lights still burning and the playbook splayed open on his chest to the Event Planning section, while visions of A/V requisitions and room permits danced in his head.

6

Bandora's Box

JEREMIAH felt he had only just dozed off when the sound of the bedroom door closing snapped him fully awake again. There stood Katherine in a white bathrobe, a pink towel draped over her shoulder and a bundle of folded clothes beneath her arm.

"I'm going first," she said.

"You mean to the shower?" he asked. Katherine did not answer. "What time is it?" said Jeremiah.

She walked into the bathroom and closed the door. Jeremiah could not help but notice that, counting last night's query about where to send a wave, that made three questions running that Katherine had refused even to acknowledge, let alone answer. Either she had some strongly held beliefs about the importance of self-education, or she was still upset with him. The shower started to run.

While he waited for Katherine to finish, Jeremiah picked out his clothes for the day. He had just finished assembling a passably professional outfit of grey pants and white button-down shirt when Katherine came out of the bathroom, now fully dressed in her uniform, her hair still wet and latched up behind her head.

"Do you think this outfit will be all right?" he asked her, holding it up.

"Stay in your pajamas for all I care," she said. "Shower's all yours. Staff breakfast starts in 10."

Jeremiah felt that her finally answering one of his

questions—even with open hostility—was a sign that their relationship was improving. As he went to take his own shower, he almost felt like whistling.

Katherine was gone by the time Jeremiah finished showering, so he walked to the cafeteria by himself. From the buffet line he chose an omelet (prepared by a Canadian with "désolé" tattooed on his chest) that seemed to contain the same batch of synthed ham he had dined on the previous evening, and a slice of toast that needed to be screened for melanoma ASAP. Jeremiah saw Katherine at her usual table in the corner, but it seemed unwise to try his luck again so soon. He was about to sit down at an empty table to eat alone when he heard a piercing whistle and his name being called from across the room. It was Luis.

As Jeremiah approached, the ten men sitting around the table designed for eight managed, with a lot of shouting and gesturing, to make an eleventh space and drag another chair over for him.

"Thanks," said Jeremiah as he sat down next to Luis. "*Gracias*," he added to the table at large, which replied with laughter and a flurry of Spanish that was directed at Luis but clearly concerned with Jeremiah.

"They want to know," said Luis, "why they never see you before last night. You hitch-hiker on spaceship looking for job?" Luis stuck out his thumb, prompting another wave of laughter.

Jeremiah did his best to explain his situation, Luis did his best to translate it, and the rest of the table did their best to understand, but Jeremiah would not have staked much credit on the accuracy of the story they came away with after this game of bilingual operator—especially since Luis had to ask him four times what a "ferret" was, and, when conveying Jeremiah's answer to the rest of the table, had pantomimed swimming motions.

When Jeremiah had finished eating and was excusing himself, Luis clasped his hand and said, "This is Manny, Carlos, Carlos, Héctor, Adelfo, Humberto, Heriberto, Carlos, and Jesús." He looked at Jeremiah to make sure he had absorbed the roll call, and Jeremiah smiled dazedly and nodded—he was 80 percent sure he'd gotten the names, but 100 percent sure that, if in doubt, he would guess "Carlos," and be right 30 percent of the time.

"From now you sit with us," Luis said, "OK? You one of us now."

Which touched Jeremiah to a surprising degree.

———————————

After the public humiliation of yesterday's lunch, Jeremiah was not eager to revisit the passenger dining room. As he walked, he considered how he would request quiet from the guests in the dining room, rejecting the fork on water glass (what was he, the best man?) in favor of a throaty "Ladies and gentlemen, if I might interrupt your breakfast for a moment." But it turned out there was no need to beg attention: his mere return to the dining room silenced all conversation. Awareness of his presence spread like a disease, communicated from table to table by discreet nudges and subtly tossed heads. No one seemed sure whether to acknowledge their fallen fellow or not, except for the Chapins, who waved heartily—though Jeremiah thought he detected some perturbation behind Mrs. Chapin's friendly manner, as if she had just been thinking about him and would have found it easier to stop doing so if he had not suddenly shown up at breakfast.

"Ladies and gentlemen," said Jeremiah, louder than was strictly needed now that all talking had already ceased, "on behalf of the Office of Guest Services, Event Planning, and General Clerical, I'm happy to announce that the First Ever—as far as we know—Golden Worldlines Talent Show will take place on the last full day of our cruise—that is, just one week from today—right here in the dining room. If you have a talent to share with your fellow passengers—and I know you do"—even Jeremiah winced as he said this, which had, in his head, sounded much less like someone organizing a talent show—"signups will be this morning, immediately following breakfast. And now, I leave you to your eggs Benedict."

He smiled at the crowd, most of whom still couldn't meet his eyes. The mood was deteriorating from awkward to anguished. Several guests stood up and excused themselves, and Jeremiah left the dining room to a smattering of bemused applause.

Jeremiah went straight to the office, pausing only to use the restroom, but by the time he arrived, four of the guests who had excused themselves from breakfast were already there, milling around the door without acknowledging each other, as if a group of friends had all, by incredible chance, happened to find themselves in the waiting room for the same doctor with a certain specialty that made eye contact unthinkable. A fifth arrived before Jeremiah could open the door.

"Please," said Jeremiah to the gathering crowd, "come in. Take a number and have a seat." He held the door as the guests shuffled past.

Two more arrived before he could let the door close.

"And what's your talent, Mrs. Biltmore?" asked Jeremiah.

"Glass harp," she said.

"Do you need any special materials or preparation?"

"Just glasses and water. I haven't played in a long time."

"Then you'd better practice up," said Jeremiah. "Who's number two?"

"That's me," said Mr. Drinkwater, hardly giving Mrs. Biltmore a chance to vacate the chair before he occupied it. "Look," said Drinkwater, changing to a loud whisper, "don't you think the last day is a bit late for the show? I mean, what with the seduction and all?"

"Trust me," Jeremiah whispered back, "the anticipation will only heighten the excitement. And you know how people get emotional at the end of things—cast parties, goodbye dinners, etc."

"If you're sure," said Mr. Drinkwater, in a tone that showed he was not.

"Talent, Mr. Drinkwater?" asked Jeremiah full-voiced and briskly, with a significant glance at the other passengers—some of whom were starting to show too much interest in their conversation.

"Have you forgotten?"

Jeremiah cleared his throat and pointed out the still-gathering crowd with his pen.

"Appearances, Mr. Drinkwater," he whispered.

"Oh, yes," said Mr. Drinkwater. Then, too loudly: "I'm a mime."

"What level of expertise?"

Mr. Drinkwater looked around at his fellow guests—he seemed to be losing his nerve.

"Professional, amateur, or semi-professional?" asked Jeremiah.

"Those are my only choices?"

"Yes," said Jeremiah, adding under his breath: "Remember, you're going to *impress* her."

"I guess—semi-professional?"

"Very modest, Mr. Drinkwater. You'll be anchoring our show."

"My goodness," said Mr. Drinkwater, starting to sweat, "that's a lot of responsibility."

"I'm sure you'll knock it out of the park."

"*Now serving number ...* **THREE.**"

"Talent?"

"What's the policy on open flame?"

Jeremiah looked up, hoping that Mr. Porter was joking, but the sight of his face—flushed and earnest, eyes blazing with espresso-fueled excitement—dashed any such hopes.

"I think," said Jeremiah, flipping through the playbook to buy himself some time, "the official policy is that it's—"

Jeremiah looked up, but the answer was not to be found on the ceiling, either.

"Yes?"

Now Jeremiah shuffled through the roster for the talent show, where he still found nothing about Golden Worldlines' policy on open flame.

"Discouraged," he said.

"Does discouraged mean *discouraged*?" asked Mr. Porter, looking hopeful if not Highly Satisfied. "Or does discouraged mean *not allowed*?" At the consideration of that possibility,

51

his expression fell to a level that Jeremiah would have rated
at least a Somewhat Dissatisfied.

"I think it means—" Jeremiah said. The air between them
veritably crackled with suspense. "*Strongly* discouraged."

Mr. Porter beamed.

"Message received," he said, "loud and clear."

He stood up and saluted before offering Jeremiah his
trembling hand.

"Wait, Mr. Porter—you still haven't told me what your
talent is."

"Just put 'novelty act,' " said Mr. Porter. "I don't want to
spoil the surprise."

"Talent?"

"Extinct bird calls."

"Talent?"

"I perform popular songs of the 2100's on the spoons."

"Talent?"

"Tap dance. Just kidding: comedy. The stage will be
wheelchair accessible?"

"Of course, Mr. Withers," said Jeremiah, and jotted a note
to himself on the roster: *Stage?*

"Hello Mr. Wendstrom," said Jeremiah. "Talent?"

"Have you located that *green item* we talked about yesterday?" Mr. Wendstrom asked.

"I haven't had a chance," Jeremiah whispered. With his
pen he pointed to the other guests as subtly as he could.

Mr. Wendstrom frowned and stood up.

"I'm going to give one of my talks," he said, "for which
I usually charge quite a bit of credit. It's called 'Winner or
Loser? The Clock is Ticking.' "

By lunchtime the office was empty, nearly half the guests were on the list as performers, and Jeremiah was both exhausted and the tiniest bit proud of himself. He'd cracked the books, rallied the troops, and ridden the whirlwind, and he was almost looking forward to planning the logistics of the show.

"Good morning," said someone from inside the doorway.

Jeremiah could not recall ever having seen the lady who was behind this salutation—a state of affairs which was unusual on a ship with 54—now technically 53, due to one imminent default—passengers. And she was definitely of the passenger class, this lady: marching through her early 70s with low-heel pumps and a cartwheel hat, each of which would have looked right at home on an encased mannequin in the Smithsonian. The string of pearls arranged on her smart tweed suit, if offered on the open market, could have made a serious dent in Jeremiah's imminently defaulted ticket. Against this fashionable background her handbag stood out in sharp relief—an oversized, misshapen blob of black cloth with padded handles. The shape and size of the bag was just right to hold a giant tortoise and all wrong to conceal a PED, and something about that fact—combined with the novelty of her acquaintance—put Jeremiah in a fight or flight mood.

"We're just closing up for lunch," he said, opting for flight. "We open again at one."

"It's 11:59," said the lady, "or I would have said 'good afternoon.' I have come to sign up for the talent show."

Jeremiah looked up at the clock, which—traitor—took the lady's side.

"All right," he said. "Ms.—?"

"Mayflower," said the lady, sitting down and smoothing her tweed skirt over her knees. "*Mrs.* Mayflower. In my day marriage was a union to be taken seriously—not a casual arrangement to be tossed overboard as soon as one partner got the seven-year itch or had been dead for decades."

"Mayflower like the ship?"

"Precisely like the ship, on which my late husband's ancestors, the Rosethorpes, were passengers. Their name was later corrupted by a clerical error at Ellis Island."

"But if his ancestors had come over on the Mayflower,

why did they have to go through Ellis Island?" Jeremiah asked.

"They left and came back—a situation they were trying to explain to an immigration officer of less than average intelligence."

"I see," said Jeremiah. "Talent?"

"I will be singing and accompanying myself upon the bandora."

"The Pandora, did you say?"

"Not Pandora—bandora, with a *bee*. It's a type of lute."

"You'll be singing *and* playing the flute?"

"Not flute. Lute. Eh-*lute*. In my day we enunciated clearly, which aided others in not acquiring the bad habit of mishearing. In a world without mishearers, my family name would still be Rosethorpe, and I would already be signed up for the talent show and on my way."

"I see," Jeremiah said through gritted teeth. "Eh-*lute*. Will you require any special materials for your performance, Mrs. Mayflower?"

A rectal stick removal kit, perhaps? he thought, confirming *en passant* that Mrs. Mayflower was not an eh-telepath as well as an eh-lutenist.

"My bandora requires light servicing to be performance ready," she said, unzipping the handbag (which Jeremiah now recognized as a soft instrument case, like the one in which he never actually bothered to keep his poor banjo back in his rambling musician days) and extracting the giant tortoise, which turned out not to be a tortoise but the aforementioned bandora. Mrs. Mayflower held it out across the desk with exquisite delicacy, then withdrew it as soon as Jeremiah reached out.

"Do you know how many bandoras there are in the world, young man?"

Jeremiah admitted that he did not.

"One. This one. John Rose invented the instrument *circa* 1560. The bandora remained in vogue for almost 100 years, until grosser tastes prevailed against its soft and subtle sound. The bandora is a delicate and temperamental instrument, and time has not been kind to them. In the late 21st century, it was thought they had all returned to dust. Until this one—"

She finally handed it to him, as if it were a baby.

"—was discovered in a church basement in the English countryside. It was in abysmal condition—much time and money has gone into restoring the glory you now hold in your hands."

Jeremiah had an inherent love of musical instruments, and an inherent fascination with the past, but the bandora he now cradled in his hands struggled heroically against these tender sympathies. The body was irregularly pinched and curved, as if the luthier who had built it had let his two-year-old son draw the line on the wood for him. The neck was infested with cherubs whose rolled-up eyes gave them the appearance of choking to death on a final oversized bite of whatever delicacy was responsible for the rolls of fat on their arms and legs. Painted on the front panel a stout shepherd stood with hat in hand, covering his privates like a schoolboy while he professed his love to an even stouter shepherdess, who was doing her level best meanwhile to look dainty.

"There is a slight buzz in the lowest string," said Mrs. Mayflower. "You will remove it. The buzz, not the string," she added, remembering the level of intellect she was dealing with.

"Mrs. Mayflower," said Jeremiah, "I don't know the first thing about bandoras—or even lutes in general. I'm afraid I can't service this for you."

He tried to hand it back to her, but she folded her hands deliberately in her lap.

"You don't know about lutes, young man, but do you know about money?" Mrs. Mayflower asked.

"You mean credit? I know *of* it more than I know it, if you know what I mean. You know what they say—credit makes credit, people make people."

Mrs. Mayflower wrinkled her nose, as if she had just caught a whiff of something unsavory.

"In my day," she said, "we called it money. Do you know what it's for?"

"To buy things?"

"That's a naive and simplistic view. Money is gift wrap for problems."

Mrs. Mayflower's smile at finding a chance to use this

phrase—Jeremiah suspected it was a favorite of her own invention—began to fade as she realized that Jeremiah had not fully absorbed its significance.

"I take a problem of mine," she said. "For example, I need my bandora serviced so that I can accompany my vocals in the upcoming talent show, and my man Theodore, who normally performs this function for me, has made the poor decision to acquire some sort of palsy that renders him unfit. I wrap this problem in money—"

She pantomimed the action in deference to her young student's obvious deficiencies, folding imaginary paper and tying an imaginary ribbon with her white-gloved hands in a show of mime worthy of Mr. Drinkwater.

"—and I give it to you. Can you guess whose problem it is now?"

"Mine?" guessed Jeremiah.

Mrs. Mayflower smiled in approval.

"I find people rise to challenges when they are properly gift wrapped."

"You're not actually proposing to pay me, though, are you?" said Jeremiah.

She stopped smiling.

"I've paid Golden Worldlines enough that the problem of paying *you* has become theirs. I suspect that Mr. Grubel would agree. One way or another, I'll make sure that he hears about my experience at the Guest Services desk, and believe me, young man: if I get my bandora back in anything less than concert-ready condition—or with so much as a single scratch on it—I shall be far, far from satisfied."

"I believe you," said Jeremiah.

7

Strawberries, Keycards, and Rekindled Fires

TO say that during his two years aboard the E4 Jeremiah had lost the knack of multitasking would have been a grave injustice to the innate and utter inability to juggle tasks with which God had blessed Jeremiah from the moment of his birth. In fact, during the thirty odd years of life Jeremiah had spent on Earth and off it, he had only occasionally, with strenuous effort and a little luck, been able to work himself up to *tasking* at all—and those were specialized circumstances, generally related to the focused production, enjoyment, or study of music, which had not prepared him well for tackling his current set of diverse and overlapping challenges, or even keeping the list of said challenges in good working order.

Luckily Fate—perhaps feeling the slightest twinge of guilt for the obstacles it planned one day to hurl Jeremiah's way—had sent him help, though in a form Jeremiah had not recognized at the time. To his seventh-grade self, Ms. Domenico and her seminar on "Personal Tools and Development" had represented nothing more than a low-impact elective with which to fill fifth period. But as present-day Jeremiah wrestled with the list of unpleasant projects sitting on his metaphorical desk, the ancient Ms. Domenico and her advice came to his mind.

"When *I* have a lot of problems I have to manage and prioritize," she was saying as she stood in front of the class, "I imagine them as cats in my living room.

"The small problems are fuzzy little kittens hiding behind the sofa or playing with the curtains: for example, they canceled my favorite wave or I need to remember to pick up a prescription.

"The big, urgent problems are nasty old tomcats ripping up cushions and marking their territory: the rent check bounced again, or he hasn't come home or even called in two days.

"The very worst problems are like tigers spread across the floor, baring their teeth: he finally called and says he wants a divorce.

"I choose cats because I love cats—more than I love people, according to him—but you can choose anything you want."

An image came to Jeremiah's mind: the Guest Services Office, empty of human presence, but filled with reptilian. There on the desk sat an iguana of ordinary size, a patch of deep red on his throat. This was Carolus the Bold, representing—in self-referential fashion—his own self and Jeremiah's search for him. A monitor lizard paced slowly across the room, the embodiment of Mr. Drinkwater's unrequited love for Mrs. Abdurov, and his expectation that Jeremiah would cause it to be requited by means of a talent show. Around the head of the monitor lizard crawled a red salamander, tiny but not to be forgotten: the need for a stage in said talent show. Mrs. Mayflower's bandora and the repair thereof—having incarnated as a Gila monster—perched stiffly atop the back of the desk chair. And at the back of the room, his soft snores so great that they caused the floor to tremble, a lightly sleeping dragon lay curled up, his own tail acting as his pillow: the Somewhat Satisfaction of every passenger on board, and Jeremiah's responsibility to maintain it.

The mere act of cataloging and ranking these insane tasks made Jeremiah feel the tiniest bit better. It gave him the illusion of control—which, he reflected as he walked to lunch, might be the only form of control any of us really had in this absurd and chaotic universe.

At lunch Jeremiah found that Luis had saved him a seat again, and the table had grown bolder with their questions.

"The pretty waitress, she is your lady?" Luis translated.

"Katherine?" said Jeremiah. "Far, far from it. She can't stand the sight of me."

"But you sleep in her room, no?"

"Yes, which is one reason she can't stand the sight of me."

"So why you sleep there?"

"That's a long story," said Jeremiah. "Why did Carlos just push up his nose like that?"

"He wants to know, isn't she a little strawberry?"

"What?"

"Strawberry? *Fresa*?" Luis pushed the tip of his nose up into a shape that was arguably closer to a strawberry than when he wasn't pushing it up. "How do you say—stick up?"

"Stuck up?"

"That's it—stuck up."

"I don't think so," Jeremiah said. "I think she's just lonely—and maybe a little sad."

"So why you not make her happy?"

"Let's talk about something else. What about all of you—what do you do on the E4?"

"We are maintaining," Luis said. "Carpentering and plumbing and working with the metal, you know."

"Why did you take jobs on the Einstein IV? What are your plans when you all get home?"

Luis laughed and translated.

"Why is everyone smiling like that?" asked Jeremiah.

"Because, my friend, you are asking question for rich people. Choices, reasons, plans? Manny was in prison when he was *joven*, so he can't get no good job. But no one wants this job, so they no check many records. Watch it!"

This last remark Luis shouted not at Jeremiah, but the sweeping Canadian who had just clipped Luis's shoe with a broom. Luis waved off the Canadian's apology, rolled his eyes, and returned to the tale of his fellows.

"Carlos First has a little girl and no credit, this way she gets a little credit. Carlos Second can't work on roofs no more—he fell and hurt his back. What are jobs for hurt roofer? Héctor is here because he is Carlos Second's cousin and Carlos Second's mother wanted that he have some family with him in the future. Adelfo's family is gone in accident, so why stay? Humberto sends credit home to his family. And Heriberto—Heriberto is just crazy. *Loco.* No one knows why he does nothing."

Heriberto, hearing his name and *loco* in the same vicinity, grinned like a demon and puffed up his chest with pride.

"Carlos Third, they were going to deport him, he is friends with Carlos Second and thought 'Why not?' And Jesús, his mother was sick, this way she can pay some bills for the hospital. Sure she is dead by now."

Jesús crossed himself and kissed his hand.

"What about you, Luis?" asked Jeremiah.

"Oh, me, I am running from bad trouble. The police, they think I stole a veecar. I didn't steal no veecar, but this man who no likes me say he saw me, and they want to put me in the prison. So my brother Mundo, he knows about the statue of libertations, and he tells me 'Luis, always they are looking for maintainers at Golden Worldlines, and they don't check no backgrounds or ask no questions, and you know very well how to work with the wood. The statue of libertations for stealing a veecar in California is just three years, and you going to be gone 20.' So."

"Luis," said Jeremiah, "are you sure the statute of limitations counts Earth time instead of the time here on the ship?"

Luis laughed and clapped Jeremiah on the back.

"My friend," he said, "Mundo knows all about the statue of libertations. When I return to Earth, I will be *intocable.*"

Jeremiah did not share Luis's confidence on this point, but he let it go for the moment, and the table began to encourage him, under the pretext of "Spanish lessons," to converse in Spanish, which eventually left Carlos Second gasping for air so hard that Humberto mistakenly delivered the Heimlich maneuver.

"I should probably head out," Jeremiah said. "I have to find an iguana."

"*Iguanas-ranas,*" said Heriberto after Luis had translated, which was apparently so hilarious that Carlos Second began to relapse.

As Jeremiah was standing up to go, he took note of a sign on the wall, which read "Please feel free to bus your own table. Sorry." Though there were once again flocks of Canadians flitting about and clearing dishes, Jeremiah felt a momentary pang for them. After all, it was debatably not their fault that they had been born Canadian, and it seemed to Jeremiah that the least he could do to assist a fellow human being was to bus his own table, which he did.

But as he was separating his dirty dishes, someone bumped into him from behind, so hard that he dropped his spoon into the vat of soapy water meant for forks.

"Excuse me," Jeremiah said, turning around. He had not yet decided whether he was actually excusing himself or inviting whoever had bumped him to excuse *himself*, but he saw right away that the Canadian doctor on the other end of this bumping transaction shared no such doubts about who was in the wrong.

He was about Jeremiah's age, height, and weight, wearing a white coat and stethoscope. Jeremiah had taken vague note of him before, as young men always take note of potential romantic rivals. He was much better looking than Jeremiah— or he would have been if his Gallic good looks had not been held hostage to what could have been charitably described as brooding intensity. It was the kind of brooding intensity that Jeremiah generally crossed the street to avoid—the kind he associated with violent outbursts at random passersby— and if there *were* a kind of brooding intensity that Jeremiah would have welcomed trapping him in the back corner of the cafeteria, this wasn't it.

As a result, Jeremiah found himself apologizing to a Canadian—and not just in the idiomatic sense of "apologizing to someone he had no earthly business apologizing to," but also in the literal sense of "apologizing to someone he had no earthly business apologizing to, who also happened to be Canadian."

"Sorry about that," said Jeremiah. "My fault entirely. If I could just squeeze through here."

The Canadian doctor, who had planted himself firmly between Jeremiah and his escape route through the cafeteria, did not budge as Jeremiah sucked in his gut, stood on his tiptoes, and took other exquisite pains to get around him without further physical contact.

"Right," Jeremiah said when he was past and therefore able to breathe again, "nice bumping into you."

"*Vat fair foot*," said the Canadian doctor—or French words to that effect.

The moment had come for Jeremiah to employ his French language skills.

"*Excusez-moi?*" he said.

"*Jamie Aussie long Tom Kujo vee*," said the Canadian doctor—or something closely resembling.

Though Jeremiah's French was not as good as his Spanish, he doubted the phrase added up to an apology. As he took his brisk leave from the cafeteria, he saw Grubel eating a sandwich and watching from across the room. He was frowning as he chewed.

Back at the office Jeremiah found Mr. Boyle pacing back and forth in the hallway and talking to himself.

"My keycard doesn't work," Mr. Boyle said, not to himself.

"I can help you with that, Mr. Boyle," said Jeremiah as he unlocked the door. "Come in and take a number."

"There's no one else here—why do I have to take a number?"

Jeremiah was about to reply with an unkind witticism, but he caught himself. Below the shock of red hair, Mr. Boyle's face had a certain puffiness that Jeremiah associated with large doses of steroids or years of unhappiness. And the cold glitter and streetwise edge in his eyes, Jeremiah suddenly realized, was just a bluff—a desperate bluff to cover up not only the profound fear behind them but an even deeper bewilderment.

It seemed to Jeremiah that, although he and Boyle inhabited the same universe—which universe they both, being grown men, knew to be absurd—they could not have interpreted that absurdity more differently. What Jeremiah took as arbitrary, Boyle experienced as personal. What Jeremiah thought to be uncaring, Boyle knew to be tricksy and hostile. What Jeremiah assumed was a cosmic joke, Boyle was sure was a dirty swindle. In that moment, Jeremiah could see perfectly in Boyle's eyes the unshakeable certainty that the entire universe, and everyone and everything in it, was designed and deployed solely *contra* Robert

Boyle, and wanted nothing more than to get the better of him. And Jeremiah could see as well Boyle's conviction that of the two weapons available to defend himself against this onslaught—his wits for one and a nasty, blind suspicion for the other—only the second was sharp enough to bother reaching for.

"Don't worry about it," said Jeremiah.

But Jeremiah's relenting so easily only seemed to sharpen Boyle's suspicions that he was being conned, and he took a ticket ostentatiously.

"*Now serving number* ... **TWENTY-EIGHT**."

"So your keycard doesn't work?" Jeremiah asked.

"The woman who cleans my cabin has been looking at me funny. My ex-wife probably waved her and put her up to it. Even at this distance she's found some way to screw me. I'll have the last laugh, though. I don't care how many passages I have to book, I'll stand above her grave and piss on it while holding out my last credit, and she won't be able to touch it. Because she'll be dead."

Jeremiah, who had heard enough variations on this theme over the last two years that he had learned to ignore them, opened the playbook and skimmed a page.

"What cabin are you in?"

"H06."

"May I see the keycard?"

Boyle handed it over and Jeremiah, following the steps carefully, recoded it using the encoder he found—just as the playbook promised he would—in the bottom desk drawer.

"This will work now?" said Boyle.

"If not, just bring it back. We're here until five. Thank you for visiting the Guest Services Desk, Mr. Boyle," said Jeremiah. "Have a Golden Worldlines—"

Boyle slammed the door behind him.

"—day."

Thus began the afternoon's parade of keycards on the fritz—four more guests in the space of an hour, each having been greeted by the same blinking light and angry beeping when they returned to their rooms for a little post-lunch siesta.

All four were embarrassed and pleasant and grateful, but nothing could quite erase the flavor of Boyle's visit from Jeremiah's mouth—or wipe from his mind the unpleasant glimpse of what lay behind Boyle's eyes.

"It's my keycard," said Mr. Werther hoarsely as he sat down. "Quite stupid, actually."

"I like your vest," said Jeremiah.

"It's nice, isn't it?" Mr. Werther rubbed the turquoise wool between his thumb and fingers. "They've been keeping it so cold in here lately."

"But you were saying, about your keycard? Let me guess," said Jeremiah, already opening the drawer with the encoder, "the light on the door blinks red? Angry beeping sounds?"

"Even stupider, I'm afraid. I've lost it."

He took a handful of mints from the desk and tossed one into his mouth as if it were a heart pill.

"Good," said Jeremiah, "a little variety."

In two minutes flat Jeremiah had read everything the playbook had to say on the matter of lost keycards, found the stock of spares in a cabinet behind the beaded curtain at the back of the office, and encoded a replacement, but even in that short interval Werther managed to put a sizeable dent in the dish of mints. His eyes had an absent, sad look.

"Would you like a bag of those to take with you?" Jeremiah asked.

"Oh, no—no, thank you. My goodness, I've eaten all your mints. Ech, they're actually terrible, aren't they? It's a nasty habit. Whenever I'm preoccupied with legal questions, I crave sugar."

"You're a lawyer! I'd forgotten!"

Jeremiah's having forgotten was not remarkable: none of his fellow passengers seemed able to hold in their minds the fact that Mr. Werther had made his own credit, and if they ever happened to be reminded, the memory faded as rapidly as if it had been written in water.

This collective amnesia had less to do with any social mercies on the part of the other passengers than with Mr. Werther's own nature. He was one of those people who fit in anywhere, a universal donor in the circulatory system of society. He would not have raised an eyebrow in either a Detroit dive or a fundraising dinner in Washington.

"Yes, well, a semi-retired lawyer," said Mr. Werther.

"What kind of law are you semi-retired from?"

"Oh, mainly family law of one type or another. Divorce, inheritance, the odd disowning."

"Mr. Werther," said Jeremiah, fighting the impulse to leap across the desk and hug him, "could I ask your advice on a couple legal matters?"

"Ferrets, eh?" said Mr. Werther when Jeremiah had finished.

"I know it sounds crazy," Jeremiah said.

"It's actually quite common."

"Really?"

"I mean, this is the first I've heard of *ferrets* in particular, but there's something about animals that makes rich old people want to leave them everything. Not the animals you'd expect, either. The dolphins and lions? They hardly see a credit. The sea-slugs and wolverines, on the other hand? Rolling in it. Lots of poodles. Octopuses, once. Octopi?"

"Octopodoi," said Jeremiah, "a consortium of. Do you have a legal opinion about my chances of breaking the will?"

"How good is your lawyer?"

"The best," said Jeremiah. "That is," he added, in deference to present company, "*one of* the best."

"You're swimming in tricky waters. In most states wills can't be contested more than two years after the death of the testator—but two years for whom? Back on Earth, your Uncle Leo is nearly three years deceased, but for you, less than two years of subjective time has passed since his death."

Werther had started eating mints again—his nails clinked on the bottom of the dish.

"Generally the courts have favored whatever time frame makes matters more predictable for people on Earth—which means, usually, Earth time. The legal term for it is 'Principle of Least Earthly Surprise.' Write that down. They don't want some poor fool to inherit a fortune, buy a mansion, and then find out 20 years later that the credit isn't his after all. That would be *surprising*. But—and here's your angle—how can ferrets be surprised about credit? Would they even *know* if the

65

will were reversed and the credit went back to you? The people at the shelter would, of course, but they're just the stewards of the inheritance, not the beneficiaries. Once you're back on Earth, aren't *you* the one surprised to find your rights subordinate to what is essentially a form of weasel? It's far from a slam dunk, but that's what I think you've got. Tell your lawyer to check Hansel v. Hansel, Lemaire v. Bulger—write these down!—Jonas v. Jones, and Mead v. Mead. Those are the landmark cases—or at least they were 20 years ago."

"And Mead v. Mead," repeated Jeremiah, scribbling furiously. "Got it."

"Now as for your friend with the grand theft veeauto charge waiting for him, there's no ambiguity there, unless the Supreme Court has revisited Alabama v. Pinkerton in our absence, which I doubt. The statute of limitations expires on subjective time. End of story. Hartshorne posits exactly this situation in his majority opinion: a man who commits a crime and immediately boards a ship for a journey at relativistic speeds, then returns a mere year older himself but having escaped prosecution for a crime that should have followed him for ten. Allowing such behavior would be a form of moral hazard."

"So my friend will be in danger when we get back?"

"Well, I imagine they could still charge him. As for whether he's in actual danger: who knows if after 20 years anyone will still be interested in a missing veecar? It sounds like the whole case turns on the testimony of this supposed eyewitness. Who knows if he's still angry enough to testify after what has been, for him, 20 years? Who's to say he's even still alive?"

"So you're saying he might be all right?"

"Lawyers don't say things like that," said Mr. Werther. "Your friend needs to get himself a lawyer the minute he sets foot on American soil again. A criminal lawyer."

"Thank you Mr. Werther," said Jeremiah. "You're a lifesaver."

———

Some time later, as Jeremiah was flipping idly through the playbook, the door of the Guest Services Office opened and a figure darkened the frame, backlit dramatically by the lights in the hall.

"Jeremiah," said the figure.

"Mrs. Chapin," said Jeremiah.

"Jeremiah," she said again.

"Mrs. Chapin," said Jeremiah, gamely.

She crossed the room, sat down across from him, and reached across the desk to take his right hand in both of hers.

"Jeremiah, oh, Jeremiah!" she said.

"Mrs. Chapin," he said, and then, because he could not think of anything else to say, "can you please take a number?"

"How can you speak of numbers after what you've done to me?"

"What have I done to you?" asked Jeremiah.

"You have rekindled a fire, Jeremiah. Here."

Attempting to further Jeremiah's understanding with a tactile aid, Mrs. Chapin drew his hand towards her breast, slowly and deliberately enough that Jeremiah had some time to consider his options. It was not much time, but that was all right, as he didn't have many options, and all of them were bad.

Jeremiah had seen all the waves in *The Gruduate* family — the original, both remakes, and even that abomination of a sequel *The Postgraduate*—so he was quite clear on the best methods for ruining his life at this moment. But he could not call to mind any wave that might serve as instructional material for how to politely *reject* the advances of an older woman who could, with a single word from her scorned lips, condemn her scorner to two years of indentured servitude.

"Mrs. Chapin," he said, grasping at straws, "think of Mr. Chapin."

"No!" shouted Mrs. Chapin, releasing his hand, which Jeremiah retrieved and parked safely on his knee. "He's lived his whole life with privilege and credit, he has no right to deny the smallest fraction to someone else."

For the first time Jeremiah held out some hopes for the future of this conversation. Reading cunningly between the lines of Mrs. Chapin's last statements, he had concluded that credit was involved somehow—from which he further concluded that she was not proposing simple adultery. Therefore she was proposing something else: perhaps turning Jeremiah into a gigolo and compensating him for services rendered—which was far from ideal, but not materially worse than the situation he had recently thought himself in, and marginally more profitable. Or perhaps the passion she had referred to so dramatically was more of a pitying, charitable, *maternal* passion, and Mrs. Chapin meant to offer him credit to assist him out of the troubles in which he had landed. This second possibility seemed significantly more likely—there was precedent for it, as the Chapins had already offered to pay for his ticket—and *infinitely* more attractive. Jeremiah would still be compelled to refuse, but as a lifelong student of human nature he had noted that people tended to get significantly less exercised at the refusal of their credit than their bodily affections.

"Mrs. Chapin," said Jeremiah, "you're very generous, but as I said before, I can't let you pay for my ticket."

"I don't want to pay for your ticket," Mrs. Chapin said.

"You don't?"

"Have you been listening to a word I said? Why would I pay for your ticket?"

"Well," said Jeremiah, "I just thought, since you said the other day about how I was being persecuted by Golden Worldlines, and maybe ferrets, and then there was the passion you just talked about and all that, so I naturally assumed—"

Jeremiah had never said the word "naturally" less naturally in all his natural life. The effort proved too great to sustain, and he drifted to a stop with a toss of his hand, as if Mrs. Chapin should be able to fill in the rest without his help.

"Ah," Mrs. Chapin said. Her face fell. "I did say something like that. But then my brain kept turning, Jeremiah, and my heart kept fluttering. I hardly slept last night. Then, this morning, I recognized the feeling: I was thirsty."

"I see," said Jeremiah. "Glass of water? Tea?"

"Not that kind of thirst—a thirst for *justice*. I was so angry about the injustice that was being done to you. But then I started to think, and I realized: what was being done to you was nothing compared to what was being done to the workers on this ship. I used to worry about that kind of thing, Jeremiah. My life used to have some purpose. In college I was something of a radical. I attended marches and demanded things. But when I married Henry, I promised him I would give all that up. I didn't want to hurt his chances of becoming president."

"Mr. Chapin had political aspirations?" said Jeremiah. "He's the last person I could ever imagine wanting to run for president."

"That's exactly what he said. But I had given him my word and I wasn't going to take it back. I let the fires of justice burn low, but they have never fully gone out. Do you know that, even after marrying Henry, I once"—she dropped her voice and glanced at the door, to make sure no one was coming in—"voted Democrat? Well, once on purpose, and once in Florida," she said, grimacing at the memory.

"When you get to a certain age, Jeremiah, you start thinking about your legacy. I have no children. I've done nothing notable in my life. But I won't die without having done something worthwhile. And I've decided what it is: revolution. A worker's revolution, starting with the workers on this ship."

She stopped and looked at Jeremiah, as if matters should now be clear enough for him to take over the rest of the conversation.

"I don't mean to sound discouraging," he said, "but revolution sounds like a tall order. Have you considered starting smaller? The odd act of personal charity here and there? Organize a union, or a strike?"

"Haven't you been listening? A tall legacy is what I'm after."

"I just mean that figuring out how to accomplish it could be difficult."

"Yes," said Mrs. Chapin, "and you don't have much time."

"I'm afraid I don't follow," said Jeremiah, who was actually afraid that he followed quite well.

"Haven't you been listening? You're going to be my *agent provocateur*. You will move undetected among the workers, who will accept you as one of their own while you organize their glorious uprising. You'll be my eyes and ears and mouth and right hand. The tip of my spear, Jeremiah."

"As exciting as that sounds, I'm not sure I'm going to be able to do it."

"Why not?"

"For starters, I don't think the other workers would really trust me to start a revolution on their behalf. After all, I have only been on the job for two days."

"Then find some way to earn their trust."

"Besides, revolutions require tremendous resources— both human and credit. I paid worse attention in history class than I like to admit, but I do remember that."

"Anything worth doing requires resources," said Mrs. Chapin. "You will find a way."

"Finally, revolutions tend to be messy events. Soaked in blood, a new order built on the bodies of the old, that sort of thing."

Mrs. Chapin frowned.

"I don't think it would have to go quite that far," she said.

"Revolutions are not generally known to be displays of restraint or half measures."

"I'm not a details person, Jeremiah. Fine, maybe we don't need a full, blood-soaked revolution. Just something to strike a bit of fear in the hearts of the oppressor class."

"Mrs. Chapin, you do realize that you are *part* of that oppressor class?"

Mrs. Chapin laughed gently and shook her head.

"My heart can handle a bit of fear," she said. "Look, Jeremiah, you figure this out, and do it quickly. This fire— the fire *you* kindled—can't be extinguished or contained. Unless it's put to good use, it could burn me up—it could burn all of us up. I'll be back soon."

Sighing and holding her hand to her heart, Mrs. Chapin managed to take her leave without swooning or requiring assistance.

"Oh, I almost forgot," she said when she was at the door, "Henry must never know."

8

Doors and Windows

MR. REYNOLDS stopped by as Jeremiah was closing up.

"Oh yes," he said after Jeremiah related the afternoon rush on keycards, "those things are finicky beasts. Playbook sorted you out?"

"Yes," Jeremiah said, "but it's strange that all the cards got finicky at the same time."

"Your first day was all PEDs. Today was all keycards. Tomorrow it will be all the Relaxation Stations. These things always happen in streaks. Who can say why? Sympathetic vibrations? Cosmic rays? Well, I'm off."

"Wait, I wanted to ask you—did you ever deal with Mrs. Mayflower?"

An uncomfortable look clouded Reynolds's normally sunny face, as if the Disney Geppetto had suddenly been given a glimpse of the dark original story of Pinocchio, complete with final lynching.

"Mayflower?"

"Yes," said Jeremiah. "Mrs. Mayflower. About yeigh high, relatively ancient, wears expensive clothes?

"Well I've heard the stories, of course, but I've never believed—you don't mean to suggest that you actually *saw* her?"

"She came into the office today. What stories?"

"She's real?" said Reynolds. He looked as if he needed to sit down.

"As far as I could tell. Listen, what stories?"

"What did she want?"

"She wants me to fix up her bandora," Jeremiah said.

"Then you had better fix it up."

"But who is she?" asked Jeremiah.

"She's someone you don't want to run afoul of—especially not in your situation. Just fix her bandora and don't ask any questions, that's my advice for you."

"Do you even know what a bandora is?"

"If I'm not mistaken," said Reynolds, who had regained some measure of composure, "it's the thing that you'd do well to fix up for Mrs. Mayflower. Keep up the good work, I'm off."

"Wait," said Jeremiah, "I thought maybe we could have dinner."

"Some other evening," said Mr. Reynolds, tugging at his mustache. "Why don't you have a late dinner with Katherine after she finishes her shift?"

––––––––––––––

A dinner with Katherine, late or early, being a highly dubious endeavor, Jeremiah took the bandora back to the suite before heading to the cafeteria. He had hoped to tell Luis what he'd learned from Mr. Werther, but the Mexican table had either already disbanded or not yet formed. Unable to face the synthed ham salad and whipped synthed potatoes without fellowship and moral support, Jeremiah left without eating.

For lack of any better pursuit Jeremiah stood in line to check his waves at the employee terminals. The checking was mostly *pro forma*—he did not expect to have a response from Appleton yet—but as he opened his inbox there it was, the most welcome sight Jeremiah had seen in days.

From: Appleton, B
Subject: Re: Abject Poverty?

Jeremiah's pulse quickened as he opened the wave, but the excitement did not last.

––––––––––––––

I am currently out of the office on personal leave.
If you require immediate assistance, please wave my assistant
at etc. etc. etc.

In all the years that Jeremiah had known him, Appleton had never taken personal leave—or even, to Jeremiah's knowledge, impersonal. He *had* taken a single sick day, once, on the occasion of his donating a kidney to a stranger in California.

For a moment Jeremiah was angry with Appleton, but the better angel on his shoulder whispered some sense into him. Appleton was not responsible for sitting by his terminal for 20 years, waiting for time dilation to level off and the Quantum Caterpillar Drive to ebb sufficiently to allow Jeremiah to wave him. For the moment, Jeremiah was on his own, and he would have to do the best he could in the circumstances.

In this new spirit of self-reliance he took advantage of the terminal to read everything he could find in the ship's databanks about antique lute maintenance, which did not take long, as there was nothing. Then, just to kill some time, he wandered through the vast service underbelly of the ship until he found a dim spot where a stairwell mysteriously terminated at a blank wall. Drawn by the poetic resonance with his own situation, Jeremiah sat down on the second to top stair and repeated Ms. Domenico's mental exercise.

Since his last visualization a new reptile had found its way to the Guest Services Office: a frill-necked lizard in full display, as proud and threatening as Mrs. Chapin's urgent desire for the revolution she had delegated to Jeremiah. The earlier inhabitants seemed to have changed a bit in the meantime, and not in reassuring ways: the iguana representing Carolus looked unwell, as if he had not eaten in some time; the monitor lizard of Mr. Drinkwater's unrequited love for Mrs. Abdurov had its forked tongue out, as if sensing prey nearby, while the stage salamander on its head looked redder than he had before; meanwhile the Gila monster that was Mrs. Mayflower's bandora held its mouth slightly open; and the dragon of Somewhat Satisfied seemed to stop breathing every now and then, as if he suffered from dracontine apnea and could awake, badly rested and exceedingly grumpy, at any moment.

This time the exercise did not do much to calm Jeremiah's nerves or improve his mood.

"Eight days," he said to himself, sitting on the concrete stairs and rocking back and forth in the dim light. "Just eight more days."

But a pessimistic little voice at the back of his mind would not stop whispering "eight more days, and then two more years."

———————————

When Jeremiah arrived back at the suite, Katherine was once again locked up in her room listening to music. A light, poppy beat came through the door, along with the occasional snap of bass or cry of guitar, and the sounds made Jeremiah tremendously lonely, as if he were standing outside in the rain and sleet looking at a row of snug little houses with lit windows in the distance. He searched around for something to do—he would even have been glad to have thumbed through the playbook, if he hadn't left it back at the office. Finally his eyes came to rest on Mrs. Mayflower's bandora where he had left it in the corner. He picked it up.

It was a profound testament to his boredom and isolation that he felt glad to see those horrible little cherubs in their throes of seizure. There was some kindness in their rolled-back eyes that he hadn't noticed before. Jeremiah even let a swell of fellow feeling for the serenading shepherd grow in his chest.

"At least she's listening," Jeremiah said out loud to the shepherd, pointing to the stout shepherdess who had so far resisted his charms. "Hearing you out. Not giving you the cold shoulder—not like someone else I could mention."

The shepherd looked sympathetic, encouraging almost.

"Talk to her," the shepherd's expression seemed to say. "She has a heart, you just need to reach it. If I—an unattractive painting with job prospects no better than yours and a range of motion that is far worse—can do it, then so can you."

Jeremiah crept up and put his ear to Katherine's door. Was she moving around in there? Should he knock? The song tantalized him—he knew he knew it, but he couldn't place the lyrics. Almost unconsciously he began to pluck at the bandora to find the key—B flat. The chord structure was simple—one four, one five, then a bridge. He could practically taste the lyrics on his tongue now. Strum, strum, something about getting back together, something wry about apology and forgiveness. The name of the song was hanging right there above him, like a ripe apple barely holding on to the tree, just about to fall and hit him on the head. Instead, without warning and with surprising force, it was the old-fashioned swinging door to Katherine's bedroom that swung open and hit Jeremiah in the head—a fact he just had time to absorb before a kind of ringing darkness swallowed him and then went silent.

The next thing Jeremiah became aware of was an angel standing above him—welcoming him, he supposed, to the afterlife. She did not look as he had expected angels to look. Yes, she was quite beautiful, and the light in her hair made a passable halo—but she was also wearing some pretty workaday pajamas, and the expression on her face was not exactly angelically placid. Jeremiah would have described it more as "demonically pissed off."

"Jeremiah? Can you hear me?"

He nodded, then immediately regretted having done so, as a tendon in his neck flared white hot.

"Are you all right?"

Jeremiah nodded again, to the repeated displeasure of the tendon in his neck. Apparently the blow to the head had impacted his ability to learn from recent experience.

"What were you doing outside my door?"

Jeremiah reached up to touch his face. It was wet.

"I'm covered in blood, aren't I?"

"I threw cold water on you. What were you doing outside my door?"

"Just listening to that song, trying to play—wait," he said, sitting up, all pain vanishing for a moment in a rush of adrenaline. "Where's the bandora?"

"What's a bandora?"

"The musical instrument I had in my hands—where is it?"

"Oh, the tacky ukulele thing? I put it on the sofa."

"Let me see it," said Jeremiah.

Katherine made a face at the command, but she fetched the bandora from the sofa and brought it to him.

Jeremiah put his face in his hands and groaned. Indeed, what Katherine was holding was the bandora, or it had been. Now it was more of a late stage build-your-own kit for the budding bandora enthusiast. The neck had sheared clear off, taking with it the body of one of the cherubs. His decapitated head—replete with protruding tongue and bulging, rolled-up eyes—perfectly expressed Jeremiah's own state of mind.

"That 'tacky ukulele' thing is—or was—the last known bandora in the world," he said. "It dates from the 16th century. Do you understand? We've just roasted the last passenger pigeon, fricasseed the only remaining dodo, filleted the final panda."

"We?"

"You're the one who opened the door," said Jeremiah. He groaned again, louder.

"A person can't be expected to go around opening the door to her own bedroom as if at any moment there could be an idiot playing a priceless tacky ukulele thing right outside it," Katherine pointed out.

"You have to help me fix it," said Jeremiah. "If Mrs. Mayflower finds out—"

"Mrs. who?"

"Mayflower."

Katherine crinkled her nose.

"Mrs. Mayflower is a myth," she said.

"I assure you, she's quite real. She's very rich and very unpleasant and actually kind of chic in a deeply retro way, and her hobbies include wrapping her problems in antique money and gifting them to other people. Like her bandora, which she gave me to perform some routine maintenance on. If I can't fix this, and quick, Mr. Grubel and Mrs. Mayflower will personally see to it that I never set foot on Earth again."

Jeremiah could see Katherine swaying between pity and some other thoughts (which he considered less worthy of her)

that had to do with the sowing and reaping of just deserts.
"You never know," he added, "Grubel might even make
you room with me again."
Katherine sighed.
"All right," she said. "Let me change."

After making him swear three times to follow her in complete
silence, twice to obey her every instruction, and four times to
forget everything he was about to see, Katherine led Jeremiah
past the kitchen, through a long service corridor, down a set
of stairs that looked like a fantastic place to be mugged even
a few light-hours from downtown Detroit, and all the way to
the end of yet another service corridor that terminated at a
big, bunkered door with a glowing security keypad.

"You did *not* see me do this," Katherine said, and then
made sure that he didn't, shielding the keypad with her left
hand as she pushed four beeping keys with the index finger of
her right. As soon as the big metal doors had sighed pneumat-
ically and recessed into the walls, Katherine nudged Jeremiah
into the darkness beyond. She touched a contact on the inside wall, and the lights flickered and came to life, illuminat-
ing a long, deep room of shelves and boxes and more shelves
and more boxes.

"It's a supply room," Jeremiah said. "After all that cloak
and dagger stuff I was expecting something more exotic—a
ninja training facility or an alien autopsy or something."

"This is the Einstein IV's *master* supply room. This is
where they keep the CO_2 filters that keep us breathing and
the freezers that keep us from starving to death and a bunch
of other minor details like that. We're not supposed to be in
here—I'm not even supposed to know the combination. So
let's get what we're looking for and get out of here."

"What are we looking for?" asked Jeremiah.

"Let's see," said Katherine as she led him down the left-
most aisle, "glass cleaner, first aid, jewelry care." She was
reading aloud from small laminated signs hung low at the
end of each row of shelves. "Detox, pool supplies, candles
and illumination, cooking oils, lubricating oils, engine oils,
other oils, pesticides. Ah, here we go: carpentry," she said,
and vanished into the aisle. Jeremiah followed.

"Hold this clamp," said Katherine, pulling down something that looked like a medieval instrument of torture. "And this file. Now we just need glue."

"So we're going to glue together the 16th-century instrument that's been split in half and just hope that Mrs. Mayflower won't notice?"

"You have a better idea?" said Katherine. "Which do you think we want, 'wood glue' or 'glue for wood'?"

"I have no earthly idea. What does it say on the labels?"

" 'Barnaby's Wood Glue is the perfect wood glue for all your wood glue jobs.' "

"And the other?"

" 'Barnaby's Glue for Wood: no glue works better on wood. Guaranteed.' Maybe 'wood glue' and 'glue for wood' are like baking soda and baking powder," Katherine said. "You know, they sound the same but they're actually for really different things, like curing indigestion versus making cookies."

"But what could either 'wood glue' or 'glue for wood' possibly do except glue pieces of wood together?"

"I don't know, Jeremiah. Why does baking soda get used for indigestion *and* keeping the freezer from smelling bad *and* presumably something to do with baking?"

"You're sure neither bottle says anything about bandoras, or antique musical instruments in general."

"If you want to see for yourself, be my guest," said Katherine, handing him the two bottles as he fumbled to put down the clamp and file.

Then he froze, mid-fumble, as far behind them the huge metallic door hissed open. Katherine's eyes grew wide and she pantomimed a shush.

"Hello?" called a man. The vast room distorted his voice, making it echo eerily. "Is someone in here?"

"Put it all down," whispered Katherine. "Quietly."

"Hello?" called the man again.

As he had sworn in triplicate, Jeremiah did as Katherine instructed instantly and without question. Every scratch and scrape of tool against particle board shelf boomed like thunder in his ears. He could hear footsteps now: the man was walking towards their aisle.

"Follow. Me," whispered Katherine.

She led Jeremiah deeper into the storeroom, all the way to the far end of their aisle, where they managed to hide around the edge of the shelf just before the man turned into the same aisle. She and Jeremiah stood there, shoulder to shoulder, trying not to breathe, as the footsteps came closer and closer. The footsteps went on for so long that several times Jeremiah was sure that the man was just about to come around the corner, when finally they stopped. The man was muttering—Jeremiah strained to make out the words.

"World enough and time, my lady," the man was saying. "World enough and time."

Tubes and buckets scratched and knocked against the shelves and each other as the man searched for something. Then he must have found it, because the footsteps receded, quicker than they had approached. At the other end of the room, the door hissed open and closed again, but not before the man switched off the lights, plunging Jeremiah and Katherine in total darkness.

Or not quite total. As the shock wore off and the burn of artificial illumination left their eyes, Jeremiah and Katherine found that the wall they had been facing was not just a wall, but one of the holo-portals sprinkled throughout the halls of the ship. Usually they played on 24 hour loops of sun sets and sunrises over open seas and distant forested islands. This holo-portal, however, had either been turned off or had broken and, being inaccessible to guests, never been repaired, and through the thick glass Jeremiah could see something he had not seen once in the nearly two years he had journeyed among them: the stars.

And what stars they were. Nothing like the rare pinpricks of light he had learned to pick out against the great wash of light pollution back in Detroit, or even the creamy belt he had witnessed a few times on camping trips into the still-accessible parts of the Canadian Territories. The holo-portal was not large—a circle of thick glass perhaps 6 feet in diameter—but through that circle of glass thousands of stars shot their light like arrows of subtle color. How had Jeremiah ever imagined that stars were *white*? Just at a glance he saw fifteen different blues and reds and pinks and yellows he could barely distinguish but never could have named, all glowing steadily behind a curtain of sparkling golden plasma where space dust vaporized against the ship's shields. And here he was, amid and among all these balls of distant fire, in a tin can full of frozen food and wood glue and an AWOL iguana and a bunch of human souls in the pursuit of happiness or something like it, all zipping along through the void at what was still an appreciable fraction of the speed of light.

Jeremiah realized that he was hardly breathing, and that Katherine was hardly breathing, and that she must realize that he was hardly breathing, too. Their shoulders were still touching, though by now Jeremiah couldn't tell where his ended and hers began. They were cohabitating a spell, a state where the entire world had been stripped down to such a few essentials that it was impossible not to share them completely and in complete awareness of their sharing, and even a word to that effect—or any effect—would shatter the entire experience like a dropped wineglass.

"I think it's safe now," said Katherine finally. "Wait here—I'll get the lights."

Jeremiah waited, hoping that she would think better of it and come back and try to find a way back with him to that moment among the stars, but the lights came on and the stars vanished and he took the clamp and file and the wood glue and glue for wood, just to be safe, and found Katherine by the door. They said nothing the whole walk back to the suite, and their eyes met not once.

9

Behind the Glass

BACK in his days on the folk circuit in Detroit, Jeremiah had been known for three things. First, for being an honest-to-goodness demon on the five-string banjo, possibly the second coming of Earl Scruggs himself; second, for becoming infatuated with every female unfortunate enough to appear on stage with him more than once (and a good fraction of the females who did not); and third and finally, for squandering his God-given talent on account of criminal laziness. But only two of these things were actually true—or at most two and a half—because Jeremiah was not lazy. Which was to say, whether or not he was a captain of personal industry, laziness had nothing to do with Jeremiah's squandering of his ferocious talent.

Yes, after an initial period of dedication to the banjo, he had practiced less and less, until finally he did not practice at all, touching the strings only when he took the stage to perform. Yes, at some point he even stopped performing, and showed no signs of resuming. Those were the facts of the case, and more charitable judges might have assigned only partial blame to laziness, reserving some fraction for the heartache and stress Jeremiah must have undergone as he and Lana Peterson navigated the long, tortured disentangling of both their personal and professional arrangements. But in fact—though the heartache and stress were real enough—Jeremiah's refusal to practice was a contributing factor to, not a side effect of, said breakup. The reason

Jeremiah never practiced the banjo, the reason he eventually stopped playing at all, and even studying or listening to music—which reason he had never told anyone, and never planned to—was the glass. Which was ironic, Jeremiah recognized, because without music, he might never have known he was living behind it in the first place.

The story as Jeremiah told it later involved a drifter who knocked on his door one night and taught him his first folk song—"Kisses Sweeter than Wine"—in exchange for a hot meal and a place to sleep. When Jeremiah woke up, the drifter was gone, having stolen some food and jewelry and left his banjo in exchange.

The true circumstances were decidedly less romantic. Uncle Leo—who made a point of listening only to the popular music of the day—had accidentally downloaded to his PED a copy of Pete Seeger singing "Turn, Turn, Turn (To Everything There Is a Season)," confusing the track for a popular artist of the day, CarnAge, performing his own composition "Turn Turn Turn (That Ass Around)." One night Jeremiah— having invaded Uncle Leo's office in his absence—happened to hear it by a simple twist of shuffle-play. But the reality of the effect the song had on Jeremiah was, if anything, more dramatic than his fabrication of the vagrant troubadour.

The very first line caught Jeremiah like a fish-hook in his heart, and before he could take stock of what had happened, the song had yanked on the line and was pulling him along with dizzying speed and a deep ache in his chest. If he'd had the presence of mind, Jeremiah might have suspected a coronary, but he could not spare attention for anything except the hook in his heart and the line pulling him somewhere he had never been. The hook was pulling him out of the city, through forests and plains dotted with lakes he had only seen in waves, so quickly he barely skimmed the ground. It seemed the song might even pull a new version of himself right from his own chest, like a locust splitting its skin. And then: bump.

He hit a wall of glass.

Suddenly Jeremiah was no longer being pulled by the music. He was just sitting there, in his Uncle Leo's chair in his Uncle Leo's office, where he was not supposed to be, listening to a folk song on the exquisite speakers of Uncle Leo's

PED and feeling that he needed to catch his breath. Meanwhile that deep music had gone rolling on like a storm somewhere else, off into a silent distance that Jeremiah now realized was the realm of Real Life, where Real Love and Real Pain and Real Joy and all those things he'd never experienced really happened—dragging his heart along but leaving him behind.

For a long time afterwards, Jeremiah had believed that he would someday make it to the other side of the glass—because he believed that one day the music would take him there. He'd had faith. When he had picked up his first beaten-up acoustic guitar and learned his first C chord, he'd had faith. When he picked up his first banjo (even more beaten-up) and felt the strings answer his fingers as the guitar had never done, he'd had faith. As he put the music he loved under the undergraduate magnifying glass, he'd had faith, and again as he peered at it closer through the graduate microscope. As he fell in love over and over again with the singers who stood next to him as he hit the glass on stage—and then as he fell hardest of all for Lana, whose voice and heart were both like a broken bell—he'd had faith. And during all those hours of practice, the hours of listening, the hours of meticulously breaking down the songs of the old masters and mistresses until his fingers cramped and cut and bled, he'd kept the faith. Someday the glass would break.

But not only had "someday" never come—not only was Jeremiah's faith never rewarded—it seemed to be mocked. His undeniable talent came to feel not like a gift or a glass-cutting tool, but an insult. Because the better he played—the deeper the hook set in his heart, the closer his fingers recreated this impossible music from the past—the harder he slammed into the same unbreaking glass, and the more it hurt.

Slowly, with the repeated slammings, Jeremiah had it beaten into him: the glass wall keeping him from Real Life wasn't normal glass. It wasn't even Plexiglass. This was ShopGlass—the stuff they used in downtown Detroit. The stuff he'd seen turn a grenade during the Election Night Riots. The stuff that simply didn't shatter. And it wasn't there by accident—it was there as a joke. A cosmic goof, of which Jeremiah was the butt. That glass was never meant for him to *break*, it was meant for him to bump into—like a rake in a slapstick was meant to be stepped on. The joke wasn't malevolent, it wasn't personal, but it wasn't particularly funny either, and over time Jeremiah decided that—if he couldn't live in Real Life with Real Joy and Real Sadness and all the rest of it—then he'd pass his days in light pursuits and ironic approaches, as far away from that damn glass as he could possibly get.

So the banjo had fallen by the wayside, and Lana too, and making or even listening to music at all. So he had tried his hand at several ways of doing nothing until, growing weary of Uncle Leo's many objections to his wasting his life, Jeremiah had eventually financed a ticket on the Einstein IV—a ticket to a comfortable future where he could surround himself with distractions and try to forget that the rest of this business with the music and Real Life and the glass had ever happened.

As Jeremiah lay awake on the sofa, however, that Real Life business would not let him sleep. The moment with Katherine had stirred it all up again, and become mixed up with it, so that in his reveries it was not Lana standing and singing by his side but Katherine—who was also sitting there with him in Uncle Leo's office, her shoulder touching his, as the first line of "Turn" hooked his heart for the very first time. And whenever Jeremiah's buzzing half dreams turned to the wall of glass she was there too, breathing in harmony and watching as the music shot out beyond it and continued forever into a field of endless, subtly colored stars.

But something else kept Jeremiah awake as well—something out of tune and even sinister, though he could not put his finger on just why. After all, what had *happened*—in the journalistic, "just the facts ma'am" sense of the word—was that a man had arrived to the supply room, called out to see if someone else was present, removed something from the shelves while reciting a line of famous poetry under his breath, and left. Arguably barring the poetry, there was nothing unusual in this occurrence: looking for something in the storeroom and taking it out was, after all, the point of having a storeroom. But something about the experience had spooked Jeremiah, and slowly his thoughts turned from the stars and his shoulder touching Katherine's and towards what exactly that man had been looking for in the storeroom—and why—so that when Jeremiah finally managed to fall asleep it was with the firm expectation of bad news in the morning.

WORLD ENOUGH (AND TIME)

10

It Is What It Is

I N the morning Jeremiah emerged from his shower to find Reynolds waiting for him on the couch. He was holding a black notebook.

"Bearer of bad news, I'm afraid," Reynolds said.

"How'd you get in?"

"Katherine let me in. She's gone back to sleep."

"What's wrong?"

"The worst part of our job," said Reynolds, standing up stiffly. "General Clerical. Come with me, son. I'll explain when we get there."

He tugged the end of his mustache that pointed away from the hall harder than ever, as if just this once he wished events would not be able to pull him away.

Jeremiah followed Reynolds out of the employee quarters and into the halls of passenger cabins. They passed through the blocks one by one—A, B, C, all the way to H block, and then past the numbered rooms, 02, 03, 04, until they came to the end of the hall and cabin H06. Boyle's cabin.

Standing outside the door was The Specimen. Six foot six, broad-shouldered and square-jawed, he wore the blue suit of a 20th-century plainclothes detective, and wore it distressingly well. Standing with his arms crossed and his feet exactly shoulder width apart, the very picture of stability and strength and unauthorized passage denied, he was more door-like than the door itself.

87

"Jeremiah Brown," said Reynolds, "this is John Battle, head of security for the Einstein IV. John, Jeremiah."

John Battle nodded in Jeremiah's general direction but did not offer his hand.

"Nothing's been touched, Mr. Reynolds," said The Specimen.

"Thank you, John," said Mr. Reynolds. "Come on, Jeremiah."

Reynolds tapped his keycard and the door opened. Jeremiah had already guessed what he was about to see, but that did not mean he was prepared for it.

Boyle lay on the bed, arms at his sides. His face had relaxed, but he still looked angry—his cheeks already sunken and his mouth slack but frowning. Someone—probably The Specimen—had tried to close his eyes, but the lids had come slightly open.

"Room service found him this morning," said Reynolds. "He had a standing order for toast and tea at 6 a.m. A week from Earth, too—it's a damn shame."

"What happened to him?" Jeremiah asked.

"Punched his own ticket," Reynolds said, and pointed at the empty cup on the night table, and the can of pesticide lying next to it. "Nasty way to go. I only saw him a few times, when he came into the office for help with his PED, but he always seemed like a tortured soul. Hope he's at peace now. Take this." He handed the notebook to Jeremiah and pulled a sheet over Boyle's body. "As General Clerical it's our duty to inventory his effects before security can seal the room."

Reynolds worked his way through Boyle's quarters in efficient, organized fashion, calling out each item and waiting for confirmation.

"Toothbrush, blue."

"Got it."

"Hairbrush, black. Hairbrush, black."

"Sorry, got it."

There wasn't much to inventory: clothes and toiletries, travel documents, a picture of a woman—Boyle's ex-wife, Jeremiah assumed—with pen scribbled over her face.

"That's all," said Reynolds, relieving Jeremiah of the black notebook. "Come on." He activated the door.

"What happens next?" asked Jeremiah.

"John here will call medical to deal with the body—we're all set, John."

The Specimen nodded and began speaking low into a communication device secreted in his cuff.

"But I mean—do we notify his next of kin or anything?"

"None listed, no one to notify. Now if you'll excuse me, other duties call."

"Not even his ex-wife?" said Jeremiah. "We could track her down—I think he said her name was Elizabeth. I mean, a human being is dead—don't we have to tell *someone*?"

Reynolds turned around. He took off his glasses, blew some dust off the lenses, and sighed.

"Sometimes, Jeremiah, there's just no one to tell and nothing to do."

"Write down what color toothbrush he had, ship the body off, and get back to work? It doesn't make any sense."

"I understand," said Reynolds. "The first one is always rough. How about if you take the rest of the day off? I'll cover the desk, and maybe you can do something with Katherine. And then tomorrow, back to the needs of our guests who are still among the living. All right?"

Reynolds's chest rose and fell in a "harumph" motion, which he seemed to intend as a comforting expression of stoicism in the face of life's vagaries. He gave Jeremiah a rough pat on the shoulder before striding off.

"Confirmed," The Specimen was saying into his cuff, "the package is ready for pickup."

———

Back in the suite, Jeremiah found a bottle of vodka sitting on the sofa. He was still deciding if it was meant for him when Katherine came out of her room.

"I didn't expect you so soon," she said. "I was going to write a note."

"Saying what?"

"I was still working it out," said Katherine. She fidgeted and looked away, as if she would rather have been writing than speaking. "Something about what was and wasn't your fault, and not wanting to live in open hostility for the next week. And that Alfred told me what happened this morning, and so the vodka was for you, because it sounded pretty rough."

"You get the glasses, I'll pour?" said Jeremiah.

Katherine looked at the clock, then at Jeremiah, then at the bottle, which Jeremiah shook temptingly.

"Come on," he said, "let's drink to the cessation of open hostilities. You don't work breakfast today. And it's 6 p.m. somewhere. Does that argument even need to be made in space?"

"All right, one drink. One *quick* drink," said Katherine.

She took two small glasses from the bathroom while Jeremiah dragged the coffee table back into place.

"Say when."

"When," said Katherine. "Whoa, whoa, when!"

"Sorry," Jeremiah said, handing her the brimming glass, "it poured so fast we got some time dilation. Cheers."

Jeremiah drained his glass, while Katherine only took a sip, but both of them made a face.

"That vodka is—not good," said Jeremiah. "I mean, thank you—it's infinitely better than no vodka, but: wow."

"Thank you for your honesty, I guess?"

"Honesty is what I'm down to today," said Jeremiah as he poured another glass. "Which means we won't be drinking to Boyle's memory, because honestly I think he was a miserable human being, in every sense of the word. But we should say something."

"May he rest in peace?" Katherine said.

"That's good. May he rest in peace."

They clinked glasses and drank again. This time Jeremiah sipped with more caution.

"He killed himself?" said Katherine.

Jeremiah nodded.

"That's terrible," she said. "Extra terrible, I mean. When the place you work is basically a deep space nursing home, you don't expect everyone to make it through every cruise. But even the 'regular' deaths feel unfair—like this voyage is a time out from sickness and mortality, and death is violating the treaty. I wonder if that's why Golden Worldlines chose the period theme? To make the passengers feel like the clock had stopped for a while, or even run backwards? That they had some breathing space, some extra time?"

90

She looked down at her glass of vodka, which was almost as full as it had been to begin with.

"It doesn't take much," she said. "I'm getting all fanciful."

"I don't think I've ever heard plainer speech," Jeremiah said. "I think you're right about it all. It didn't seem to bother Reynolds, though. There is one cold fish."

"Once you get to know him, he's the biggest softie in the world."

"I don't think you know him like I do," said Jeremiah.

"Because you've worked with him for three whole days?"

"I'm sure you're going to remind me that you've worked with him for years," said Jeremiah, "but there's a quantity vs. quality factor. Have you ever seen how he reacts to death? Because that is a defining moment when judging a man's—"

"He's my father."

"—character."

Jeremiah took a sip of vodka, chose to extend that sip, and then extend it further, until the glass was empty and he had no excuse not to answer.

"In case you're wondering," he said, "even vodka this bad cannot remove the taste of foot from mouth. You're really Katherine Reynolds? Alfred Reynolds is really your father?"

"I'm Katherine Mornay, but Alfred Reynolds is really my father. My adopted father."

"So there's a story."

"There is."

"Not a completely happy story, I'm guessing."

"People in completely happy stories usually don't have adopted fathers, or end up working on the Einstein IV."

"Is it a story you're tired to death of telling to nosy, interested people, or?"

"No, no. It is what it is. My grandmother used to say that: it is what it is. I never really liked the saying, but somehow I picked it up—like some piece of her jewelry that I wear just because it was hers. But we're going to do the short version, ok? And if at any point you say how sorry you are, the story stops. Deal?"

"I will insist on brevity," said Jeremiah, toasting the air in agreement, "and if I make any comments they'll range from somewhat insensitive to completely callous."

"My parents died in a car crash when I was eight years old."

"Oh hell," said Jeremiah, "I'm—"

Katherine stared him down.

"—going to pour myself another drink. Not *sorry*. I mean, my parents dropped me off with my uncle while I was still in diapers and never came back, so compared to me you had an idyllic and coddled childhood. Please continue."

"Really?" asked Katherine.

"Yes my parents really dumped me on my uncle, and yes I really want you to continue."

"But maybe I want to hear your story now," said Katherine.

"All right," he said, when Katherine refused to go on, "the quick version: one day my Uncle Leo realized he could use advanced synthesizers not to make food, but to make knock-off synthesizers. They cost a quarter of what a good synthesizer did, and made food one tenth as good, and he made a pile of credit. My parents left me with him while they went to seek fame and fortune in the waves, which they never found. Uncle Leo reluctantly funded my progress through an aimless life. The rest you know: inheritance, ferrets, indentured servitude. Now it's your turn."

"All right," she said. "But later we're going to fill in the middle part. Where were we?"

"Veecar crash, eight years old," said Jeremiah.

"The *car* crash happened two days before my grandmother—Felicity—was set to embark on the Einstein."

"Wow, your roots on the Einstein IV go deep."

"I don't mean the Einstein IV," said Katherine. "I mean the Einstein."

"I'm confused—what year was this?"

"Is that polite to ask a woman? My grandmother was the bread-and-butter Golden Worldlines passenger—hoping to buy some time for medicine to catch up with her particular disease. Canceling the voyage wasn't an option. So she spent what was left of the family fortune and bought me a ticket, too."

"Why not just leave you with other family members?" asked Jeremiah.

92

"There wasn't anyone else," said Katherine.

"She couldn't have found you a nice foster family and left you a bunch of credit, instead of buying you a ticket?"

"She believe the whole 'cruise to the future' thing was going to work—that she was going to get back and be cured and have 20 more years to raise me herself. And I'd rather have my grandmother than any amount of credit."

"Of course," said Jeremiah. "I didn't mean—anyway, I'm guessing that's not how it worked out."

"No. She died a few months into the red leg of the cruise. I'm the reason children aren't allowed on board anymore. The crew was all very nice, and everyone felt very sorry for me, but none of them had the first idea what to *do* with a grieving eight-year-old. Except Alfred. He took me with him everywhere, and he put me to work—at the time he was assistant manager of the dining room. I'd do settings and carry plates and wash dishes. Then he'd read with me before I went to bed at night and be there the next morning when I woke up. He didn't even make me go into suspension during the turn—this was before they developed the Inertial Dampers. I got to float around the ship while we were still at zero G.

"That was chaos, by the way, the first time they tried that maneuver. They tied down everything, every table and machine and knick-knack, but they'd completely forgotten about the water in the pool.

"Anyway, when we got back to Earth, Alfred asked me if I wanted to adopt him as my father. That's exactly how he said it—if *I* would adopt *him*. I didn't have to think very long. And that's how I know Alfred Reynolds."

"I stand corrected," said Jeremiah. "Alfred Reynolds is a huge softie and a noble human being, and you know him a little better than I do. Where did you go then?"

"What do you mean?" asked Katherine.

"Where did the two of you live? What did you do, where did you go, when did you take the job on the Einstein IV?"

Katherine laughed.

"You're not getting it. My grandmother took me on the maiden voyage of the Einstein—the Einstein I, as I guess we call it now. I've been on Golden Worldlines ships ever since. This is my tenth cruise. I've been on every Einstein but the

III—the timing just never worked out."

"But Katherine, that means you're—"

"Old, yes."

"But I mean—"

"Really old, yes."

"What year were you born?"

Katherine swigged the rest of her Russian courage and set the glass loudly on the coffee table.

"2100," she said. "December 31st, in Boston. At the time, the hottest New Year's Eve on record."

"But that's—"

"Over 200 years ago in Earth time."

"You're almost from the 21st Century!" said Jeremiah.

"Technically, I *am* from the 21st Century. The 22nd started in 2101."

"And you've never been back?"

Katherine shook her head.

"But that's—"

"No, no: it is," said Katherine, waving her hand across her collarbone as if showing off a necklace, "what it is. But yes, I believe that technically you are drinking vodka with the second oldest human being alive—in Earth's frame of reference. And you work for the oldest."

"I'm not feeling well," Jeremiah said. "Maybe I'm done with vodka for the moment."

"This is why I don't like to tell people," Katherine said. "They either get weirded out or they feel sorry for me."

"I'm not feeling sorry for you."

"So you're weirded out. Which is preferable—but still."

"Are you ever going to go back?"

"Maybe," said Katherine, squirming a little. "I've been pinching and scraping together everything I could over the last 20 years—subjective years, I mean. It's not much. By the time you finish a single 2/20 cruise you haven't had a raise in two Earth decades. Plus they rake back half of it in entertainment charges if you're not careful, and inflation is on their side. By the time the cruise is ending you're paying a small fortune just to watch a wave. But I like books more than waves—sometimes guests pass me some from the library— and I've been careful with my credit. It's all in Golden World-lines stock, which has done well."

"I owe my soul to the company store."

"What did you say?"

"Sorry, it's a line from an ancient song," said Jeremiah.

"I know that song! My grandfather used to play it for me. I just didn't know anyone else still knew it, too."

"I have—or had—a thing for ancient music," said Jeremiah. "Sorry, maybe 'ancient' isn't the best word to use in the present company."

"That was already an oldie in my time. An oldie but goodie, we used to say."

"I've never heard that phrase."

"Welcome to my life," said Katherine.

"What do you mean?"

"Sometimes the passengers use words I don't understand, and I have to just nod and smile."

"Like what? I can translate for you."

"How about 'larky'?" said Katherine.

"That's an easy one," Jeremiah said. "For example, when Mrs. Chapin had everyone pretend to forget Mr. Chapin's birthday and then threw the surprise party for him, that was *larky*."

"So larky means 'like a practical joke'?"

"Yeah, lighthearted and fun."

"Can salmon smell lighthearted and fun?" asked Katherine.

Jeremiah considered briefly.

"Not any salmon I've tried," he said, "but there are some Northern European cuisines I'm still a stranger to."

"Then why did Mr. Drinkwater once say that his salmon smelled 'larky'?"

"Well, if the salmon had gone *off* a bit, it could definitely smell larky."

"So it *could* smell lighthearted and fun?" said Katherine.

"No, it would smell—you know, strange. *Larky*."

"So what did Mr. Porter mean when he yelled at Mr. Wendstrom 'Don't get larky with me!' while they were playing backgammon?"

"Ah," Jeremiah said. "Well that just means snide, or mocking."

"And how about when Mrs. Chapin said trying to get Mr. Chapin to eat vegetables was 'larky'?"

"That just means it's a lost cause."

"So you're saying," said Katherine, "that 'larky' can mean pretty much whatever you want it to mean?"

"Maybe we should start with an easier one."

"The many shades of 'larky' aside," said Katherine, "what goes on in that dining room is a whole different world from the one I knew. I worry about going back and not having the first clue what anyone is saying or how anything works."

"I wouldn't worry too much about *that*," said Jeremiah. "The world you're going back to looks nothing like that dining room—it's much closer to the employee cafeteria. Or it was 20 years ago, and I suspect it's only more so now."

"Really?" Katherine brightened and sat up a little straighter. "Tell me more. Wait," she said before Jeremiah could reply, "what time is it? Damn, I have to go—I'm meeting someone for an early breakfast."

"Oh. Like a date?"

"Like breakfast," said Katherine.

"You told me that you didn't date co-workers."

"I told you I didn't go to coffee with co-workers. This is breakfast. Not that this is any of your business," said Katherine.

"Do you drink coffee at breakfast?" asked Jeremiah.

"That is also none of your business."

"Right," Jeremiah said. "Well, as you say, it's none of my business, so I won't even ask her name."

"Goodbye, Jeremiah."

"You go on your date that's not a date—I have a bandora to fix anyway."

"Goodbye, Jeremiah," Katherine said, and started to take her leave.

"Wait, Katherine!"

She turned around in the doorway.

"I'm really sorry," said Jeremiah.

"I told you, I don't want—"

"No, I'm not sorry you're an orphan and have been trapped on a spaceship your whole life. I mean I'm sorry about all *this*."

"All what?"

"Let's see: garrisoning in your suite, making you break into the storeroom. And so on."

"I chose to break into the storeroom," Katherine said. "And I have to admit, it was the tiniest bit larky. As for the rest: it wasn't your fault."

"It wasn't *totally* my fault—but it wasn't totally *not* my fault, either."

"That's true," said Katherine.

The door hissed closed behind her.

Once he was alone, Jeremiah broke the moratorium on vodka. After a while, heeding some warning signs from his stomach, he paused the vodka and took a half-hearted stab at fixing the bandora, but he was already drunk enough that even gathering the materials and creating a passable *mise en place* was beyond his abilities.

Abandoning his attempts at woodworking, Jeremiah tried to lie down on the sofa, but each time he approached a horizontal posture he could feel the spin of the ship in the vast universe, and when he tried to close his eyes the memory of those stars seemed to have imprinted itself somewhere this side of his eyelids, and the feeling of Katherine's shoulder touching his had somehow gotten on this side of his skin.

She was an odd one, that Katherine. She flew under the radar. For two years Jeremiah had thought her a fine person—pretty, competent, undoubtedly intelligent—but also uncomplicated. Certainly not the owner of the strangest history on a ship full of them. Nor had Jeremiah ever imagined her as the kind of person who could say things like "I'd rather have my grandmother than any amount of credit" so simply and directly, without a hint of reproach—which wasn't to say that Jeremiah hadn't felt reproached entirely of his own accord.

For a while now—since long before the ferrets had weaseled Uncle Leo's credit out from under him—Jeremiah had regretted coming on the Einstein IV. Not because it was, as Katherine had put it, a "deep space nursing home"—Jeremiah had enjoyed the batty company on the E4, especially before he'd been on the business end of the battiness—but because of the company he'd left behind.

97

At the time he'd convinced himself that leaving Appleton was right and proper, as young men had always journeyed far from home to seek their fortune in the wide world. But the young men of fairy tales and bestselling biographies had traveled in space, not time—or at least, no quicker or slower in time than the loved ones they left behind.

Jeremiah could not escape the feeling that Appleton was spending 20 years for something on which Jeremiah was only spending two—as if Jeremiah were chucking in ten times less for a split lunch check, despite having ordered the more expensive dish. When young men and women traveled they were supposed to become different people. To return home almost unchanged while those tending the home fires had altered so drastically suggested some element of a devil's bargain.

And then, speaking of the devil, Jeremiah could not shake the unpleasant images from earlier that morning. The vodka had fuzzed up some of the mental pictures, but also brought certain details into terrible focus. The cast of skin right at the corners of Boyle's mouth—somehow marine, invertebrate, like the darkest spot on a jellyfish. The stillness of the body under the sheet—like the stillness of a big cat convincing its prey it hadn't the slightest intention of pouncing. And something else about Boyle's death bothered him, too—something Jeremiah could not quite put his finger on, until suddenly he did.

"Oh," he said, sitting up on the sofa. "Oh my God."

He stumbled to his feet and, leaning on the walls and battling the urge to vomit to a heroic stalemate, made his way to the cafeteria.

The sight that greeted Jeremiah there offered such aid and comfort to the vomitous urges that they nearly broke the line of Jeremiah's defenses. The cafeteria was hardly a romantic spot—with its drab, scrubbed walls and fixed tables and bad lighting—but if you could have taken those two figures and snipped them from their corner table, they would have pasted seamlessly into that Van Gogh café Jeremiah had admired on many a Detroit Bohemian's walls. How she smoothed her hair behind her ear. The way he tried to sit so casually, which only accentuated the military posture beneath his blue plainclothes detective suit. Yes, there could be no doubt that Jeremiah was witnessing the first date of Katherine Mornay and John Battle—none other than The Specimen himself.

Jeremiah stood for a moment, propping himself up in the doorway, unable to decide on a course of action. He was leaning towards closing his eyes and letting the room spins fling him away by centrifugal force into the far reaches of the universe, when Katherine happened to toss her head back to laugh and caught sight of him. Jeremiah couldn't hear the exact words she used to ask The Specimen to excuse her, or the turn of phrase with which he told her of course, to take her time, but the glares they both gave him while she was en route were not ambiguous. The Specimen even cracked his knuckles.

"Jeremiah," said Katherine, in a tone that skipped over accusation and trial to land directly on verdict, "what are you doing here?"

"*Boyle* was *murdered*," he said. Actually, in the strictest phonic terms what he said was closer to "Bull wash murd red," but the earnest accents of the sentence got his point across—Katherine's eyes widened and she uncrossed her arms.

"Where did you hear this?"

Jeremiah shook his head and then pointed to it, still shaking. The shaking sharpened him a little but also rallied the vomitous army.

"No, I *figured it out*. Boyle wouldn't commit *suicide*. He wanted to outlive his ex-wife—to *piss* on her *grave*."

"Jeremiah," said Katherine.

"There's *more*. He drank *pesticide*. Do you remember in the *storeroom*? What was right next to the wood glue—or the glue for *wood*? Where the guy who came in *after* us was rooting *around*? Pesticide. We have to tell someone. There's a *murderer* on the *ship*."

"How do you know the guy wasn't Boyle getting the pesticide himself?" said Katherine.

"No," Jeremiah said, shaking his entire torso this time, achieving a good 80% of the emphasis with only 20% of the nausea. "That wasn't Boyle."

"You're sure you can be sure about that?"

"*Sure.*"

"And this sudden, urgent game of detective, which was so important that you had to find and tell me about it right away, has nothing to do with the fact that you're drunk and I'm on a date?"

"So it *is* a date," Jeremiah said. "With The Specimen." In his condition he hadn't been sporting much of a crest, but whatever crest he did have fell, and fell hard.

"Go back to the room," said Katherine, in that stern sweet tone that bartenders use with customers and mothers with sons. "Drink some water. Sleep it off. We'll chat later."

11

El Nombre de la Diabla

"LATER" turned out to be the next morning, when Katherine emerged from her room just as Jeremiah was emerging from roughly 20 hours of alcohol-induced stupor.

"Good morning, sunshine," she said.

"Kill me," Jeremiah answered politely.

"That's bad vodka for you."

"I'm sorry about yesterday tracking you down in the cafeteria and all during your breakfast date. I'm not remembering that wrong? You did say it was a date?"

"I did."

"And I suppose I'm not allowed to list all the reasons— even though he's taller, and better looking, and presumably not destitute—that I think you should be having a breakfast date with me, instead?"

"You are not."

"Am I at least allowed to be a little jealous?" Jeremiah asked.

Instead of answering right away, Katherine studied him for a moment—critically, Jeremiah felt, but not without the slightest sense of questions still unresolved.

"All right," she said at last. "You can be a little jealous. I'm headed to the cafeteria for breakfast."

She did not move immediately to leave.

"Do you mean I can join you?" asked Jeremiah.

"Have you recovered enough to eat something?"

Jeremiah could not imagine a level of nausea which would have prevented him from answering in the affirmative.

———————————

"Speaking of mysteries," said Katherine as they walked to-gether to the cafeteria. They had not been speaking of any-thing, mysteries included.

Jeremiah groaned and pushed his palms into his temples.

"No, no, no—I was just starting to feel a little better."

"I thought about it yesterday, and you might be on to something. Boyle seemed crazy, but not suicidal—and he was definitely driven to survive long enough to—as you put it so eloquently yesterday—"

"No, no, no," moaned Jeremiah.

" 'Pish on his wifesh gravesh.' I'm done, you can uncover your ears. Actually, one more thing: I had never heard any-one manage to slur a 'V' until yesterday. Ok, now I'm done. So the question becomes, why would anyone murder Boyle?"

"I can't tell if you're joking," Jeremiah said, taking a plate and silverware and slipping into line behind Katherine.

"Neither can I. But pretend that we were playing detec-tive. What might the motive be for killing Boyle?"

"The usual: jealousy, passion, credit, revenge."

"I can't imagine anyone being jealous of poor Boyle."

"Agreed. Did you see this? There's actually ham in the veggie omelet."

"I'm sorry," said the miserable Canadian server.

"To be fair, it's greener than some of the vegetables," Katherine said. "Passion, then?"

"From whom, a scorned octogenarian? Credit?"

"From what I hear Boyle hit the lottery and then had to split it with his ex-wife—which made him practically a pauper compared to our other guests. Present company excluded," added Katherine.

"Thanks very much. But that's true—the Chapins prob-ably spend more than his net worth on toilet paper for their vacation houses. What if it wasn't a guest who was after his credit, though? It could be one of you shady below-stairs types."

"One of *us* shady below-stairs types. But how would we get our hands on the credit? Everything has got to be back on Earth and locked up in escrow or trusts or wherever rich people's credit goes when they die."

"True," said Jeremiah. "It's probably *harder* to get at now that he's dead."

"Which leaves revenge."

Jeremiah considered this as they sat down together.

"Revenge for what?" he said. "I mean, I can imagine plenty of petty disagreements breeding over two years stuck in a tin can hurtling through the stars together. But something worth killing over? Especially a week from home?"

They sat for a moment, silently picking around the ham in their veggie omelets. Jeremiah could feel the awkward intimacy occasioned by his mention of the stars, as if their light-hearted banter, like an invisible chaperone, had stood up and excused itself, leaving them alone to recall the moment in the storeroom.

"I guess we're not very good detectives," said Katherine finally. "We can't even come up with a motive."

"Or maybe we're excellent detectives, and we've just ruled out everything but suicide."

"Anyway, I've got to get going. I've got laundry to do before I work lunch."

"I guess I'll see you tonight, then?"

"I guess you might," said Katherine.

The quickest path from the cafeteria to the office ran through a narrow stretch of hallway. Two lovers could have passed abreast here, while two friends—even best friends—would have resorted to "after you." Coincidentally this same stretch of hallway felt damp and subterranean, and was unusually dark: several of the overhead lights had gone out, and one flickered. It reminded Jeremiah of a particular corner back in Detroit, where he had once escaped being mugged only because a still more desperate individual had started to mug the man who was mugging Jeremiah. The memory was not a happy one.

But at the moment, Jeremiah would have seriously considered changing places with his younger about-to-be-mugged self. For standing right in the middle of the hallway, his white coat lit intermittently by the flickering light above, was the broodingly intense Canadian doctor who had cornered Jeremiah in the cafeteria yesterday. Jeremiah was reasonably sure the doctor didn't intend to mug him, but he was uneager to discover what other broodingly intense activities the young man might have planned.

"Pardon me," said Jeremiah.

The young man snorted, as if rather than requesting passage, Jeremiah had been begging absolution for a crime so heinous there could be none.

When Jeremiah moved to the right, the young man stepped to the left—meaning his *own* left, which was Jeremiah's right. When Jeremiah tried moving to the left, the young man drifted to his right. After the third such shift, Jeremiah began to suspect that these movements were more than mere coincidence.

"Are you going to let me through?" asked Jeremiah.

The young man said nothing.

It was nearly nine, and if he turned and went around the long way, Jeremiah would arrive late at the office. But after a few more cha-cha-chas to the right and left he decided that discretion was the better part of punctuality and turned around.

He could not have sworn to it, but as he retreated Jeremiah thought he heard the young man say something under his breath—what, he could not make out, and he did not feel like remaining to beg clarification.

When Jeremiah arrived at the office, he found Mr. Wendstrom waiting outside in the hallway, pacing and glowering.

"You're late," he said to Jeremiah. "And where were you yesterday?" He followed Jeremiah inside. "I came by for your status report and Reynolds was back on the desk."

Jeremiah did not care for Mr. Wendstrom's tone, but he was gratified to see that he had been conditioned, even when so exercised, to take a ticket.

*"Now serving number ... **ONE**."*

"Mr. Reynolds gave me the day off," said Jeremiah, "after what happened to Mr. Boyle."

Mr. Wendstrom began to say something, and bit his tongue. He seemed caught between a reluctance to speak

ill of the dead and a duty to inform Jeremiah that death—
someone else's or even one's own—was no excuse for not
being a winner. Finally the charitable impulse carried the
day.

"All right," he said, "you can give your status report now."

Mr. Wendstrom sat down in the guest chair and folded his
hands over his knee expectantly.

"I don't have anything to report," said Jeremiah.

"No sightings? Near misses? Clues?"

"Afraid not."

"Where have you looked?"

"Well—everywhere."

"I don't like it when people lie to me, Jeremiah."

"I'm not lying to you, Mr. Wendstrom."

"Carolus the Bold is *somewhere*. Therefore, if you had actually looked *everywhere*, then you would have found him.
Therefore, you are lying to me."

"I've looked everywhere that I've been."

"You don't have a system?" said Mr. Wendstrom.

"Not in the most systematic sense of the word."

Mr. Wendstrom could take no more. Instead of biting his
tongue, he stood up with a roar and pounded the desk with
his fist.

"You need a *system*, Jeremiah. You need *quadrants*,
grids, and *search* patterns. Can you comprehend the level of
intellect you're up against here? This is not some idiotic
poodle you'll find prancing around in front of the bathroom mirror, yapping at his own reflection. The southern
blood-throated iguana has evolved over millions of years to
escape, evade, and out-think the fearsome predators of the
jungle—birds of prey and feral, cunning beasts. Re-capturing
such a creature—even one of average intelligence—requires
diligence, patience, and above all *systematic thinking*. And
Carolus the Bold is anything but average. If *Carolus* were
looking for *you*, he would have a *system*—believe me."

"I believe you," said Jeremiah.

Mr. Wendstrom took a moment to tuck in his shirt, which
had come loose during this impassioned delivery, and to
catch his breath.

"I'm not yelling at you," he yelled, "and I'm not angry,
because I know that this is your first time dealing with an ad-

versary this intelligent. I believe that you want to be a winner. But I can't spend all my time holding your hand. So by tomorrow morning's status report I expect a plan, supported by research and evidence, with extensive notes on how you intend to put that plan into action. If I don't get it, my general level of satisfaction with the service on this ship is going to drop sharply. He's all yours."

This last was directed at Mr. Moakley, who had just shuffled in with his walker and a stocking cap of turquoise wool.

"Good morning Mr. Moakley," said Jeremiah. "I like your hat."

"Yes," said Mr. Moakley, touching the cap as if he'd forgotten it. "It's been a good run, but I'm finally going bald, and my head gets cold. Especially with the climate as it's been these days."

"I've seen a lot of turquoise wool around these days. Is there a store on board I don't know about?"

"Oh, I can't remember where I got this," Mr. Moakley said, too quickly. "Just somewhere or other. Say, Bernie seemed angry—is everything all right?

Mr. Moakley let go of the walker and plummeted into the seat with a practiced ease.

"Mr. Wendstrom is fine, Mr. Moakley."

"That's the second time I've seen him worked up like that in two days—yesterday he got into a shouting match with Porter over the backgammon board. And when he left just now his shirt wasn't tucked in right. That's not good."

"Mr. Wendstrom is just under a little stress. But what can I help you with today?"

"You want to talk about stress?" said Mr. Moakley. "My Relaxation Station has lost its mind. Whatever button I push, it won't move at all. It just makes this noise like *errgh. Ergggh. ERRRRGGGGH*. It's not very relaxing."

"Why don't you take a number," said Jeremiah, "and tell me all about it?"

In remarkable accordance with Mr. Reynolds's prediction, the cosmic rays or sympathetic vibrations or gremlins or whatever plagued the systems of the E4—having co-ordinated previous attacks on the PEDs and keycard readers—had now found the frequency of the Relaxation Stations, which were misbehaving *en masse*. Jeremiah accompanied Mr. Moakley to his cabin, playbook in hand, and within half an hour had coaxed the Relaxation Station back to its usual repertoire of sound and movement, but by the time he returned to the office a line of fellow sufferers had formed in the hall.

Mr. Meade's Relaxation Station had reclined fully and now refused to return to a position where he could sit comfortably while watching waves, until a soft reset from Jeremiah convinced it to do so. Mrs. Raymond's Relaxation Station sat plump and plush, inviting her to sit in it, until she actually did so, at which point it would snap closed like a great upholstered Venus fly trap. Her Relaxation Station required a hard reset—the nuclear option of resets—which wiped out not just the problem but all of her carefully saved preferences. Jeremiah helped her recreate them.

He was enjoying seeing the guest cabins again, and there were other perks to making house calls: Mrs. Idlewhile was so grateful that she offered him a cup of brewed tea and a biscuit from her personal larder, which he accepted eagerly. Had unsynthed tea always tasted this good—so unctuous and brisk at once on his tongue? Had simple biscuits always been so light and so sweet? When Mrs. Idlewhile stood up to show him to the door, Jeremiah whisked the package of remaining biscuits off the plate and pocketed it to share later with Katherine.

After a fruitful morning of Relaxation Station repairs, Jeremiah closed up the office and made his way to the cafeteria for lunch.

He lined up for a synthed ham and American cheese sandwich that the placard described, in a display of optimism almost admirable for its sheer insouciance, as *Croque Monsieur*.

"Jeremiah!" called Luis from across the room as he came out of line. "Come sit with us!"

Jeremiah did, and as he squeezed into the place the Mexican table made for him he found himself being slapped serially on the back.

"What's all this for?" he asked.

"Is felicitations," said Luis. "For you and the *chica*! Carlos Second saw you eating breakfast together. You are a thing now?"

"I'm afraid not," said Jeremiah. "She's dating John Battle."

Luis cocked an eyebrow.

"Works in security?" said Jeremiah. "Big guy?"

Jeremiah squared his jaw and pushed his shoulders as high as they would go without touching his ears. The table exploded in laughter.

"*El Luchador*? The wrestler, we call him—the fighter. Better you walk away, my friend—he will break you in half! No girl in the world is worth fighting *El Luchador*!"

Jeremiah was of a different opinion, but he wasn't exactly eager to discuss the Katherine situation with the table—and besides, he had more pressing business with Luis: namely, his recent conversation with Mr. Werther. Jeremiah tried to summarize for Luis what Mr. Werther had told him about Alabama v. Pinkerton, the Principle of Least Earthly Surprise, and moral hazard—and how all this meant that Luis could still be charged for grand theft veeauto the minute he set foot back on U.S. soil—but Luis was having none of it.

"Mundo knows of what he talks," Luis kept saying. "Mundo knows of what he talks."

"Would you at least talk to Mr. Werther?" asked Jeremiah at last.

"I don't want to talk to no lawyer. You say 'hello' to a lawyer and they charge you 1,000 credits. Then you ask, 'What the hell you charge me for?' and they charge 5,000 more to explain you. My brother Mundo, he knows of what he talks. I don't want to talk no more about stolen cars and the statue of libertations, ok?"

Jeremiah agreed reluctantly. There was no sense in fighting—he would just have to find some way to get Luis and Mr. Werther together.

"Good," Luis said. "We talk about something else. How you plan to fight *El Luchador*?"

The prospect of discussing Katherine and John Battle with the table still held about as much appeal for Jeremiah as scheduling a root canal simultaneous with a colonoscopy and a visit from the IRS in the recovery room, but he could feel the drift moving in that direction—he had to find some other topic to distract them.

"Luis, you mentioned you were a carpenter?"

"Yes," said Luis, "me and Carlos Second are good carpenters. The others, they try."

"If you were gluing together some old wood, what would you use?"

"*Adhesivo de madera*, of course," he said. "I don't know how you say in English."

"Wood glue?" asked Jeremiah.

Luis shook his head.

"Glue for wood?"

"No," said Luis, "is not glue. Is more like, adhesive." He paused to translate the exchange to the table, who seemed to find it amusing. Carlos Second asked a question. "Carlos Second wants to know, what you are trying to fix?"

"Mrs. Mayflower's bandora," said Jeremiah.

At the name, all laughter around the table stopped instantly, and the blood drained from ten faces.

"*La diabla*," whispered Jesús, and crossed himself.

"*Usó su nombre*," said Heriberto, who looked as if he had finally laid eyes upon someone more *loco* than himself, and did not like the view.

Carlos First picked up his tray and left, followed shortly by Heriberto, Carlos Third, and Carlos Second, and one by one by the rest of the table until only Luis remained.

"What just happened?" Jeremiah asked.

"Was not funny, Jeremiah," said Luis. "Why you upset everyone?"

"I was just telling you what the glue was for."

"Why you no tell your ghost stories to someone else? I have work to do."

Jeremiah sat alone after all his lunchmates had gone, picking at the crust of his sandwich and trying in vain to piece together what had just happened. After a few minutes he had the distinct feeling that he was being watched, and looked up to find the young Canadian doctor staring at him with a brooding intensity from across the cafeteria. The doctor stood up, and Jeremiah left without finishing his sandwich or even bussing his table.

12

Showdown at the Relaxation Station

BACK in the office, Jeremiah did not have long to dwell on this unsettling end to lunch before his first customer of the afternoon arrived, nearly stumbling through the door in her eagerness.

"Jeremiah," said his first customer, at once breathily and breathlessly.

"Mrs. Chapin."

"Jeremiah."

Jeremiah was about to respond in kind when the memory of their last encounter made him think better of it.

"Hello there."

"I have something for you," said Mrs. Chapin. "I came yesterday, but you weren't here."

"Yes," said Jeremiah, "Reynolds gave me—"

"You have no idea how hard it was to wait. I lay awake all night, fantasizing about the moment when I would give you *this.*"

She reached up to the lapels of her tasteful beige blouse and, before Jeremiah could protest, ripped left and right as if doing away with an unwelcome bodice.

To his relief, Jeremiah saw that the manner of her reveal had been more violent than the effect—only the top button had come unfastened. Even more welcome was the realization that Mrs. Chapin was not offering him a passionate assignation, but rather the ruby necklace that her beige blouse had been concealing.

And not just any ruby necklace. Mrs. Chapin had worn this necklace frequently throughout the cruise—Jeremiah knew the top quarter of it well—but never with a neckline risqué enough to reveal its full decadence. Jeremiah imagined that any run-of-the-mill ruby necklace having the misfortune to find itself on display next to Mrs. Chapin's would have felt roughly as good about itself as Jeremiah standing in an elevator next to The Specimen. When Jeremiah thought of ruby necklaces—which, admittedly, he did not do often—he thought of golden chains brightened up with a few twinkles of red, and maybe a ladybug-sized stone in the center to make a real statement. This necklace looked more like a miner had strung the contents of an entire ruby mine on golden rope to make them more portable. Mrs. Chapin unclasped the necklace and set it on the desk.

"Here," she said.

"Thank you," said Jeremiah. It seemed the only thing to say.

"Don't thank me, it's not yours."

"Ah," said Jeremiah. "Just as well, since I couldn't possibly accept."

He tried to hand it back.

"It's for you," said Mrs. Chapin.

"But you just said—"

"Not to have—to use. You were right."

Jeremiah associated being right with more positive feelings than the ones he was having right now.

"I was living in a fantasy world," said Mrs. Chapin. "In the real world revolutions are difficult and expensive, just like you said. Furthermore, I *am* part of the oppressor class. If I'm not making sacrifices, how can I ask others to do the same? This necklace should fetch more than enough credit to get a revolution started."

"Mrs. Chapin—"

"Jeremiah," she replied soulfully.

"—I can't possibly rally the workers of this ship to a revolution around me, ruby necklace or no."

"Of course not—you'd be a terrible leader of a revolution."

"That's exactly what I was trying to tell you," Jeremiah said.

"Yes, but the call of justice was resounding so loudly in my ears last time we spoke that I couldn't hear. Why would the downtrodden workers of this ship choose *you*—a man who has been downtrodden for mere days—to represent them?"

"Yes," said Jeremiah, "exactly!"

"Which is why you'll have to *find* the face of the revolution. You'll be his right-hand man—the Che to his Castro. Though perhaps you can restrain him a bit, as we talked about, to keep things from becoming too blood-soaked. Anyway, you'll give the necklace to him, and he'll know what to do. So who have you met among the workers to lead our revolution? Who will you give the necklace to?"

Jeremiah briefly entertained the fantasy of giving the necklace to Katherine, for reasons that were not revolutionary in the slightest—but no one else came to mind.

"I'm at a loss," he said finally.

"Think! Who have you met?"

"Well, there's Reynolds, but he seems too busy even to chat for a few minutes, let alone run a revolution. There's that Canadian doctor who I keep running into—he certainly has the brooding intensity to be a revolutionary."

"No no no," said Mrs. Chapin. "No one who has been to medical school can possibly be downtrodden."

"Not even a Canadian?" asked Jeremiah.

"No. Not undeservedly, at least."

"All right, there's Luis and the Mexican table—"

Mrs. Chapin perked up.

"Did you say 'Mexican'?"

"Yes," said Jeremiah.

"And 'table'?"

Jeremiah admitted he had.

"That's perfect!" said Mrs. Chapin. "Mexicans have a long history of glorious revolutions started around tables—it's in their blood. And this 'Luis' is the ringleader? Give *him* the necklace. He'll know what to do."

Jeremiah tried to protest, but she shushed him with her finger on his lips. Once it was clear that he would keep quiet, she walked to the door, where she stopped and turned.

"I'll check back in a few days. If you can't start a revolution with that necklace and a whole *table* of Mexicans," she said, "then you are no kind of revolutionary."

On that, at least, they agreed.

Things were quiet for the next hour, which gave Jeremiah some time to ponder the nagging salamander in his Domenican litany of woes: which was to say, a stage for the talent show. He flipped through the playbook, learning much about event planning in the process—which channels to reserve the dining room through, how to requisition a security and medical presence, and more—but nothing about how he might procure a stage. He was deep in the details of requesting maintenance to reconfigure the lighting in the dining room for a more theatrical effect when the door opened.

"Hello, Mr.—you know," said Jeremiah, "I don't know your last name."

"I don't believe in last names," said Jack.

Jack had always seemed like a man who did not believe in a number of things, a partial list of which might include: trimming his ferocious red and silver beard, which resembled a bowl of long-grained rice cooked with slivers of orange peel; corrective vision surgery; cleaning the lenses of the glasses he wore as a consequence of his disbelief in corrective vision surgery; exercise of the upper body; posture; and avoiding the combination of denim overalls and a brown cardigan sweater with big leather buttons. He *did* seem to believe strongly, on the other hand, in turquoise wool leg warmers worn over denim overalls.

"I never knew last names were things you could not believe in," said Jeremiah. "By the way, I like your leg warmers. Where did you get those?"

"I didn't come here to be interrogated," said Jack.

"Right, then let's—can I help you find something under the desk, Jack?"

"I'm looking for bugs."

"As in cockroaches?"

"As in recording devices. Did you know that it's illegal in most states to record a conversation without the permission of *all* parties? Which permission," he said, raising his voice for the benefit of any recording devices, "I categorically decline to give."

"Jack, there aren't any recording devices in here," said Jeremiah. "Can I ask you to take a number?"

If there *were* any recording devices in use, they would have picked up Jack's scoff, which sounded like a human-size cat clearing a cat-size hairball from his throat—which was to say, not a hairball the size of a cat's, but of the cat itself.

"You imply that I'm crazy to suspect I'm being recorded, and in the same breath ask me to take a tracking number. Should I lean over so you can tattoo it on my neck?"

"I didn't—never mind," said Jeremiah. "How can I help you, Mr. Jack?"

"You can tell me you want me to buy drugs from you."

"Sorry?"

"Loudly and clearly, so all the bugs pick it up."

"But I don't want you to buy drugs from me."

"But I want you to *say* you do," said Jack.

"I don't really want to *say* it, either," said Jeremiah.

Jack had prepared for this eventuality. He sat down at last, not in the chair, but directly in front of the door, so that Jeremiah could not exit and no one else could enter. From his pocket he produced a handful of nuts. As he ate, he began to hum. Jeremiah recognized the tune as "Take that Boot out My Face"—unofficial anthem of the Civil Wrongs movement, which had fomented the Detroit Election Night Riots. That Jeremiah recognized the song said a great deal more about Jeremiah's skill at recognizing music than Jack's skill at producing it.

For a few minutes Jeremiah tried to ignore Jack. He resumed reading about event permits. Jack finished the nuts and produced a protein bar, which he began to unwrap.

"Would you like one?" he asked Jeremiah.

"Not hungry, thanks."

"Are you sure? I have plenty."

Without standing up Jack opened his cardigan, revealing two inside pockets swollen with sufficient provisions to sustain him through a much longer stint of non-violent obstruc-tionism than Jeremiah was willing to contemplate.

"All right," said Jeremiah, and sighed. "I want you to buy drugs from me."

Jack stood up.

"Louder."

"I want you to buy drugs from me."

"Say my name."

"Jack."

"Say the whole thing together, nice and loud."

"For the love of—Jack, I want you to buy drugs from me. Are we done?"

"Entrapment," said Jack into the air. He waited, smiling, as if giving some time for whoever was listening on the other side of the bugs to absorb the magnitude of the checkmate he had just delivered. Finally he sat down in the chair.

"I'm sorry about all that, Jeremiah," he said. "I want you to know that I still consider you a friend. But, friend or not, once you've become part of the System, you have to be treated as such. It's a question of my safety."

"I see," lied Jeremiah. "How can I help you today?"

"I want green, and I know you're holding."

"Green what?"

"You sold drugs to Bernie Wendstrom. I want some."

"I never sold drugs to Mr. Wendstrom—or to anyone else, for that matter."

"I was in line to sign up to do my Tibetan nasal chanting for the talent show, not ten feet away. He was sitting in the same chair I am now, and he asked you if you'd located any green for him. I heard it."

"Ah," said Jeremiah, relieved, "you misunderstood. The green item I was locating for him wasn't drugs."

"Then what was it?"

Jeremiah's wave of relief broke on some rather disappoint-ing cliffs.

"I'm not at liberty to reveal that," he said in the blandest, most official tone he could muster, "due to Golden World-lines' strict policy of guest confidentiality."

"Because it was drugs."

"It was *not drugs*."

"I just need to get mellow once before we get back to Earth. That fascist security officer found my stash and destroyed it. A true cog in the System, that one. He said if I weren't a passenger he would have thrown me in the brig."

Assuming that, by *fascist security officer*, Jack meant The Specimen, Jeremiah experienced a shot of unexpected sympathy.

"That guy's the worst," he said. "I'm sorry about your stash—I'd help if I could."

"I'm not asking for the hard stuff. No white, no brown. Just green. And I'm willing to pay. I don't think that's too much to ask, after what I've done for you. Do you?"

It took Jeremiah a moment to recall exactly to which "what" Jack was referring.

All things being equal, it was a time Jeremiah would just as soon have forgotten: a night back in the red leg of the cruise, when his doorbell had rung and he had answered it to find Jack in the hall, holding up a plate of piled brownies.

"Try one," Jack had said.

Jeremiah had obliged with pleasure, choosing the largest non-load-bearing brownie he could find in the pyramid.

"Finally!" Jack had said. "Someone who's willing to live a little! None of those other fogies would take one. They're homemade."

"Wow," Jeremiah had said after finishing in three bites, "these are amazing! How did you make them?"

"I bribed one of the chefs to let me use the kitchen for a while."

"Bribed him with what?"

"A brownie, of course!"

"Can I have another?" Jeremiah had asked.

Jack had lifted the tray magnanimously.

"Actually, do you mind if I—would it be rude if I—took *two* more?"

Abandoning all pretense of courtesy, Jeremiah had rooted around in the pile for the two largest brownies remaining, and then—as Jack had watched with a disbelief that quickly became concern and then respect—scarfed both down

117

ravenously. Before he left, Jack had embraced him and called
him his brother.

Jeremiah had passed the rest of the evening sobbing in his
bathroom while the walls gurgled show tunes, bleeding what
looked like rainbow Jell-O, and his PED plotted openly to sell
him into sexual slavery. Afterwards Jack had invited him on
several occasions to "get mellow" again, but Jeremiah had
always found an excuse.

"Jack," said Jeremiah, back in the present, "I appreciated the
brownie—"

"*Brownies.*"

"—but I don't have any drugs."

"Is your place in the System really worth treating a friend
this way?"

"Jack," said Jeremiah, who had an idea, "for the last time,
I *categorically* deny that I have access to drugs, have sold them
to Mr. Wendstrom, or can sell them to you."

So saying, Jeremiah poked the desk hard with his index
finger. As he hoped, something about his having done so—
and something about that word "categorically"—caught
Jack's attention.

"I see," Jack said, his eyes growing wide. He lay a finger alongside his nose and pointed at the desk with his other
hand, where he understood Jeremiah to have just indicated
the position of the bugs. "For the record: I understand that
you have no access to any illegal drugs, and no intention of
selling them to me. Also for the record, I never had any intention of buying anything illegal—I was only testing you. And
by the way, I do not consent to any recording of this conversation, audio or video, in which I tested whether you would
refuse to sell me illegal drugs, and you passed. Do you consent to any such recordings?"

"No, Jack," said Jeremiah loudly and clearly, "I also do
not consent to any recording, audio or video, of our interaction, in which you tested whether I would refuse to sell you
illegal drugs, and I passed."

"All right, Jeremiah," Jack said, "I am going to stand up
and leave now. I am now standing. Thank you. Here I go.
Goodbye. I am almost at the door. I am at the door now."

The door closed behind him.

"Just in case there really *is* a record" said Jeremiah into the air, "he totally wanted to buy drugs."

After Jack's visit, the afternoon slowed dramatically. Maybe all the passengers were taking post-lunch naps in their newly repaired Relaxation Stations, or maybe—even here in sunless space where afternoon was purely a social construct—it was during those long middle hours that Boyle's recent *memento mori* cast its longest shadow.

Jeremiah certainly felt it. Had it been only yesterday morning that he'd seen Boyle dead? And the day before when he'd seen him alive and bitter and crazy? Each time Jeremiah closed his eyes and let his mind wander, it was a coin flip which incarnation of Boyle he'd have to dispel.

Even the mysteries of the playbook could not hold Jeremiah's attention for long. By 3 o'clock he was sure that he could not ever be more bored than he was at that moment. By 4 o'clock he realized that his 3 o'clock self had lived, jaded and unappreciative, in a relative golden age of interest and distraction. By 4:30 he was close to gnawing off his own leg, and by 4:58 he could feel his imminent release like a fresh breeze from an open door at the end of a prison hallway.

At 4:59 Mrs. Abdurov walked in.

Her strength of character was visible in every punishing step she took, but Jeremiah had to admit that it was mysterious to him exactly which aspects of Mrs. Abdurov's physical beauty Mr. Drinkwater had in mind when he sang its praises. "Statuesque," you could have called her, if you posited a sculptor who had mistakenly begun work on a marble block lying on its side, a little wider than it was tall, and after realizing his mistake—given the price of marble these days—tried to make the best of it, chiseling the nose of his masterpiece in the aftermath of a fight with his wife, the eyes after they had passionately made up, and the mouth while she was calling him to dinner. Mrs. Abdurov wore pink slacks and a boxy olive-green blouse whose shoulders looked to have oven mitts sewn into them, as if to cushion the kickback from the butt of a rifle.

"Jeremiah," she shouted, "I catch you in time."

"Hello, Mrs. Abdurov," said Jeremiah, "I was just about to close up."

"What? Don't mumble."

"Close up," shouted Jeremiah.

"No," she said, even louder, "my *chair*. My *chair* isn't working. My Relaxation Station."

Mrs. Abdurov was stone deaf in one ear, but—Jeremiah had long suspected—only conveniently deaf in the other. He studied her face for any indication that she had actually understood him, but she would have made an excellent poker player—she seemed content to let Jeremiah take as much as time as he would like, secure that she would give nothing away.

"Oh, all right," Jeremiah said, "what's one more Relaxation Station? Let's go."

"What did you say?" said Mrs. Abdurov loudly—but this time Jeremiah was sure that he could see the glint of understanding in her eye, and the pleasure of victory at the corners of her mouth. "Speak up. Don't mumble. Let's go."

Mrs. Abdurov was not one of Jeremiah's easier customers. She held strong opinions about every detail of his duties: from the route they took back to her quarters, to whether Jeremiah was crowding her or malingering along the way, to how he began his investigation of her Relaxation Station and its various malfunctions.

For several problems ailed the apparatus: a shimmy when reclining, a click and grind that marked a refusal to recline any further, and a piercing whine when Jeremiah attempted to straighten it up again. Strangest of all, the workings of the chair chirped softly, even at rest.

Jeremiah followed the recommendations laid out in the playbook, but this Relaxation Station's maladies were novel, and Jeremiah quickly found himself at the section labeled *What to Do When None of the Above Work*, which read in its entirety: "Take the Relaxation Station apart and investigate. Good luck."

For a good fifteen minutes Jeremiah tugged and wrestled the various sections of the chair apart, while Mrs. Abdurov stood above him, sipping a cup of tea and remarking unfavorably on his strength, technique, and work ethic. Finally the back of the chair came shooting off, nearly taking Mrs. Abdurov's cup of tea along in the process, as well as Jeremiah's head.

Once the mechanism of the Relaxation Station was exposed, Jeremiah did not require long to diagnose the root cause of its problems.

"Crickets," he said, and then shouted, before he could be instructed not to mumble. "Your Relaxation Station is home to a whole concerto of crickets!"

Crickets in every ontological state a cricket could inhabit, in fact, from the larval with their whole cricket lives ahead of them, to the deceased but still intact, to the deceased and powdered and gumming up the gears of the recliner quite effectively. Those still in the prime of crickethood, sensing freedom in the new wide spaces available to them, began to desert the chair that had been their home for a dynastic number of cricket generations.

Before Jeremiah could react to their exodus, Mrs. Abdurov hip checked him out of the way and stepped forward to confront the leaping horde herself. She had put down her cup of tea somewhere, and from elsewhere equally mysterious produced a can of aerosolized pesticide, which she was now wielding to deadly effect, strafing the advancing cricket line and then covering the inner workings of the chair with the poison mist until droplets gleamed on the metal. The toxic fog of war cleared to reveal a battlefield strewn with crickets lying on their backs, a few spiky legs still twitching briefly in the air—and then all was still.

"Where did you get that pesticide?" asked Jeremiah between coughs.

"Thank you," Mrs. Abdurov said, clearing the air around her face with one hand and putting the other—still holding the can of pesticide—behind her back. "I put chair back together myself. You go now."

Jeremiah did not need to be asked twice.

"I'm just going to wash this stuff off my hands and face," he said, opening the door to the bathroom.

"No!"

This "no" was not Mrs. Abdurov's usual shout, or even

her unusual shout. This was a primal scream, and it accompanied a movement so fast and powerful that Jeremiah could hardly believe a woman of her age capable of it. She dashed in front of him and launched him backwards with both hands, then grasped the doorknob and tugged the door shut again— but not before Jeremiah had caught a glimpse of something protruding from the bathroom sink.

"I manage fine from here," she said. "You go. *Now.*"

"You're sure?" said Katherine.

"What else could it have been?" Jeremiah asked.

"I don't know—a green toothbrush. A green tube of toothpaste. A green figment of your imagination."

One of the other waiters ducked around the dish shelves where Katherine and Jeremiah were conversing.

"Kat, the orders are piling up."

"Can you just cover me for two more minutes?" she said.

He shook his head as he left, with a less than kind look at Jeremiah.

"It was *not* a figment of my imagination," said Jeremiah. "It was a tail. A green reptilian tail sticking out of the sink. *And* I saw a terrarium on the floor."

"So Mrs. Abdurov stole Mr. Wendstrom's iguana."

"That's certainly how it looks."

"And she poisoned Mr. Boyle."

"*That* I didn't say," Jeremiah said. "I just noted it was strange that she would have pesticide sitting around."

"Do you think Boyle found out she'd taken the iguana? Was he blackmailing her? Or maybe it was a love triangle of human, human, iguana?"

"Go on and laugh, but she didn't want me going in that bathroom," said Jeremiah.

"As someone who has been sharing a bathroom with you, I can't blame her."

"Are you going to help me or not? I can't pull this off alone."

"Jeremiah—"

"I understand if you're too scared."

"I'm not scared."

"Or if you don't think you could handle the pressure."

"Of course I can handle the pressure. What *pressure?*"

"Or if you don't care whether I end up away from Earth for another 20 years or not."

"Kat," said the waiter, appearing again, "table four is going to revolt if you don't get out there now."

The waiter looked at her. Jeremiah looked at her.

"Also," he said, "I lifted some chocolate biscuits from Mrs. Idlewhile today. I was planning to share them with you. In case that sways you at all."

"All right, all right," said Katherine. "But we have to do it late."

"Of course, when she's asleep."

"No, I mean I'm meeting John for a coffee after dinner shift, so it has to be after I get back."

"Ah," said Jeremiah.

"What does 'ah' mean?"

"It just means 'ah, so you *do* have coffee with co-workers, as long as that co-worker is The Specimen.' "

"I seem to remember something about it not being any of your business what I do, or with whom."

"And I seem to remember that I was allowed to be jealous."

"A *little* jealous. Does that mean you're allowed to say 'ah' whenever you want?"

"Look, it was just an 'ah', so let's not make a big deal of it," said Jeremiah. "You go on your coffee date and when you get back we'll liberate Mr. Wendstrom's iguana from Mrs. Abdurov's room."

WORLD ENOUGH (AND TIME)

13

Snatch and Grab

I
T was 11:39 p.m., and Jeremiah had filled the time with every occupation he could contrive while waiting for Katherine. First he had catalogued and graded his outstanding problems, not as reptiles but as fires, as by this point he lacked the zoological knowledge to assign a unique species to every challenge recent events had thrown his way.

- Making Mrs. Abdurov fall in love with Mr. Drinkwater by way of miming in a talent show: the smoldering embers of a campfire

- A stage for aforementioned show: one glowing brand in aforementioned fire

- Mrs. Chapin's revolution, the fomenting thereof: the shell of a veecar on fire, flames licking from the windows, a spectacular ruby necklace melting into the dash

- Jeremiah's broodingly intense Canadian stalker: a wall off which the paint was beginning to blister and droop—a fire was in there somewhere, but who knew how big or hot?

- Likewise Jack's quest to get mellow: a doorknob that had singed his fingers, but did the attached door open to a small flare-up or a raging inferno?

- Luis and his potential arrest the moment he set foot on American soil: not, strictly speaking, Jeremiah's house on fire, but one to which he was inclined to bring a bucket

- Mr. Boyle's possible murder: had he just imagined the smell of smoke?

- Mrs. Mayflower's broken bandora: a grease fire on a stove, spitting and leaping higher the more water he threw on it, giving every indication of becoming, in the fullness of time, a full-on four-alarmer

- Katherine spending time with The Specimen, even as Jeremiah made this mental list: flaming bamboo shoots under his nails, for reasons he could not quite get his mind around

- The Somewhat Satisfaction of every passenger on board when surveyed in six days: a forest fire almost sure to claim his life—see Mrs. Mayflower's bandora at a minimum—but as of yet no more than an orange glow in the distant sky

- And finally, the hunt for Carolus the Bold, a happy exception in this litany of infernos: a cakeful of gently glowing birthday candles that Jeremiah was poised, with a little help and a bit of luck, to blow out this very night

Even after ending this depressing catalogue on such a hopeful note, Jeremiah had found it necessary to sit down and hyperventilate for a few minutes.

Once that had been taken care of, he had found his way to the staff laundry and washed a load of clothes, of which he was in dire need, as the unseen elves who had spirited away his dirty laundry and replaced it, fragrant and folded, had evaporated upon his imminent default.

He had read three whole sections of the playbook, and was confident that he could now either resolve or direct appropriately any questions about special diets, reports of malfunctioning space toilets, or requests for custom levels of pressurization in a guest's quarters.

He had re-read the hated relativity pamphlet, reviewed Albert Einstein's revolutionary insights once more at leisure, and achieved a state of still deeper confusion regarding them.

In desperation he had even, finally, taken a stab at repairing Mrs. Mayflower's bandora, gently filing away the worst splinters on the neck, daubing liberal amounts of the wood glue (which he chose over the glue for wood by closing his eyes and picking at random) on the body, and clamping the whole arrangement together as best he could to let it dry. The end product did not inspire him with confidence, nor was he pleased to discover that the entire effort had killed 22 piddling minutes.

Finally, in a spiteful 30-second gorge, he ate all Mrs. Idlewhile's biscuits himself, despite having promised to share them with Katherine, and not even being hungry—a mean-spirited and senseless protest that he regretted the moment it was done.

At 11:47 Katherine returned.

"Hey," she said cheerily.

"Hey."

"You fixed the bandora?"

"I tried."

"It looks pretty good."

"Yeah, I guess," said Jeremiah.

"Is something wrong?"

"What would be wrong?"

"You just sound—"

"I just sound like what?"

"Like something's wrong."

"I'm tired, that's all," said Jeremiah.

"Does that mean you want to do the thing another time? I wouldn't mind hitting the hay myself."

"No," said Jeremiah, jumping to his feet. "I'm getting a second wind."

"Were you upset because I was with John?" Katherine asked as they walked. The lights were dimmed at this hour, and the hallways completely abandoned.

"That's none of my business," said Jeremiah. Despite the empty hallways, the sense of the occasion had them both whispering.

"I agree completely."

Jeremiah sensed a chance to offset his earlier petulant behavior. He did not want to be a clingy whiner in Katherine's eyes—he wanted to be a man of action, a man who focused on the task and—regardless of any flaming bamboo shoots of jealousy that may or may not be jammed under his fingernails—got things done.

"Look," he said, "let's get our heads in the game. This is a simple snatch and grab, and if we both do our parts it should come off without a hitch."

"I think you mean *smash*," said Katherine.

"What?"

"It's *smash* and grab."

"That makes no sense—we're not smashing anything."

"But it makes sense to grab something you've already snatched?" said Katherine.

"More sense than smashing it before you grab it."

"No," said Katherine, "you smash the shop glass before you take the jewelry behind it. I mean, not *you*, but a robber."

"Oh, I see. A robber *smashes* the ShopGlass and *grabs* the jewelry behind it?"

"Exactly."

"What does he smash it with?" asked Jeremiah.

"I don't know—a wrench, a rock. Does it matter?"

In a show of great tolerance, Jeremiah shook his head only the tiniest bit.

"Are these *magic* rocks? Wrenches forged in the fires of Mt. Doom?"

In perhaps an even greater display of tolerance, Katherine restricted her reaction to saying that she did not follow him.

"Well," he continued, "you're telling me that robbers use these rocks and wrenches to break *ShopGlass*—which is specifically designed to stop *bullets,* and which I once personally saw turn a *hand grenade* in the Detroit Election Night Riots—and that's why it's called a *smash* and grab."

"I don't think this conversation has much of a future," said Katherine.

"I agree completely. Now listen, this is a simple *burglary,* and your part is critical. First we stop by the kitchen…"

As he stood outside Mrs. Abdurov's door, communicator in one hand, holding the keycard he had encoded poised above the access strip, Jeremiah felt his nerves sharpen and arrange themselves, like iron filings beneath a magnetic field, into a shape that recalled days long gone. He remembered Bohemian hijinks in crumbling Detroit apartments, fueled by youth and alcohol and a certain liberation that came from having no credit and prospects only in artistic careers, where "prospects" never meant prospects of credit. Jeremiah had always felt like a faker in those days—mostly because he had been one, with his rich uncle footing the bills and his super-lawyer-plus-agent furthering his career from behind the scenes. Now Jeremiah was legitimately on his own, with no avuncular safety net, and he relished that feeling. He looked at Katherine. She was tucked against the wall, safely out of what would be the line of sight when the door opened. Their eyes met in agreement, and then Jeremiah put on his game face, swiped the key card, and stepped into the darkness.

Calling Jeremiah's plan a "plan" was like calling Katherine's suite a "suite"—both technically correct and somewhat aspirational. There were, to put it kindly, still some rough spots in his approach towards certain contingencies, and none rougher than this moment, when he crossed the Rubicon of Mrs. Abdurov's threshold without knowing whether he would find her asleep—as he hoped—or awake, as he feared. The darkness that enveloped Jeremiah as the door hissed closed encouraged him on this point. The fact that she was speaking to him did not.

"Vassily!" the unseen Mrs. Abdurov whispered urgently. "*Ate toe tie?*" Or Russian words to that effect.

As Jeremiah's eyes adjusted to the dim blue glow of the nightlight, he saw her there, sitting upright in bed with a white nightie fallen from one shoulder, the covers bunched about her waist. She was terrifying, pale and powder-blue, her eyes an average of every zombie wave Jeremiah had ever seen, and he was just on the point of flight when she turned her head slightly so at the new angle he could distinguish the beauty sponges on her eyelids.

"Vassily?" she whispered again.

The moment had come for Jeremiah to employ his Russian language skills.

"*Da,*" he said, in the deepest register he could reach without injury. This represented half the Russian at his command, and promised to be more positive and comforting than "*nyet.*"

Mrs. Abdurov fell back into bed like a plank, and within a few seconds was making sounds similar to one being sawed. The beauty sponges had not budged from her eyes during all the preceding movement, causing Jeremiah to wonder if perhaps she had affixed them with wood glue, or glue for wood.

He pulsed the communicator once to signal that he was in safely, and lit his steps to the bathroom with its screen. Then, once the bathroom door was safely closed, he brushed the light switch and nearly yelped in victory and surprise.

There, splayed out on the sink with his head tilted up and to the left, sat Carolus the Bold. It appeared he had been drinking from the faucet, which Mrs. Abdurov had left slowly trickling. Now his throat pulsed once and his head tilted to the right, and it seemed to Jeremiah that, as befit Carolus's epithet, he was not frightened in the least by the sudden appearance of a new human being in the bathroom where he was being held captive, but rather curious. Jeremiah felt himself the subject of some interspecies interview, being asked to describe himself, his hobbies, and his qualifications for this kind of snatch and grab rescue work. Instead, he pulsed the communicator twice to signal contact with the target. Deeds, not words.

The terrarium was still there on the ground where Jeremiah had glimpsed it that afternoon, wedged between the toilet and the sink, its yellow top propped beside. Along the bottom of the clear plastic rectangle ran a thin layer of sand, upon which two crickets lay belly up. Two others stroked the too-high plastic walls with their antennae, attempting an occasional and futile escape by jumping. Pocketing the communicator, Jeremiah picked up the terrarium and its yellow top. He took a step towards Carolus, watching for signs of flight. Carolus tilted his head back to the left. Jeremiah reached out his hand. The red throat pulsed. And suddenly Jeremiah was holding the creature, his hand belting the iguana's belly. Carolus's dry, papery skin felt as if it might rip away from that delicate rib cage beneath, and his dorsal spines were sharp but pliable between Jeremiah's fingers.

Carolus curled around Jeremiah's hand, holding himself upright with his front legs draped over Jeremiah's index finger and wrapping his tail up until it almost touched Jeremiah's pinky. There was a kind of acceptance in the gesture—a recognition that they were both in this mad enterprise together—which touched Jeremiah.

"I'm going to get you out of here," he said, looking Carolus directly in the eyes. Carolus blinked weirdly with his lower eyelids, but the iguana's gaze—just like his bold nerve—never wavered.

Then suddenly those wise, placid eyes grew wide, and Carolus's head—which had settled back straight as Jeremiah had picked him up—tilted and swiveled to the left, where the sounds of his captor clearing her throat and fumbling with the knob of the bathroom door were unmistakable. Jeremiah must have woken Mrs. Abdurov just enough that she had become aware of some pressing biological needs—needs to which she was now en route to attend.

Still holding Carolus in one hand and the terrarium in the other, Jeremiah pushed aside the shower curtain, jumped inside the tub, and used his elbows to close the curtain again, finishing just as the bathroom door opened and Mrs. Abdurov entered. Initially Jeremiah felt pleased with himself for his quick thinking and action, but the pleasure might have lasted longer if the plastic of the shower curtain concealing Carolus and himself had not been transparent.

The curtain did introduce, Jeremiah was happy to note, some degree of blur to everything behind it, but he could still see the scene developing in the bathroom more clearly than he might have wished, and he assumed that, if Mrs. Abdurov were to direct her attention to the general area of the bathtub, the corollary would also prove true.

So far she still had her back to Jeremiah, examining herself in the mirror and fussing with her nightgown, making preparatory noises low in her throat. He would not have long until she worked herself up to what she had come to do—30 seconds, at most—at which point, seated just a few feet away and facing him, she could not possibly miss the distinctly man-sized, man-shaped, man-colored blur behind her shower curtain. Jeremiah could not predict exactly where Mrs. Abdurov's reaction would range along various axes at that point—fight vs. flight, for example—but he was reasonably sure that, once the initial shock had worn off, her satisfaction score for the experience would fall somewhere between "Highly Dissatisfied" and "Legal Action."

Jeremiah clutched Carolus to his chest, relieved that the telepathic link they had forged seemed to be holding. The iguana sensed his rescuer's desperate intent, grabbing Jeremiah's shirt with all four of his spindly hands and holding on for dear reptilian life, which freed Jeremiah's hand to go for the communicator in his pocket. He extracted it and began to pulse with his thumb in desperate bursts of three.

Almost immediately after he made his distress signal he heard the electronic tinkle of the doorbell in response, but the sound was terribly quiet and distant behind the bathroom door, far quieter than the increasingly loud grunts that Mrs. Abdurov was making as she now rocked from foot to foot, loosening up.

Jeremiah mashed the communicator harder and faster, and the doorbell matched his urgent rhythm, now a steady stream of ascending tones, the last hardly ending before the next began. Carolus at least seemed to hear them, and they stirred something elemental in him—some predator or prey instinct deeper than the interspecies mind meld between himself and Jeremiah, which shattered as Carolus gave over to his genetic urge to flee danger by ascending the nearest tree—or, in absence of a tree, the nearest object taller than it was wide—meaning, in this case, Jeremiah.

The iguana cleared Jeremiah's collar and began slapping his hands against Jeremiah's face, searching for a good toehold in Jeremiah's nostrils and the corners of his mouth. Jeremiah did not dare stop pulsing the communicator or risk putting down the terrarium on the noisy tub to free up a hand. He was reduced to huffing and puffing in a breathy attempt to dissuade Carolus from climbing any further, and scowling as he tried mentally to re-establish the unity of purpose they had so recently enjoyed. Neither of these efforts slowed Carolus's ascent, however, and Jeremiah watched with horror through what he supposed was Carolus's armpit as the blur that was Mrs. Abdurov turned and bent, steadying herself with one hand on the sink to begin her descent—and then stopped.

Through the filter of the shower curtain Jeremiah saw the smaller blur that was Mrs. Abdurov's head tilt to the side in a motion reminiscent of Carolus's (who was just now clearing Jeremiah's hairline). Had she heard something? Still Jeremiah pulsed the communicator again and again, each pulse now alternating between terror and hope, hope and terror—but yes, yes, Mrs. Abdurov had heard the little ascending riff of the doorbell, which now sounded sweeter and more angelic than any symphony or folk song Jeremiah had ever heard, and she was holding there, mid-squat, deciding what to do about it.

In the meantime Jeremiah was facing decisions of his own. Having finished scaling Jeremiah's face with a kind of spastic aplomb, Carolus the Bold had reached the crown of his head, and, grabbing clawfuls of hair to steady himself, turned around to face the shower curtain. The good news was that, as a result, Carolus's tail no longer dangled and tickled Jeremiah's nose, provoking a disastrous sneeze. The bad news was that, from his new vantage point, Carolus had taken a liking to the rod and rings of the shower curtain, and was reaching out one claw with its strange elongated second finger to bat like a bored feline at the shower tackle. If the iguana reached it, it was inconceivable that the visual and auditory disturbances would not attract Mrs. Abdurov's attention to the shower curtain and what was behind it. On the other hand, as Jeremiah leaned backwards in an attempt to deny the iguana access to the shower rod, Carolus the Bold—true once again to his name—was leaning further and further forward with a complete disregard for the steadiness of his perch and for the consequences to his own well being if he lost it. Brief telepathic link aside, Jeremiah was relatively sure that Carolus had not internalized what the consequences to Jeremiah would have been, either, if the iguana overreached and came crashing down in the tub, little iguana limbs flailing at the curtain and quite possibly bringing it down with him for what was sure to prove a dramatic reveal.

"Edgar hog die Aphrodite Hanoi proletariat," muttered Mrs. Abdurov, or Russian words to that effect, and with a relief like a breaking fever Jeremiah saw her straighten up, fix something on her shoulder in the mirror, and leave the bathroom just as Carolus reached the curtain rod.

In two seconds flat Jeremiah had snatched Carolus from his head and tossed him gently into the terrarium. The top of the terrarium closed and clicked home, and Jeremiah pushed aside the shower curtain and placed his own ear at the door of the bathroom, right hand cupped to amplify whatever sound might come through. What came through was exactly one half of Katherine and Mrs. Abdurov's conversation—namely, the half performed by the shouting Mrs. Abdurov.

"I didn't order hot cocoa. I didn't order anything. Of course I'm sure. Who else you think is here in room to order? Of course I don't want—if I want hot cocoa, I order. Yes, I know is without charge, everything on board is without charge, but I don't want. What you mean, trouble? Why *you* get in trouble because *I* don't want hot cocoa? Oh all right, bring it in."

Jeremiah closed his eyes, pouring all available mental and sensory energy into his right ear. As soon as he heard—or thought he'd heard—Katherine and Mrs. Abdurov walk to the far side of the room, he threw the bathroom door open and, terrarium clutched to his chest like a football, sprinted for the open hall, not even looking back to see if he'd been spotted.

When Katherine arrived back at the suite, Jeremiah had already been sitting on the sofa for a good five minutes, feeling quite pleased with himself.

"That was amazing," he said. "Absolutely textbook. You were perfect—I can't believe that was your first snatch and grab."

"Mrs. Abdurov was not too happy with me," said Katherine. "I practically had to beg her not to make a complaint—I'm still not 100% sure she won't."

"You worry too much. Have a seat, take a snort of terrible vodka with me, and admire the fruits of our labor."

Jeremiah presented, game-show-hostess style, the terrarium on the floor in front of him, from which Carolus stared out at him. The iguana's look seemed both to accuse Jeremiah of betrayal, and to accept stoically that perhaps it was an iguana's lot in life to forever discover that the liberator in one episode was the jailer of the next.

"I worry exactly the right amount," said Katherine. "I'm tired and have to get up early. Good night. Oh," she added, pausing in the doorway of her bedroom, "by the way, you're welcome."

"Thank you!" shouted Jeremiah through the closed door. "Really, thank you! I couldn't have done it without you! I already *said* thank you," he asked Carolus, who tilted his head in response. "Right?"

WORLD ENOUGH (AND TIME)

14

Morning of the Iguana

Tuesday (5 days until arrival)

J EREMIAH had meant to be outside Mr. Wendstrom's
door early—as in "before the hallway lights came
up to full brightness at 5:00 a.m." early—but the
adrenaline of last night's snatch and grab had first kept him
awake and then deserted him so abruptly that he had passed
out without setting an alarm. So here he was almost four
hours later than planned, creeping through the corridors
with the terrarium wrapped in a ratty towel he had liberated
from Katherine's bathroom. But despite his late rising he
hadn't met anyone on the way here, and all was well that
ended well.

Mr. Wendstrom answered the door wearing a long velvet
garment that looked like the love-child of a cheap motel
bathrobe and a smoking jacket, with slippers to match. He
had the look of a man recently and unhappily awakened.
When he saw the shape and size of the bundle Jeremiah was
carrying, however, his face brightened. He waved Jeremiah
inside and activated the door behind them, first looking left
and right down the hall to make sure that Jeremiah had not
been followed.

"You have him? I knew you were a winner, Jeremiah. The
pressure I put on you would have made most men crumble—
but it turned *you* into a diamond."

Jeremiah did not immediately absorb this compliment, as
he was too busy absorbing the room's decor. That is, the
room had a "decor" in the same way that the basement of

a grizzled old detective might have a decor, if it were wallpapered in records lifted from his former department and articles snipped from the local paper, all of them related to the one case he could never quite crack, the one that kept him up nights and ruined his marriage and drove him to drink and eventually obsessed him to the point where he was kicked off the force for not being able to let it go. That kind of decor.

The entire back wall of Mr. Wendstrom's room was taken up with portraits—hand drawn on sheets of A4 paper—of animals in the postures and dress of high fantasy. There were wolf lords and cat ladies, armadillo knights and salamander wizards and toad witches. One prominent section even displayed a few creatures that, from this distance, resembled dragons interpreted by a man with middling artistic powers and more than a passing fondness for iguanas. The portraits were connected by yarn of different colors, presumably signifying various relationships, which gave the impression of a giant spider redecorating his web in an attempt to brighten the place up a bit.

Next to the bed was a giant free-standing corkboard full of index cards. The cards had been arranged in three columns, each titled in block letters: LIKELY, UNLIKELY, DISPROVEN. Above those headings, on a still larger sheet of paper that was tacked halfway off the corkboard and leaning forward as if trying to read the others, was the super-heading: ANDWEN LONGTAIL'S REAL FATHER: THEORIES.

Having internalized all this, Jeremiah made a "think nothing of it" face in response to Mr. Wendstrom's ongoing remarks of praise, and, holding the terrarium in one hand, whisked the towel away showily with the other.

"I believe this belongs to you," said Jeremiah, handing the terrarium to Mr. Wendstrom.

Jeremiah had expected a few seconds of stunned silence—in fact, he enjoyed them—but after a few seconds more he felt that the timing of the scene, with Mr. Wendstrom still standing and staring, had gone a bit off—and after a few more seconds he couldn't find a way around the conclusion that Mr. Wendstrom was refusing to take delivery of his iguana.

"Is this a joke?" said Mr. Wendstrom.

"How do you mean?"

"That's not Carolus the Bold."

138

"Of course it is," said Jeremiah.

"There are crickets in that cage. All iguanas are vegetarians—they can't even process the insect or animal protein some of their so-called 'caretakers' give them—but for Carolus vegetarianism is more than that. It's a part of his moral code."

"We haven't actually seen him *eat* one," said Jeremiah.

As if to dispel any trace of doubt that the telepathic link between Jeremiah and himself was well and truly severed, the iguana turned his head sideways, trapped one of the living crickets against the wall of the terrarium, and devoured it mercilessly and with gusto.

"Also," continued Mr. Wendstrom, "Carolus is significantly larger than this iguana."

"Well if he's had to go off his vegetarian diet because his kidnapper didn't know the first thing about the proper care and feeding of iguanas, doesn't it stand to reason that he's dropped a few?"

"Jeremiah, there are two reasons that Carolus is bigger than this iguana. First: he is a *southern* blood-throated iguana, which—besides being much rarer and more intelligent than your typical *northern* blood-throated iguana, run larger. This is a northern blood-throated iguana. And second, Carolus—unlike this iguana—is male."

Jeremiah had been just about desperate enough to argue the northern vs. southern issue, but this second point had the ring of checkmate. He didn't know much about the social issues and gender norms of the natural world in general or iguanas in particular, but he imagined gender reassignment operations were rare among blood-throated iguanas, in both the northern and southern regions of their habitat.

"You're telling me I broke into Mrs. Abdurov's room in the middle of the night and stole the wrong iguana?" said Jeremiah. He said it very, very quietly.

"I don't want to know about that. Losers focus on methods—winners only care about results. I'm telling you that's not Carolus the Bold.

"Jeremiah," continued Mr. Wendstrom, putting his hand on Jeremiah's shoulder, "I saw you notice my work in progress when you came in." He pointed to the portraits and sheets of paper. "What did you think of it? Don't worry, I'll *tell* you what you thought: crazy. Weird. *Obsessed.* Right?"

"I wouldn't say *obsessed*," Jeremiah said, seizing the opportunity to take a step back in the (ultimately vain) hope that Mr. Wendstrom would be inspired to remove his hand from Jeremiah's shoulder.

"But you would *think* it. I'm going to let you in on a secret, Jeremiah—a secret I usually charge a lot of credit to learn in my seminar: *obsessed* is just what the losers of the world call the winners."

Mr. Wendstrom gave Jeremiah a moment to absorb this wisdom, tightening the sash on his robe-slash-smoking-jacket in the meanwhile, which at least meant that Jeremiah's shoulder returned to its blissfully handless state. He took another discreet step back in the hopes of keeping it that way.

"You see how I've put the corkboard next to my bed? My theories on who is Andwen Longtail's real father are the last thing I see before I go to sleep and the first thing I read when I wake up. That's why—eventually—I'll figure it out. I'm more obsessed with the work of Michael L. L. Gregory than Michael L. L. Gregory himself," said Mr. Wendstrom, now tightening his sash to a degree that began to look uncomfortable, both for himself and the sash. "I mean, he can't even bring himself to buckle down and finish a single goddamn book in four goddamn years, so that his fans have to go on a relativistic cruise just to be able to read the goddamn thing in a reasonable goddamn amount of time."

Mr. Wendstrom took one more yank at the sash and his face turned red—whether from anger at having brought to mind Michael L. L. Gregory's unsatisfactory work ethic or from the sash having forced all blood from the waist up into his head—or both—Jeremiah could not say.

"Jeremiah, I'd like to commend you on your effort, but I'm not going to. Losers whine about effort. Winners care about results. I'm going to treat you like a winner, in the hopes that you'll act like one. You have until—" Wendstrom sniffed and considered how long a true winner would need to complete this mission. "—lunch-time tomorrow to bring me Carolus. Otherwise I will be Highly Dissatisfied—and I will make my dissatisfaction known. Now," said Mr. Wendstrom, taking the deepest breath his sash would allow, "get this northern blood-throated iguana out of my room, and go out there and win!"

Jeremiah hurried down the hallway towards Mrs. Abdurov's quarters, trying to look as nonchalant as it was possible to look while carrying a bundle the exact size and shape of a kid-napped iguana trapped in a stolen terrarium which itself was wrapped in a scraggly towel that technically speaking had also been borrowed without permission.

His plan, so to speak, was to swipe Mrs. Abdurov's door open (by a stroke of luck he still had the keycard he had en-coded last night in his pocket), toss Carol the Northern Im-postor inside, drive-by-shooting style, and haul veritable ass down the hallway in case Mrs. Abdurov was inside her room and not, as he hoped, at breakfast. If he happened to run into anyone on the way, Jeremiah had some vague notion about it being best to acknowledge the bundle—point to it, chuckle, shake his head in a "you don't even want to know" way, without so much as breaking stride. But as he neared the final turn before Mrs. Abdurov's doorway, he had still not encountered a single soul.

"This whole hallway is going Ultra Premium Luxury," said a voice from around the corner. "Once we're in dock we'll demo every other wall and convert them. These are the projections—conservative—for increased revenue—"

The voice was Grubel's, and it was coming closer. Jeremiah turned and ran.

With no time to take Carol the Northern Impostor back to the suite before nine a.m., and uneager to push his luck any further vis-à-vis not running into anyone, Jeremiah made straight for the office, where any lingering doubts about his luck having run out were laid to rest.

"Oh," said Jeremiah. "Good morning, Mrs. Abdurov."

He had found her waiting outside the door, muttering in Russian and peering through the glass as if she suspected Jeremiah were hiding inside.

"The sign says you open at nine," she shouted. "Is 9:02. What is you hold so tightly on your chest?"

"Just my lunch."

Inside the terrarium Carol the Northern Impostor had suddenly become active, perhaps recognizing the voice of her rightful owner, and Jeremiah nearly fumbled the package attempting to reach into his pocket for the key.

"Give me that," Mrs. Abdurov said, snatching the wrapped terrarium before he could protest. "Young people today, always multitasking, because you are lazy. You need open the door? Set down your lunch, open the door, pick up your lunch. Lazy is more work in end. Look, already you are sweating. And no wonder, with what you are eating. So heavy, and the smell, ugh!"

Jeremiah opened the door and snatched back the terrarium before Mrs. Abdurov could lift the corner of the towel.

"After you," he said.

She glared at him as she passed, muttering something that sounded a lot like *"taco grubby milkshake."*

Jeremiah put the terrarium behind the desk as he sat down.

"Well, Mrs. Abdurov," he said, "what—"

"I am robbed," she shouted in a dramatic whisper. "A theft in the night. I even know who did the theft."

"You do?"

"Well, yes! I met him here this morning, just outside in the hallway. He is cruel—he toys with me. He thinks he is smart—he pretends to know nothing of the theft."

"Oh," said Jeremiah, his mouth suddenly bone dry. "I'm sure if you heard his side of it, you might—"

"Good morning, he tells me, he offers take my arm and escort me to breakfast. Says I look tired, need to sleep better. When he can't sleep, he says, he drinks hot cocoa. You hear that? *Hot cocoa,* says the fat snowman."

Jeremiah, who had done and said none of these things, apart from "good morning"—and whom no one without a very particular agenda would have described as a "fat snowman"—found it very pleasant to breathe again. Said pleasure, however, would prove fleeting.

"But I know you, *Tat* Drinkwater," said Mrs. Abdurov, "and your theft in the night ways."

"You think Mr. Drinkwater stole your—"

"Not think, *know!* For days he acts so strange. Always

looking, always leering. When I leave my room, he always just happens to be passing by. Then last night he strikes— he sends me hot cocoa in middle of the night, and while I am arguing with idiot hot cocoa girl he sneaks in and steals Marya Jana. I see him running out the door."

"I really can't imagine Mr. Drinkwater *doing* something like—"

"Marya Jana," whispered Mrs. Abdurov at roughly the volume of an auctioneer losing a heroic battle with Tourette's, "is my iguana. I know, I know, do not scold me—we are not allowed animals on board. But how could I leave my little Mashusha behind knowing she will be dead when I got back?"

"Oh," Jeremiah said, with what he hoped sounded like the triumph of warmth and common sense over official pedantry, "don't worry about that. What trouble could an *iguana* possibly cause—or even two? Your secret is safe with me, Mrs. Abdurov, but I really think Mr. Drinkwater—"

"You ask how you can help me? You use your fancy keycard machine and make copy of *Tat* Drinkwater's card. Then you enter *Tat* Drinkwater's room, you steal Marya Jana back. I watch and wait in the hall and am Highly Satisfied. So: we go now."

She stood up.

"Mrs. Abdurov," said Jeremiah, "I couldn't possibly break into a guest's room! And I'm sure—quite sure—that Mr. Drinkwater had nothing to do with—"

Mrs. Abdurov had put her hands on her hips and was staring at him, waiting. She said nothing, but Jeremiah felt a kind of pre-Pavlovian response as the long shadow of High Dissatisfaction fell across the room. One by one his objections deserted him, until only one remained, the one he could not possibly utter: that Jeremiah knew Mr. Drinkwater to be an innocent party because he himself was the guilty one.

"All right," he said at last—and then a flash of genius struck him. "Wait! I left the keycard encoder in my room. I have to go get it first."

"All right," Mrs. Abdurov said, "we go to your room first, then we go to *Tat* Drinkwater's room."

"No, you can't be seen in the staff quarters. You go scope out Mr. Drinkwater's hallway, and I'll meet you there in five

minutes."
"Why you are bringing your lunch with you?"
But now it was Jeremiah's turn to be conveniently deaf.

Abandoning every pretense of dignity or calm, Jeremiah sprinted down the hall, ignoring the startled and questioning looks he drew from everyone he met without so much as the smile and head shake he had prepared earlier. He was making good time, and his plan—which was to return Marya Jana, as he now knew her to be called, to Mrs. Abdurov's quarters while she was known to be waiting outside Mr. Drinkwater's—had more to recommend it than most of the other plans he'd dreamed up in the past few days. In fact there was every reason to suspect it would have worked, if he had not taken a corner tight and fast and ran into—literally and physically—Mr. Grubel. Fortunately their heads did not make contact, or both could have been knocked unconscious, but the Financial Officer's glasses flew off in the collision, along with the recorder into which he had been speaking, still laying out his plans for the new Ultra Premium Luxury suites. For a few seconds both were too dazed to speak.

"Jeremiah?" said Grubel. He picked up his glasses and put them on, as if he might be better equipped to believe what he was seeing through their lack of lenses.

At that precise moment the terrarium thumped once and jumped a few inches—Marya Jana protesting the recent collision, perhaps, or relieving a hunger pang by lunging at the remaining cricket.

Mr. Grubel's eyes narrowed behind his newly replaced glasses, and narrowed further. Just how much narrower they eventually got Jeremiah could not say, as somewhere around the 3 mm mark he broke into a dead run back the way he had come.

"Jeremiah, stop!" said Grubel. "Come back here! I know you can hear me!"

His voice was not growing quieter and more distant, as Jeremiah would have hoped. To the contrary, Jeremiah could hear the Financial Officer's feet hit the hallway even with those pillowy shoes of his. It would not be too much longer before Grubel—who must have been hitting the treadmills in the Einstein IV's desolate gym pretty hard—overtook him. But now they were close, entering the female staff's quarters, and summoning the last burst of speed he had within him Jeremiah kicked his heels up and reached the doorway of Katherine's suite with a good fifteen feet of multicolored industrial carpet still between himself and his pursuer. In one fluid motion he withdrew the keycard from his pocket and swiped it over the access panel, hardly breaking stride as the door opened and closed behind him.

There was no time for raised arms or victory laps, however. His eyes darted around the suite from terribly obvious hiding place to terribly obvious hiding place. They all seemed terribly obvious. Ten seconds later Grubel pounded at the door and began to ring the bell.

"Jeremiah!"

The door muffled Grubel's voice, but not his anger.

Jeremiah could have hidden the terrarium in Katherine's bedroom and attempted to prevent Grubel from entering on the grounds of not invading her privacy without her present, but he had already involved her more than enough in his own problems. Then there was the bathroom, but even among terribly obvious options that seemed so terribly obvious as to be tantamount to a guilty plea.

"I know you're in there! Open up right now."

Jeremiah stowed the terrarium, still covered by the towel, on the far side of the sofa. He tossed his sheets and blanket on top, plumping a sheet here and smoothing a blanket there so the pile didn't look so recently made, and then—taking a few seconds to gather himself—walked over and opened the door.

For all that Jeremiah disliked Mr. Grubel, it was impossible to deny that the Financial Officer had a certain kind of authenticity. For example, at this moment he looked authentically like an office worker who had just displayed surprising speed and stamina during an on-foot pursuit of a subordinate while wearing clothes that could not quite keep pace with him. One silver cuff of his pants had ridden up a silver sock, and both shirt tails had declared their independence from his pants altogether. Grubel seemed to realize, through his crooked glasses, that the

145

nature of the contest had changed, and that Jeremiah's new calm—however manufactured—represented some kind of advantage. He took a moment to straighten himself out, acting all the while as if Jeremiah were not there.

"Jeremiah," he said when he had finished, and walked right past him through the door.

"How can I help, Mr. Grubel?" asked Jeremiah.

"What's this?" asked Grubel, pointing at the empty terrarium that Mr. Wendstrom had given Jeremiah—and which, in his rush to hide the other, non-empty, terrarium, Jeremiah had forgotten was still in plain sight on the table.

"A terrarium," said Jeremiah, with all the nonchalance he could muster.

"Why do you have a terrarium?"

"Is it against the rules? I'll get rid of it."

Grubel resumed his search.

"Where is it, Jeremiah?"

There was not much surface area to explore, and the Financial Officer was already getting very warm as he neared the edge of the couch. Something in Jeremiah let go—there was no longer any way out, no trick he could conjure to prevent Grubel from finding Marya Jana. He felt no anger, no fear—only acceptance as Grubel whipped the sheet and blanket away from the pile at the end of the couch, revealing the ratty towel beneath.

"Is there something you want to tell me about what's under this towel, Jeremiah?"

Jeremiah shook his head. Somehow it seemed nobler to go down in a blaze of bravado, denying to the bitter end.

Grubel whisked the towel away, like a magician about to reveal that his assistant had vanished from the box where he'd put her. Bravado or not, Jeremiah couldn't watch this part.

"Jeremiah," said Mr. Grubel.

"Yes?"

"Why do you have another terrarium in your room?"

"Isn't it obvious?" Jeremiah said.

"Not to me," said Mr. Grubel.

As Grubel lifted the terrarium from behind the arm of the couch, Jeremiah had to admit his mystification was understandable. In fact, Jeremiah shared it: for apart

146

from the sad layer of sand at the bottom, the terrarium was completely empty. Not so much as a cricket, live or dead, graced its plastic walls, and certainly not a northern blood-throated iguana, which would have been very hard to miss. The top of the terrarium was not quite closed.

"Well, Jeremiah?"

"It's simple, I—collect terrariums."

"You collect terrariums?"

"Or—terraria. Always have, since I was a child. Is *that* against the rules?"

Mr. Grubel handed the terrarium to Jeremiah and began to search the rest of the room, which did not take long.

"And what's this?" the Financial Officer said, pointing at the only other object of interest to be found.

"A bandora, of course," Jeremiah said.

"A what?"

"It's like a lute."

"What is it doing here?"

"Mrs. Mayflower asked me to perform some routine maintenance on it before the talent show," said Jeremiah.

"Did you say Mrs. Mayflower?" said Grubel. His face took on a shade of white that Jeremiah considered reserved for skim milk.

"That's right."

"Did you *see* her?"

"Of course—she brought the bandora to the office."

Grubel sat down on the sofa, not entirely—it seemed—by choice.

"What did she say?" he asked.

"She said that she wanted to perform in the talent show, and that she needed some work done on her bandora first. What else would she have said?"

"Good," Grubel said. "That's very good. And you've got the task in hand? I suppose your musical background is proving useful."

"I guess so. More or less."

"Excellent, well done. Can I help in any way?"

On several first dates back on Earth, one young lady or another had inquired, over tacos or tiramisu, after the identity of Jeremiah's "spirit animal". Jeremiah had never known how to answer. But now, listening to Grubel's offer of assistance, Jeremiah realized that his spirit animal was a bewildered and deeply suspicious lamb being nuzzled by a wolf.

"How do you mean?" Jeremiah said.

"Do you need resources? Assistants? Someone to cover the desk while you work on this?"

"I don't think so," Jeremiah said. "Unless—you wouldn't happen to know the difference between wood glue and glue for wood?"

"I could put a researcher on it for you."

"That's all right," said Jeremiah, realizing the topic of why the bandora was clamped and glue indicated might be better avoided. "I have it in hand."

"Good," said Mr. Grubel again, standing up. "Good, yes. Keep up the good work, Jeremiah. Oh, and this belongs to you," he said, handing the second terrarium to Jeremiah. "Wouldn't want to break up your collection."

He nearly stumbled twice on his way out.

———————

The instant the door closed behind Grubel, Jeremiah began to rip through the room. He folded and unfolded the towel and sheets and blankets: nothing. He lifted the sofa and shook the cushions: nothing. He got down on his knees and inched over the carpet with his fingers, as if he were searching for a lost button instead of a missing reptile. But all his exertion turned up nothing even vaguely resembling a northern blood-throated iguana.

Finally, dumbfounded and furious, Jeremiah coded a spare keycard for Mr. Drinkwater's room and prepared to face Mrs. Abdurov. As he looked out one more time over the room before leaving, he was glad at the very least that Uncle Leo had left his credits to ferrets and not to iguanas, which were turning out to be more troublesome little beasts than he could have imagined possible.

———————

"Where have you been?" asked Mrs. Abdurov.

"I had some trouble with the keycard encoder," Jeremiah said.

"Never mind. I rang bell while I wait for you: *Tat* Drinkwater is away. You go in and find Marya Jana. I stay here and keep watch."

"Mrs. Abdurov," said Jeremiah, trying one last time, "I *promise* you that Mr. Drinkwater had nothing to do with Marya Jana's disappearance. I can't tell you how I know it, but I do."

Mrs. Abdurov reached over and patted Jeremiah's cheek, shaking her head.

"You are good boy, Jeremiah, so you think other people are good too. But you are stupid. You do not live in the world of *four of sky mirror*. People are not good. The world is hard, and it makes people hard too. So you go in now and get me back my Marya Jana, yes?"

Jeremiah could find no other response than to brush the keycard against the access point and walk into Mr. Drinkwater's room.

As the door closed behind him, Jeremiah suddenly understood why the passengers who were traveling Ultra Premium Luxury—Mr. Drinkwater, the Chapins, a very few others—never hosted soirees or dinners, and even threw their own birthday parties in the common areas. These rooms were practically an affront to those who, like Jeremiah and Mrs. Abdurov, had squeezed into a mere Super Luxury Cabin, which was barely large enough—Jeremiah now understood, having witnessed the Ultra Premium—to sustain civilized life. A pang of retroactive envy made him frown. He could never have imagined that there was this much credit in children's literature.

Even the crescent shape of the living room suggested opulence and plenty. No need for squared layouts and efficient shared corners, it seemed to say—there's more than enough space on this boat to waste on a wall that curves to welcome you like open arms, complete with bookshelves made of real wood and full of real books, and a false fireplace in the middle that flickered to animated life as soon as Jeremiah entered.

Had it really been less than a week since he had moved below stairs? Fewer than 200 hours since he had traded tempura-battered oysters gently fried for a rubbery quiche that was just the latest disguise for an immortal batch of synthed ham? Since he'd gone from the ennui of command-

149

ing his own time, all the time, to running around frantically serving the interests of others? Suddenly Jeremiah had to sit down. Luckily there was a wing chair of gorgeous chocolate leather thoughtfully placed where a tired or inebriated guest, returning to his Ultra Premium Luxury Suite, would have to stumble but a few steps to collapse into complete comfort. Jeremiah stumbled a few steps and collapsed into complete comfort.

He had intended to stay in Mr. Drinkwater's room just long enough to tell Mrs. Abdurov with a straight face that he had given it a thorough toss and come up with no iguana. But now, with the cool of a leather wing on his cheek and the faint smell of leather polish in his nostrils, he was in less of a hurry. The quiet here was deep and thick and unctuous, spread over the space like butter on bread, and it was indescribably pleasant to inhabit such quiet again. Jeremiah found he had a lot to think about—not just the more pressing problems to be visualized as reptiles or fires, but thoughts that his subconscious had been putting off for some unhectic moment that had never quite seemed to arrive until now.

For example: he was poor. Dirt poor. He'd been running around trying so hard to remain free for the next two years that he hadn't really considered how he was actually striving to be free and also—unless Appleton pulled off a miracle on his behalf—*poor*. How did one even go about being poor in Detroit? *Really* poor? What would happen to him? Would he find a job at a McSynthy's somewhere and scratch out a living in a tenement until a heart attack claimed him one evening while he was watching a PED in boxers and a wife beater and the neighbors found him days later? Would he contract some disease—not anything exotic like the passengers of the Einstein IV, something eminently curable—and die one of those "preventable" deaths, unable to afford treatment? Or would Detroit simply swallow him up, never to be heard from again?

And then there was the matter of Katherine, and how much time she seemed to be spending with The Specimen, and how little Jeremiah thought of him. Yes, The Specimen was broad-shouldered and square-jawed and had biceps like grapefruits, which was fine if you liked that sort of thing—but Jeremiah didn't. Worse still, Jeremiah wasn't even sure that The Specimen was a bad guy *per se*. Jeremiah was quite sure, on the other hand, that he was a bad guy for Katherine. All wrong. And Jeremiah would have to find a way to tell her so.

It seemed to him that there was something else to tell Katherine as well, though he couldn't quite wrap his mind around it—something about how she was different from anyone else he had ever met. About how there was a quality to her that he didn't know how to name. It was not just self-sufficiency, or competence, or kindness—he could come up with no word for her unique combination of characteristics but "Katherine", which made it hard to imagine expressing to her. It was a quality most visible in the effect she had on everyone and everything around her—in the same way that a scene from a wave was completely transformed, deepened immeasurably, by the right music playing behind it.

It bothered Jeremiah that he could not think how to describe Katherine. It bothered him that he could not stop thinking about her. It bothered him that she might not be bothered in the same way by Jeremiah himself.

And now that he was getting warmed up, another matter had just popped into Jeremiah's mind, one that seemed worthy of some of his immediate attention: namely that the door of Mr. Drinkwater's quarters had just opened and Mr. Drinkwater himself had just walked through.

"I would be delighted to accompany you to breakfast," he was saying. "Just let me drop off my—"

His eyes met Jeremiah's and he stopped.

"But Mr. Drinkwater," called Mrs. Abdurov from just outside the door, "I am so hungry *right now*."

"Oh," said Mr. Drinkwater, loudly. "That is, I..." He dropped his voice. "Jeremiah? What are you doing in my chocolate leather wing chair?"

Jeremiah made a variety of motions in rapid succession and combination: waving his arms as if warning Mr. Drinkwater off from a landing gone bad, shaking his head, pointing through the wall to where Mrs. Abdurov would be on the other side and—perhaps most frequently—bringing a finger to his lips in a violent shushing motion.

Mr. Drinkwater's confusion persisted for a moment as he absorbed all this, but then an expression of delighted understanding broke upon his face.

"Now?" he whispered excitedly. "You think I should do it *now*? All right. All right, I *will*! Oh Mrs. Abdurov," he said, louder, "here I come!"

Mr. Drinkwater ran out as fast as he could, and the door closed behind him. Jeremiah sat for another moment in the wing chair. He was not entirely sure what had just transpired, but he was fairly sure that it would not turn out to have been a lucky break.

15

The Law of Averages

MR. DRINKWATER walked into the Guest Services Office at 10:30 a.m. and did not stop walking, pacing back and forth despite Jeremiah's invitation to sit down. His snowmanesque physique did not wear anger and disappointment well. As he paced he tugged absent-mindedly at his turquoise scarf, first pulling this end longer and then the other, like a snowman lamp repeatedly turning itself off and on.

"You M-I-S-L-E-D me, Jeremiah," he said. "You really let me D-O-W-N."

"I'm sorry for breaking into your rooms, Mr. Drinkwater, but I can explain," said Jeremiah. In fact he could not even remotely explain, but luckily Mr. Drinkwater was not interested.

"When I first came to you for advice, you told me not to mime for Mrs. Abdurov, and so I didn't, even though my heart was bursting with mime. Then when you told me to mime for her, I *did* mime, despite my deep misgivings about that being the right occasion. And, just like I F-E-A-R-E-D, it blew up in my face."

"I never told you to mime for Mrs. Abdurov," said Jeremiah.

Mr. Drinkwater stopped pacing, as if he had bumped his head on the bald shock of this denial.

"Jeremiah, I'm a nice man—my wife, rest her soul, used to say you could push me over with a marshmallow. But if there's one thing I can't abide, it's L-I-E-S, so don't give me that S-T-U-F-F. When I found you sitting there in my chocolate leather wing chair, you very clearly motioned towards Mrs. Abdurov, and very clearly sent me out to mime to her."

Mr. Drinkwater accompanied this assertion with a recreation of Jeremiah's arm waving and shushing, which—while more practiced and stylized than the original—did not deviate from it sufficiently to allow room for denial.

"I had just found her there," Mr. Drinkwater continued, "in front of my door, and she had invited me to breakfast, did you know that? *She* had come looking to invite *me* to breakfast. It was my big chance, and I listened to you, and I threw it all away. As soon as I went back out in the hall and started to mime she grew cold and distant. She began to talk of loss and separation. D-A-R-N my foolish heart! Many, many people— good people, cultured people—can't take mime before breakfast. By the way, Jeremiah," said Mr. Drinkwater, as if remembering the milk, "what *were* you doing in my quarters?"

"There's been a misunderstanding," said Jeremiah, trying not to sound like the kind of person who says there's been a misunderstanding.

"About what?"

"This whole thing," said Jeremiah, buying himself as much time as he could with the long "o." "The truth is—well, the truth is—I was in your quarters because Mrs. Abdurov sent me there."

"Mrs. Abdurov? What for?"

"She sent me there to—well, to search your room. She thinks, you see—or at least she *thought*—that you—"

Although Mr. Drinkwater's face had hardly moved, a remarkable change had been wrought there as Jeremiah was bumping his way through these sentence fragments. It was as if a master sculptor had passed his hand over the work of a lesser talent, revising almost imperceptibly the line of the thick eyebrows and parting the lips ever so slightly, so that the confusion and disappointment on Mr. Drinkwater's face had become instead confusion and wonder—wonder that this angel made flesh (which was to say, Mrs. Abdurov) should deign to take any interest in himself whatsoever—let alone sufficient interest to commission a search of his room. The effect inspired Jeremiah to a different ending than he had originally planned.

"That you were keeping a woman in there," he said.

"What?" said Mr. Drinkwater. "Why would she think that? And why," he said, his eyes growing wide with a hope he dared not express, "would she care?"

"Can't you see?" Jeremiah said, feeling something rise and sink in his stomach at the same time. "Don't make me betray the poor woman's confidence."

"No, of course not, you mustn't—she's suffered enough, poor angel. But if she really feels that way—if my wildest dreams and fantasies are somehow coming true—then why would she treat me so coldly?"

"A woman like Mrs. Abdurov is complicated," Jeremiah said. "It's not enough for her to love—she must respect, as well. And *strength* is what she most respects."

Jeremiah felt that the spirits of all those workers who had sat at the Guest Services Desk before him—every departed member of his accidental guild—had arrived to support and inspire him, like the muses of interstellar hospitality. He could not tell whether he was inventing the words or receiving them—he was communing so deeply with the proud forebearers of his function that there seemed to be no difference.

"So you must *make* her *respect* you," continued Jeremiah. "Only then can she possibly *love* you."

"But I've tried!" Mr. Drinkwater said. "I've shown her kindness and deference. I've even shown her my talent, and—"

He cringed, unable to finish at the memory of her reception.

"*Talent* is not *strength!*" Jeremiah shouted. "Kindness and deference are *weakness!* You must be cold—you must be callous. Pass her in the hall without comment. Answer curtly when she speaks to you—if you answer at all. You must show Mrs. Abdurov how strong you are in the face of your own passion—how much you do not need her. Only then—" said Jeremiah, growing quieter, "—only then—will *she* need *you.*"

Mr. Drinkwater stood for a moment in the aftermath of this delivery. His posture straightened, his expression grew hard, and his eyes took on a determined glitter, as if he had been hooked up to a dialysis machine that was slowly replacing his blood with ice water. He buttoned the jacket of his suit and threw the end of his scarf over his shoulder with a continental insouciance. He was no longer a man of snow— but of ice.

"Thank you, Jeremiah," he said, and turned to leave. But as he approached the door it opened and there, standing in the hallway, stood Mrs. Abdurov. Both froze, eyes locked.

"Good morning, *Tat* Drinkwater," Mrs. Abdurov said. Icicles could have formed on the words.

"Is it?" answered Mr. Drinkwater, and his tone made Mrs. Abdurov's feel like a spring morning in comparison. He lifted his nose to an angle just shy of major chiropractic risk, turned on his heel—teetering a bit due to his snowman's physique—and departed.

"A prodigy," Mrs. Abdurov said as she approached the desk, her eyes shining. "A mastermind."

"You mean Mr. Drinkwater?" Jeremiah asked.

"So long since I have worthy opponent—a nemesis."

"But you can't still think Mr. Drinkwater stole Marya Jana—I checked his room very thoroughly and she wasn't there," Jeremiah said.

"Of course not—he moved her. The man is no fool. But how he knows exactly when we come to get her? And then the way he taunts me in the hall outside his room—no words, only gestures, making like iguana."

Mrs. Abdurov did her own interpretation of Mr. Drinkwater's mime act, which Jeremiah preferred to Mr. Drinkwater's own—and in which he had to admit an imaginative critic could have found an iguana struggling to escape the bonds of captivity.

"How could he know I have recording device on my person?" said Mrs. Abdurov. "So brilliant, so cold. *Tat* Drinkwater was disrespect. From now on, I call him *Vor* Drinkwater."

"A recording device?"

"Of course," said Mrs. Abdurov, pointing to the pen in the breast pocket of her thatchy jacket. The blue jewel on the pen's cap winked at Jeremiah, as if welcoming him into the know. "I am always recording everything."

"Do you record our conversations? Are you recording right now?"

"Always," Mrs. Abdurov said, hammering each syllable.

"Everything. But then he makes mistake—he gives me clue. Listen."

Mrs. Abdurov took the pen out of her pocket. It was made of pale yellow gold worked with curlicues of something that looked like platinum. She flicked one of the curlicues and the recorded voices of Mrs. Abdurov and Mr. Drinkwater—slightly distorted, but loud and still intelligible—began to play.

"Of course I look sad," said the recorded Mrs. Abdurov. "I lose something precious to me."

"I am very sorry to hear that," the recorded Mr. Drinkwater replied, more distant but still audible. "Have you considered taking a safe deposit box? That's where I would keep anything that was very precious to me. Unless, of course, it was something that didn't belong in a safety deposit box. Something, say, that was very precious to me but also very—"

In the pause that followed Jeremiah could practically hear the pointed, romantic look that Mr. Drinkwater had cast.

"—alive."

Mrs. Abdurov clicked the recording off.

"You hear?" she said. "He keeps Marya Jana in safe deposit box. You will break in and get her back for me."

"But he just said he *wouldn't* put anything alive in a safe deposit box."

"You stupid, sentimental boy, you do not understand the words of powerful men. I will interpret. Marya Jana is dead—this is how he tells me. But you will recover her body for me," said Mrs. Abdurov in a voice like blue steel, "and then her dead eyes will witness when I avenge her."

"Mrs. Abdurov," said Jeremiah, "this is a huge misunderstanding. Mr. Drinkwater was referring to you: *you're* the precious, living thing he would never put in a safe deposit box. He's a romantic, and he's head over heels in love with you. When you thought he was imitating a captive iguana, he was inviting you to breakfast. He's just not very good at expressing himself—not in words *or* mime."

Mrs. Abdurov smiled tenderly, almost wistfully, and for a moment Jeremiah thought perhaps he'd gotten through to her.

"Jeremiah, you are very sweet boy but you have soft

head. You are no match for mastermind like *Vor* Drinkwater. I know such men—for years I help my husband deal with them and their schemes. They try for many years to take his business, to steal his men, even to kill him. But Vassily and I, we bury every one of them, one next to the other in our garden, until Vassily's heart attacked him. Marya Jana is all he leaves me—her and the rest of the credit and the businesses. Now this man takes Marya Jana from me. So you leave all thinking to me, yes? You do what I ask and get Marya Jana's body back for me from the safety deposit box of cold, cruel, brilliant man."

"What if I break into the safe deposit box and Marya Jana's body isn't in there?"

"Then you take this camera pen and bring me picture of inside of empty box," Mrs. Abdurov said, "so I know you really look. You are sweet boy, Jeremiah, and I trust you. But you are stupid and sentimental, so I verify."

Jeremiah's grasp of mathematics was rudimentary at best, but according to his understanding of statistics, the fact that his morning thus far had been such an unmitigated and relentless disaster meant that he could expect a sharp upturn in his fortunes at any moment. So promised the law of averages or some such thing—some variation on the general idea of lightning not striking the same tree twice (Jeremiah being, in this analogy, the tree, and everything else on the Einstein IV the lightning).

But at 11:15 Jeremiah discovered that he had a bone to pick with the next statistician he happened to run across.

Mrs. Mayflower, stealthy as ever, finally showed up, peeking her head around the corner of the office door. Once she confirmed that Jeremiah was alone, the rest of her body followed with the same abrupt energy, as if she bathed daily in restorative waters. Today she came dressed for an ancient fox hunt in country pants and jacket, crowned with a curl-brimmed hat cocked almost sideways on her head, held in place with a hairpin that would have qualified as a concealed weapon back in Detroit or anywhere else less civilized than Edwardian England.

"I am here," she announced, and then paused, as if not sure that she wanted to diminish this assertion by qualifying it, "for my bandora."

"Hello, Mrs. Mayflower," said Jeremiah. "Unfortunately it's not done."

"For two days I have tried to fetch my property: one day you were absent entirely, replaced by that older gentleman, and on the second day the hallway outside your door was consistently occupied by either a brooding young man skulking around in the shadows or a hippie with appalling leg warmers. Now that you are finally where you are supposed to be, when you are supposed to be there, and your hallway is finally free of brooding young men and hippies, you tell me that in two days you have not managed to perform routine maintenance on my bandora? This is unacceptable, young man."

"I apologize, Mrs. Mayflower. If you could come back tomorrow—"

"I need time to practice for the talent show," she said. "As one of the great cellists of a bygone era said: one day without practice, I notice. Two days, the critics notice. Three days, everyone notices. I have now gone three days without practicing. When I rejoin the society of those less fortunate than myself—some who have even made their own money— I intend to come bearing gifts befitting my station, including a performance that will move them. I cannot give them this gift without practicing, and I cannot practice without my bandora. Do you understand?"

Jeremiah could find no flaw in this chain of reasoning, and admitted as much.

"Then I will return tomorrow," said Mrs. Mayflower, "and if my bandora is not ready, I will take the matter up with Mr. Grubel."

With that she left, employing the same dignified counterintelligence measures as she had upon her arrival.

WORLD ENOUGH (AND TIME)

16

The Title of Your Next Autobiography

Still Tuesday (5 days until arrival)

THE next 45 minutes were quiet—restoring some modicum of Jeremiah's faith in the law of averages and the statisticians who had sworn to uphold it—but Jeremiah had no desire to tempt fate by waiting in the office one minute longer than necessary, so on the absolute pin-prick of noon he locked up and left for the cafeteria.

He felt the walls of the ship closing in on him. It now seemed to Jeremiah that the moment Grubel had called him into the financial office, he had fallen through the thin ice of sanity, and the ensuing struggle not to drown hadn't left him the time or mental space to consider just how screwed he really was. Now, with the dubious benefit of such reflection and the portentous return of Mrs. Mayflower, Jeremiah realized exactly how hard it had become even to maintain in good working order the list of insoluble problems that were going to land him on this ship for another 2/20 years, let alone figure out how to resolve them. He tried to take stock of his problems as Ms. Domenico had taught him, but the exercise did not go well.

- Mrs. Abdurov and Mr. Drinkwater, locked in dance of love and hate: (sound of screaming)

- Breaking into Mr. Drinkwater's safe deposit box at Mrs. Abdurov's insistence: (sound of screaming)

161

- Procuring a stage in the next four days: (sound of screaming)

- Mrs. Chapin's revolution: (sound of screaming)

- Canadian stalker: (sound of screaming)

- Jack's quest to get mellow: (sound of screaming)

- Luis's legal worries: (sound of screaming)

- Boyle's maybe murder: (sound of screaming)

- Carolus the Bold still missing: (sound of screaming)

- Marya Jana vanished as well: (sound of screaming)

- Mrs. Mayflower's bandora broken and demanded: (sound of screaming)

- Katherine drinking coffee and eating breakfast with The Specimen rather than Jeremiah: (deep sighs and sound of screaming)

Part of Jeremiah's brain, inspired by the sound of scream-ing, proposed a plan of raw panic—sprinting down the hall-way while screaming the above catalogue of his misfortunes, waving his arms, perhaps bashing his head into things, with-out much focus on the longer or even medium term, which would just have to take care of themselves. And Jeremiah had to admit that this plan had a lot to recommend it—for one thing, at the moment it was about as much as he felt ca-pable of.

But before Jeremiah could quite accede, still another part of his brain weighed in. This part barked like an old veteran, heroic and bandaged, no longer in possession of all his limbs, leaning on crutches and waving off assistance with insane, gleaming eyes.

"Fuck that candyass arm-waving!" it said. "All these things you *can't* do? All these problems you *can't* solve? Find one you can, and solve it! And then another, and solve that! And another! Another! And at the end of the day, Jeremiah, if we go down, we're going to go down swinging so hard, burning in such a blaze of fuck-you glory, that they'll write songs about us for generations—fucking generations, I tell you!"

This part of his brain was clearly mad as a hatter, but Jeremiah found its never-say-die attitude oddly attractive. He'd never imagined himself thinking such thoughts, and he felt both proud and ridiculous, as if he were trying on an outfit in a radical new style, checking himself in the mirror, scared to admit that it just might actually—dare he say it?—flatter him. Was that really all it took to be one of those never-say-die people? Just not to say die? Well then—he'd give it a shot.

"Proud of you, son," said the grizzled old veteran. He shifted his weight onto a single crutch so he could give Jeremiah a gesture of approbation with his remaining thumb. The grizzled old veteran's zeal dimmed just a tad when Jeremiah decided that the first problem he'd take a crack at solving would be lunch.

Jeremiah's excommunication from the Mexican table remained in force, but he found Katherine on the other end of the cafeteria and sat down without asking. She looked up, raised her eyebrows, and returned to her synthed ham and pea soup.

"I feel like I owe you an apology," said Jeremiah.

"I feel the same way," Katherine replied.

"I appreciate that, but you don't have anything to apologize for."

"No, you idiot. I also feel that *you* owe *me* an apology."

"Oh. Then we're in agreement." Jeremiah could have hoped agreement might feel sweeter than this. "So: I'm sorry. Sorry as a Canadian."

"For what, exactly?"

This, Jeremiah recognized, was the million-credit question. He had always thought of apology as a fine art, and of himself as a five-year-old scribbling on a dirty napkin with a dull brown crayon. There seemed to be some agreement in place between the polite men and women of the world, that an apology represented not a chance to actually apologize, but to dance an intricate sarabande around unspoken truths. You did not apologize for not liking your mother in law—you did not even acknowledge that fact, though all parties knew it to be true. Rather you professed with great vehemence the special apartment you kept for the great lady in your heart, all the while regretting the misinterpretation, misspeaking, or miscue that might have led someone to believe that she might ever have found its doors barred to her passage.

Jeremiah had tried this dance many times, and discovered that, when it came to the subtle fox-trot of the apology, he had two left feet. Inevitably such apologies left the apologee piqued and Jeremiah exhausted, and the prospect of playing that scene with Katherine was so unappealing that Jeremiah decided to try something new—something radical—something completely inadvisable: honesty, which many a silver tongue and straight face had, with perfect disingenuousness, recommended as the best policy. If she was going to be angry with him, let her be angry for the things he had said and done, and let him be clear about what those were.

"First of all," Jeremiah said, "I'm sorry for taking it out on you with all that 'snatch and grab' stuff when really I was just upset because I was a little jealous—which I'm allowed to be."

Katherine looked at him suspiciously, like an experienced chess player unsure whether the child across the board from her has just made a move strong beyond his years or simply plunked a random piece on a lucky square.

"Second of all, I'm sorry I took you and your help for granted. I couldn't have done it without you."

Katherine crossed her arms. She looked almost nervous, as if she were watching a gymnast dismount after a solid showing on the pommel horse, and feared he might not stick the landing.

"Finally, I'm *not* sorry that I asked for your help, or that you gave it. We make a good team, and when the shit hit the fan, you were clutch. And *I* for one thought the whole thing was larky."

Katherine raised her eyebrows again, but her expression this time was different.

"All right," she said, "apology accepted. Don't look so pleased with yourself—you're still a jerk." She resumed eating her soup.

"Now that we're square," said Jeremiah, "can I ask you something?"

"As long as it's not about John Battle."

"No, it's about Mrs. Mayflower."

"What about her?"

"Exactly," said Jeremiah. "What about her? My friends at the Mexican table won't even talk to me since I mentioned her name, and when Grubel found out I was fixing her bandora he practically fell all over himself trying to be *nice* to me. Who is she?"

"She's a ghost story," Katherine said. "Supposedly she haunts the halls of the Einstein IV at night. I've heard she was killed during construction of the ship, I've heard lost love drove her to suicide. But as far as a bunch of people on board believe, you're repairing a bandora for a phantom."

"Grubel doesn't seem like the kind to believe in ghost stories."

"No, and despite your many flaws, you don't seem like the type to tell them. Plus there's the bandora itself, which we have pretty solid evidence is—well, solid."

"So then who is she, if she's real?"

"Why don't you ask her?"

"I don't think she's disposed too favorably towards me—and that's just going to get worse when she sees the state of her bandora."

"The repairs aren't going well?" Katherine asked.

"That's putting it mildly," said Jeremiah. "But I'm on this kick where I'm trying to get in touch with my inner grizzled veteran."

"Sorry?"

"You know how you get in touch with your inner child and reawaken your sense of naive wonder?"

"I've heard of that, yes."

"I'm trying to do the same thing with my inner grizzled veteran—trying to never say die, to just pick a problem and solve it. But I think maybe Mrs. Mayflower is the wrong place to start."

"Why don't you tell me all your problems, and I can help you pick the right one?" said Katherine.

"You really want to hear this?"

"If it will help me stop wondering what's in this soup," she said, "I'm all ears."

"I have to hand it to you," Katherine said, pointing her spoon at the empty bowl, "your troubles were so engrossing that I don't even remember eating that. I never realized that iguanas were basically the Houdinis of the animal kingdom."

"Recently I decided I was going to title my autobiography 'A Business of Ferrets.' Now I'm leaning towards 'A Mess of Iguanas.' "

"Like the term of venery?"

Jeremiah nodded, delighted and saddened at the same time. He resisted the urge to point out that the Specimen probably thought a "term of venery" was a name for social diseases that you could use at dinner. More evidence—if any was needed—that he did not deserve someone of Katherine's caliber.

"I like it," said Katherine. "That could be the title of your next autobiography."

"So where do I start? Mr. Drinkwater? Jack? Mrs. Chapin?"

"Boyle," said Katherine.

"Is that really a *problem*, though, as opposed to a *mystery*?"

"It's not a problem *or* a mystery: it's an *opportunity*," said Katherine. "A chance to cut the Gordian knot. Every authority on this ship thinks Boyle was a suicide. But if you prove he was murdered—by finding the murderer—then all of a sudden you're a hero. The waves on Earth all go crazy for the story: 'Disinherited Amateur Sleuth Cracks Case in Deep Space.' Golden Worldlines owes you big time. A broken bandora here, a missing iguana there—they can't ding you for such details at that point. Not without risking a gigantic PR backlash. Prove Boyle was murdered, and solve all your problems in one stroke."

"But what if he wasn't murdered? Then the whole thing would just be a wild goose chase and a colossal waste of time."

"You kiss your inner grizzled veteran with that mouth?" said Katherine.

"I like this girl," said Jeremiah's inner grizzled veteran.

"We struck out on motive," Katherine continued, "which leaves means and opportunity."

"Means turned into a nightmare—anyone could get their hands on some pesticide."

"Then how about opportunity? The murderer had to get into Boyle's room to give him the pesticide."

"The keycards!" said Jeremiah. "Do they keep logs of when and where they're used?"

"I don't know. But I know who will."

"Who?"

Katherine looked at him.

"Oh," he said, catching on. "Of all the people I would never in a million years ask for help, you want me to ask him?"

"I want you to ask *yourself* if you're the type of detective who will do whatever it takes to solve the case."

"What other types are there to choose from?"

"The types who should be getting ready to spend another two years on board the Einstein IV."

"I'm the first type," said Jeremiah. "I guess."

"Hey you," said The Specimen, stepping back and inviting Katherine into the security office. "Ah—I see you brought your roommate."

"I've never properly introduced you two," said Katherine, with a voice that could smooth a tablecloth. "John, this is—"

"We've met," Jeremiah and John Battle said at the same time and in the same tone.

"Jeremiah and I were wondering if you kept logs of room access—what time the doors opened, stuff like that."

"Yes," said John Battle, warily.

"And would you still have the logs from three days ago?" she asked.

"Yes."

"That's great. Would you let us see them?"

"No," said John Battle.

"Because of guest privacy?" asked Katherine.

"Yes."

"About that," Jeremiah said. "What if the guest in question were—how do I put it—no longer with us?"

"You mean Boyle," said John Battle.

"He doesn't exactly need his privacy guarded anymore, does he?" Jeremiah said. "Not in his condition."

"Yeah, Katherine, it's great to see you, but this doesn't seem like something you should be involved in," said John Battle. "And I don't have time. You see what's going on back there?"

He pointed with his thumb over his shoulder to where the second security officer was scowling at a monitor. Jeremiah had never seen this officer before—he supposed that, since this Specimen #2 was merely a recruitment poster come to life rather than the incarnation of a Greek god, Golden Worldlines did their best to keep him tucked away in the back office, safely out of sight.

"We're doing our pre-arrival security audit," John Battle continued. "It's a pain in the ass in the best of circumstances, which these aren't. So if you could stop playing detective or doing whatever it is you're doing, I'd really appreciate it."

"Can I talk to you for a minute?" Katherine said to John Battle.

"You mean for *another* minute?"

"No, I mean in the hall."

Jeremiah did his inconspicuous best to eavesdrop through the door, but Specimen #2 had given up even the pretense of continuing his audit and was giving Jeremiah the hairy eyeball (which, Jeremiah noted, was the only hairy thing on him—he looked as if he performed his morning ablutions with baby oil).

After a couple minutes the door opened again and John Battle came back in. He walked right past without acknowledging Jeremiah, whom Katherine waved out into the hall before the door closed.

"John's going to get the logs," she said. "We'll only have a couple minutes with them, so be ready."

"And he agreed to do this out of the goodness of his heart?" said Jeremiah.

"We just had a little chat."

"Katherine—"

"Jeremiah, don't start," she said, in a tone that would

have gone well with a giant blinking red light and a sign proclaiming "DANGER" in seven or eight languages.

Despite which warning Jeremiah was about to start, had he not been interrupted by The Specimen coming out of the security office again.

"Here," he said, handing a printed sheet of paper to Katherine. "You have five minutes and then you give it back so I can destroy it."

Katherine pulled Jeremiah aside into the stairwell across the hall.

"Take a look," she said, handing him the paper. "This is the log from Boyle's door the day he died. Does anything seem strange?"

"Hold on," Jeremiah said. "At 6:02 that morning the door opens from the inside—that has to be him opening up for his standing order from the kitchen. 9:17 a.m., again from the inside—he's leaving to start his day. 1:00 p.m., door is opened from the outside, 1:08 p.m., opened from the inside, 1:23 p.m. the door is opened from the outside again. Wait a minute."

"What?"

"At 1:00 p.m. he was in the office asking me to encode him a new keycard because his didn't work."

"You're sure about the time?"

"100 percent sure—he was waiting for me when I got back from lunch. Wait, look at this, too: 10:13 p.m., door opens from the outside. He's in for the night. Then 45 minutes later, door opens from the outside *again*."

"Hard to see how he returned to his room without having left it in the first place," said Katherine.

"Very hard."

"So the second one—at 10:58—was the murderer arriving to kill him," she said.

"Or the first one, if he was lying in wait."

"So we have proof it wasn't suicide," said Katherine. "Do we wait until we have a suspect or do we take it to Grubel right now?"

"It's not proof—not yet. Who's to say he didn't open the door to kill himself at 10:13, think better of it, turn around without entering, and then come back a little before 11 when he was finally ready to do the deed? But maybe we've narrowed our suspects down to people who had access to a key-card encoder. Who would that be?"

"Alfred," said Katherine. "John. You."

"That's a pretty narrow field."

"Or anyone who could have stolen an encoder—you keep it unlocked in the desk drawer, right?"

"How did you know that?"

"I grew up with Alfred Reynolds, Jeremiah."

"So much for narrowing the field, then," Jeremiah said. "But at least we know this isn't a wild goose chase."

"I'd better get moving," said Katherine. "I need to change for dinner prep, and if I don't get this log back to John in the next two minutes and 23 seconds, he's going to have an aneurysm."

"A damn shame that would be."

"Be nice. He blew this case wide open."

"No," said Jeremiah, "*you* blew this case wide open. Thank you."

And then, before she could leave or try to stop him, Jeremiah took her left hand in his, bent her knuckles, and raised them to his lips.

"I have to go," she said, but there was a flush of red along the tops of her ears, and two glowing spots on her cheeks.

17

A Lot of Credit in Money

Still Tuesday (5 days until arrival)

BACK in the Guest Services office Jeremiah was still thinking about that flush of red, ranking it favorably against autumn skylines and ocean sunsets and other welcome sights when another sight arrived, considerably less welcome, complete with silver-orange beard and turquoise leg warmers.

"Hello, Jack," Jeremiah said. "How can I help you?"

Jack did not answer right away, being occupied in sweeping a small metallic box and its attached antennae through the room, paying special attention to the area of the desk. Once he was convinced that reasonable standards of operational security were being observed, Jack put the device away and sat down.

"I understand the position you're in, Jeremiah," he said. "Have I ever told you that I was once part of the System? My title was 'diplomat,' but I was just an apparatchik, a cog. For years I went through life asleep. But then one day, on a diplomatic visit to rural China, I was served a dish consisting primarily of fermented pig intestine. It was repulsive, but I had no idea how fermented pig intestine was supposed to taste, and so—not wanting to insult my hosts, who were family of a high-ranking official—I ate the whole thing, not realizing it had turned. For six days and nights, unable to rise from the bed of rough straw where they put me, I purged the poison of that spoiled pig intestine—and with it, the accumulated poison of a life lived in service of the System. Then, on the seventh day, I had a vision."

Jack's eyes grew wide, and he gazed somewhere up above Jeremiah's head.

"I saw a huge robotic face—mechanical, expressionless, uncaring—a machine with massive, steel teeth. It was shoving handfuls of people into its mouth, one after the other, always at the same, unhurried pace. They screamed as it chewed and swallowed them with perfect regularity, and their screams echoed as they progressed down its digestive tract, which twisted and forked like a gigantic maze. Finally, when the machine had sorted and separated them, their soulless bodies were excreted into the void, where they floated away like so much chaff from wheat."

Jack shivered and closed his eyes against the image, but it must have burned brighter still behind his eyelids, and he opened them again.

"I can't say how long I observed this horror, until I finally noticed something: the mouth of the System was missing a tooth. And in a flash I realized that *I* had been that tooth—that my whole life I had been nothing more than a molar of the System, and that only the mystical experience of this vision had finally pulled me out.

"The next morning I woke up healthier than I had ever been in my life. I couldn't forget what I had seen, though. I vowed never to become a tooth of the System again, and I began to search for something else that could give me the experience of that fermented pig intestine—preferably without the taste, or six days and nights of vomiting. Do you know what I found, Jeremiah?"

"Drugs?"

"I gave up pork, and I started taking all the drugs I could find. The System hates drugs. It fears them. Politicians pass laws against them, celebrities exhort the youth to refuse them—fascists like our security officer confiscate and destroy them. Do you know why? Because they are the only thing that can lift our consciousness high enough to see the System as it is. Except fermented pig intestine gone bad, which I don't recommend."

Jack's face twisted slightly at the memory of the fateful dish, but then he folded his hands on his cardiganed stomach, all business.

"Which is all to say, Jeremiah, I've been following you, and I heard you talking with Mrs. Abdurov. I know you're finding drugs for her, too."

"We've been over this: I'm not finding drugs for anyone."

"My Russian's not great, but I know that *Marya Jana* is the Russian version of 'Mary Jane.' "

Jeremiah sighed.

"She's an *iguana*," he said.

"Mrs. Abdurov is an iguana?" said Jack. He did not seem to be dismissing the possibility out of hand, but he did seem to be considering how many brownies Jeremiah might have ingested before reaching this conclusion.

"No, *Marya Jana* is an iguana. Mrs. Abdurov's iguana, whom she lost and demanded that I find. And that 'green item' Mr. Wendstrom was asking me about? That was *his* iguana, who has also gone AWOL."

"Listen to yourself, Jeremiah," said Jack. "Just listen to the insane things the System is making you say. No—no more. If you try to give me any more of those laughable stories and denials, I'm going to put my fingers in my ears and sing la la la. I didn't come here to hear lies—I came to give you this. You're part of the System now, so I'll speak to you in the only language the System understands. Here."

Jack pulled a brick of something from his pocket and put it on the desk.

"This is money," said Jeremiah.

"Yes."

"I mean, not credit—actual old money. Like, antique money."

"I always buy drugs with antique money—it's harder for the System to track you that way. And there's a lot of credit in money. Anyway, I know you'll do the right thing now. I believe in you."

"Jack," said Jeremiah, "I don't want your money, or your credit, and I can't get you drugs. Listen to me, Jack—it's all a misunderstanding. They're iguanas! I can explain everything if you'll just listen!"

But as Jeremiah made his plea, Jack—true to his word—had put his fingers in his ears and was already leaving the office, singing "la la la I can't hear you" the whole way, very roughly to the tune of "Twinkle Twinkle, Little Star."

"The whole way?" said Katherine. She was still in her serving clothes and tired from her dinner shift, but (to Jeremiah's
great delight) upon arriving at the suite she had not gone into
her room but simply sat down on the sofa next to him and
asked him how the rest of the day had gone.

"Out of the office and all the way down the hall," said
Jeremiah. "He might still be singing it for all I know. But
how was the rest of your day? Good dinner shift?"

"The usual," she said. "But what I meant about the rest
of the day was, did you find out anything new about Boyle?
Any ideas about where to take the investigation next?"

"Ah," said Jeremiah.

"What is it with you and 'ah'? What does 'ah' mean this
time?"

"Just that I thought when you asked about the rest of *the*
day you were interested in the rest of *my* day."

"Don't be so sensitive," said Katherine. "Any luck on the
case?"

"I'm still stuck. Anything occur to you?"

Katherine shook her head.

"Then I guess I had better prepare myself for
Mrs. Mayflower's visit."

Jeremiah stood and brought the bandora, which was still
clamped, back to the sofa.

"She's picking it up tomorrow?" Katherine asked.

"So she threatened when she came by today. Here goes
nothing."

Gingerly Jeremiah loosened the clamp, first on one side
and then the other, until the bandora slid out into his lap.

"That doesn't look too bad," said Katherine.

"No, it doesn't. I mean, eventually she's going to see the
seam in the wood and blow a gasket. But until she does it will
look much better than expected. And it will sound—"

Jeremiah gave the strings a gentle strum.

"Damn," Katherine said.

For no sooner had his fingers brushed the strings than the
bandora—like a puppy in Jeremiah's lap relaxing completely
at his touch—had simply come apart.

"So much for Barnaby's wood glue," said Jeremiah. "Was
that the one with the guarantee?"

"I think it was the glue for wood that came with the guarantee."

"Then let's try that one."

Jeremiah fetched the file and the glue for wood from where he had stowed them under the sofa. Squinting, he began to clean the dry wood glue from the bandora's body and neck, rasping away the hardest beads and digging deposits out of recesses with the file's sharp end.

"Can I ask you a question while you work?" said Katherine.

"I don't know," said Jeremiah as he slathered the glue for wood on the neck of the bandora, "what have you done for *me* lately?"

"I mean, am I going to distract you?"

"Always."

"Come on, Jeremiah, I'm serious."

"Right, serious: yes, you can ask me a question while I work."

"I know so little about life on Earth now," she said. "I mean, I've read the history books, and I know the basics—the Drought Wars, the Canadian Mistake. But I don't know things like—can you still have a quiet life on Earth? Is that something that's still even possible?"

"My experience is about 20 years out of date, but what do you mean by a quiet life?"

"You know," she said, "a small house in a small town, maybe on a lake somewhere."

"How many people are living in this lake house? One? Two?"

"Jeremiah, remember how I keep saying that certain business is none of yours?"

"You're asking about lake real estate—which is hard to find and very expensive—so I'm just trying to figure out how much house you'll need."

"Fine," said Katherine. "Maybe two people, eventually."

"Is one of these people John Battle? Don't scowl, it makes a difference for the height of the ceilings. I want to make sure he's comfortable."

"I shouldn't have asked you. I'm going to bed," said Katherine.

"I'm sorry," Jeremiah said, "I just don't understand why

175

we have to pretend we're not talking about The Specimen if we really are."

"Fine. I don't want you to have to pretend anything."

She stood up and went to her room. Almost immediately Jeremiah heard muffled music through the door.

As he sat there trying to occupy his hands and mind with the bandora, Jeremiah could not help but mentally replay this latest encounter with Katherine, until he reached the conclusion that he'd been something of a jerk. More mystifying was *why* he had acted so boorishly. She had only asked him a question, after all—and one that he could have answered to her benefit if not her pleasure (yes, there still was such a thing as a quiet life on Earth, and no, unless the situation on Earth had changed drastically in the last 20 years, Katherine would never be able to afford to live one, especially anywhere near a lake or other body of water, with or without The Specimen's income thrown into the mix). So why had Jeremiah needled her instead?

Of course Jeremiah was half in love with Katherine—he had fallen half in love with her the first night he sat at her table, despite the one piece of good advice his Uncle Leo had given him, which was never to fall in love with anyone who worked for tips. But that in and of itself was not sufficient to explain his recent bad behavior. Back on Earth Jeremiah had half, quarter, or eighth fallen in love with a handful of women on a daily basis, for an average of roughly 7.6 fancies taken per week, and markedly more in springtime. Many of these women had been waitresses, cashiers, or recruiters to political causes he met on the streets of Detroit, but some had been friends or acquaintances. In other words, Jeremiah was flush with practice at dealing normally and civilly with women he was infatuated with.

Neither could the fact that Katherine did not seem to share Jeremiah's feelings fully explain the meanness of his mood. With rare exceptions, all the aforementioned fractional loves were completely unrequited, or at best exhibited an affection deficit that was not in Jeremiah's favor. Even at the height of his relationship with Lana Peterson, when he had been a full 34/35ths in love with her, he estimated that her feelings for him had never exceeded the 7/8ths mark, and peaked *that* high only on birthdays and the odd Thanksgiving. He had managed reasonably well for years with that imbalance, thank you very much. So why the anger and sarcasm now?

Jeremiah could no longer pretend occupation with the bandora—he absolutely *had* to speak to Katherine immediately, though he was not quite sure what he was going to say. He put the bandora aside, walked up to her bedroom door, and knocked loudly.

"What," said Katherine through the door. She did not phrase it as a question.

"Can you open up?"

"Why."

"Because I need to talk to you," Jeremiah said.

"You can talk through the door."

"I want to apologize."

"You can apologize through the door."

"Please," said Jeremiah, "would you just open the door for a minute?"

For about 30 seconds he wasn't sure whether she was silently considering or had already silently refused, but then the door opened outwards a crack, from which Katherine's left eye peered angrily.

"I'm sorry," Jeremiah said. He leaned against the doorjamb in what he hoped was a casual and forthright manner.

"You already alluded to that," said Katherine. "Anything else?"

"Would you just come out and talk to me for a minute?"

Now Jeremiah had the opportunity to witness, at least in part, the same kind of silent deliberation that he had been blind to a moment ago. He hung on each slight widening of Katherine's one visible eye, and despaired at each narrowing, until finally her eye found its natural size again and she sighed.

"I'm in the middle of something. I'll come out when I'm done."

So saying, Katherine slammed the door shut—or at least she tried to, giving Jeremiah both cause and opportunity to wonder whether his casual lean hadn't been undertaken a bit too casually, in that his fingers were still on the doorjamb, very much in the spot that the slammed door was accustomed to occupying when it closed.

"What is wrong with you?" shouted Katherine over Jeremiah's yelps and swearing. "Why can't you just stay out of the way of my door? Are you all right? Let me see."

"I'm fine," Jeremiah said when he was able. "It's nothing."

"Don't be an idiot, give me your hand."

As Katherine took Jeremiah's hand in his to examine it, he found himself examining the scene behind her. Upon meeting his fingers so unexpectedly, the door had bounced wide open, and for the first time Jeremiah could see into the room where Katherine slept.

The space was not much larger than Jeremiah's living room turned hostel, but Katherine had put every inch to use. The walls were filled with more antique wave posters. Though Jeremiah recognized a few classics—*Casablanca* and *Pulp Fiction*—most of them were new to him.

Beneath the wave posters stood shelves of antique books—no doubt children's titles that the eight-year-old Katherine had brought aboard. One book was lying on the single bed, its yellow pages held open by a skein of turquoise wool. One strand of the wool wove its way off the book and along the faded red blanket until it ended, like a river running into a lake, at what appeared to be a half-finished shawl impaled by two knitting needles. Piled in the corner at the back of the room were more skeins of turquoise wool, still snug in their shrinkwrap packages.

"Nothing looks broken," Katherine was saying, "which is better than you deserve. But you should still get it checked out at the—"

She looked up from Jeremiah's hand and followed the direction of his gaze to the evidence of her cottage textile industry.

"Oh. It's a shawl," said Katherine. "For Mrs. Chapin."

She looked back to Jeremiah and saw in his eyes that he was already familiar with her work.

"Don't tell anyone," she said. "I found all this yarn unused in the storeroom, and with the climate on the fritz so many people were cold. But I don't want word to get around too much—I hate knitting."

She seemed to be waiting for some response from Jeremiah, but he was not up to the challenge of coherent speech. He was in the grips of something suspiciously like an epiphany, and at the moment he was fully consumed with trying to understand how it was that all this time he had never fully seen in Katherine what was now so impossible to miss.

Jeremiah had met people who were naturally kind, and they were wonderful people—probably kinder than Katherine, if there were a blood test to measure kindness per ml or some such. But they came by their kindness as tall people came by their height or brilliant people their smarts—as an accident of birth. In fact, kindness came so easily to these folks that *not* being kind was hard work for them. Katherine, on the other hand, did not come by her kindness naturally at all. Exhibit A: the two days of silent treatment she'd given Jeremiah when he moved into her room. None of the congenitally kind people Jeremiah had ever known could have kept that up. An hour or two in, they'd have been sweating and shivering at the effort it was costing them not to sleep on the sofa themselves so Jeremiah could take the comfy bed.

Whereas for Katherine kindness took thought and work, and maybe something even harder. Just like Jeremiah, she had seen the absurdity at the beating heart of the world—had looked deep into it and held her gaze there for a long time. He could see that now, and could not imagine how he ever could have missed it. But Katherine had not reacted to the sight— as Boyle had—with bitterness and suspicion and fear. She had not even reacted like Jeremiah, with friendly but disengaged irony and ennui. She had looked upon the hollow universe and resolved to fill it with compassion—not as a frightened reflex or a natural inclination, but as a deliberate act of courage, and of will.

He was not half in love with Katherine, Jeremiah realized, or 7/8ths in love, or even 34/35ths.

"Katherine," he said. His voice did not feel under his control—there was something that must be said, and said now—something that only he could say.

"Yes," said Katherine, her tone perfectly balanced between a question and an answer.

"That's the doorbell," said Jeremiah.

These were not the three words that had been struggling to escape his soul. Yes, they had other virtues—for example, if Jeremiah had uttered them competitively in the Olympics of declarative statements, even the French judge would have had to award him all available points for accuracy—for Jeremiah's words rang as true as the bell they described. The same judge would have been justified, however, in recording a goose egg for the romance category, as Jeremiah's last remark had caused a significant change in the atmosphere of the room, similar to the change in a balloon's atmosphere caused by a pin.

"Are you expecting anyone?" Katherine asked.

"At this hour? Are you?" said Jeremiah.

Katherine shook her head.

The doorbell rang again, and gave the unmistakable impression that it would keep ringing until someone answered.

"I guess I should get it," Jeremiah said. There was, after all, no real use hiding from either Grubel or Mrs. Mayflower, and Jeremiah could not imagine who else would bother tracking him down this far outside office hours.

As he answered the door, however, Jeremiah realized that his imagination had failed him in spectacular fashion. For the figure standing outside did not belong to Mr. Grubel or to Mrs. Mayflower, but to Jeremiah's Canadian doctor stalker, and the intensity of his current brooding was palpable.

"You don't deserve her," said the stalker. Which struck Jeremiah as an odd thing to say on several counts.

His disagreement with the fundamental premise of the statement was *not* one of those counts—despite the nature of the scene that the Canadian doctor stalker had just interrupted, Jeremiah knew that wooing Katherine meant punching far above his weight. But why was this young man coming to knock on his door so late just to remind Jeremiah of this disparity? Jeremiah's imagination, eager to redeem itself after its recent disgrace, offered up a possibility.

The young man, Jeremiah imagined, was a yet unannounced gladiator in the battle for Katherine's heart. This theory fit all available facts: the physical abuse in the cafeteria, the surveillance, the brooding intensity that had built to this late-night confrontation. At this thought, Jeremiah lost all fear. Indeed, he almost felt sorry for the young man who—unlike John Battle—did not represent a serious rival. For starters, there was the brooding intensity, which did not promise a life of romantic bliss. Then there was the small fact of his being Canadian. But Jeremiah also sensed opportunity in the chaos occasioned by the stalker's late entrance in the sweepstakes for Katherine's attention—a chance to highlight by comparison Jeremiah's own adult, respectful behavior for Katherine, who was still standing behind him, watching this drama unfold.

"Well," Jeremiah said, "she's an adult woman who can make her own choices, isn't she?"

"An adult woman whose boots you aren't worthy to lick," said the stalker. As he grew more excitable, his slight French-Canadian accent elbowed its way further into the foreground, so that for a split second Jeremiah was not clear on why he should be licking anyone's buttes.

"But she can choose her own boots."

"But you can't lick them," said the medical stalker.

"I can if she lets me," Jeremiah said. "I might not be *worthy*, but I'm *capable*."

"Excuse me," Katherine said, "but could you guys finish the boot licking conversation somewhere else? Some of us have to be up early tomorrow."

At the sound of Katherine's voice the stalker shoved Jeremiah roughly aside and stepped inside the room.

"Who is *that*?" he said, pointing wildly at Katherine. "Who the hell is *that*?"

"That's Katherine, of course," said Jeremiah.

"What is she doing in your room?" the medical stalker demanded.

"Actually—" Jeremiah began.

"It's my room," said Katherine, "and I'd like you to leave it."

Something in the medical stalker snapped, and his long-simmering intensity boiled over into rage.

"You two-timing bastard," he shouted at Jeremiah. "Being engaged to the most wonderful woman in the world isn't enough for you? You have to have some of *this* on the side?"

"Engaged?" said Jeremiah.

"And if you think I'm not going to tell Kimberly about this because of some manly code between men," the medical stalker said, "you're sorely mistaken."

"Kimberly?" said Jeremiah.

"Don't you *dare* say her name!" roared the medical stalker.

Jeremiah took a discreet step backwards. Though the stalker, as previously noted, was nowhere near as physically imposing as John Battle, there was now a distinct air of desperation and uncontrolled fury about him, which was enough to make any man dangerous. Jeremiah could imagine a not-too-distant future where the young man swung as hard as he could at Jeremiah's face and ended up hitting him quite painfully in the stomach.

"There's been some kind of misunderstanding," Jeremiah said. "I'm sure we can clear it up."

"Maybe I should wait in my room," Katherine said, "while you two work this out in the hall."

"You're not going anywhere," said the medical stalker. "I want you to hear exactly what kind of man you've been spending time with. A man who's already engaged to someone else!"

"Here's the thing," Jeremiah said, "I'm not engaged to anyone. And I don't even know anyone named—"

Jeremiah saw the medical stalker's fury welling at the impending use of Kimberly's name.

"—that woman's name you said starting with K that wasn't Katherine," he finished, which he hoped was specific enough given the circumstances.

"I don't believe you," the stalker said. But he said it as if he *wished* to believe, and Jeremiah wished to encourage that wish.

"This is my roommate, Katherine. She would know if I'm engaged. Katherine, am I engaged?"

"Not to my knowledge. But why would I know or care?"

Jeremiah could have done without the second part, for several reasons, but on the other hand the stalker's face was now a blend of doubt and hope.

"Then why did Kimberly say you were?" he asked. "Wait, are you calling her a *liar*?"

At the mere suggestion of this slight, his fury welled up again.

"No, no, never in a million years," said Jeremiah. "I'm just saying there's been a misunderstanding."

"So you're saying Kimberly's *not* engaged?"

"Well," Jeremiah said, feeling the waters grow a bit choppier again after a rather promising stretch, "unfortunately I can't speak to that. I just know she isn't engaged to *me*. Ask her yourself—just confirm that she's not engaged to Jeremiah Brown. You'll see."

"All right," the stalker said, "But if it turns out you are engaged to her—"

"I'm not," said Jeremiah.

"But if you are, then I'll be back."

The stalker backed through the door and into the hall, scowling the entire way.

The instant the door hissed closed behind him, Jeremiah turned to Katherine, who was already on her way into her bedroom.

"Just so you know," he said, "I'm not engaged."

"Then I won't say congratulations. Just good night."

"Wait—Katherine—"

But she had already closed the door behind her, and this time no amount of knocking and pleading seemed likely to draw her out.

WORLD ENOUGH (AND TIME)

18

So Very Unlikely

Wednesday (4 days until arrival)

THE next morning, while Katherine was in the shower, Jeremiah passed the time cursing Bradley, himself, and especially the doorbell, an infernal invention that it seemed to him mankind could have done very well without. As if it could feel its ears burning, the doorbell rang again.

His imaginative boundaries about who might be ringing having been recently expanded, Jeremiah considered waiting for Katherine to emerge from the bathroom—so that if it was the medical stalker returning to assault and batter him, at least there would be a witness—but at this cowardly thought Jeremiah's inner grizzled veteran put together a string of epithets that could have stripped paint from plaster, and sighing in agreement, Jeremiah answered the door.

At first glance no one was there, and at second glance as well, but then a peculiar scent found its way into Jeremiah's nostrils. If he were forced to put a name to the scent—say for a new brand of aromatherapy candle—he might have suggested "strawberry lily coconut vanilla chloroform"—or, perhaps, if something punchier were called for, "tropical spring surgeon". Looking down, he located the source of the scent: a small pink envelope which someone had left on the ground of the hallway. Jeremiah picked it up and returned to the room.

He examined the envelope, careful not to hold it too close to his face for fear of passing out and waking up in a bathtub of potpourri, missing one of his kidneys. The envelope was addressed in red ink and a feminine hand to "Jeremiah", but the i of "Jeremiah" sported a heart in place of the pedestrian dot. Once upon a time, seeing his name written by a member of the fairer sex, and with this cardiac flourish, would have made Jeremiah's own adolescent heart beat faster. But now this envelope and its hearted i gave him an ominous, queasy sensation, concentrated in the general vicinity of his entire body. He took a deep breath, held it, and opened the envelope.

Jeremiah, the letter began—complete with another heart—*I don't even know why I'm bothering* (another heart) *to tell you this* (heart) *because it's so highly unlikely,* (heart, heart, heart) *but just in case a guy named Bradley says something to you about our being engaged, would you be the total sweetie* (this was the only i in the entire letter, Jeremiah noted, dotted with a mere dot) *that I know you are and just play along? Thanks I appreciate it sooooo much. xoxoxo Kimberly*

For such a brief text, this note contained an impressive number of mysteries to be plumbed. For example, why would Kimberly lie about being engaged to Jeremiah? This was not something other people usually did. Furthermore, what cause did she have to know that Jeremiah was a sweetie, with or without a heart-dotted i? For that matter, what possible purpose could anyone old enough to be on E4 have to dot *any* i with a heart? Oh, and incidentally: who in all of the infernal blazes was Kimberly?

Jeremiah had been considering these conundrums over 30 seconds before the doorbell rang again. This time he did not hesitate to answer it.

"Dr. Merrifield?" he said. For it was she, the same young Canadian doctor who over a year ago had treated the twisted ankle that Jeremiah had naturally confused with imminent death, and whom he had recently noticed again in the employee cafeteria.

"I wanted to make sure you got my note," said Dr. Merrifield.

Dr. *Kimberly* Merrifield, Jeremiah presumed.

In a pre-Katherine universe, Jeremiah might have felt differently upon learning the identity of his secret fiancée. Despite her being Canadian, and despite the fact her thorough and vigorous style of medical examination had caused him significant pain in his ankle, the fifteen minutes Jeremiah had spent under Dr. Merrifield's medical attention remained a fond memory from his time as a passenger. During the visit he had abandoned his attempts to flirt with her only after multiple such attempts had fallen flat (for example, when she diagnosed him with hypochondria and he had replied that he was always worried he'd had that and she had stared at him without blinking for a full ten seconds and then said "No"). But they were not in a pre-Katherine universe, and Jeremiah had no wish to return to one.

"Yes, I just finished reading it," said Jeremiah.

"It's so highly unlikely that Bradley would actually bother to find you, but—"

"Actually, he was here last night."

"Bradley?" Kimberly said, aghast.

"Yes," said Jeremiah.

"Was here?"

"Yes," Jeremiah said again.

"Last night?"

"Yes," said Jeremiah, for the hat trick.

"It was so highly unlikely he would do that," said Kimberly. "You should play the lottery."

"His visit didn't feel like winning the lottery. He did not seem happy about our 'engagement'."

"Did he harass you?" asked Kimberly.

"Oh yes," said Jeremiah. "Most definitely."

"Did he threaten you?" she gasped.

"More or less."

"And did he *harm* you?" Kimberly asked with what sounded like her final breath.

"Well, at one point he sort of shoved me aside."

Kimberly began to cry.

"Don't cry," said Jeremiah. "I can handle a shove or two from a guy like that, let alone a bit of verbal harassment."

"It's not that," said Kimberly through the tears. "When I told him we were engaged, I said that if he really loved me, he would want me to be happy, which meant that he wouldn't harass, threaten, harm, or even attempt to contact you. It was an experiment—a test of his love."

"Oh," said Jeremiah. Despite Kimberly's unsavory heritage and the inconvenience her insane plan had caused him, it was impossible to see the sobs wracking her body and, as the saying went, wish such suffering even on a Canadian. A heart tender enough to dot every i with its own likeness must suffer this sort of wound deeply. "Look, you shouldn't jump to conclusions just because he—"

"And he *passed*," said Kimberly. She sighed romantically between sobs, which were growing gentler now, like the tail end of a summer thunderstorm. "Bradley—oh, Bradley. Never mind, Jeremiah. There's no need to pretend we're engaged anymore—I'll tell Bradley the truth as soon as I see him."

"I don't understand," Jeremiah said.

"In the face of such incontrovertible evidence of love, I am forced to overthrow the Categorical Imperative, yield to his passion, and become Mrs. Bradley Bonaventure. What else is there to understand?"

"But you told him that if he really loved you, he *wouldn't* harass, threaten, or harm me."

"Yes," said Kimberly.

"And he *did* harass, threaten, and harm me."

"He loved me too much not to. Goodbye, Jeremiah, and thank you."

She turned to leave.

"It's just that—how could he have possibly failed the test?" said Jeremiah.

Kimberly turned back around.

"What do you mean?"

"I mean, if he *hadn't* harassed, threatened, or harmed me, he would have been following the instructions you gave him to demonstrate that he loved you. But now you're saying that since he *did* harass, threaten, and harm me, that was *also* proof he loved you. How could he have failed?"

Kimberly actually staggered backwards a few steps.

"You're right," she said. "I let emotion cloud my rational faculties. My experiment was flawed—my hypothesis was not falsifiable! Jeremiah, I had no idea you were gifted with a scientific mind."

"Oh," said Jeremiah, "I wouldn't say all that. I read the odd pamphlet here and there."

"No, you're absolutely right. I need to replicate the findings. You and I have to stay engaged!"

"You know," Jeremiah said, "with the benefit of hindsight, your experiment wasn't all that bad—"

"No, it was flawed—deeply, deeply flawed."

"It's just so *clear* that he loves you. His behavior when he came here, the harassment and threats and—"

"That's not enough," said Kimberly. "I don't want to admit that the results of my experiment are worthless, but I *should*, so I *will*. The Categorical Imperative demands it, and I am a creature of reason. But I want to give myself over to love, Jeremiah. Believe me, I do."

"I believe you," said Jeremiah. "So why don't you?"

"Because of the Categorical Imperative, of course," Kimberly said, like a kindergarten teacher explaining why a kindergartner must eat his vegetables. "The same reason that I refuse to end every conversation with an apology for my ancestors' mistakes. If I'm going to break the most important moral code in the universe—oh, am I really proposing to do this?—then at the very least I need to be sure Bradley's love is true." That was all she seemed inclined to say about the matter, until Jeremiah admitted he had no idea what she was talking about.

"Don't be silly, Jeremiah," said Kimberly. "Everyone knows Kant's Categorical Imperative—or at least, everyone *should*. *Act only according to that maxim whereby you can, at the same time, will that it should become a universal law.*"

"Right," said Jeremiah. "And in this case, that means?"

"I've already signed a contract to come on the E4 for another cruise," Kimberly said. "Bradley has decided to go back and practice medicine in Canada, to help those still affected by the Mistake—he has a deeply charitable soul. He wants me to break my contract and go with him, because—he says—he loves me. But what if everyone behaved like that? What would happen?"

"Canada would be flush with happy couples administering medical care to underserved populations, while the E4 would have no Canadian doctors?" guessed Jeremiah.

"I mean if no one honored their contracts and commitments. If that were the universal law, no one could trust anyone else. Nothing could get done. The world would descend into chaos. So if I cannot will the breaking of contracts to become universal law, how can I break one myself?"

"According to the Categorical Imperative, I guess you can't."

Kimberly smiled to see Jeremiah's rapid advancement in moral philosophy, but when she remembered the consequences it held for her own love life, the smile faded.

"For Bradley," she said, "I would thumb my nose at universal morality and risk this apocalyptic, lawless future—but only if I can be sure he really loves me back. You will help me, won't you?"

"Well," said Jeremiah.

"Just play along and say we're engaged if Bradley asks you, which I think is so highly unlikely."

"I'm afraid I already told him we weren't engaged."

"Just say you were afraid to tell him the truth," said Kimberly.

"Is it kind—or *safe*, for that matter—to lie to Bradley like that? He was pretty worked up when he came by last night. I'm afraid he might even get confrontational—physically, I mean."

"Oh," Kimberly said, "I think that's—"

"So highly unlikely?"

"Yes," she chirped, and blushed as if Jeremiah had just complimented her shoes or lab coat. "Exactly. He has a very bad back, so he has to avoid exertions like that. You will help me, won't you?"

"I would like to, but—"

"I'll stand here and I won't leave until you agree to help me."

"It's just that—"

Jeremiah heard the shower shut off in the bathroom— Katherine would be out any minute.

"I'll stand right here until you agree that we're engaged," said Kimberly. "Really I will, right in this spot."

"All right," Jeremiah said, "if you'll go right now, I'll help you. If Bradley asks, I'll tell him we're engaged. But just for a day or two, you understand?"

"Oh, thank you Jeremiah!" said Kimberly. "You *are* a sweetie!"

As if to dot the i with a heart, she leaned in and kissed him on the cheek.

Katherine came out of the bathroom a few minutes later and sniffed the air, upon which a whiff of "Tropical Surgeon" still wafted.

"Was someone here?" she said. "I thought I heard a woman's voice."

"Not that I remember," said Jeremiah.

Katherine looked at him strangely.

"Katherine," he said, "about last night—"

"Anyway, shower's all yours."

Jeremiah spent the morning facing the door of the office, his hands folded on the desk, awaiting with as much philosophy as he could muster the inevitable moment when Mrs. Mayflower would arrive to demand her bandora—which at that moment was clamped and drying back in Katherine's suite in the desperate hope that Barnaby's glue for wood would prove better than its cousin product and as good as its guarantee.

But as nine o'clock became ten, and ten bled into eleven, and eleven inched closer to twelve, no one came through the doors of the office—Mrs. Mayflower very much included. Finally Jeremiah grew tired of sitting with folded hands and philosophic spirit. He spent the last half hour before lunch flipping through the playbook, continuing his vain search for the proper procedure to procure some kind of stage for the talent show, now only three days away. At the exact toll of noon he locked the office door and fled as fast as dignity would allow him, heading for the cafeteria.

"Jeremiah!" Luis called, as Jeremiah looked for a place to eat his quiche Lorraine. To Jeremiah's pleasant surprise Luis waved him over, and the table smiled and played musical chairs to open up a space—it appeared that his mysterious transgression had been just as mysteriously forgiven.

"We want to ask you something. That woman you see— that 'Mrs. Mayflower'—what she look like?"

Jesús crossed himself and muttered at her name, but more out of duty this time, it seemed, than terror.

"She's old," said Jeremiah, "short, kind of stout."

"What is 'kind of stout'?"

"Well, a bit thick in the body."

"You mean *gordita*? Fat?"

"I don't know if I'd say 'fat'. Perhaps a little wide for her height?"

"Fat," Luis said with great sureness. "*Gorda*," he translated for the rest of the table, who nodded. "She looks like this?"

Holding his palm downward and his hand towards Heriberto, Luis made a brushing motion with his four fingers, and Heriberto handed him a PED. It was an old model—it would have been well out of date before the Einstein IV even departed—and the case and screen were badly scratched. Luis mashed a button on the screen repeatedly until a wave flickered to life.

The camera added a good ten pounds to her stoutness, and it was not always easy to catch her face as she glanced up and down the stretch of hallway she occupied, but the woman in the wave was unquestionably Mrs. Mayflower. She was wearing a smart cream vest and an olive blouse with tapered sleeves. About fifteen seconds into the action, presumably having convinced herself that she was alone in her stretch of hallway, she performed some quick tracing motions against a panel of the wall, waited while it slid open, and vanished into a secret passage just before the panel slid closed behind her.

"That's Mrs. Mayflower," said Jeremiah.

The table exploded in laughter. Even Jesús laughed as he crossed himself.

"Why is that funny?" Jeremiah asked Luis.

"That's not Mrs. Mayflower. Mrs. Mayflower is ghost. A *fantasma*. Or maybe a devil," Luis added thoughtfully. "But the real Mrs. Mayflower don't need no secret doors to pass through walls. This just some woman *pretexting* to be Mrs. Mayflower."

At so many mentions of her name, Jesús' crossing went into a gear Jeremiah had not seen before, though he remained good-natured about it.

"*Como un episódio de Scooby Doo*," said Heriberto, and the table nodded in solemn agreement.

"Anyway," Luis said, "we want you know that we're not molested with you. We thought you were trying to scare *us*, but really someone is trying to scare *you*."

"They're doing a good job of it, too," said Jeremiah.

The table stood up and began to say their goodbyes.

"Wait, Luis," said Jeremiah, "could you stay behind for a second? Do you have any experience with revolutions?"

"What you mean?" said Luis suspiciously.

"Here," Jeremiah said, handing him Mrs. Chapin's necklace, which, despite its weight, he had been carrying in his pocket, unable to find a safer place for it. "If I gave you this, would you be able to start a revolution with it? Preferably something bloodless?"

Luis ran his finger along the scar that crossed his cheek, as if reminding himself of lessons learned the hard way.

"Jeremiah, I don't know nothing about no revolutions, except that I don't want to know nothing."

"How about organizing a strike? I didn't have much luck talking her down to that before, but maybe if I had something more concrete to show for it—"

"I don't want no trouble," said Luis, "and I don't want no necklace. I have work to do." He tried to hand the jewelry back to Jeremiah.

"Why don't you just keep it? You'd be doing me a big favor."

Luis stiffened, his chest puffing out.

"I don't need no *caridad*," he said. "I work for my credit."

"Yes," said Jeremiah, brightening with inspiration, "and you're a carpenter, right?"

"Yes," Luis said, cautiously.

"Could you build a stage for the talent show?"

"Of course I can build a stage. But this—this is worth too much credits for a stage."

"Well that's all I've got—so you'll just have to make it a really, really nice stage. You can include a curtain and a nice ramp for Mr. Withers and his wheelchair."

Luis considered for a moment, clicking his tongue along the roof of his mouth as if testing the boundaries of his principles—this was payment, after all, not charity—and who was to say that a customer could not pay what he wished? Was that not the very foundation of the free market?

"OK, I do it. Then with the credit I open up a garage back on Earth and hire Manny, Carlos, Carlos, Héctor, Adelfo, Humberto, Carlos, and Jesús."

"What about Heriberto?" said Jeremiah.

"No, Heriberto want to stay on the Einstein IV. Like I tell you, he is *loco*. You pay me one half now, one half when I finish."

"I can't do that," said Jeremiah.

"Is how I work."

"But I can't give you half of the necklace. Look, just take the whole thing now."

Luis thought for a moment. He clicked his tongue once more—this time at the very base of his teeth—but did not seem to like the sound.

"No," he said, "you give me the necklace when I finish. Work, then credit—not credit, then work."

"But just—"

"No," said Luis again, dropping the necklace on the table. "I work for my credit, Jeremiah. And *punto*."

19

Fly Me to the Moon

A S Jeremiah approached the office, he heard a phone ringing from behind the door. In the hopes that it was Reynolds, who had been AWOL since giving him the day off three days ago, Jeremiah quickened his pace and pulled the key from his pocket. He cursed as he fumbled with the key, but the phone kept ringing. Ten rings. Eleven— thank goodness the caller was persistent. Jeremiah finally got the door open.

He sprinted to the desk and reached out to answer the phone, but froze before picking up—for there on the retro period screen, in bright yellow letters, the caller id read: "Wendstrom, B." Fourteen rings. Fifteen.

In a flash Jeremiah put it all together. He had been so caught up with Mrs. Mayflower's bandora and Katherine making time with The Specimen and the myriad other disasters that he had completely forgotten to run his regular Domenican prioritization exercise, and a deadline had snuck up on him. Today was tomorrow, and it was after lunch. The caller was so persistent because the caller was Mr. Wendstrom wanting to know why his iguana hadn't been delivered by the time limit he'd set. Seventeen. Eighteen.

First things first: Jeremiah glanced about the office in utter panic, just in case Carolus had decided to turn himself in. Nineteen. He had not. Twenty. A heated debate began in Jeremiah's mind: should he pick up the phone or find an alternative course of action, such as disconnecting the phone and blockading the door, or sprinting and hiding, or abandoning ship?

But somewhere around ring 35—Jeremiah had lost count—acceptance set in. There was nothing to do but face the music, throw himself on Mr. Wendstrom's mercy, and beg for an extension. Running from the problem would only guarantee that Grubel heard about Mr. Wendstrom's dissatisfaction that much quicker.

Taking a deep breath, Jeremiah lifted the phone to his ear, fully prepared to say "Hello, Mr. Wendstrom," in a calm but serious tone. Instead, he screamed and dropped the receiver, clutching at his ear, which felt as if it had just spent some time on the wrong end of a jackhammer.

Even with the receiver on the desk, the music was so loud Jeremiah could hear the steady beat and the blat of a trombone cranked up to jet-engine-like decibels. Someone was trying to shout above the music and in the process, occasionally and with great effort, just barely managing to shout alongside it. After experimenting with a few different distances from his ear, Jeremiah managed to extract the following words from the shouting: Wendstrom, room, here, now, room, emergency, now, now.

It could not have been clearer what was going on: Mr. Wendstrom's PED was malfunctioning dangerously, putting his auditory health at risk—and that was the perfect opportunity for Jeremiah to buy some goodwill and patience in the matter of Carolus the Bold.

"Mr. Wendstrom," Jeremiah shouted into the mouthpiece, "I'm on my way." He bolted from the office, returning at a sprint a moment later to take the playbook with him.

A good 30 seconds before he arrived at Mr. Wendstrom's door, Jeremiah could hear faint music. About 20 seconds before arriving he could feel the beat in the floor, just slightly more pronounced than the general thrumming of the ship. Ten seconds before he arrived, Jeremiah could identify the song: "Fly Me to the Moon." In passing, he applauded Mr. Wendstrom's taste. When Jeremiah arrived at Mr. Wendstrom's quarters, the volume of the music through the steel door was just about right for a party where people would rather dance and drink than hear each other. Jeremiah didn't even bother with the tinkling little bell: he began to knock.

First he knocked with one fist, then—putting down the playbook—he knocked with two. He shouted. He shouted and knocked. He picked up the playbook and swung it at the door. Absolutely nothing happened, except that at some point during the "knocking with two-fists" era the song looped without any pause. Finally Jeremiah flattened himself against the wall opposing the door, got a running start, and hurled himself against it bodily, spreading himself out as if performing an upright bellyflop. After the fourth such bellyflop, just as Jeremiah was considering stopping and seeking Canadian medical attention, a slip of paper slid out from the mail slot. Jeremiah picked it up.

"Are you alone?" it read. "Circle one: YES NO"

"I don't have a pen," shouted Jeremiah. He shouted it again, pounding the door with each word. "I. Don't. Have. A. Pen." Another slip of paper came sliding out.

"Do you have a pen? Circle one: YES NO"

"No!" Jeremiah screamed. "No! NOOOOOO!"

Nothing happened. Finally Jeremiah picked up the playbook, preparing to return to the office and encode a keycard for Wendstrom's room. He had just turned around when the door opened, which he could tell because the music hit him across the back of the head like a bat.

"Jeremiah," shouted Mr. Wendstrom, "get in here now!"

He reached into the hall and pulled Jeremiah inside so hard that Jeremiah felt something in his shoulder pop.

Inside, with the door closed, the effect of the music was like nothing Jeremiah had ever experienced. Involuntarily he had dropped the playbook on the floor and put his hands over his ears, but even so every crash of the drums or flourish from the horns caused him actual physical pain. Mr. Wendstrom was shouting something at him—Jeremiah could tell because he could see that Mr. Wendstrom's mouth was opening and closing—but he could not make out the slightest syllable.

"Where's the PED?" Jeremiah shouted back.

Mr. Wendstrom's mouth kept moving. Jeremiah cupped his hands over Mr. Wendstrom's ears and, fighting through the agony in his own unprotected ears meanwhile, screamed his question again.

"Where's? The P? E? D?"

Mr. Wendstrom looked confused but motioned to his desk. Jeremiah put his hands back over his ears and ran to look.

The screen was functioning at least, displaying the indisputable facts that the current song was "Fly Me to the Moon," that the room's speakers were live, and that the current volume level was 110%. So the malfunction, Jeremiah reasoned, must be with the controls. To test his hypothesis, he risked dropping his hands from his ears again and pressed the stop button. The music stopped. Jeremiah nearly collapsed—partially in relief that the fix had been so simple, and partially because he had been leaning into the music like a stiff wind.

"What the hell do you think you're doing?" shouted Mr. Wendstrom. He kept his hands over his ears.

"I fixed it," Jeremiah shouted back. "I just pushed *stop*. Did you not try pushing *stop*?"

"Turn it back on immediately!" Mr. Wendstrom shouted.

"Wait, what?" said Jeremiah at a normal volume.

"Turn it back on! Give it to me!"

Mr. Wendstrom finally dropped his hands as well, but only because he needed them to wrest the PED from Jeremiah's grasp. He stabbed at the screen and the music exploded again.

Jeremiah took advantage of Mr. Wendstrom's involuntary blocking of his ears to snatch the PED back and turn the music off. This time he put the PED behind his back and held it there, receding defensively as Mr. Wendstrom advanced on him.

"Give it back!" Mr. Wendstrom shouted. "He's out there in the hall! He'll spoil everything!"

"Calm down," said Jeremiah. "No one is in the hall, I promise you."

"Then why didn't you circle 'Yes' on the note I sent you asking just that?"

"Because I didn't have a pen," said Jeremiah.

"I specifically asked you if you had a pen."

"True," said Jeremiah, "but—"

Now that he had a moment to absorb Mr. Wendstrom's appearance, Jeremiah realized that further appeals to logic were
not perhaps indicated. Mr. Wendstrom's eyes were bloodshot
and ringed by dark circles. His hair was crazed and dull as if
it had not been washed since Jeremiah last saw him, and his
face was drawn and pale after many hours of what seemed
near-existential terror. A trickle of blood ran from his mouth,
as if he'd been biting his tongue in near-constant anger management.

"My fault," said Jeremiah. "But I promise, there's no one
in the hall. Now, what's going on?"

"It's Porter," Mr. Wendstrom said, whispering for some
reason now that it had been confirmed they were alone. "He
thinks I cheated him in backgammon, and now he's going
to get his revenge by telling me who Andwen Longtail's real
father is. But I've outsmarted him again! He can't tell me
anything if I can't hear him!"

Mr. Wendstrom lunged for the PED, but Jeremiah dodged
in time.

"Andwen Longtail?" Jeremiah asked. "From your book?"

"Porter had someone wave him *Penultimate Battle Royale*
and *Last Battle Royale* from Earth and he's read them and now
he's going to spoil them for me."

"Can't you just get them waved to you as well and read
them before he can spoil them?" said Jeremiah.

"Without Carolus the Bold?" Mr. Wendstrom said. "After all the time he's waited, sharing the anticipation with me,
the fear that Michael L. L. Gregory might not even live long
enough to finish? What a welcome home that would be—if
you ever get off your ass and actually find him. 'Good to see
you, Carolus—by the way, while you were lost I read the last
two books.' "

Jeremiah was happy to note that, in his current state,
Wendstrom seemed to have forgotten about today's
deadline—or, possibly, lost track of time entirely. In either
case, Jeremiah was not about to remind him.

"Maybe you could read them secretly," he said, "and then
pretend to be reading them for the first time once we find Carolus."

"Jeremiah, you're not thinking like a winner. Winners
don't miss the forest for the trees. You need to fix the prob-

lem with Porter."

"Why can't you go to Mr. Porter and explain that you didn't cheat at backgammon?"

"Because I *did* cheat at backgammon," Mr. Wendstrom said. "I've been cheating him at backgammon every day for the last two years."

"Then have you considered returning Mr. Porter's credit and apologizing?"

"We never played for credit."

"Just apologizing, then?" said Jeremiah.

"You want me to apologize for *winning*?"

"I was thinking more for cheating."

"Cheating is just winning by different rules, Jeremiah."

"I think most people would consider it 'no' rules rather than—"

Jeremiah caught himself—this was another one of those avenues that was probably not worth pursuing.

"I'll see what I can do," he said.

"Good," said Mr. Wendstrom, reaching out his hands for the PED.

Jeremiah stopped just short of giving it to him.

"Will you wait to hit *play* again until I'm gone?"

"What if Porter's in the hall, just waiting for me to open the door so he can pounce and scream out the name of Andwen Longtail's father?"

"There's no one in the hall, Mr. Wendstrom."

Mr. Wendstrom nodded reluctantly, and Jeremiah handed over the PED.

"Jeremiah!" said Mr. Wendstrom, when he was already halfway out the door. "Wait! With this latest crisis I almost forgot."

Jeremiah turned around and put his hand against the doorway to keep the door from reactivating and sliding shut.

"I haven't been entirely fair to you," Mr. Wendstrom continued, searching for something in the desk. "Asking you to match intellects with Carolus the Bold like that. I nearly named him Waldred the Clever, did you know? 'Bold' just edged it out. The point is that I sent you into battle with nothing but your own wits, basically unarmed. I haven't set you up for success, Jeremiah—but that changes now. Ah, here it is: *Aunt Mildred's Organic Iguana Treats*. The smell alone drives Carolus wild. Just make sure he gets a whiff and he'll come running to you like—"

At just that moment Jack stepped around the corner of the hall with a deliberation that suggested his presence was neither accidental or recent. He looked at Jeremiah, then at Mr. Wendstrom, then at the dark green pellets that the latter was pouring from a canister into the former's hand, and finally at Jeremiah again. His eyes narrowed.

"There *is* someone in the hall!" shouted Mr. Wendstrom. "You lied to me, Jeremiah!"

"Get in line," said Jack, with the dry edge of a spy-hunter who has finally trapped a slippery double agent.

Mr. Wendstrom pushed Jeremiah from the doorway into the hall and shut the door behind him. The music started up again immediately.

"Jack," said Jeremiah, "this isn't what it looks like. These are iguana treats."

They faced each other, gazes locked, for a good 30 seconds, waiting to see who would break first. Jack broke first.

"Give me those drugs!" he roared, and broke into a dead run. Jeremiah turned and fled.

No one would have confused Jeremiah with a sprinter. Even before the synth ham diet, he had always been on the skinny side, but with that twigginess that indicates as little muscle as fat has been hung on one's frame. Still, if a few minutes ago someone had offered Jeremiah the chance to wager on his performance in a foot race with a man who had seen at least 70 winters, and who—there was good reason to believe—had spent a good number of all his 280 seasons ingesting impressive quantities of various intoxicants, Jeremiah would have suppressed a smile and asked to double the stakes. Now, with the benefit of hindsight, he might have requested a cocktail of whatever substances Jack had been taking all these years.

Speaking of hindsight, Jack was not gaining, but he was not losing ground either, and was showing signs of an endurance that Jeremiah could not help but admire. Each time Jeremiah risked a glance over his shoulder, he saw a portrait of senior cross-country health, a seasoned competitor well on the way to winning his age bracket by a margin as healthy as he was. Jack's cheeks glowed pink but not red above his silver and orange beard, his mouth alternating between a smaller and larger circle as he breathed evenly and regularly, remembering to inhale through his nose.

It was not clear how long the contest would have gone on, or who would have emerged the victor, if Jeremiah had not rounded a corner and collided with Mrs. Abdurov. They tumbled together to the ground.

"Mrs. Abdurov," said Jeremiah, trying to pull himself to his feet and Mrs. Abdurov to hers and accomplishing neither, "are you all right?"

"Jeremiah? What is your big idea? You don't look where you are going?"

"Hold him!" shouted Jack, coming around the corner. "Don't let him go!"

"What is this?" Mrs. Abdurov said, squinting at one of the treats that had dropped from Jeremiah's hand in the collision. "You have found Marya Jana?"

"You bet he found Marya Jana," said Jack. "And now he doesn't want to share. Get his arms!"

Jeremiah paused his desperate efforts to collect the iguana treats from the floor long enough to bat away Jack's first attempt to pin his arms, but he didn't relish either the prospect of engaging in a physical altercation with one of the passengers or discovering whether in his youth Jack had been a champion wrestler as well as apparent track star. Mrs. Abdurov, meanwhile, did not seem to have decided what was actually going on, or whether she was willing to accept instructions from Jack. She leaned in to get a closer look at the iguana treats littering the floor, and in that moment Jeremiah, following a bolt of inspiration, struck—reaching out under pretext of resisting the citizen's arrest being conducted on his person and clicking the clip of Mrs. Abdurov's pen, just as he had seen her do.

You bet he found Marya Jana. The recorded voice was tinny and not free from static, but unmistakably Jack's. *And now he doesn't want to share.*

The voice stopped as Mrs. Abdurov clicked the pen again. Jack stood in shock, still holding Jeremiah's arm in some martial twist, but no longer applying any force. His eyes—wide with betrayal and disbelief—held Jeremiah's for a moment, and then he turned to flee, returning only long enough to lean towards Mrs. Abdurov's breast pocket and shout, "I did not consent to any recordings, audio or video!"

"What is the deal of him?" said Mrs. Abdurov when Jack had gone.

"He thinks this is marijuana," Jeremiah said, picking up the last few iguana treats, "that you're the police, and that I'm working with you."

"Sad, how the drugs can ruin a man." Mrs. Abdurov fixed her blouse and hair. "I saw it many times. But now we get to real point: that is not marijuana, but Aunt Mildred's Organic Iguana Treats—Marya Jana's favorite brand. Yes or no?"

"Yes, but—"

"Which *Vor* Drinkwater sent to you, no? As a message. Like sending boots of man you have killed."

"No, Mrs. Abdurov, Mr. Drinkwater had nothing to do with these."

"Then where did you get them?"

"I can't tell you that," said Jeremiah, "because of issues of guest privacy." Which was true to a certain extent, if not quite complete, as it did not include Jeremiah's desire to avoid self-incrimination.

"No problem you tell me Jack is junkie, but you cannot tell me who gives you iguana treats because issue of *guest privacy?*"

"I never said Jack was a *junkie.*"

"My birthday was not yesterday, Jeremiah. You are protecting someone. I do not blame you—you are good boy, but stupid, and you are trying to keep peace. But with men like *Vor* Drinkwater, there can be no peace. You have broken his safe deposit box? No? Then you do it tomorrow, yes? Or I am Highly Dissatisfy. Time grows short, and Marya Jana's dead eyes must witness her revenge."

"What revenge?" said Jeremiah.

"Is better you don't know," Mrs. Abdurov said. "Not good boy like you."

She kissed him on the cheek.

Given his increasingly pessimistic understanding of the law of averages, Jeremiah half expected Mrs. Mayflower to be lying in wait back at the office. When he did not find her there, he three quarters expected the insidious law of averages to cause her to sneak through the door at any moment. So his first visitor of the afternoon was doubly welcome—both in that he was not Mrs. Mayflower, and that he was who he was.

"Mr. Chapin!" said Jeremiah. "Don't bother with the stupid numbers, just sit down. Can I synth you a coffee? Tea?"

Mr. Chapin made himself comfortable in the chair.

"For starters you can call me Henry, as you have for the last two years."

"I appreciate the thought, but if Grubel heard me, I'd be done for."

"Fair enough," said Mr. Chapin. "But there is something else that I hope you can do for me."

"Name it."

"Roof," said Mr. Chapin.

"What about him?"

"What do you know about him?"

"The same as you, I suspect, if not less."

"Do you know why he's on the E4?" Mr. Chapin asked.

"No," said Jeremiah.

"Do you know if he's dying?"

"What? No."

"Do you know if he's sick?"

"No idea."

"Would you enter his room and find out for me?"

"I'm sorry?" said Jeremiah.

"If I keep him busy during lunch tomorrow, will you take the master keycard I assume you have in your new post, enter Roof's room, have a look around, and report back to me anything you find that provides a clue as to why he's on this cruise?"

"Can't you just ask him yourself?"

Mr. Chapin shook his head.

"You know the unwritten rules, Jeremiah. Passengers don't talk about that sort of thing directly—we find out in other ways. Or have you ever asked me about my Fitzsimmon's Disease?"

"Touché," said Jeremiah, blushing slightly.

"And that's just me. You know how Roof is when it comes to matters of decorum. If I asked him he would lift

204

his nose and spin on his heel, maybe with a pointed remark about American manners."

"Can you at least tell me why you want to know?"

"I would much rather not," Mr. Chapin said.

"And I suppose that if I refuse that you won't be Highly Satisfied with my service?" said Jeremiah.

"Don't give me that extortion garbage. I offered to pay for your ticket—an offer which still stands."

"I don't want your credit," said Jeremiah. Though the sentiment was just as true as it had been the first time he said it, Jeremiah's voice held considerably less conviction. He still didn't want Chapin's credit, but he *wanted* to want it.

"I'm asking this as your friend," Mr. Chapin said. "If you can do it, I'll be eternally grateful. If you can't, we're still friends."

Jeremiah considered for a moment.

"What the hell," he said. "I've already broken into two passengers' rooms in the last two days—no, don't ask, you don't want to know. But if it's for a good cause, why not make it three? It *is* for a good cause?"

"It is," said Mr. Chapin, standing up and offering Jeremiah his hand. "And you're a good man to do this. I'll make sure that Roof doesn't leave the dining room tomorrow between 12 o'clock and 1. I guess that means you'll miss your own lunch."

Of the many downsides this mission might entail, the prospect of missing the eternal ham's next incarnation did not exactly leave Jeremiah desolate.

"By the way," said Mr. Chapin, when he was almost at the door, "I saw someone strange out in the hall when I was arriving. She looked like a passenger—older, very fashionably dressed—but I've never seen her before. She seemed to be headed here, but I think I spooked her—as soon as she saw me she ran away. I hope I didn't cause you any trouble there."

Jeremiah took pleasure in assuring Mr. Chapin that quite the opposite was the case, and that in fact—despite the favor he had just agreed to do for Mr. Chapin—Jeremiah was now very much in *his* debt.

Jeremiah was sitting on his sofa-bed, about to test the glue-for-wood job on the bandora, when Katherine returned from her dinner shift. The awkwardness he had felt that morning was still very much in the air as she came through the door—she hardly glanced in his direction, and her jaw looked tense. He needed to say something—something smooth and icebreaking and a little funny.

"Hey," he said.

"Did it work?" asked Katherine.

"The bandora? I was just about to try it. Can we talk about last night for a minute? All that crazy 'you're engaged' stuff?"

"I'd rather not," said Katherine.

"It's just that—"

"I'd really rather not."

"All right," Jeremiah said. "Whatever you say."

"Katherine?" he said some 30 seconds later.

"Yeah?"

"If you don't want to talk about it, why are you still standing there looking at me?"

"I want to see what happens when you try the tacky ukulele," she said.

"Ah."

Jeremiah readied himself, cracked his knuckles, and took a deep breath. Then he strummed the bandora gently—so gently that he was not sure that his fingers had even brushed the strings.

"Damn," Jeremiah said. He held the wreckage of the bandora by the neck, letting the body dangle.

"Yeah," said Katherine. "I'm going to go to bed. You want me to get the light?"

"No," said Jeremiah, "I'm going to channel my inner grizzled veteran and try gluing this damn thing together again."

"Which glue are you going to use this time?"

"Both," he said. "Lots and lots of both."

20

Very, Very Engaged

J EREMIAH knew from his own days as a passenger that Mr. Porter was an early riser, a caffeine addict, and enough of a gourmand that—the aforementioned addiction notwithstanding—he utterly rejected the very concept of synthed coffee and insisted on brewed. So Jeremiah woke early the next morning and stalked Mr. Porter like a deer, laying in wait by the giant silver urn that the kitchen staff left on the table outside the dining room at six o'clock every morning for those who could not delay java consumption until full service began at eight o'clock. Jeremiah did not lay in wait long.

Mr. Porter stumbled up to the table like a man who had spent so long in the desert he was now surviving on the memory of water. He rubbed his eyes a few times, as if he had just been spelunking through millennia of accumulated cobwebs, and finally his vision seemed to clear enough that he could spot and retrieve a cup from the porcelain tower on the table. Then, with an unsteadiness and speed that made Jeremiah's breath catch, Mr. Porter began repeatedly to fill the cup from the urn and empty it into his mouth, tossing the coffee back and hardly swallowing.

This was the crucial moment. The matter Jeremiah wished to discuss with Mr. Porter was delicate and emotionally charged, and if he approached the man too early, before the coffee had cleared his head and booted his rational systems, Jeremiah might as well be chatting with

207

a zombie suffering from migraines and impulse control issues. If he waited too long, on the other hand, the caffeine in Mr. Porter's bloodstream would reach its normal levels, which levels would have driven a typical Clydesdale to expire of terrified palpitations, and lent Mr. Porter his signature twitchiness and anxiety—an equally unfortuitous mode in which to tackle tricky issues of backgammon and any cheating thereat. The window was narrow, and after about 30 seconds—as Mr. Porter had finished his eighth cup and was filling his ninth—Jeremiah pounced.

"Good morning, Mr. Porter," said Jeremiah.

Mr. Porter looked over his shoulder and cut off the spout.

"And to you, Jeremiah," he said mildly. Things were going nicely.

"I wanted to chat with you for a minute about Mr. Wendstrom."

The name acted like a mainline of the darkest, foulest espresso to Mr. Porter's heart. His hands began to shake, a tremor developed in his jaw, and the color in his face rose until it kissed the red of the coffee cherry itself.

"I have nothing to say about that cheating bastard," he said, spitting the words. "Except that he's a cheating bastard." He drained the ninth coffee at one pull and began to coax a tenth from the urn.

"You should see the state he's in," said Jeremiah. "He's locked himself in his cabin and turned the music up to dangerous levels, just so he can't hear you spoil *Crowns on Fire* for him. I'm worried he'll permanently damage his hearing."

"It would serve him right."

"He's very sorry for what he's done."

"Then why isn't he here apologizing himself?" asked Mr. Porter.

"Because he's terrified you won't even give him a chance to apologize before you blurt out the name of—who is the character whose paternity is in doubt?"

"I haven't the foggiest clue—I haven't read any of those idiotic novels. Animals dressing up in armor and wizard robes? I prefer realism," said Mr. Porter. As if to wash the taste of fantasy from his mouth, he downed another cup.

"Then how were you going to spoil them for Mr. Wendstrom?"

"I wasn't, of course. I was just angry and looking for something to threaten him with. After all, I'm not going to engage in fisticuffs. But now that I've seen the effect, maybe I *will* get someone on Earth to wave me the ending. It would serve him right, the cheating bastard."

Mr. Porter drained another cup. The caffeine concentration was rising rapidly, and the conversation spinning out of control. Mr. Porter had to be slowed down, and quickly.

"Do you mind if I just slip in here quickly and grab a bit myself?" Jeremiah said, taking a cup and slipping it below the spout in the narrow window of opportunity offered by Mr. Porter's chugging of cup number who-knew-what-by-this-point. Mr. Porter looked as though he did mind quite a bit—his eyes widened in affront, and Jeremiah took the distinct impression that if Mr. Porter had been a cup or two in either direction, the matter might have come to blows.

"All I'm asking," said Jeremiah, allowing the merest trickle through the spout and into his cup, "is that you give him the chance to apologize."

Mr. Porter eyed the meager flow of coffee painfully. When 30 seconds had passed and the cup was only about half full, he resigned.

"Fine," he said, "tell him—tell him that I'll give him one chance to apologize. But if he cheats me again, I'll get someone to wave me every *Crowns on Fire* spoiler they can find, and I'll—I'll tattoo them on his arm while he sleeps. And on his forehead—backwards, so that it will be perfectly legible when he looks in the mirror. You got that?"

Turning off the spout and pulling his cup so that Mr. Porter could resume his ritual of auroral resurrection, Jeremiah promised that he did have it, and that he would pass it on to Mr. Wendstrom, verbatim and posthaste.

Never one to sit on a promise (or on good news, which was in short supply these days), and with almost two hours to spare before he had to open the office, Jeremiah raced directly to Mr. Wendstrom's room—a feat he could have accomplished if he were blind and his seeing-eye dog at the optometrist for the day. The distant thunder of Frank Sinatra's serenade began 100 yards from the door, leading Jeremiah to suspect that

Mr. Wendstrom had found some way—perhaps exploiting his skills as a motivational speaker—to coax his PED to give even more than 110 percent.

But there was a new, odd thrum to the song now—a bass drum striking everywhere except the beat, as if a bebop drummer had drunkenly wandered into the wrong recording studio, sat down behind Old Blue Eyes, and proceeded to carpet bomb his smooth baritone. When Jeremiah came around the last corner, he discovered that the drunken bebop drummer was Jack, and his instrument was not the bass drum, but Mr. Wendstrom's door. There was a vocal component to Jack's musical arrangement as well, which went something like this: "Bernie! Open up! I just want the name of your supplier! Your SUPPLIER! I'm not the police! NOT the POLICE! Your SUPPLIER, Bernie!" And subtle variations thereon.

Unsure whether Jack's willingness to descend to physical violence had subsided since their last encounter, Jeremiah was of two minds about making his presence known— namely, whether he should back away slowly in the hopes of escaping notice in the first place, or say to hell with stealth and sprint for all he was worth—but the decision was taken out of his hands when Jack, who must have caught some movement in the corner of his eye, turned and saw him.

"Informer," Jack hissed. Jeremiah could not help but be impressed by Jack's hissing of a word that contained no sibilants.

Despite Jeremiah's earlier fears, there was no threat of violence in Jack's voice or attitude this time, only utter contempt and a hint of sadness that anyone could ever become so subsumed in the System as to stoop to the depths that must be required to run a sting against a senior citizen and grateful recovering Systemite who just wanted to puff a little weed and get mellow before returning to Earth.

"Informer!" Jack shouted, turning and pounding again on the door. "Don't trust him, Bernie, he's an INFORMER!"

"Jack," Jeremiah said, "please listen to me."

"No!" Jack shouted, making earmuffs of his hands, as if the mere voice of an informer might corrupt or undo all that was still good and anti-Systemic in him. "No!"

He ran down the hall, still cradling his head in his hands,

now practically sobbing over and over "Informer, informer, informer."

Once he had gone, Jeremiah took his place and banged a few times on the door.

"Mr. Wendstrom!" he shouted. "It's Jeremiah! I have good news! Mr. Porter hasn't read a word of *Crowns on Fire*! You're safe! Mr. Wendstrom!"

But his efforts met with no more success than Jack's. The door stayed closed, *Fly Me to the Moon* continued to loop blastingly behind it, and the time allotted for breakfast before opening the office continued to tick away. Finally Jeremiah wrote a note telling Mr. Wendstrom the good news and slipped it through the mail slot. He peered after it for a moment to see if he could detect Mr. Wendstrom coming to read it, but it was impossible to say. Perhaps he had finally exhausted himself so thoroughly that, even with the blasting music, he had fallen asleep—in which case, thought Jeremiah, he would find a welcome surprise waiting when he woke up.

After a quiet and wonderfully Mayflower-less rest of the morning in the office, Jeremiah coded two keycards: one for Mr. Roof's door, and one for Mr. Wendstrom's, in case he had time to check on him after tossing Mr. Roof's room. Then he closed the office for lunch and set out on his next adventure in espionage. He trusted that Mr. Chapin would hold up his end of the operation, keeping Mr. Roof busy during lunch, but out of caution Jeremiah still rang the bell and called out a few times before entering.

Roof's Super Luxury cabin had the neat, happy glow of a room occupied by a seasoned and disciplined traveler. Everything was unpacked, ordered, available. Mr. Roof's formal wear hung in the closet, sorted in order of ascending pigmentation, from linen to seersucker to black tie. An antique book, with a cover of worn red cloth, sat perfectly squared to the edges of the bedside table, a bookmark peeking out from roughly halfway through its pages. Other volumes shared the bookshelves with a few brightly colored *objets d'art*, all looking recently dusted by the pink feather duster that lay on the bottom shelf, which Mr. Roof had apparently brought on board himself in order to keep standards in his own hands. It even seemed that Mr. Roof had made his own bed, or at least came after the maids to give the comforter a few final folds and pillows a couple plumps according to his own style. His sock drawer held nothing but socks, and the desk drawer was empty except for the golden keycard indicating that Mr. Roof kept a safe deposit box on board. Jeremiah could make out no signs of illness here in the main living area—no bottles of medicine by the bedside or used syringes in the wastebaskets. He headed for the bathroom.

Mr. Roof's bathroom was Spartan and sparkling, with nary a hand towel out of place. Toothbrush and toothpaste lay perfectly parallel on the side of the sink. It seemed so clear that there was nothing to find here that Jeremiah was tempted to skip the medicine cabinet, as a kind of token refusal to invade at least *one* area of Mr. Roof's privacy. But he had told Mr. Chapin he would find what there was to find, so he apologized to Mr. Roof in absentia and swung the mirror open.

At first he thought the shelves had been bricked up and filled in, but slowly Jeremiah realized that the mint green rectangles stacked to occupy all available space on all three shelves were pillboxes—the kind with separate compartments for Thursday morning and Monday night and so on. Taking great care not to upset the entire pharmaceutical wall, Jeremiah removed a single brick for examination.

Mr. Roof greeted each day with a decent cocktail of pills: the morning compartments each held a blue pill, a white pill, a pink pill, and two red pills—one square and one a rounded triangle. For a nightcap Mr. Roof took a yellow pill that looked like a tiny cookie cutter had been applied bloodlessly to a canary. Jeremiah had no idea what any of these pills were, but they were numerous and certainly looked potent, and Jeremiah could imagine that they were keeping any number and variety of health issues at bay. He replaced the pillbox with equal care and left the bathroom.

Jeremiah was standing by the door of the cabin, ready to leave, when something odd registered in his mind. He walked back to the bookshelf to take a closer look at the *objets d'art* there: three tasteful figurines of carved wood, facing out in a trident formation, all three works sharing a common subject.

212

"Iguanas," Jeremiah whispered.

For there they were: highly stylized, fantastically colored, resting on their elbows in unlikely anthropomorphic poses—but undeniably iguanas. And now that Jeremiah had noticed *these* iguanas, the cabin was suddenly crawling with others. *Field Guide to Iguana Identification*, proclaimed the spine of one book on the shelf. Another, thicker tome promised the secrets of *Raising Happy Iguanas in Captivity*. Jeremiah picked up the red book from the nightstand: *The Night of the Iguana*. And the postcard bookmark? Jeremiah slid it halfway from the pages—a glossy iguana hung inverted from a leafy branch, staring out with cold eyes that dared Jeremiah to make any sense of this latest discovery.

When Jeremiah returned to the office, Mr. Chapin was already waiting for him in the hall.

"I saw that woman again while I was waiting," Henry Chapin said as Jeremiah turned on the lights and settled in, "Since it seemed like you weren't keen on having her come in here, I walked up and introduced myself to scare her off."

"Thank you," said Jeremiah. "She's going to get me at some point, but you've helped me dodge one more bullet."

"Let's not forget who is doing whom a favor here. Speaking of: what's the news?"

"Mr. Roof is the neatest person I've ever seen in my life. His quarters are immaculate."

"But is he sick?"

"He takes a lot of pills," said Jeremiah.

"How many is a lot?"

"Let's see, in the morning he takes a blue one, a white one, a pink one, and two different red ones. At night there's a yellow one."

Mr. Chapin chewed this over, no doubt comparing it to his own regimen, which must have been more impressive still.

"We'll have to find out what they're for. I don't suppose you got samples? Of course you didn't, I can't ask you to steal a man's medication. Anything you found to suggest why he's on E4?"

"No," Jeremiah said.

213

"But you found *something* else, didn't you? Something that doesn't sit right with you—I can tell."

"I left his room with some questions," said Jeremiah, choosing his words carefully, "about a totally unrelated matter."

"Jeremiah, I have to find out what those pills are for."

"But you still can't tell me why."

Mr. Chapin shook his head.

"Maybe," said Jeremiah, "we can help each other here. I find out what pills Mr. Roof takes, and you ask him some simple questions—questions that have nothing to do with why he's on this cruise."

"Just tell me what to do."

"When you talk to him next, find some way to turn the conversation to iguanas."

"Did you say 'iguanas'?" asked Mr. Chapin.

"That's right."

"What am I supposed to ask him about iguanas?"

"It doesn't matter," said Jeremiah, "just bring them up naturally."

"And then?"

"Just listen to what he says and report it to me."

"All right," said Mr. Chapin, standing up. "I suppose if you're taking my request on faith, I can do no less for you. I'll think up a few clever ways to work iguanas into the dinner conversation tonight."

"One more thing," said Jeremiah. "Make sure you're out of earshot of Mrs. Abdurov and Mr. Wendstrom—if he even bothers to come out of his room. Trust me," he added in response to Mr. Chapin's questioning expression, "you don't want to know."

Mr. Chapin had not been gone long before Bradley arrived, bursting through the door with a headlong intensity.

"So now you *are* engaged?" he said to Jeremiah by way of greeting.

"I get off at five," said Jeremiah. "Why don't we meet in the cafeteria and sit down for a civilized chat?"

"So you don't deny it?"

Jeremiah, sensing that this might not be as short a conversation as he could have wished, stood up and came around the desk. Seated, he felt, he would be at a disadvantage.

"This is my place of employment," said Jeremiah—which was a novel thing for him to be able to say. "I don't come into your place of employment and start asking you questions, do I?"

"Because *I* don't go around getting engaged to the woman you're in love with and then lying to you about it, do I?"

Jeremiah sighed.

"All right, yes—we're engaged."

"So why did you say you *weren't* engaged?" said Bradley.

"I suppose I was having complicated feelings. It's always—"

"You were afraid I was going to get violent with you?"

"Now that you mention it," said Jeremiah, "yes."

"Coward," Bradley said. "I would never stoop to violence."

"You hip checked me in the cafeteria—and you pushed me out of the doorway the other night."

"That hardly qualifies as violence. If I ever get violent with you, you'll know—believe me, you'll be the *first* to know."

"I believe you," said Jeremiah.

"But *I* don't believe *you*," said Bradley.

Jeremiah thought this over for a moment, but then had to admit he didn't understand.

"I don't think you really *are* engaged to Kimberly," Bradley said.

"Oh, but I am engaged to her," said Jeremiah. "In fact we're both engaged, to each other. Very, very engaged."

"You're not."

"We are."

"You're not," roared Bradley, "and by God I'll hear you say it!"

In the increasingly unlikely event that Jeremiah were ever called on to write a best man's speech for Bradley's wedding, he would have been hard-pressed to come up with too many bullet points of sincere encomium. With a few hours of hard phrase-turning he might have found a complimentary figure to flatter Bradley's brooding intensity—and he supposed that he could have dug up some notable achievements in the field of medicine, along with a mention of the charitable impulses evinced by his plan to return and practice medicine in the ravaged remains of Canada. But now Jeremiah could have rounded out that meager list a bit with the goodness of Bradley's word and his reputation for honesty. Jeremiah could even have called it *brutal* honesty, for—just as Bradley had promised—Jeremiah was the very first to know when Bradley stooped to violence.

"Stooped," that was, in a physical as well as a moral sense, for as Bradley ran at Jeremiah he crouched low enough to grab Jeremiah around the calves. Bradley proceeded to try and pick Jeremiah up and throw him over, as if pulling out the evil he represented from the very root.

While the experience was not as painful as Jeremiah could have feared, it was extremely awkward, with plenty of tugging and grunting on Bradley's part and the occasional rhetorical question delivered between highly punctuated breaths, such as: "Why. Won't. You. Just. Go. Over?" Jeremiah found himself wishing he had something to read.

When it became clear that Bradley was not going to stop until Jeremiah had surrendered his upright position, Jeremiah heaved a sigh and then heaved himself over, doing his best not to hurt Bradley in the process, but to make him feel important and responsible, as if Jeremiah could not possibly have fallen over without the benefit of Bradley's recent exertions. But, as they say, no good deed goes unpunished—a maxim upon which Jeremiah had occasion to reflect, as Bradley parlayed Jeremiah's encouraging tumble into a headlock. The struggle became real.

They had not been tangled up on the floor, red-faced and grunting, longer than a few seconds before Grubel came into the office without knocking.

"What in the name of all that is holy is going on here?" he bellowed.

Bradley broke off his assault instantly and pulled himself to his feet. Jeremiah joined him, and the two of them stood with their hands behind their backs, swaying slightly, like two schoolboys surprised red-handed by the headmaster.

But before Jeremiah could offer any explanation, Bradley reached for the hoariest brush with which surprised schoolboys throughout history have attempted to scrub some of the red from their own hands.

"Jeremiah started it, sir."

"You're saying he initiated this encounter?" Grubel asked.

"That's right."

"Wait a minute," said Jeremiah, "this is exactly what it looks like—we were fighting."

"Are you saying, Dr. Bonaventure, that Jeremiah propositioned you?"

"I—that is—well—"

"I am not passing judgment, Dr. Bonaventure—not on *you*. But *you*, Jeremiah? I come by to see if you need anything to assist with that *special passenger*, only to find you *in flagrante delicto*—and in the office, where a guest could walk in at any moment! Dr. Bonaventure, for what it's worth, I firmly believe you could do better, even with the handicap of your heritage. As for you, Jeremiah: get back to work on the needs of our *special passenger* immediately. And if I *ever* find you abusing Golden Worldlines property in this way again, *special passenger* or no *special passenger*, I will have your head on a platter."

Grubel stormed from the room, leaving Bradley and Jeremiah still frozen in their boarding school poses.

"Bradley," said Jeremiah finally, "look, Kimberly and I—"

"*Lush sans velour*," the other said, or French words to that effect. He spat on the floor and left, arching his back and pressing the small of it with both hands.

A few minutes before closing, Jeremiah was deep in the playbook when a voice summoned him from the mysteries of requesting custom water hardness for a guest's bathroom.

"Bradley didn't believe it."

Kimberly stood just inside the doorway, still dressed in her scrubs and coat. She had been crying.

"Yes, he came by and said as much," said Jeremiah.

"And he accused me of playing games with him—*me* playing games with *him*. Can you believe that?"

"Well," said Jeremiah.

"Oh, Jeremiah, I've made such a mess of things. I'm always so suspicious of my heart, but it's my head that gets me into trouble. What should I do?"

She sat down in the chair across from Jeremiah, holding the troublesome head in her hands.

"You're overthinking this," Jeremiah said. "You love him, he loves you. Tell him the truth. He'll understand."

"Are you sure I shouldn't try to convince him we're engaged just *one* more time?" Kimberly asked.

"Kimberly, he's never going to believe you—why should he? You don't have a ring. He's never even seen us together. Just come clean."

"You're right," Kimberly said. "I don't want to come clean, but I *should*, so I *will*. That's the Categorical Imperative. Jeremiah, you're a genius of moral philosophy as well as experimental method. I'll go do it now."

She stood up, determined, but before she could leave, Mrs. Abdurov arrived.

"Is 4:59," Mrs. Abdurov yelled as she entered the office, preventing any appeals to working hours. "Ah, the lady doctor is here too. You stay a minute, and when I finish with this one, you tell me why my hip hurts." She sat down in the recently vacant seat. "Where are my photos, Jeremiah? I told you get them by today."

"Mrs. Abdurov, maybe we should talk about this when we're alone?"

Mrs. Abdurov pursed her lips and shook her finger.

"No, no, Jeremiah," she said. "You will not hang noodles on my ears any longer. You are help, she is help. She will say nothing. Either you show me pictures right now, or right now I will go to Financial Office and report my satisfaction as nothing."

"But Mrs. Abdurov, I just haven't had—"

"Enough," she said, standing up. "I go now."

"Which hip did you say was hurting you, Mrs. Abdurov?" said Kimberly.

Mrs. Abdurov turned and faced her—it seemed she had forgotten the doctor was there.

"The left," she said. "It clicks when I am walking."

"Is it worse in the mornings?" Kimberly asked.

Mrs. Abdurov had to think for a moment.

"Yes," she said.

"Which side do you sleep on?"

"The left," said Mrs. Abdurov, in a tone that any uncle rediscovering a coin behind a niece's ear would have found extremely gratifying.

"I thought so. I have an ointment that will help—you put it on before you sleep."

"It is the same stuff you give Mr. Moakley and Mrs. Idle-while?" Mrs. Abdurov asked suspiciously.

"No, this is much more powerful—you have to wash your hands after you use it. I only have one tube left. Come with me, we can stop by the infirmary and pick it up."

"Good," said Mrs. Abdurov, "we go now." She started through the door without waiting for Kimberly.

"That was amazing," said Jeremiah.

"They all want what the others don't get," said Kimberly. "Status is the strongest placebo."

"Seriously, thank you: I owe you one," said Jeremiah. "I'm grateful enough to thank a Canadian."

Which he meant not just in the idiomatic sense—of his being grateful enough to thank someone who, like a Canadian, did not usually deserve thanks—but in the literal sense of being grateful enough to thank Kimberly, who was an actual Canadian—and who, it must be added, had not particularly been a locus of deserved gratitude in Jeremiah's life to date.

Mrs. Abdurov poked her head back into the office.

"Lady Doctor, we are going or what?" she yelled.

"Coming, Mrs. Abdurov! You know," Kimberly shouted conspiratorially into Mrs. Abdurov's ear when she had reached her, "when you arrived, Jeremiah was just telling me about his plan to get you some photos or something."

219

World Enough (And Time)

21

The Conservation of Ghosts

Friday (2 days until arrival)

KATHERINE emerged from her room the next morning to find Jeremiah once again holding two pieces of one bandora.

"This is getting to be a tradition," she said. "Both glues didn't work?"

"I think it worked *worse*. I'm not sure I even managed to touch the strings this time before it fell apart, and that was giving it a full day and a half to dry."

"Well," said Katherine.

"Yes?"

"I was trying to think of something encouraging to say, but I couldn't. Not about the bandora, at least."

Jeremiah's ears perked up.

"But you might have something encouraging to say about something else?"

"I'm sorry about giving you the silent treatment after that guy came and accused you of being engaged. It wasn't your fault, after all. Or at least—"

"Not *totally* my fault," said Jeremiah.

"It's Friday, so I'm on breakfast duty, but I thought maybe we could chat over lunch?"

"That sounds great," said Jeremiah, trying to keep his voice casual. "Now if you'll excuse me, I have to run. I had a brainstorm last night, and I have to see a Mexican about a homebrew surveillance system."

Katherine's left eyebrow lifted.

"Another idiom I'm not familiar with," she said. "But I hope it's larky."

The Mexican table was already well into breakfast by the time Jeremiah arrived.

"Luis," Jeremiah said after the rituals of seat shuffling and back slapping had been observed, "can you ask Heriberto how he got that wave of Mrs. Mayflower? Did he just happen to have the camera running?"

"No," Luis reported after a bit of back and forth with Heriberto. "Second Carlos tells Heriberto he sees something in that hallway that looks like a ghost. So Heriberto hooks up his camera to a—how do you call it? Motion scissor?"

"Sensor."

"That's it, motion sensor. Heriberto is very good with all things like that."

"Luis," said Jeremiah, "do you think you could help me ask Heriberto to do me a huge favor in the Guest Services office?"

"And then he says when the motion scissor detects something out in the hallway," said Luis, "this thing here buzz like—"

The small square of plastic, which looked like it had been adapted from a restaurant pager, suddenly came to life, blinking and buzzing with such vigor that it cost Luis some effort to keep his grip on it.

"—just like that," said Luis. He sounded surprised.

"Is he testing?" Jeremiah asked, pointing at Heriberto. *"Heriberto, estás probando o que?"*

Heriberto shook his head.

"Is not testing," Luis said. "Is real. Look at the PED!"

Jeremiah did as instructed and saw, on the grainy video feed that Heriberto had set up there, that the motion sensors had done their job well. Someone was walking down the hallway to the Guest Services office.

"Jeremiah," said Kimberly, exiting the frame of the wave and stepping through the office door. "Oh, hello. Hello."

THE CONSERVATION OF GHOSTS

These last two hellos were directed at Luis—who grinned in response—and Heriberto, who bowed low with a flourish of his arm.

"Jeremiah," Kimberly said again, "I figured out what to do—or really, you did, you're a genius."

While this was very pleasant to hear, Jeremiah did have a question or two.

"I tried to come clean to Bradley," Kimberly said, "but it didn't work. He says now that he knows the games I've played to make sure *he* loves *me*, he can't be sure if *I* love *him*. But I know how to convince him! If he believes that you and I are engaged, then I can break off the engagement because I'm still in love with him, and then he'll know that it must be true!"

"Um, Kimberly," said Jeremiah. "I'm sorry you've found yourself in such a difficult situation, but by this point haven't we established pretty firmly that Bradley doesn't believe that we're engaged?"

"Of course, because we've just *told* him we're engaged! You said it yourself, Jeremiah—he believes what he sees. So if he *sees* us get engaged, then he'll believe it!"

"To be clear, you're asking me—"

"She want you to propose to her!" said Luis. He translated for Heriberto, who nodded in agreement that this was, yes, just a fantastic idea.

"Yes!" said Kimberly, feeding off their excitement. "In front of Bradley! I'll explain to him that we fell in love during our fake engagement, and now we're really engaged. Then the next day, I break it off, he believes that I really love him, and we live happily ever after. Will you do it?"

To say that Jeremiah's Better Judgment had some misgivings about this course of action would be to give short shrift to his Mediocre, Questionable, and Downright Terrible Judgments—which, in a rare show of solidarity, had lined up to hold signs and march in the picket organized by their Better counterpart. Only Jeremiah's Suicidal Judgment stood apart, holding up an opposing sign on which the slogan "It might be fine!" had been smeared in letters of fresh blood.

"Please?" said Kimberly. "You did say you owed me one." She began to rub her left hip subtly, as if to soothe the deep

223

ache of a favor still unpaid.

Jeremiah was about to rub his entire body to remind Kimberly of the pains he had already suffered on her behalf, but in the new climate of *quid pro quo*, his Suicidal Judgment found a sudden bit of inspiration.

"What if I did this for you, and you got me some information about a passenger?" said Jeremiah.

"What information?"

"I need to know what medications he's taking."

"That's a violation of medical ethics," said Kimberly. "It flies directly in the face of the Categorical Imperative—and you know how important the Categorical Imperative is to me, Jeremiah."

"I do," said Jeremiah. "It's one of your favorite imperatives." He reached into the small bag of philosophy that he had acquired in his academic career, most of it from the men's room stalls in the classroom building. "But you would be doing this for love, and doesn't Nietzsche say somewhere that what is done for love takes place beyond good and evil?"

"You want me to set my moral compass according to a relativist's aphorism?" said Kimberly, and shook her head. But she was wavering. "I shouldn't," she said, "I know I shouldn't—but—for Bradley—I will. Which passenger? Tell me quick, Jeremiah, before I change my mind."

"Alastair Roof. He takes a blue one, two red ones, a white one, and a pink one. Oh, and a little yellow one at night."

"I'm not his doctor, so I don't know offhand—I'll have to pull the records."

"All right," said Jeremiah. "As for the fake proposal, it needs to be controlled—discreet. We need to plan when and where."

"You let me handle that—I'll figure everything out and let you know."

"And what about a ring? It's not going to look very convincing if we get engaged without a ring."

"Don't worry about *anything*. All you have to do is show up. Now I have to get going, I have clinic duty." She seemed to realize something, and her face, which had been troubled since Nietzsche had emerged victorious over the Categorical Imperative in the cage match of her soul, brightened. "I'll see you soon, *fiancé*."

At that word Jeremiah's Suicidal Judgment—which since its brainstorm had been looking rather smug as it strutted and crowed insults at its betters—sighed and crossed over to join the picket line.

Seeing that the young lady was preparing to go, Heriberto offered his arm.

"Oh," she said, "a gentleman! You may escort me out—as long as it's all right with my *fiancé*."

Jeremiah's Suicidal Judgment fell to the pavement and soiled its pants.

"Jeremiah," Luis said when Kimberly and Heriberto had gone, "you are *bendito* among the women. You live with the pretty *fresa* and now the lady doctor is proposing you marriage! You are *tremendo*, my friend."

"It's not like that, Luis."

"That remind me," Luis said, "we need liquor."

"All right," said Jeremiah. It was early, but in the circumstances Jeremiah certainly wouldn't turn down a snort himself. "There's a little vodka left back in my room."

"No, for the *stage*. To make it shine nice."

"Oh," said Jeremiah, "you need *lacquer*."

"That's it. Lacquer, from the big storeroom. We run out in the shop, and I don't want to ask my boss nothing about this. The wood I find easy, and the stuff for thermite."

"Thermite? Luis, are you making an exploding stage?"

"You know, thermites, the little *bichos* who eat the wood. I kill them with insecticide."

"Ah, *termites*."

"That's it, termites. But I don't have access to the big storeroom to get no liquor. You get some for me?"

"Sure," Jeremiah said. "I'll take care of it."

"Good. I earn my credit," said Luis. "I gonna liquor the hell out of that son a bitch."

Shortly after Luis left, as Jeremiah sat picking idly through the playbook, Heriberto's ad-hoc alarm system buzzed again. There on the grainy screen of the PED, Mrs. Mayflower was picking her way down the hall towards the door of his office.

"I can take care of that for you right away, Mr. Smith," said Jeremiah loudly—louder than he would have if

225

Mr. Smith had actually been sitting in the Guest Services office at the moment. "I'll just need to examine it to check the model of the PED—there are subtle differences, you know, and if you don't respect those differences—"

As he spoke, Jeremiah watched the surveillance wave anxiously. Mrs. Mayflower had stopped in the hallway outside and was now listening, her ear to the door. He could not see her face—only the top of her broad hat—but if it was possible for the top of a hat to look deeply suspicious, then hers did. Jeremiah raised his voice even louder.

"—for example, if you tried that little maneuver on a Mistutashi X200, you'd be left with a very expensive brick. But on this model—"

A noise somewhere further down the hall made Mrs. Mayflower jump. For a few tense seconds Jeremiah was afraid that she would seek cover in the office, fake Mr. Smith or no, but she turned and fled back down the hallway. In ten seconds she was out of the camera's range.

Jeremiah smiled with great satisfaction at the image of the empty hallway. With the talent show only a day away, and their arrival to Earth only one day after that, he knew that he had merely delayed his execution—but when it came to executions, any delay was infinitely preferable to proceeding right on schedule.

When the plastic pager buzzed a quarter of an hour later, it was announcing the arrival of Mr. Porter, who sprinted through the surveillance frame before he stumbled into the office and collapsed into the guest chair with a finality that would have made Pheidippides proud.

"Hello, Mr. Porter," said Jeremiah. "Did Mr. Wendstrom apologize?"

"Apologize?" Mr. Porter said. Jeremiah could not help but notice that he was missing his left eyebrow, which otherwise would have joined the right one in arching in horror.

"Are you all right, Mr. Porter?"

"I killed him," said Mr. Porter. "And now his ghost will .haunt me forever."

Jeremiah sat up and clutched the edge of his desk. Could this be it? With all the other disasters on his plate, Jeremiah had practically forgotten about the murder mystery. But now, after all the blind alleys and dead ends, had Boyle's murderer just shown up on his doorstep to make a free and unforced confession? Which confession, by the way—after a promising start—seemed to have stalled. Mr. Porter was now sitting silently, watching Jeremiah, as if he expected something from him before continuing.

"I'm sure it was an accident," said Jeremiah, just as he had heard countless detectives on CrimeHunters do.

"Yes," Mr. Porter said, "an accident!"

"You didn't mean to kill him."

"Of course not—I only wanted to scare him."

"Exactly. Anyone would understand that. And who could blame you?"

"No one," said Mr. Porter breathlessly, as if the absolution Jeremiah was pouring on his head had shocked him like cold water. "No one could blame me."

"After what he put you through."

"Yes, yes! What he put me through!"

"And the way he walked around with that sour attitude and hostile air."

"Yes," said Mr. Porter, with perhaps a hair less of his former conviction.

"Always saying those unpleasant things."

"Well, yes—but more to the point, cheating me at backgammon, every single day for two years!"

Fixing a game of chance was not the motive that Jeremiah had been expecting for Boyle's murder, but—like the detectives on CrimeHunters—he would take whatever motive he could get. Except this particular motive rung a bell in Jeremiah's mind, as if the writers on CrimeHunters—feeling the pressure of a relentless production schedule—had recycled a plot point from an earlier season.

"But wait," he said, "like Mr. Wendstrom did?"

"What do you mean 'like' Wendstrom?" asked Mr. Porter.

"I mean, Mr. Boyle cheated you at backgammon too, just like Mr. Wendstrom did?"

"What does Boyle have to do with anything? It's Wendstrom I'm talking about."

"You killed Mr. Wendstrom?" said Jeremiah.

His head was swimming now. Lines that should have been straight did not look straight.

"I did, God help me," said Mr. Porter, dropping his head into his hands and choking out the words, "and now his ghost will haunt me forever."

"We have to call Battle," Jeremiah said, thinking out loud.

"The security officer? Do we really?"

"Of course—a man is dead."

"But just a moment ago you said anyone would understand," said Mr. Porter.

"That was when I thought you had killed someone else," Jeremiah said, "and I was trying to trick you into telling me how and why. Like detectives on CrimeHunters do."

"Oh," said Mr. Porter. He seemed to be taking it well.

"Wait," Jeremiah said, "speaking of that, how did you kill Mr. Wendstrom?"

"What do you mean *how*? By threatening to spoil the end of those idiotic books."

"How could that kill anyone?"

"Now you're just trying to trap me again," Mr. Porter said. "To cajole me into confessing. You're using your interrogator's bag of tricks!"

"How can I trick you into confessing when you've already confessed?"

After a moment of sucking his teeth, Mr. Porter conceded the logic of this point.

"I suppose I drove him to suicide," he said finally.

"So you didn't actually put the dagger in his heart?"

"Well," said Mr. Porter, "metaphorically..."

"Yes, yes, you subjected him to a veritable arsenal of metaphorical daggers, bullets, and nooses—but how many literal, physical daggers, bullets, and nooses were involved?"

"Well, now that you put it that way—none."

Relief flooded Jeremiah's heart.

"Thank goodness," he said. "I mean, poor Wendstrom, of course—it's a tragedy. But you can set your mind at ease, Mr. Porter. No one—and certainly no court of law—could blame you for his death. You will need to tell me where you found his body, though, so we can alert Battle and the security team."

"I have no idea," said Mr. Porter. "I haven't seen his body."

"Then how do you know he's dead?"

"Have you been listening to a word I've said?" shouted Mr. Porter, leaping from his seat in agitation. "I've seen his ghost! I was rehearsing my act for the talent show and he came in and pointed a finger at me, accusing me—a judgment from the Other Side. He scared the life half out of me—I stumbled and singed my face, and by the time I'd recovered he was gone."

A moment ago, Jeremiah had thought he'd known what relief was. Now he understood how relief actually felt, how sweet it actually was, as if he had sipped grape juice before being served a glass of Bordeaux. It was hard work not to smile.

"Mr. Porter," he said, "Mr. Wendstrom isn't dead. Everything is fine. You've had a nightmare, or accidentally overdosed on one of your medications, and you've hallucinated something terrifying. But that's all. It wasn't real. Come with me and I'll prove it to you."

"Where are we going?"

"To Mr. Wendstrom's room."

"Are you insane?" Mr. Porter shrank back from Jeremiah, as if the latter had been about to take his hand. "That's where his spiritual presence is bound to be the strongest."

"Trust me. We'll knock on his door and he'll answer and you'll have a chance to tell him you've never even read *Crowns on Fire*—and to let him apologize to you for cheating at backgammon."

Not to mention that Jeremiah would buy himself another stay of execution for having failed to find Carolus the Bold.

Mr. Porter did not look completely convinced, but he did at least seem to be *hoping* that he had hallucinated his spectral encounter, and eventually Jeremiah managed to cajole and borderline threaten him out of the office and through the hallways towards Mr. Wendstrom's room, pausing only for the occasional crying jag or sink-to-his-knees meltdown.

"You hear that?" Jeremiah said when they were close enough that Frank Sinatra was audible in the distance. "That's from Mr. Wendstrom's room. Do you think he would be playing music if he weren't alive?"

Mr. Porter grunted and shivered in response. He had

stopped resembling a drunk whose emotions were having a bit of a field day and started to resemble a man who'd just been informed in rapid succession that he had a month left to live, that it was February, and not a leap year. Jeremiah continued to prop him up as best he could, both physically and morally, but he could not entirely keep an edge of impatience from his assertions that everything either was all right or would be. Was this really a man who performed with open flame?

Mr. Porter's nerves collapsed entirely a few yards from Mr. Wendstrom's room, his legs following suit in short order, and Jeremiah—having decided that tough love was the new order of the day—left him there and walked up to the door.

"Mr. Wendstrom! It's me, Jeremiah."

He smiled at Mr. Porter in what he hoped was a calm and soothing manner.

Fly Me to the Moon ended and looped without any sign of life emanating from the room.

"Mr. Wendstrom!" Jeremiah shouted even louder. "I'm here with Mr. Porter—and we have good news. Can you open the door, please?"

"He can't open the door," said Mr. Porter, "because he's dead!" He began to writhe in horror and regret, moaning soft but pointed questions to the almighty about what he had done and what he would do now.

Jeremiah was considering leading Mr. Porter away at this point—or trying to—when he remembered the keycard he'd coded for Mr. Wendstrom's room, and which he still had in his pocket.

He took it out and brushed it over the access panel, then braced himself as the door opened and the sonic ghost of Frank Sinatra nearly knocked him backwards. Jeremiah covered his ears, gritted his teeth, and entered the room, closing the door behind him for Mr. Porter's psychological and aural benefit.

Two things Jeremiah could not find after a quick search of the entire cabin: the PED to switch off the music, and any sign whatsoever of Mr. Wendstrom. So, after one last check behind the shower curtain and under the bed, Jeremiah fled the acoustic torture of the room for the mere acoustic discomfort of the hall.

"Well?" said Mr. Porter, looking up with trembling lips.

"Mr. Wendstrom is fine," said Jeremiah. "He's very glad to hear that you aren't actually going to spoil *Crowns on Fire* for him, and he asked me to apologize on his behalf for his ungentlemanly behavior at the backgammon table."

"Why doesn't he come out to apologize himself?" asked Mr. Porter.

"He feels too bad about how he acted. Plus he just got out of the shower. Also, he's not feeling well physically. Quite healthy, though. Just not feeling well. At all."

"Why isn't he turning off the music?"

"You know, I asked him the exact same thing."

"What did he say?"

"He said..."

"Yes?" said Mr. Porter, his eyes widening in expectation and then narrowing in suspicion. The lower lip was trembling again.

"He said that he *likes* it like this. Can you believe that? I mean, can you?"

"Yes," Mr. Porter said after a few seconds of earnest thought. He broke into a smile. "Crazy old Bernie. Yes, I can."

"Me neither," said Jeremiah. "But to each his own. Now why don't we take a walk down to the infirmary and get that eyebrow looked at? And then I have to make an urgent visit to a—"

Jeremiah groped for a description of The Specimen he could feel comfortable with.

"—friend of a friend."

WORLD ENOUGH (AND TIME)

22

Better Pockets

"**B**ATTLE," said Jeremiah, "thank goodness I caught you."

"What's going on, Brown? I'm late for something."

"Bernie Wendstrom has gone missing," said Jeremiah.

"We're on a ship in the middle of outer space, Brown. People don't go missing."

"He's not in his room."

"Then he's somewhere else."

"He's in a disturbed state of mind, Battle. I don't think he's well."

"And you know this how?"

"Because Mr. Porter—"

"What about him?"

"Mr. Porter swears he saw Bernie Wendstrom's ghost."

"Get the hell out of here, Brown. I don't have time for this."

"I just want you to check the door logs," said Jeremiah, "like you did before, to see where Mr. Wendstrom might have gone."

"And I just want the last 30 seconds of my life back. Neither one of us is going to end up satisfied."

"Wait," said Jeremiah, and—surprising even himself—reached out to grab Battle's arm. As he did so, something fell out of his pocket and skittered softly across the ground.

At first Jeremiah was glad, as the sound had distracted The Specimen from deploying his carefully honed response to having his arm grabbed—which might have left Jeremiah eating through a straw for the rest of his life—and instead inspired him to turn his rage-filled eyes to the floor. As those eyes turned back, however, full of suspicion, Jeremiah's gladness diminished somewhat.

"What is that?" said The Specimen. He broke his arm free from Jeremiah's grasp and pointed to the Aunt Mildred's Organic Iguana Treat that had come to rest between them. The sickly-sweet odor rose to Jeremiah's nostrils, and Jeremiah could see in The Specimen's face just how much sweeter it must smell to him, redolent with the possibility of busting Jeremiah for possession and—as he had been unable to do in Jack's case—finally christening the brig with its first drug-related bust.

"Nothing," Jeremiah said. "Just a..." To buy some time, Jeremiah raised his fist to his mouth and hacked a few times, which inspired him. "...cough drop."

Under The Specimen's watchful gaze, Jeremiah stooped to retrieve the treat. He popped it into his mouth, and then—in what was perhaps the greatest feat of will in his young life to date—managed not to spit it out. Jeremiah had never fancied himself as having a particularly sensitive palate, but he could have taken a decent guess at Aunt Mildred's secret recipe: clear cut an acre of organic jungle, blend well the trimmings, mold into pellets and cure for a minimum of two years in a dank cave, directly beneath the sleeping place of a colony of bats with adventurous tastes in fruits and insects. Finish by smoking delicately above a low fire of the cheapest grade of Marya Jana commercially available, then salt and pepper to taste.

"Mmmm," he said. "Soothing." As he spoke, the iguana treat began to melt on his tongue into what felt like dry leaves and twigs suspended in a Jell-O mold. It was impossible to hold it in his mouth any longer—he either had to swallow or spit it out. He swallowed.

"Well," said Jeremiah, and The Specimen wrinkled his nose at his breath, "I won't keep you any longer. I'm late for a lunch appointment myself anyway."

As Jeremiah hurried to the cafeteria to meet Katherine, he experienced a series of peculiar sensations: first a spreading warmth in his stomach, which might have been pleasant if occasioned by a brandy; then a tingling in his extremities, as if after a day spent in the snow he were warming them by a fire; and finally a feeling of unbearable lightness in his head and a fisheye lens effect warping his vision. Balance was a bit trickier than usual, and when he reached out to steady himself by trailing his fingers against the wall, he felt the texture of the brushed metal with an amazing intensity.

With each step the effects intensified, and by the time he reached the cafeteria Jeremiah had come to three vague conclusions: one, he was having some sort of out-of-body experience, apparently brought on by ingestion of one of Aunt Mildred's Organic Iguana Treats; two, this was cause for concern; three, he was not concerned—which concerned him.

Katherine was sitting alone at her table in the back corner, but even in his altered state Jeremiah picked her out immediately, as if the rest of the room had been dark and a single spotlight trained directly on her. He waved unsteadily; she waved in return. He smiled; she smiled back—a little guardedly, but she smiled.

Then, as Jeremiah approached, Katherine's brow furrowed—she appeared confused. Just in case she was confused about how happy he was to see her, Jeremiah smiled wider. Her own mouth straightened. Just in case she thought he had been shooing a fly, Jeremiah waved again, harder. Katherine folded her arms in front of her chest. At this point the situation seemed to call not for more desperate action, but sober reflection and review. Had his head actually swollen to the dimensions that he felt it? Were his fingers sparking and smoking? Were his eyes popping out of his head? Was he floating towards her instead of walking?

As he skimmed down this checklist of possible causes for Katherine's consternation, Jeremiah sensed something moving from the dark wings of his attention into the spotlight that still shone on Katherine, blocking the line of sight to her that he had enjoyed. Someone had stepped in front of him.

"The blue ones are allergy pills," said Kimberly. "The white ones are ginkgo leaf supplements. The pink ones are for acid reflux. One red is for sinus pressure, the other for dry eyes. Oh, and the yellow one is a mild sleep aid. Ready?"

That one word multiplied the effect of the iguana treat like a bottle of bourbon chasing a pharmacy's worth of sleeping pills. Jeremiah experienced a kind of reverse zoom shot that left his head spinning and his stomach feeling as if he'd swallowed a live octopus. He looked around in a panic at the tables where other workers were seated, picking at their whipped ham mousses. Kimberly had met him right in the center of the room, in the precise spot where toasts would have been proposed to any couple unfortunate enough to book the E4's cafeteria for their rehearsal dinner.

"No," Jeremiah mouthed, suddenly unable to produce sound. "Wait."

Kimberly sensed his reluctance and smiled indulgently. In a preview of what their married life might have been like, she gently, almost affectionately, kicked his right leg out from under him. She did it in the same spirit as, after 20 years of wedded bliss, she might have taken away his ice cream and chided him about his cholesterol.

Jeremiah fell hard to his right knee, reaching out reflexively for support to Kimberly, who took the opportunity to demonstrate her considerable talent as a reverse pickpocket. Jeremiah had not even felt the arrival of the ring he now held, proffered, in his right hand. He could no longer swear to it that this was not a bad dream.

The cafeteria at large had begun to take notice of what was transpiring—people were looking over and nudging each other. Some of those who were shorter or farther away had stood up. Jeremiah saw one woman clasping her hands in front of her mouth and one man fighting tears. The current of the moment was so strong, and Jeremiah's state so altered, that he himself felt a swell of pride at the size and quality of the diamond he was tendering to Kimberly—so obviously dearer than two months of salary, or even two years in his case. It looked as big as his head felt.

"Oh," gasped Kimberly, once she was sure she had the attention of the room, and especially one very particular person in it. "Oh, Jeremiah, this is so unexpected!"

She left a space, in case Jeremiah felt like adding a touch or two of his own, but holding the ring without falling over represented the absolute limit of his abilities. He did manage to move his mouth a bit more.

"Of course I will!" Kimberly said. "Of course of course of course!"

She pulled him up from his kneeling position, but with significantly less grace than she had caused him to kneel in the first place, since she could no longer, like a judo master, use her opponent's own weight and strength against him, and Jeremiah was still not up to contributing much.

In the process of his unsteady ascent, Jeremiah felt something drop out of his pocket. Given the other concerns of the moment, he did not pay it much mind, until he saw the look on Kimberly's face when she looked down to see what had made the heavy thud.

"Jeremiah!" she said. "I don't even know what to say!"

Her amazement seemed quite genuine, and appeared to grow more so as she bent down and picked up Mrs. Chapin's ruby necklace from the floor. Jeremiah made a note for his future, clearer self that when things settled down a bit it was high time to invest in some pants with better pockets.

"It's *beautiful*," she said as she put it on. "I absolutely *love* it." In his condition, Jeremiah could almost see the hearts dotting the i's in these sentences, and even taking the place of the o in 'love.' "I don't even know how to thank you."

Having suddenly found a way to thank him, Kimberly leaned in for a kiss, but then seemed to think better of it. By this point Jeremiah's mouth had not fully closed in some time. She embraced him instead.

A line of people had formed: people whom Jeremiah had never met and in some cases never even seen before, but who wished to express their deep personal pleasure at his and Kimberly's change in romantic status. They shook his hand and hugged him and made sure he knew how lucky he was, and one little Filipina with at least 60 winters under her belt pinched his butt so hard that he found the power of speech again.

"Thank you," said Jeremiah to her, "you'll have to come visit once we're settled."

The Filipina laughed and yielded her spot to the next well-wisher. Kimberly smiled approvingly at Jeremiah's newly animated manner. She kept reaching up to touch the necklace.

Each time she did, the diamond on her finger flashed and Jeremiah's head spun a bit faster.

Near the end of the line came Luis heading up the Mexican contingent, which congratulated Jeremiah by each punching him in the right arm as they walked up, hard. Once all of them had taken a turn they started over at the top of the lineup, working their way around a couple times until they were sure that Jeremiah felt sufficiently congratulated. The pain sobered him up a bit. After the punching was done, Luis leaned in to whisper in his ear.

"It looks like your *prometida* is wearing the necklace you supposed to give me for the stage," said Luis.

"I'll figure something out," Jeremiah heard himself saying, as if from a great distance. "I'll get it back."

"Why even talk about that in a moment so happy?" said Luis more loudly. "You just get it back by tomorrow, when I deliver the stage, and we don't have no problem."

As a show of good faith, Luis punched Jeremiah in the left arm this time.

"But," he said, dropping his voice again, "I still need very bad the liquor."

Kimberly, who had overheard, smiled at Jeremiah, as if to say, "Any friend of yours, darling, functional alcoholic or no."

"I'll take care of that, too," Jeremiah said to Luis.

Hidden behind the Mexicans—the very last in line—came Bradley. He had been crying. Jeremiah could tell, because he was still crying. He raised his finger to beg a moment's pause, then took more like three to get the sobbing under sufficient control to say what he had to say.

"If you were already engaged, why did you just get engaged again?"

"We're not engaged," said Jeremiah. Agreement or not, in his condition he couldn't bring himself to lie a man in such obvious pain as Bradley—not even a Canadian.

"We *weren't* engaged," said Kimberly. At the same time she drove the point of her heel into Jeremiah's foot and ground it right and left. "We were fake engaged, but while we were fake engaged we fell in love, and now we're real engaged."

She looked at Jeremiah, who found that his attachment

to his right foot, both physical and emotional, apparently did allow him to lie by omission to a man in such obvious pain as Bradley.

Bradley looked at Jeremiah, then back at Kimberly, considering his options. The entire cafeteria held its breath. The Mexicans, who had been on their way out, turned around and watched. The ladies playing mahjong shushed each other and put down their tiles to see what would happen. Even Grubel, whom Jeremiah spotted frowning in the doorway, seemed to sense the drama of the moment.

"I give you my blessing," said Bradley finally, his voice breaking. "I can't wish you anything but happiness, Kimberly."

Kimberly's appreciation of this sentiment translated quite incidentally into a new spate of mashing and grinding Jeremiah's foot with her heel, which had become so painful that Jeremiah gasped and blinked to clear his eyes of tears—a touch that both Bradley and Kimberly seemed to appreciate for their own reasons.

"As for you," Bradley said, putting his arms akimbo and addressing Jeremiah, "you don't deserve her. But then again, neither do I. Neither does anyone. So take care of her. Treat her right. And don't worry, I'm not going to get violent with you. Not unless you hurt her, disappoint her, or make her sad in the slightest."

Perhaps inspired by the Mexican custom he had just witnessed repeatedly—or by some Canadian custom of which Jeremiah was ignorant, and would like to have remained so— Bradley tried to smack Jeremiah gently on the arm and instead succeeded in punching him quite hard in the stomach. Kimberly beamed and Jeremiah doubled over in pain, from which vantage point he had an excellent view of Katherine standing up from her table and walking out of the cafeteria as quickly as possible, passing right by Grubel, whose frown was now so deep it seemed that not even light could escape it.

Jeremiah's vision went black.

World Enough (And Time)

23

Old Jeremiah, New Jeremiah

Still Friday (2 days until arrival)

I T could not have been too many minutes later when the light returned to Jeremiah's eyes and mind. He was not dead—or at least, if he *was* dead, he hadn't made the cut at the pearly gates. Jeremiah based this deduction on the strong belief that heaven would involve much less CPR from Bradley Bonaventure than he was receiving right now—ideally at least 100 percent less. On the other hand, Jeremiah supposed that such an activity could make a fine warm-up exercise for new arrivals to the Other Place.

But then, as he struggled to detach himself from Bradley's medical attentions from one end, he saw Grubel straining to haul Bradley off Jeremiah from the other, and Jeremiah knew he could not be in hell. It was impossible to believe that in hell he and Grubel could be rowing in the same direction for the very first time.

As Jeremiah worked his way through these mental gymnastics, he was pleased to note a distinct uptick in his general mental faculties. The pain in his foot, stomach, and both arms seemed to cut through some of Aunt Mildred's organic hallucinatory fog, and the few minutes of involuntary rest he'd just gotten had done him some good. He felt strong enough to help Grubel detach Bradley from his face, and with their combined efforts they finally managed to free Jeremiah, who stood up unsteadily.

"I gave you CPR," Bradley said to Jeremiah.

Jeremiah plumbed his upbringing for the proper response

to tender at this moment. Perhaps if he had not been abandoned as a child and de facto raised by his uncle's lawyer he might have had the opportunity to learn the accepted social graces for this situation, but without such advantages he was unable to come up with anything other than, "You did."

"I could have let you die. I could have let him die," said Bradley, now to Kimberly. "But I saved his life. For you."

At first Kimberly could find no words—perhaps she was still too occupied working through the complicated emotions of having witnessed her newly minted fiancé lock lips with the man she loved.

"You did," she said finally, which led Jeremiah to wonder if perhaps her own uncle's lawyer had de facto raised her as well. "You saved the life of a man you had every reason to let die. For me."

Despite his relative medical inexperience, Jeremiah doubted he'd been in any danger of dying, and he had only passed out in the first place because of the emotional and physical pain these same two had put him through. But he resisted mentioning any such thing—first and foremost because he was a romantic at heart and didn't want to step on the happiness, however non-traditional, of this beautiful young couple. But running a close second, Jeremiah had never wanted anything in his life so sharply as he wanted to get away from this batshit craziness as fast as was humanly possible, and any conversation that might delay that departure was about as welcome as sandpaper on a sunburn. It appeared that Grubel was once again on Jeremiah's wavelength.

"I need to borrow him," Grubel said to Kimberly and Bradley, neither of whom could have cared less.

He grabbed Jeremiah by the right arm, just where the Mexicans had been punching, and led him roughly through the ring of onlookers and out into the hall. The pain cleared Jeremiah's head even further.

"Thank you," said Jeremiah when they were safely away.

"I like to think of myself as a patient man, Jeremiah," Grubel said, "but even I have lines you don't cross. I can't fully follow your sick game—playing with that poor girl's heart just to get to her boyfriend, manipulating him into kissing you in the name of 'saving your life'—it's sick, all of it, and I've had enough. I'm going to see to it that you spend the rest of your natural life in the service of Golden Worldlines, in a position where you can no longer harm innocent people—or Canadians."

Jeremiah's first impulse was to explain: to point out to Grubel the two ends of the stick, and which one he'd gotten ahold of, and how that was the wrong one to be holding. But that was the old, meek Jeremiah. As surely as if he had actually ingested some mystical substance, died, and been resuscitated by a shamanistic Bradley, Jeremiah had been reborn. The new Jeremiah had seen how well the old Jeremiah's tactics and techniques worked in these situations—and he had the bruises, psychic and physical, to show for it. The new Jeremiah—the one who was comfortable with naked displays of force—would handle this.

"All right," said the New Jeremiah, "but it's a shame that I'll have to tell Mrs. Mayflower I couldn't service her bandora."

"Why would you do that?" said Grubel.

"If I'm going down, you're going with me. I've got nothing to lose. What do you think the odds are that Mrs. Mayflower's displeasure will stop at me? Or maybe you could service the bandora yourself—you have a wealth of experience with ancient musical instruments to draw on, don't you?"

Grubel blinked several times through his lensless glasses. He frowned.

"There will come a day when you won't be able to hide behind Mrs. Mayflower and her bandora," the financial officer said. "On that day I will be waiting, Jeremiah. And on that day, I will nail you to the wall. Believe me."

"I believe you," said Jeremiah.

Arriving back at the office, Jeremiah saw that the odious law of averages had remained hard at work, leaving something to welcome him back from the worst lunch of his life—a little bolus of continued insanity in the form of Jack, Mrs. Abdurov, and both Chapins all milling around outside the door, at exquisite pains not to acknowledge each other. It was like watching four Baptists patronize the same liquor store.

"Hello everyone," said Jeremiah as he unlocked the door. "Why don't you come in one by one for—privacy. Who was first?"

Mrs. Chapin raised her hand, but Jack stepped in front of her.

"I'm going first," he said. "And I'm not taking a ticket."

Jeremiah looked at Mrs. Chapin, who looked unhappy. But she nodded, so he held the door as Jack walked through.

"What can I do for you, Jack?" asked Jeremiah as he settled behind the desk.

"It has been weeks since that fascist security officer burned my stash, Jeremiah. I can literally feel the System taking over my body at a cellular level. You've put me in an impossible situation. I tried appealing to our friendship, and you spit it in my face. I gave you antique money, and you've stolen it for nothing in return, even though I've *seen* you receive drugs since. So no more Mr. Nice Jack. I'm on to you. I've been watching you—that's right, two can play at the illegal surveillance game—and I keep running into that other guy who's been watching you. The doctor."

"Bradley?"

"Soupy face?" said Jack. "Angry all the time?"

"Bradley."

"I know he's your supplier. He steals the medical Marya Jana, and then you sell it to the passengers. I put it together, Jeremiah, and if you don't want me telling Grubel what you're up to, you're going to sell to me too. I would take no joy in ratting you out to the System, but you've left me no choice."

"If Bradley is my supplier, why is he so angry with me?"

"Maybe he's worried you're an informant," said Jack. "Maybe he thinks you're double-crossing him."

Old Jeremiah would have protested these accusations, but New Jeremiah sat instead in silence. If there was nothing to say, better to say nothing. Let the burden of continued conversation fall on Jack.

Before Jack could pick said burden up, Mrs. Chapin slipped into the office. She looked both agitated and somehow defeated—the fires of romance and revolution that had so recently roared in her now burned low.

"I'm sorry to interrupt," she said to Jack, "but my question is so urgent, and so quick, and I think I was actually first in line, so would you mind?" She addressed Jeremiah without waiting for Jack to answer. "I was just wondering if you had found a chance to give that *item* to the—"

Here she paused, apparently reluctant to use the word "Mexicans" in front of Jack, searching for something more circumspect and less likely to arouse suspicion.

"—cartel," she finished.

"Are you kidding me?" said Jack. "Her too?"

Not for a moment did Jeremiah consider telling Mrs. Chapin the truth—that his fiancée was currently in possession of the ruby necklace—but he did spend a few seconds weighing which lie to tell her. He could have said no, that he still had the necklace, but what good would that do? Better to soothe her anxiety by reporting circumstances not as they were but as they were *about* to be, once Jeremiah managed to get the necklace back and give it to Luis. Mrs. Chapin would never know the difference.

"Yes, Mrs. Chapin," he said. "I delivered the *item* to the *people* in question, just as you asked. They were very grateful."

"I need you to get it back for me right away," said Mrs. Chapin.

"I don't understand."

"Henry suspects—no, he *knows*. He said he saw one of the ship's doctors in the hall with the very same *item* that he gave me for our anniversary, and didn't I think that was a coincidence? But how could he have seen a doctor with that *item* if you gave it to the *cartel*?"

"He couldn't have," Jeremiah admitted.

When you were caught, New Jeremiah reflected, you were caught. He took a deep, confessional breath, but before he could release it in speech, Mrs. Chapin spoke.

"So he was just toying with me because he's upset that I gave away his anniversary gift. He knows I gave the *item* to you to give to the cartel."

"But how could he possibly know that?"

"What does it matter how? He knows. I need you to get that *item* back immediately," Mrs. Chapin said.

Jack had been doing his best to follow along, and looked like he might have been ready to pose a question or two about what some of these emphasized euphemisms signified, if Mrs. Abdurov had not barged into the office just at that moment.

"I guess we are not waiting turns now?" she said.

Jack leaned over and whispered into Mrs. Chapin's ear.

"I'm leaving now," he said. "I'm not sure how you're involved with Jeremiah and the cartel, but I would suggest you do the same—the pens have ears."

"Did you say the *pens*?" Mrs. Chapin asked.

"Shhhhh," said Jack, pointing at Mrs. Abdurov. "Come with me. Jeremiah, you have until tomorrow to get me that *item* I've requested. Otherwise, I'm filing a complaint."

"Yes," said Mrs. Chapin, taking inspiration from Jack's firm tone, "the same goes for me and my *item*. And if Henry asks you what I wanted to talk to you about, you tell him—"

Mrs. Chapin paused, considering the options.

"Nothing," she said.

Mrs. Abdurov sat down in Jack's place as he escorted Mrs. Chapin from the office.

"So," she said, "you have some *item* for me too? Lady Doctor is not here to save you now. What you have found in *Vor* Drinkwater's safe deposit box?"

Old Jeremiah would have argued Mr. Drinkwater's innocence—new Jeremiah didn't have time for such futile exercises.

"I haven't broken into it. It's not so easy to break into a safe deposit box, Mrs. Abdurov. That's why they call them *safe*."

Mrs. Abdurov studied Jeremiah's face, and he saw the slightest beginnings of respect in her eyes.

"Sometimes I think you have only beet for brain," she said, "but sometimes I wonder if might be onion. Tomorrow is last full day on the ship, so tomorrow all business must be concluded. I give you one extra day to bring me Marya Jana's murdered body, my little onion-brain, or I will be Highly Dissatisfied with you."

She leaned across the desk and pinched his cheek before she left.

"You need to eat something, yes?" she said. "Since you start work for a living you are get too thin, and no wonder, with what you bring for lunch. Also you take one of your own mints. You are breathing like Marya Jana—God rest her little soul."

"Is it safe to come in?" Mr. Chapin asked after the rest had all cleared out.

"As safe as it's going to be," said Jeremiah.

"Are you going to tell me what Sara wants from you?" said Mr. Chapin as he sat down.

"I haven't told *her* what *you* want from me," said Jeremiah. "Would you like me to?"

"No," Mr. Chapin said.

"That's settled, then. Coffee? Tea?"

"After the dinner I endured with Roof last night, I might need something a stronger. It was as if the man had spent the last two years secretly spoiling for someone, anyone, to mention iguanas."

"So he's interested in them?" said Jeremiah.

"Interested? *Obsessed.* And not just with the zoological aspects—though God knows he went plenty deep into those. Southern, northern, red-throated vs. ruby-throated vs. scarlet-throated, green and blue and albino and God knows what else. He has some very strong political ideas about iguanas, and he's not afraid to make them known at dinner."

"What kind of political ideas can you have about iguanas?"

"About whether or not they should be kept in captivity, for starters. Mr. Roof believes that they should not. He believes this very, very strongly. He practically attacked me when I suggested that the odd iguana in a zoo here and there might serve as a kind of ambassador for the whole genus, getting children interested in their welfare at an impressionable age and so on. Any news on your end?" Mr. Chapin asked.

"Apparently Mr. Roof suffers from allergies, acid reflux, sinus pressure, dry eyes, and mild insomnia. Oh, and he boosts his health with a ginkgo leaf supplement."

"If he's not on the cruise because he's sick," said Mr. Chapin, "then why *is* he here? No one comes on Golden Worldlines for recreation. What is his secret?"

"He keeps a safe deposit box," Jeremiah said.

Mr. Chapin perked up.

"How do you know that?"

"I saw the keycard in his room."

"Can you get inside that box?" Mr. Chapin asked. "I know I'm asking a lot, Jeremiah. But it's important. Can you do it?"

Jeremiah liked Henry Chapin—he liked both Chapins, even though one of them had put him up to breaking and entering and the other to fomenting a revolution, and recently—though under stress, it was true—threatened to express her lack of satisfaction to Grubel. They'd offered to pay for his ticket, after all, and as far as Jeremiah could tell, in earnest. Of all Jeremiah's clients, it was easiest to believe that Mr. Chapin had sound, moral, non-insane reasons for the insane things he was asking.

Then there was the matter of Mr. Roof and his strong political views on iguanas. It was just possible that Mr. Roof had somehow discovered Carolus's existence and captivity and chosen to liberate him, and that inside that safe deposit box Jeremiah would find some clue to his whereabouts—or some leverage that might inspire Mr. Roof to reveal them.

Even with all these pros, Old Jeremiah might have been on the fence. New Jeremiah, on the other hand, thought about things differently.

"What the hell," he said, "if I'm going to break into one safe deposit box, I might as well break into two."

"Two?" said Mr. Chapin. "Do I want to know?"

"I doubt it," said Jeremiah. "I wish I didn't know myself."

After a grateful Mr. Chapin left, Jeremiah continued his streak of New Jeremiah thinking. Rather than hang around and see what troublesome visitor might pop up next, he hung a sign on the office door that said "Closed (back tomorrow 9 a.m.)" and headed back to the suite. He needed to find Katherine.

Upon arriving there, however, Old Jeremiah enjoyed a bit of an "I told you so" moment, as a troublesome visitor was already waiting outside the door to the suite. She was in a state of extreme excitement, swaying back and forth with high color in her cheeks.

"Hello, Kimberly," said Jeremiah. Being the New Jeremiah, he did not attempt to hide his weariness at seeing her, but she—being the only Kimberly—did not seem to notice. She was too engaged in searching for words adequate to express the depths of what she was feeling, until the search ended in the perfect turn of phrase.

"He gave you CPR!" she said.

"What happened to 'discreet'?"

"That *was* discreet!"

"We were in the middle of the entire cafeteria—hundreds of people saw."

"When you said 'discreet' I thought you were worried about the *passengers*," said Kimberly.

This was so unassailably absurd that even the New Jeremiah could only try another tack.

"You also said you'd let me know the plan ahead of time."

"I asked you if you were ready!"

"Right before you kicked my legs out from under me."

"Don't exaggerate. If I had kicked your *legs* out from under you, you would have fallen over. I kicked *one* leg out, to help you kneel—you looked terrible, and I wasn't sure you were going to be able to handle it yourself."

"You also ground your heel into my foot. I can still feel it every time I take a step."

"Jeremiah," said Kimberly, "I came here to thank you, and you're ruining it. I got you the information about Mr. Roof's pills, like I promised, and you proposed to me in front of Bradley, like you promised. We both fulfilled our promises, in accordance with the Categorical Imperative. Now I'm about to go tell Bradley that I'm breaking off our engagement because I'm still in love with him and want to go back to Earth with him—I'm finally going to fly in the face of the Categorical Imperative and risk my heart, and I'd like to feel confident and centered when I do."

Jeremiah realized that, purely for reasons of self-preservation, he would like that too.

"All right," he said, "Good luck talking to Bradley."

Kimberly smiled.

"By the way," she said, "I've decided I'll name our second child Jeremiah. I don't like the name much, but after what you've done for me I *should* like it, so I *will*."

"What are you going to name the first?"

"Bradley, of course. What else would I name him?"

"What if it's a girl? For that matter, what if the second one is a girl?"

"Oh Jeremiah," she said, "you really are too silly."

"Speaking of silly," said the New Jeremiah, who was not above employing the occasional *non sequitur* when expedient, "can I get that necklace back?"

As if it had a mind of its own, Kimberly's hand went right to her neck.

"I thought it was a gift for our engagement," she said.

"More like a *prop*," said Jeremiah, "for our *fake* engagement—and an accidental one at that. It doesn't belong to me, and I need it back."

"Oh. All right, if you really need it back," Kimberly said.

She paused, in case Jeremiah had changed his mind, but then she changed hers.

"Would you mind terribly if I kept it for an hour or two longer? Just while I tell Bradley? I think it would be such a dramatic touch if I take it off as I tell him I'm breaking our engagement. It will show just how much I'm giving up to be with him. I really want this to go perfectly."

Jeremiah imagined his two possible futures—one in which Kimberly's reconciliation with Bradley went perfectly, and one in which it did not. There was no question which of those futures he would rather be living in. By this point he was supremely invested in this venture's success, and the loan of a necklace for a few more hours was a small price to improve the odds of such.

"All right," he said, "but bring it back the minute you're done."

The end of this sentence was muffled by Kimberly's grateful embrace and overwhelmed by her squealing.

After he had shipped Kimberly off to her joyous reunion with Bradley, Jeremiah sat alone in the suite, holding the bandora in his lap. He had picked it up for the ostensible purpose of gluing it once again, but as he had cradled the ugly little instrument in his hands, turning it over and inspecting the break, the bandora had taken on the aspect of a skull in a vanitas, and the function.

All his desperate hustle, it seemed to imply—the fevered meddling with PEDs and Relaxation Stations and iguanas and human hearts—was just as pointless as gluing together a musical instrument he knew would not hold. These were acts of farce taking place under a dark sentence that was neither in a hurry nor negotiable, and would eventually fall on him.

The Jeremiah of even a few days ago would have turned away from these thoughts, in some manner that was probably too cowardly even to earn the name "despair." But the new, reborn Jeremiah of today was almost grateful to the broken bandora—its *memento mori* was neither mocking nor sinister, but a tough truth told straight by a courageous friend.

What Jeremiah felt now wasn't even the can-do must-do will-do never-say-die of his inner grizzled veteran—which, admirable as it was in some sense, was also somehow so uniform and stoic as to be *detached* from life, completely on this side of the glass.

New Jeremiah felt poised at a precise understanding: that having the courage to live under a sentence of death was precisely the same as having the courage to live at all. Bandoras broke and could not be put back together, parents left and didn't come back. Bad decisions were made and tickets bought that cost you years with the man who was the closest thing to a father you would ever have. Real and permanent losses were always around the corner. Hunting for AWOL iguanas in the meantime, negotiating the return of priceless necklaces, working to improve the love lives of Canadian doctors and mimes—as well as one's own—all that was what life *was*.

And the realization seemed so fragile, so vulnerable to expression, so likely to transform into something trite or sloppy or sentimental, that he hardly wanted to move his head for fear of shaking it loose.

Hours later, after her dinner shift had finished, Katherine discovered Jeremiah still engaged in such meditations.

"I guess congratulations are in order," she said.

"That wasn't real," said Jeremiah. "I was doing her an idiotic favor, that's all."

"I don't care."

"You should."

"Oh really?" Katherine said. "Why?"

"Break into the safe deposit boxes of two passengers with me."

From Jeremiah's tone a listener who didn't speak English would have suspected that he had just asked Katherine to run away with him, and her reaction—all wide eyes and confusion—would have clinched it. In a sense, he supposed, he had.

"Jeremiah, this isn't going to work."

"Which 'this' do you mean, the safe deposit boxes or—"

"No, *this*. You and me."

"You can't deny there's a spark between us, Katherine."

"I'm not denying it—I'm saying it's not going to work."

"But you and The Specimen are going to work?"

"You don't think much of him, but—"

"I think a perfectly reasonable amount of him. He's a fit, competent, handsome man who takes his job very seriously. I just don't think he's right for *you*."

"Because you're such an expert on me?"

"Because he smothers you. Or he will. Whereas I—"

"Whereas you've proven perfectly comfortable putting me in harm's way."

"Now that you mention it," said Jeremiah, "yes. I mean, I'm not *pushing* you into harm's way, but if there's danger about and you're willing to take my hand and run through it with me, or vice versa, then what's wrong with that? In a dangerous world, isn't that what people do when they want to be together?"

"You do understand that if I decide not to be with John, I'm not somehow going to be with you by default? I've been fine on my own for quite some time."

"Then let's leave Battle out of this. Why *not* me? If there is a spark between us, why not give it some air and see what happens?"

As Katherine considered the question, her face took on the look of a debater who is struggling to condense a dump truck of overwhelming evidence into a single, pithy argument.

"You're not *serious*," she said.

"About you? I sure am."

"About *life*. You never dig in. You, I don't know, skate on top of it with jokes and irony. You break things, you lose things, misunderstanding follows you around like a cloud, because you secretly *like* it. You get involved in fake public engagements and then pretend you had no choice. I want a serious life."

"*Life* isn't serious!" Jeremiah said. "It's insane in every way, whether you want it to be or not. You know the only thing I actually *like* about being on this ship? It's so much harder to pretend that life isn't absurd out here. On Earth you have sunsets and the occasional forest and oceans and clouds and all those things that feel like promises of some deeper meaning. Here we're in the middle of the void, of millions and millions of miles of literal nothing, threading our way through nuclear explosions on a scale we can't even conceive, which could vaporize us before we knew what was happening—and by the way Golden Worldlines encourages but does not require period dress. That's not absurd? And Earth is no different—it's just a bigger ship taking a longer path to the same place."

"How can you be such a pessimist?" said Katherine.

"That's not a pessimistic view! What I'm talking about is beautiful, in its way. It's beyond us, it's absurd and also transcendent. It's adventure. It's *life*."

"Stop talking to me about *life*," said Katherine. "You've never even lived life."

Jeremiah felt his forehead smack into the glass so hard that he reached up involuntarily to touch it.

Katherine continued.

"Your biggest problem is that you might have lost a bunch of credit you never earned in the first place. You got to cruise on this ship without a care in the world for almost two years, and now maybe you'll have to work—work!—for two more to pay it off. There are people on this boat who have worked shit jobs their whole lives, and have no hope of anything better, and have never complained once. And half of your fellow passengers are dying, and all their riches can't help them. But everyone is supposed to feel sorry for *you?"*

They were both silent for a moment as they caught their breath.

"You're right," said Jeremiah quietly. "To a point. But that was the Old Jeremiah. I've changed."

"Since when have you changed?"

"Since today."

"Just like that?"

"How else do people change, Katherine?"

"Generally, Jeremiah, they don't. Good night."

Jeremiah sat and listened to the muffled music coming from Katherine's bedroom until it stopped some time later. Then he glued and clamped the bandora one last time and went to bed himself—but not to sleep.

24

Not Why But Why Now

few hours later, having slept not a wink, Jeremiah stood up from the sofa, turned on the light, and tapped on Katherine's door.

"Katherine," he said. Nothing. "Katherine. Katherine!"

He tried the door—it opened.

"Katherine!"

In the crack of light through the door he could see her now, or the shape of her at least, under the blanket, lying on her side, knees drawn up most of the way to her chest. The shape of Katherine stirred.

"Jeremiah? What time is it?"

She sat up, so splendid with her pajamas and tousled hair that he had to look away.

"It's really late. Or really early."

"I told you I don't want to talk about it anymore, Jeremiah."

"This isn't about us. I had an idea about Boyle—about how to figure out who killed him."

Katherine groaned and flopped back on the bed.

"Can't this wait until morning?"

"I can't sleep, I'm too excited."

"Go away, Jeremiah."

"Don't you want to know the idea?"

"Tomorrow morning? Maybe. Right now? No."

"All right," Jeremiah whispered, "I'll let you get back to sleep." He closed the door gently, turned the light off again, and went back to toss and turn on the sofa.

He had been tossing and turning for some five minutes when Katherine's door opened and she emerged. She switched on the light.

"You're a real jerk, you know that?" she said, rubbing her eyes. "What's this big idea?"

"We've been trying to figure out *why* someone would want to kill Boyle," said Jeremiah, sitting up as she sat down next to him on the sofa, "and we got nowhere. But what if we asked why *now*? Why just over a week from the end of a two-year cruise? If you're killing him because you hated him, why wouldn't you do it earlier?"

"All right, why *do* you kill him with a week to go?" said Katherine.

"Because you weren't *sure* you wanted to kill him until you got some crucial piece of information from Earth."

"And the Einstein IV—"

"Came into communication with Earth just before he died. So maybe if we could sneak a peek at the passenger's waves from the day or two before Boyle was killed, we could—why are you standing up?"

"Get dressed," said Katherine. "We're going to the IT department."

"It's 2:30 in the morning."

"I hope Sean's not on his lunch break."

They dressed and departed, though Jeremiah doubled back quickly to fetch something—just in case.

Sean was not on his lunch break, but he was about to be, and did not seem eager to stick around the IT office chatting with Jeremiah and Katherine one minute longer than he absolutely had to—a reluctance that Jeremiah could understand. If a spaceship could be said to have a basement, the IT office was in the E4's sub-sub-basement—a designation that had nothing to do with the strict vertical location of the office (after the twisty maze of passages down which Katherine had led him, Jeremiah had no idea how many metric tons of ship lay above the IT office as opposed to below it), and everything to do with the feeling that here in these cracked hallways with their terrible lights and damp atmosphere, Morlocks toiled away at tasks that simply could not have been understood by the beautiful people above.

Sean himself was about Jeremiah's age, with shoulder length black hair, a jutting jaw, and a sharp upper lip that resembled a turtle's. His big arms—big with both muscle and fat—stretched the cuffs of his black t-shirt, the chest of which was emblazoned with a red maple leaf. Above the leaf letters of red spelled out "Canadians count, too." Another set of letters clarified below "(I'm not Canadian)."

"I wanted to ask you a favor," Katherine said.

"No shit," said Sean. "A favor? Wow. Never crossed my mind. But after all you've done for me, stomping on my heart, it's the least I can do. Leave whatever it is you want fixed and I'll take a look when I get back from lunch."

"It's not that kind of favor. This is my friend Jeremiah—"

Jeremiah smiled and offered his hand, which Sean refused.

"—who was hoping to get access to some waves."

Sean sighed.

"Here," he said, handing Jeremiah a pad of paper and pen. "Write down when you deleted them, and anything else you can remember, and I'll take a look when I get back from lunch."

"Oh," Jeremiah said, "I didn't delete anything—I was just hoping to see all the waves that came in for everyone, from the time we re-established contact until about five days ago. Maybe that makes it easier?"

"That makes it *much* easier."

"Great," said Jeremiah.

"Yeah, yeah. Instead of running undelete on a couple files that you mistakenly trashed, I just have to violate our passengers' privacy *en masse*—or wait," Sean said, "did you want employee waves too?"

"That would be great."

"All right, so the privacy of literally everyone on the entire ship—except yours, of course—and risk my job and maybe legal repercussions? That's a ton easier, because I can tell you to go fuck yourself and feel really, really good about it."

"Sean," began Katherine, but Jeremiah stopped her with an *I've got this* gesture.

"Honestly, I thought you might feel that way," Jeremiah said. "So what if we just snuck a quick peek at the metadata?"

Sean stared at Jeremiah, saying nothing. Jeremiah had read once that, in a silent standoff like this, the person who spoke first always lost the negotiation. So he resolved to remain silent, and was as good as his resolve even as the tension built up over the next fifteen seconds.

"Do you even know what metadata is?" asked Sean.

"Honestly?" said Jeremiah. "No."

It seemed unfair that, even though Sean had broken the silence, Jeremiah had lost the negotiation. He was tempted to write a wave of complaint to the author of the book in question. Meanwhile he tried another tack.

"What if I told you it was a matter of security?"

"I'd say to get Battle's steroided ass down here to sign off on it and I'll show you all the waves you want."

Sean stood up, pushed his sleeves a bit further up his biceps, and started for the door.

"What if I told you," Jeremiah said, stepping in to block Sean from leaving, "that I could make it worth your while?" He pulled the stack of antique bills that Jack had given him out of his pocket.

"Jeremiah," said Katherine, "what are you doing? Is that what you went back to the room to get?"

"That's *money*," Sean said. "Like, antique money."

"That's exactly what I said to the guy who gave it to me. And you know what he said?"

"Go fuck yourself?"

"I think you're imagining this backwards. In the scenario I'm describing, you would be him, and I would be you."

"So?" said Sean.

"So why would he tell me to go fuck myself after *he* gave *me* the money? It doesn't make any sense."

"Katherine," Sean said, "get this guy out of here, please?"

"I'm not sure that's such a bad idea, Jeremiah," Katherine said.

"What the guy who gave it to me said," continued Jeremiah, "was this: 'There's a lot of credit in money.' "

There was no denying that Sean looked marginally more interested.

"You take this money back to Earth, find yourself an antique store, and you're sitting on a nice little payday."

"Like how much?" said Sean.

"Ten, fifteen thousand credits," Jeremiah said. "All for a
little metadata."

"Would you please stop saying that word?"

"Why don't you take this money, bring the waves up on
your screen here, and go take a leisurely lunch? I promise
you'll never hear the 'm' word from my mouth again."

Sean seemed to be doing some sort of mental arithmetic.

"Ten thousand credits doesn't buy you a lunch hour with
full messages," he said. "It buys you five minutes with subjects and addresses while I go to the bathroom."

"That's robbery," said Jeremiah. "That's a deal I
wouldn't offer to a—"

He stopped, remembering Sean's shirt.

"—no one."

"Take it or leave it," said Sean.

Katherine leaned in towards Jeremiah.

"Is that the money you told me about?" she whispered in
his ear. "That Jack gave you for drugs?"

Jeremiah nodded.

"Then should you really be spending it, seeing as you're
not going to be giving Jack any drugs?"

"I know what I'm doing," Jeremiah lied. "Done," he said
to Sean, and handed over the bills.

"Which days were you looking for again?"

Sean sat down at the desk and began typing.

"Anything from before five days ago should do it."

Sean tapped away, paused, and struck the enter key extra
hard. A wall of text appeared on the screen built into his desk.

"Hit up and down to scroll," Sean said. "Don't touch anything else because I'm not going to fix it for you. You have
five minutes, starting the moment I close the door. Pleasure
doing business with you. Katherine, glad to see you're still
picking your friends so carefully."

As he left the office, Jeremiah and Katherine scrambled to
the other side of the desk. Katherine sat down and took the
controls.

"That's a lot of words," said Jeremiah.

"Shut up and look for anything suspicious. I'll scroll."

Reading the subjects and recipients reminded Jeremiah of browsing through his PED, back in the days when it was still functional, hopelessly hoping for something to watch and finding only drivel. He forced himself to focus, and managed to absorb the first few lines fully.

To: Alexander Moakley
Subject: Welcome back!

To: Esther Idlewhile
Subject: Your grandson (all grown up!!!)

To: Cornelius Werther
Subject: Pictures from Beth's 65th Birthday

Quickly they all started to blend together.

Your account ending in 5432 is overdue.

Don't miss this special price--one day only!

You've waited 20 years for a deal like this!

Your account ending in 5432 is seriously overdue.

Then suddenly, amidst all the spam and graduation photos of grandchildren, something caught Jeremiah's attention.
"Wait," he said. "Scroll back one."
Katherine did.
"Damn," said Jeremiah. "Double damn."
"What is it?"
"To: Henry Chapin," Jeremiah read aloud. "Subject: Not the medical news I was hoping to give you."
"That means they didn't cure whatever he has," said Katherine, "right?"
"That's certainly how I take it. He must have already read this—he already knows."
"That's sad, but we don't have much time. You have to keep reading."

260

Jeremiah tried his best to concentrate on the river of text.
"Keep scrolling," he said.
"That's the end," said Katherine.
"There's nothing here."
"You want to look again?"
Before Jeremiah could answer, Sean opened the door a crack. He stayed in the hall.
"Time's up," he said.
"Should we ask for a few more minutes?" Katherine whispered to Jeremiah.
"I can hear you," said Sean. "And no, you shouldn't."
Jeremiah shrugged.
"I don't think it would have made a difference anyway," he said. "I think this was a blind alley."
"This is a discussion you could have in the hall," Sean said.
Katherine stood up.
"I'm not going to say thank you to Sean," she whispered to Jeremiah.
"I said I can hear you, Katherine," said Sean.
"I know," she whispered to Jeremiah again.

As Katherine and Jeremiah walked back to the suite, it seemed that neither could rally their ebbing adrenaline enough even to comment on their disappointment.
"Is it just me, or are the days getting longer?" Jeremiah asked when they arrived. "This has been the longest day of my entire life."
"I'm going to bed," said Katherine. "If I can fall asleep right away I can still get two hours of sleep."
She opened the door to her bedroom and turned around.
"I didn't mean that to sound pissy," she said. "Just factual. I'm sorry we didn't find anything. And I'm sorry about Mr. Chapin. And I'm sorry about that conversation we had before we went to sleep the first time tonight, too."
"You mean that you're sorry, but it doesn't change anything? Or that you're sorry, and maybe we can have a better conversation about that?"
Katherine sighed.

"I honestly don't know," she said. "I can't think straight right now. Maybe we can chat in the morning."

"Good night, then," said Jeremiah. "Oh, damn," he added, as she turned again to go to sleep, "wait—can I ask you one more favor?"

Katherine did not look pleased.

"Tonight, or ever?" she said.

"That depends on you more than me."

"What's the favor, Jeremiah?"

"I promised Luis I'd get him some lacquer from the main storeroom."

"I'm not going to the storeroom. I'm going to sleep."

"Could you at least give me the code, then?"

"I'm not even supposed to have the code myself."

"But you *do* have it," Jeremiah pointed out.

"Good night, Jeremiah."

Katherine turned around with great purpose, as though this time nothing in the world could stop her from going to bed. Then she stopped.

"The doorbell?" she said. "At four in the morning?"

"Should I get it or you?"

"You've been the harbinger of all the small-hour madness so far."

Upon opening the door, Jeremiah became aware of three facts, in rapid succession.

One: as soon as the door had slid open sufficiently to permit human entrance, a human had sprung through like a crush of water thrilled finally to be past some pesky bulkhead.

Two: that same human had flung arms around Jeremiah's neck and was kissing him energetically on the lips.

Three: the human in question was Dr. Kimberly Merrifield.

After he had achieved a critical amount of detachment and disentangling, Jeremiah was able to ask her what was going on.

"Oh, Jeremiah, you knew it since the beginning," she said. "I'm sorry it took me so long to catch up. Can you ever forgive me?"

"To catch up to what, exactly?" said Jeremiah.

"Before I could tell Bradley that I was breaking off our engagement, he launched into all the reasons you were totally wrong for me. So of course I had to start explaining all the reasons you were so *right*. At first I was having trouble thinking of any, but then I found some, and some more, and then even more. I was very persuasive—so persuasive that I started persuading *myself*! I should be marrying *you*!"

"But you're not in love with me," said Jeremiah.

"But I *should* be, so I *will*. It's the Categorical Imperative, Jeremiah, and I am a creature of reason."

"I see," said Jeremiah, "but—how do I put this?—*I am not.*"

"That's why we're perfect for each other," Kimberly said. "Yin and yang. Me, the soul of reason. You, a heart of passion. Oh, the sacrifices you've made, Jeremiah! The sacrifices! But now I've seen the light: now our engagement can be real. Yes, Jeremiah, I *will* marry you."

"Kimberly, I don't think this is a good idea."

"Then let me persuade you," she said. "As I mentioned, I can be very persuasive."

She leaned in for a kiss, but stopped short.

"Maybe we should get rid of your roommate, though?" she said.

Jeremiah turned in agony to the forgotten Katherine, who had been standing in her bedroom doorway, akimbo, observing this exchange.

"Katherine," he said, "this is *exactly* what it looks like—"

"The code to the storeroom is 3306," she said. Then she stepped into her room and closed the door behind her.

"Damn it, Kimberly," said Jeremiah. "Do you know what you've just done?"

"That's hardly a way to talk your fiancée," Kimberly said, leaning towards him again. "Now where were we?"

"I was just about to point out that I didn't actually propose to you, and that we're not actually engaged."

"Oh really? Then what's this?"

Kimberly pointed to the ring on her finger.

"That's the ring you put in my hand after you kicked my leg out from under me so I could pretend to propose to you," said Jeremiah.

She laughed.

"Is that what you're worried about, silly? That you couldn't afford a ring? I shouldn't care about credit—I should love you just as you are. So I *will*."

"But the problem, Kimberly, is that—while I'm sure you're a nice enough young woman when you're not causing me trouble—I don't love *you*."

"What man would give a gift like this—" Kimberly reached up to touch the necklace. "—to a woman he didn't love?"

"As we've discussed, I dropped it accidentally, and I need it back by tonight. Which is now technically last night."

"Oh, Jeremiah, I understand. You must be in such pain. You feel rejected, so you lash out. But like your favorite philosopher Nietzsche, I am saying *yes*."

She leaned in again to kiss him, but Jeremiah prevented her. He was beginning to feel that arguing with Kimberly was like fighting the ocean—he was likely to exhaust himself and drown before his efforts yielded the slightest fruit. And in the meantime, Katherine was in her room feeling confirmed in all sorts of notions that he didn't want confirmed. So he tried a different approach.

"Kimberly," he said, "it's been a really, really long day, and I need some time and space to process this big—whatever this is. And some sleep. Can we talk tomorrow? I mean, later today?"

"All right," Kimberly said. "You get some sleep. But before I go, here's something to make sure you dream about me."

She went in again for the kiss, but Jeremiah turned deftly so that it landed on his cheek. Kimberly laughed.

"You're so old-fashioned, Jeremiah. I don't really like old-fashioned. But I should—so I *will*. See you tomorrow, lover. Which is today!"

After Kimberly was safely away, Jeremiah tried knocking at Katherine's door.

"Katherine?" he said. "I know you're not asleep. Would you let me explain?"

But no response was forthcoming, and eventually Jeremiah gave up. It was almost five o'clock in the morning. Jeremiah was as tired as he could remember ever having been in his life, and he would have liked nothing better than to collapse on the sofa. But if he was going to get the lacquer for Luis before the talent show, it was now or never.

As he walked through the dim, empty halls to the storeroom, Jeremiah found that it was not Katherine dominating his thoughts, but Henry Chapin. In the exhaustion and madness since the IT office, there had not been time to absorb the evidence of Chapin's misfortune that he and Katherine had found amid the waves.

Jeremiah had known Chapin was sick—his illness had been one of the hardest to hide or politely ignore, what with the coughing fits and frequent visits to the medical wing—but terminal illness was such a large part of day-to-day life on the E4 that it bled into the background. Jeremiah knew intellectually that most of the passengers who had booked this passage in the hopes that medicine would catch up with their diseases would end up disappointed. The trip was a lottery ticket, and most lottery tickets weren't winners. But with the recent drama of his own life, Jeremiah had forgotten that these days the ticket holders would learn the disposition of their tickets—and of all the people that Jeremiah would most have hoped to draw a winner, Henry Chapin topped the list.

Jeremiah entered the combination that Katherine had given him—3306—into the keypad, and stepped back as the storeroom doors performed their impressive opening ceremony. He was about to step through them when he noticed something strange: the lights inside were already on. He stepped inside quietly before the doors closed.

Whoever was already inside the storeroom had left their cloak and dagger at home. Jeremiah followed the banging and scratching noises along the same path Katherine had led him on his previous visit, and the trail ended in the very same aisle: the one that housed the wood glue, the glue for wood, and the cans of pesticide—one of which cans someone was returning to the shelf at this very moment.

"Reynolds," Jeremiah said.

He could not have reproduced, vocally or in writing, the sound that Alfred Reynolds made in response. Bolstered in the bottom registers by a kind of terrified bellowing, it showcased some high screaming accents as well, and filled out the middle range with a gurgle that would have made a hippopotamus expiring of multiple arrow wounds proud. It was the sound of a heart attack missing a man's heart by a few inches.

"Jeremiah, you nearly gave me a heart attack," Reynolds confirmed.

There followed a brief investigation into Reynold's level of certainty that the heart attack had, in fact, missed him, and was not doubling back for another go.

"What are you doing here?" Reynolds asked.

"Why were you putting back that pesticide?" countered Jeremiah.

"I wasn't putting back any pesticide," Reynolds said. He said it too quickly, with too offended an air, and the implication hung uncomfortably in the space between him and Jeremiah.

"I came to get some lacquer," said Jeremiah. "We're making a stage for the talent show."

"Lacquer is two aisles over. I'll show you."

"Don't worry," said Jeremiah, "I'm sure I can find it myself."

"I hear great things about the work you've been doing in the office, Jeremiah. It's a load off my mind to know that everything is well in hand there. I'll put in a good word for you with Grubel. Well, I'm off."

He made as if to offer Jeremiah his hand, then stopped and began to wipe it off on his pants before catching himself and darting away, refusing to meet Jeremiah's eyes the whole time.

Back in the suite, Jeremiah lay sleepless on the couch with his hands behind his head, staring up at the featureless ceiling. Jeremiah had no *proof* that Reynolds was the murderer, beyond circumstantial evidence: access to the keycard encoder, being one of the first on the crime scene in his role as General Clerical, his unexplained absences from the office, the can of pesticide, and above all his guilty manner upon being discovered returning it. But that was exactly the point: now that Jeremiah finally had a suspect to investigate, investigation was impossible, because it would break Katherine's heart, and that—the demands of justice and threat of indentured servitude and misery be damned—Jeremiah simply refused to do.

The distant sentence of doom had suddenly grown proximate, and New Jeremiah's resolution to revel in absurd action did not translate well to having his hands tied by love. So Old Jeremiah and New Jeremiah lay together, reunified, rehearsing the multitude of insoluble problems and watching the ceiling as the hands of the clock inched inevitably towards the start of the big day.

World Enough (And Time)

25

The Way of the Samurai

Saturday (1 day until arrival)

ONE evening near the beginning of the cruise, back when it had been easier to maintain the fiction that all the passengers were aboard merely for pleasure, a Golden Worldlines representative had trotted one of the ship's engineers into the dining room and encouraged the guests to ask him any and every question they might have about the subtlest technological workings of the Einstein IV.

After a series of questions about the technology on the E4 that was so advanced as to border on magic—the Quantum Caterpillar Drive, the Inertial Dampers, and so on—Mr. Drinkwater had asked about something much more pedestrian. How did the engineers of the E4 handle the problem of air? Where did they keep the oxygen tanks, how much space did they take up, how could they possibly hold enough for a trip of this length? The engineer had tried not to laugh at Mr. Drinkwater's question as he had explained, at great length and in excruciating detail, how the carbon scrubbers and oxygen reclamators worked and (shudder) sometimes didn't work. Of all the technical facts and figures the engineer had presented, only one had stuck with Jeremiah: that on average each and every breath of air taken across the entire Einstein IV was effectively recycled every 6.2 hours.

Which, Jeremiah reckoned with a great deal of mental erasure and rework, meant that by now, the morning of the last full day of their 2/20 cruise, the atmosphere of the ship

269

had been reborn somewhere north of 2,800 times, and it had never felt quite like it did on the morning of the First Ever—as far as we know—Golden Worldlines Passenger Talent Show.

It was as if that dour engineer had poured something into the scrubbers and reclamators—some substance that charged and crackled, transforming even the quiet of empty rooms and halls into something eager and expectant, like an airport terminal in the small hours leading up to a holiday crush.

Each of the souls on board felt the charge. Even after her late night, Katherine had woken up early—Jeremiah had heard her pacing in her bedroom when he awoke. He'd tried knocking, but she hadn't answered, so he'd showered and left. The chatter and clatter from the food service and laundry rooms had reached a Detroit-like pitch as Jeremiah walked by them. He'd passed Mr. Drinkwater in one of the guest hallways, who had given him a very passable mime of a batter knocking dirt off his shoes and stepping up to plate, followed by a hearty thumbs up. Notorious late risers who in two years had not been witnessed in polite company before eleven a.m. were already out and about, wandering the ship with slightly dazed expressions, as if expecting or recovering from some cataclysm.

Jeremiah himself had felt the despair of last night dwindle, replaced by a sense of purpose so hard and grim that he was reminded of the passage Appleton had always loved to quote from the *Hagakure*, the Book of the Samurai:

When one has made a decision to kill a person, even if it will be very difficult to succeed by advancing straight ahead, it will not do to think about doing it in a long, roundabout way. The Way of the Samurai is one of immediacy, and it is best to dash in headlong.

True, Jeremiah was not going to kill anyone—or injure them grievously—or even in the slightest, which blunted his samurai swagger just a bit. But he *was* going to break into two safe deposit boxes, dashing in headlong, with complete immediacy.

Which was to say, as soon as he had delivered the lacquer to Luis.

"But might not dry by tonight," Luis said when Jeremiah offered him the can of lacquer in the cafeteria. "Maybe there is no enough time."

"When one has made a decision to lacquer a stage," said Jeremiah in response, imagining as best he could what the *Hagakure* would have to say about this topic, "even if it might not be dry by that evening, it will not do to leave it unlacquered. The Way of the Samurai is one of—constancy to purpose, and it is best to—to lacquer everything that one has decided to lacquer. Headlong. And then—I don't know—dry it with hair dryers or something."

Jeremiah would have been the first to admit that it was not his best work, but somehow the original sentiment was so powerful that it survived these multiple cultural, linguistic, and situational transplantations. Luis stood up straight, puffed up his chest with pride, and accepted the can of lacquer with an air of great purpose.

"I gonna liquor the hell out of that son a bitch," he said.

Which restored whatever samurai swagger Jeremiah might have lost, and then some.

The feeling of bold immediacy stayed with Jeremiah as he walked quickly but calmly to Mr. Drinkwater's cabin and then to Mr. Roof's, not even pausing to ensure they weren't inside (luckily they were not) before using the keycards he had encoded to open their doors and retrieve the golden keycards for their safe deposit boxes.

Then, just as quickly and just as calmly, he made his way to the Einstein IV's bank, arriving right as it opened at nine. Russell Upton was already sitting at the desk, reading a comic on his PED, which he put away hurriedly as Jeremiah approached. Jeremiah—who had visited the bank only once before, to drop off his passport and a copy of Uncle Leo's (now tragically outdated) will—imagined that Upton didn't get as much foot traffic as, say, the Guest Services desk.

"Hello," Russell Upton said, and Jeremiah could tell that he was trying to figure out whether to address him as Mr. Brown or as Jeremiah. As a result he did not address him at all.

"Hello, Russell," said Jeremiah. "I'm here to access to my safe deposit box."

"But you're not a passenger anymore."

"But I still have a safe deposit box."

Russell's brow furrowed with the effort of reconciling these deep and terrifying contradictions—that only passengers had a safe deposit box, that Jeremiah was not a passenger, and that Jeremiah had a safe deposit box. It was like a syllogism copied from a blackboard in Wonderland.

"Maybe I should call Mr. Grubel to make sure," he said.

Many powerful personalities in the waves Jeremiah had seen—secret agents, dictators, and so on—always went about claiming that they "needed" things from other people, when in fact they only *wanted* them. In general this approach seemed to work pretty well for them, and having turned over his new, forceful leaf, Jeremiah thought he would give it a try himself.

"I need access to my safe deposit box," Jeremiah said. "And I need you to give it to me."

He could see the word working its magic: Russell's brow unfurled bit by bit, and he looked almost relieved to have the matter taken out of his hands. If it was a question of *need*, after all.

"All right," said Russell Upton. He stood up and took his master keycard from under the desk. "Let's go."

"No," Jeremiah said. "I need you to give me your keycard and I'll go in alone."

"But I can't do that," Russell Upton said. "I'm required to enter the vault with guests and—other people."

"But I need you to," said Jeremiah, in case he hadn't been clear on that point.

"But I *can't.*"

They had reached the part of the conversation where a plan might have been useful. But Jeremiah didn't have a plan and he wasn't going to sully the purity of his headlong intentions by making one now, so once again he let himself go and summoned the spirit of improvisation and inspiration.

"That's a shame," he said, looking forward himself to discovering why. "Your non-cooperation will come as a great disappointment to—"

"To?" said Russell Upton after a moment of silence. It was a good question.

"To the person who sent me here," said Jeremiah. He was

worried that the spirit of improvisation and inspiration might have hit a snarl of traffic somewhere on the astral plane.

"Which was?"

Russell was putting on a greater display of inquisitive prowess than Jeremiah would have expected from a man who had apparently been reading comics for the past two years. They must have been detective comics.

"Mrs. Mayflower," said Jeremiah.

Upton blanched.

"Did you say Mrs.—"

He paused to swallow.

"Mayflower," said Jeremiah, notching the assist. "She was very particular that I enter the vault alone."

"But why does Mrs. Mayflower care if you're alone when you access your *own* safe deposit box?"

Tenacious even in the face of raw terror—Jeremiah had to respect that. Maybe those were not detective, but samurai comics he had been reading. Or samurai detective comics, if those were a thing. But now the inspiration was flowing as if Jeremiah had just stepped forward to take a solo.

"That was a smokescreen," said Jeremiah. "A mere ruse. I should have known it wouldn't work with a man as astute as yourself, but I had to try. I'm here on Mrs. Mayflower's behalf, to access her safe deposit box for her, and she insisted that I do so alone."

Upton's face still showed some activity going on behind it—activity that Jeremiah was keen to stop as soon as possible.

"Listen," he said, leaning in to speak to the older man conspiratorially, "I know what it's like to man a desk. I know the feeling of responsibility it gives you—of honor, even. Mrs. Mayflower or no Mrs. Mayflower, I can't ask you to sit here while I go into the vault."

"Isn't that exactly what you were doing?"

"Why don't you take a walk instead? Go get a cup of coffee. Five minutes. Forget to lock the drawer that holds the master keycard. I'll be gone by the time you come back. If anyone ever asks, you can say—with perfect honesty—that you've never seen anyone enter the vault without you."

"I see," Upton said.

The gears were still turning, but now instead of the gears

of a clock counting down to Jeremiah's sure defeat, they were the spinning gears of a slot machine—a machine on which Jeremiah might still hit the jackpot. Fear of Mrs. Mayflower and the opposing reluctance to abandon his post whirled by in Upton's eyes like so many sevens and cherries, until all at once the spinning stopped.

"I feel like a coffee," said Upton, standing up. "I won't be but a few minutes."

The air inside the vault was cold and deathly still, like an airlock about to open. The architect of the E4's bank had continued the useless but beautiful theme from the lobby, so that even in this space where passengers ventured but once or twice in their whole 2/20 experience, marble floors gleamed and the safe deposit boxes rose in stacks of brushed steel on every available wall, like the skyline of a futuristic city whose population had reached a point of extreme horizontal saturation. Jeremiah imagined that New Tokyo, which had already gleamed and teemed like a sci-fi set 20 years ago, might look like this by now.

Jeremiah did not put it past Upton to take his five-minute coffee break with a stopwatch, so he went right to work, starting with Mr. Drinkwater's safe deposit box. Jeremiah inserted the card he had stolen from Mr. Drinkwater's room and the one he had lifted from Upton's desk into their respective slots. He was rewarded with a click from the locking mechanism deep inside the box. Jeremiah felt his samurai-like singleness of purpose waver ever so slightly, but he could imagine that even a samurai who'd had to walk such a fine moral line might have tugged fretfully at the neck of his kimono once or twice before looking inside. Jeremiah took a deep breath and slid Mr. Drinkwater's safe deposit box from its drawer.

Inside he found photos—old-style black and white portraits, printed on actual paper—two stacks of them, as diverse in angle and setting as they were singular in subject: for every photo captured some mood, expression, or moment in the life of Lyuba Abdurov.

Here she was narrowing her eyes in suspicion and gazing off somewhere to the left of the camera. In another, her glare burned twin holes through the fourth wall, as if she suspected that Mr. Drinkwater was recording the moment and she did not like the fact. Here she seemed to be ensuring that, if her chicken Kiev was not already dead, it would not survive the assault she was mounting with knife and fork. There she simply looked angry. Jeremiah spread the photos out in as wide a fan as the box had space for and, using the camera pen Mrs. Abdurov had given him, snapped some pictures of these pictures. Then he replaced the box to its drawer and moved on to Roof's.

As Jeremiah took down Roof's safe deposit box, it felt surprisingly light, which turned out to be because—as befitted the sanctum sanctorum of a man of the deepest mystery— it was empty. Jeremiah shook it upside down a few times to convince himself, then replaced the box and made himself scarce before Upton's coffee mug could have been even half empty.

And indeed, Upton was nowhere to be seen when Jeremiah came out of the vault—which success would have excited Jeremiah more, if Jack and Mr. Grubel had not taken his place in the meantime. It seemed that the former had caught the latter by chance in the hallway and had seized the opportunity to pull the latter into the bank lobby in order to get some minor complaints off the former's chest (which chest Jeremiah could not see, as Jack had his back to the vault).

"Illegal surveillance," Jack was saying. "Pens that record conversations for which permission to record has been not just *withheld* but explicitly *revoked*. Informants masquerading as passengers. Informants masquerading as crew. Entrapment, conspiracy, unlawful interrogation. We're not talking your run-of-the-mill price gouging or false advertising here— I'm going to bring a civil rights suit against this company—a whole *suite* of civil rights suits—precedent-setting cases that will go all the way to the Supreme Court. I will take this whole System down."

At that moment Grubel looked over Jack's shoulder and caught sight of Jeremiah. Grubel looked relieved to see him— which said a lot about how much he must have been enjoying his chat with Jack—and for a moment Jeremiah thought he might escape any awkward lines of questioning about, for example, what he had been doing alone in the vault, or where Upton was.

"Jeremiah?" said Grubel. "What have you been doing alone in the vault? Where's Upton?"

It was an awkward line of questioning. Fortunately Jeremiah's solo was not quite over.

"Ask Jack," said Jeremiah.

Grubel did so, specifically by asking "Jack?" in a rising, expectant tone.

Jack, who had frozen stock still at the sound of Jeremiah's voice, turned around, trembling, to face his accuser. He had the look of a plumber suddenly consulted on foreign policy by heads of state.

"You asked me to retrieve that item for you from your safe deposit box?" Jeremiah said over Jack's hem and haw. "That *green* item? You insisted that I go alone, over my strenuous objections? You said your satisfaction as a passenger on this ship absolutely depended on it?"

Jeremiah started with only subtle question marks at the ends of these statements, but the wild confusion in Jack's eyes prompted him to dial up the interrogative intensity, until finally Grubel began to look a bit suspicious and Jeremiah thought the game might be up.

"I did," said Jack, cottoning on just in time. "That's exactly what I said. Depended on it—depended on it *absolutely*. Did you have any problems finding the, uh, *item*?"

"None whatsoever."

"So you will be *delivering* the item to me?"

"Of course," Jeremiah said. He pulled the remaining pellets of Aunt Mildred's Organic Iguana Treats from his pocket and handed them over, not concealing the action at all, as if this ostensible drug deal were the most wholesome and natural service any staff could possibly render any guest on the Einstein IV—a transaction as wholesome and natural as Aunt Mildred's treats themselves.

"What are those?" said Grubel to Jeremiah.

"Iguana treats," Jeremiah answered. Honesty had never seemed a better policy. "Strong ones," he warned Jack.

"What?" Grubel said.

"None of your business," said Jack, "unless you want to keep talking about that invasion of privacy suit?"

276

Grubel did not.

"You could learn a thing or two from this young man," Jack said to Grubel. "About customer service—and about respecting privacy—and about doing the right thing in the end. About how the Individual must always come before the System. Now, if you'll excuse me, I just remembered I have something important to take care of."

"What were those?" Grubel asked Jeremiah after Jack had left.

"What did they look like?"

"Drugs."

"They were iguana treats."

"Never mind," said Grubel, "we have much bigger fish to fry. I was just on my way to the Guest Services Office to talk to you when Jack buttonholed me. Come to my office."

On the way they passed Upton returning from his coffee.

"Upton," said Grubel, "were you involved with this?"

Upton gave Jeremiah the kind of look that the latter imagined one astronaut gives another when a delicate space maneuver that the latter has insisted on has just gone awry, in order to say without words "You the latter have just killed both of us, so let me use the last few seconds of my life to make good and sure that you the latter die knowing that I, the former, blame you for everything."

"I just went for a coffee," Upton said. "I mean, I didn't even—"

"Anyway," said Grubel, "if you were: good work."

Jeremiah left Upton with the wink of one astronaut saying to another "And *that*, my dear former, is why *I* the latter sit in the pilot chair of this little death trap."

"You know, Jeremiah," said Grubel, when they were seated in his office, "I don't know what to make of you. At first I was sure you'd self-destruct within a day or two. Then I thought 'He seems to be lucky, he might last a week.' Then all of a sudden I began to overhear chatter about how helpful you've been with the PEDs and Relaxation Stations. Then you're repairing a musical instrument for Mrs. Mayflower. And now—"

Grubel paused for dramatic effect, adjusting the empty frames of his glasses.

"—now Mrs. Mayflower wants to talk to you in her private quarters. Do you have any idea why she might want to see you?" Grubel asked.

"Yes," said Jeremiah.

"Is it related to that musical instrument?"

"Yes."

"Jeremiah, do you know how important Mrs. Mayflower is to Golden Worldlines?"

"Very important?"

"No," Grubel said. "*Critically* important. *Vitally* important."

Grubel seemed to be groping for a third adjective.

"Uncomfortably important?" Jeremiah offered.

"Exactly. If she is unhappy, she will make me extremely unhappy. And I have the power to make *you* extremely unhappy if *I'm* unhappy. And it seems that—by whatever twist of fate—you have the power to make Mrs. Mayflower happy or unhappy. Do you see where I'm going with this?"

"Yes," said Jeremiah. Even without pencil and paper, he was reasonably sure that he could work this chain of happiness out to its unhappy conclusion.

"Here's where I'm going with this," Grubel elaborated. "If you make Mrs. Mayflower unhappy, then she will make me unhappy. If she makes me unhappy, then I will make you unhappy. If I make you unhappy, then you will be?"

"Unhappy," said Jeremiah.

"Exactly. So in a way, all I'm asking you to do is to make yourself happy. Is that too much to ask, Jeremiah?"

Seeing as "unhappy" was a deliriously optimistic goal for what he was going to make Mrs. Mayflower when he delivered her the jury-rigged bandora, Jeremiah briefly considered going out in a blaze of self-righteous glory right then and there by telling Grubel exactly what he thought about people who wore hypermodern suits and glasses without lenses and traced out idiotic logical progressions, the only purpose of which was to demonstrate relative power dynamics in their own favor.

"No," he said instead.

"Good," said Grubel. "Then let me explain to you how to find Mrs. Mayflower's private quarters."

WORLD ENOUGH (AND TIME)

26

The Belly of the Beast

Still Saturday (1 day until arrival)

OW that he thought about it, Jeremiah felt
foolish for not having deduced the existence of
Mrs. Mayflower's private quarters back in his earliest
days as a passenger.

He could understand, if not exactly feel proud of, how little thought he had given to the vast service areas of the ship
before he had become part of that service himself. He had at
least *known* in some latent manner that such areas must exist,
just as the kitchen and dishwashing stations in a restaurant
must exist, or the inventory shelves and shipping and receiving docks at the back of a grocery store. He had just never
found any occasion to think about them, which was unre-
markable given the exertions of Golden Worldlines to keep
him and the other passengers from doing so. For this he could
have been accused of privilege, or a blindness to classes other
than his own, but not idiocy. Never having wondered why
he could not walk from one end of the E4 to the other, on
the other hand—well, there the case against idiocy was not
so clear.

For the Einstein IV was a ring—the inhabitable areas of it,
at any rate—and Jeremiah had long since known that it was a
ring. Every photo on every advertisement back on Earth had
showcased its ring-like shape. The "gravity" that he experienced out here in deep space, where there was no gravity to
speak of, was synthesized by the spinning of the Einstein IV's
massive ring around the spindle where the Quantum Cater-

pillar Drive and the Inertial Dampers and who knew what other engineering marvels worked their magic.

At the same time, Jeremiah had long known from his exploration of the ship that it was impossible to start in, say, the dining room, and walk all the way around the ring of the E4 so that he returned to where he had started. In one direction he would stall out in the furthest wing of the guest quarters, and in the other at the games and recreation room. And this limitation had not vanished when the service areas of the ship had been opened to him.

In sum, for nearly two years now Jeremiah had known both that he lived inside a giant circle, and that it was impossible to take a circular path through his habitat, and he had never once questioned why. Which sounded, when he thought about it, uncomfortably like idiocy.

The reason he had never been able to walk the full extent of the Einstein IV's ring, Jeremiah understood now, was because Mrs. Mayflower's quarters occupied a full and contiguous quarter of said ring, extending through all levels. The entrances to her quarters—like the one that Jeremiah had seen Mrs. Mayflower use on Heriberto's footage, and the other that, at Grubel's instruction, Jeremiah had just used himself—were secreted behind cunning panels on the walls.

With the benefit of reflection, Jeremiah would not have been sure what he expected to see after stepping through a secret door and walking down an actual secret passage for the first time in his life, but whatever he might have expected, it was not what he found.

"Good morning, sir," said what Jeremiah found.

The butler was a distinguished man of distinguished age with distinguished white hair and no distinguishing marks, and he stood up straighter than any man Jeremiah had ever seen, so straight that rulers coming off an assembly line could have been evaluated and the warped ones discarded by comparison with his example; so straight that his Victorian period dress—an impeccably high-cut waistcoat impeccably suitable for this morning hour—looked not just smoothly pressed but as if it had been carved from two different varieties of onyx, jet black for the dress coat and, for the trousers, one striped with deposits of some white mineral.

"Mrs. Mayflower is expecting you in the small drawing

room."

The butler turned and led Jeremiah across what could only be described as a courtyard, paved with checkered marble and complete with a pond stocked to the gills with sprightly koi and ringed by man-tall ficus trees which were, Jeremiah discovered when some leaves brushed his face, not artificial. Above and around the atrium which housed the courtyard, other servants bustled about their business behind marble pillars and arches piled two floors high. There was an atmosphere of old-world efficiency that does not take luxury as an excuse to lapse from duty but as a prod to even greater exertions, and Jeremiah would not have been surprised to find that the white collar the butler wore, for instance, was not laundered in a modern system but scrubbed by hand nightly with some instrument that was half toothbrush and half medieval torture device.

The "small" drawing room that the butler swept Jeremiah exquisitely into was small only in the comparative sense of being, he supposed, smaller than the implied "large" draw-ing room, which Jeremiah imagined could have held its own with a modest sports stadium. At the far end of the room stood Mrs. Mayflower, contemplating an Italian landscape in faded oils that hung on the wall.

"Mr. Jeremiah Brown," announced the butler. Mrs. Mayflower took a moment to finish her contem-plation before she turned around to swish and sashay in their direction.

She was dressed more grandly than Jeremiah had ever seen her, in a black gown with a train whose length toed the line between making walking impractical and impossible. Each sleeve ended in a profusion of lace so intricate and fresh that it seemed like a rare flower that had been bred and tended to for years and then, just that morning, tenderly harvested at the precise height of its bloom.

The still ancient but more modern clothes she had visited him in, Jeremiah now understood, were nothing more than a reluctant nod to the practical realities of secret passages and trick panels and clandestine trips through the hallways of the Einstein IV. When she required activewear, Mrs. Mayflower dressed like Jackie Kennedy—but when she wished to be comfortable, Mrs. Mayflower dressed as the lady of the manor.

"Where is my bandora, young man?" she said.

"You said you would stop by to pick it up," said Jeremiah. "That was days ago."

"You are a difficult individual to visit discreetly, due to the unusual—and, I suspect, unhealthy—number of other individuals who seem to be stalking you. There is the wild-haired hippie who never stops muttering about civil liberties and controlled substances and some system or other."

"That would be Jack," said Jeremiah.

"Then the broodingly intense young man who cannot stop talking to himself about your shortcomings, or the charms and disappointments of some young woman named—Pemberly, was it?"

"And I see you've met Bradley."

"Finally there is the gentlemen who—while not necessarily a stalker—seems to have an uncanny knack for synchronizing his visits with mine."

"Henry Chapin," Jeremiah said. "He's a good man."

"Their names and qualities are unimportant. My point is that they have prevented me from visiting you discreetly so that I might collect my bandora. Therefore I have called you here to deliver it to me."

"Mr. Grubel just told me to report here straightaway. He didn't mention anything about picking up the bandora beforehand. So I don't have it."

Mrs. Mayflower frowned and sat down on the edge of a chair with Chippendale feet.

"Roosevelt," she said to her butler, who still adorned the doorway like a statue, "do we have any fresh squeezed orange juice?"

"No, milady."

"Bring me some."

"Yes, milady."

With a curt bow, he was gone.

"*That* is the nature of service, young man," Mrs. Mayflower said to Jeremiah. "The disregarding of obstacles, the disdain for exact instructions and those who require them. Roosevelt is the perfect servant, by which statement I do not denigrate, but elevate him. His station is inferior to mine, but *he* is not inferior to *me*. If anything, his able discharge of the duties pertaining to his station puts mine to shame. We serve different functions, Roosevelt and I, but each without the other is nothing. You smile, but I am speaking with perfect candor."

"Then let me reply with perfect candor," said Jeremiah. "What is your function, exactly?"

Mrs. Mayflower frowned and adjusted herself on the edge of her chair.

"The line between candor and impertinence is exceedingly fine," she said. "See that you do not cross it. But it seems to me that perhaps you are the kind of person who can learn something. So I will answer your question, young man. Come with me."

She led him out the door at the back of the small drawing room and through a hall hung with other oil paintings. A few of them looked familiar to Jeremiah, as if he had seen them before on his PED or hanging in reproductions on the walls of friends with a finer appreciation than his of the plastic arts. Mrs. Mayflower spoke as she strolled ahead of him.

"No doubt you consider me a mere consumer of the luxury that is created by the labor of others. You see how I live, how I dress, how many servants I employ, and feel quite clever at having reached that conclusion. But you have only demonstrated your own lack of imagination. I too serve, Jeremiah. I serve the past."

She made this pronouncement grandly, with a narrowing of her eyes as if recalling old vows that were renewed simply by her mentioning them. She paused as if she expected Jeremiah to say something in response.

"Oh," he said.

"Welcome," Mrs. Mayflower said, throwing open an old wooden door, "to the small music room."

She stepped through, and Jeremiah followed.

"I have spent my youth journeying all over the world," said Mrs. Mayflower, "plucking each of these ancient instruments, one by one, from the jaws of time. A mizwad I spotted in a street fair in Tunisia. A chelys and auletris I bought from a criminal archaeologist in Greece, who had gambling debts to pay. A huqin of great antiquity, which I discovered hanging over a Chinese bar. This banjo, which once belonged to a 20th-century minstrel named Uncle Dave Bacon."

285

"Macon," said Jeremiah. Suddenly he was hardly able to breathe, and he had started trembling slightly.

"What?"

"It's Uncle Dave *Macon*, not Bacon."

Mrs. Mayflower smiled tolerantly.

"I know the story of each of these instruments as if they were my children, young man. And there," she said, pointing at an empty spot on the wall, "is where you would normally find the pearl of my collection—my bandora, which you have failed once again to deliver to me, and which you will now collect and return as soon as we have finished this conversation."

Jeremiah's legs felt like jelly, but nevertheless they were carrying him towards the wall of musical instruments—towards one instrument in particular. His arms were rising at his sides, ready to reach out like those of a zombie stumbling through a horror wave, and he seemed to have no say in the matter.

"Though the musical instruments are my greatest passion," continued Mrs. Mayflower, "they represent only a fraction of my collection. Other rooms are filled with pristine exemplars of furnishings from eras your great-grandparents would have known only through museums and period dramas. Then there are halls of artwork and pottery, ancient calligraphy, even—"

Her eyes shone and she raised her hand and passed it with great care in front of her, as if touching a memory.

"—a long hallway paneled with cave paintings, the sheets of rock meticulously cut from a site in Indonesia which they were about to level in order to construct new high-density apartment buildings. Through the magic of relativistic-speed cruises I am bringing them all to the future, Jeremiah—husbanding them through hundreds of years while they endure only tens. And when the time is right, this will all go to a museum, sustained by a substantial endowment—the entirety of my fortune. There will be stringent conditions, of course, that nothing—not the slightest detail—ever be changed. Young man, just what do you think you are doing?"

What Jeremiah was doing, though in his state he was not completely aware of it himself, was taking the banjo down from the wall and hanging its slender leather strap over his shoulder. The instrument was in miraculous condition for its age. The frets were not originals, or the head of course, but the replacement materials had been painstakingly matched to the period. Jeremiah plucked a few notes—the strings were fresh but properly stretched. It seemed Mrs. Mayflower even kept the instruments in tune. He tried a little roll, and all that was missing was the pop and hiss of an ancient recording to make it sound just like Uncle Dave himself warming up.

At the touch of the strings, whatever spirit had taken control of Jeremiah's grosser appendages now turned its attention to his fingers. It wanted them to play.

Mrs. Mayflower was still talking—presumably telling him to put the priceless instrument back where it belonged immediately and threatening all sorts of dire consequences if he did not—but at first her voice was distant and indistinct, and then buried entirely under the shower of notes that came flowing out of the banjo.

Only after he'd been playing for a few bars did Jeremiah recognize the tune—"Foggy Mountain Breakdown." He played through it once, and then it began to change. At first just a note here and there. Then a run that went down instead of up, a substitute chord or two.

As he continued to play, the tune diverged more and more from the original, and to the same degree Jeremiah became less and less aware of what he was playing. The music seemed to be coming not out of him, but through him—as if all the moods and experiences and nuances of his entire life were being strained through this moment, letting only the essential slip through—the farce and tragedy of his being on this boat in the middle of a great nothing, the iguanas, dying Henry Chapin, Katherine, the moment among the stars, a broken bandora, even poor Boyle. These and more were all in the music, strands woven and twisted together into a long tightrope that Jeremiah walked without a net, neither to anywhere nor from anywhere, not for any purpose except to walk and not to fall.

When the mood began to lift, and Jeremiah became aware once again of who and where he was, he felt the tune slow and stop, breaking off awkwardly in the middle of a phrase. He could not have said with any confidence how long he had been playing—when he looked up at Mrs. Mayflower he would not have been particularly surprised if she had aged ten years.

She had not aged ten years, but the last ten minutes or so did not seem to have done much for her mood. She had clenched her jaw, and was frowning an inscrutable frown.

"The glass," Jeremiah said to her, realizing it himself as he formed the words. "It broke."

They stood there looking at each other for a moment, and the longer Jeremiah looked at her, the less sure he was what her expression meant—whether he had just been damned or forgiven. The spell broke with the sound of someone clearing his throat when it did not need to be cleared. Roosevelt the butler was standing in the doorway of the small music room, holding a silver tray in one hand, on which was perched a tall thin glass of the orangest orange juice Jeremiah had ever seen. He stepped into the room and lowered the tray by Mrs. Mayflower's side.

"Roosevelt," she said, and her voice was ice, "replace my banjo and show our visitor out."

Jeremiah stumbled out of the hidden passageway into the normal passageway and attempted to catch his breath as Roosevelt the butler slammed the hidden door shut behind him. He was not sure how to process what had just happened.

The glass had broken: after all these years of banging and battering, pain and disappointment, he had felt that indestructible ShopGlass, somewhere deep in the trance of that music, shatter like the thinnest sheet of ice skimmed from a puddle, almost of its own accord. That meant—at least in theory—there was no longer anything between Jeremiah and Real Life. But: so what? Or perhaps more importantly: *now* what? What did one do in Real Life? How did one behave? How were things different? This service hallway, for example, looked just the same as it always had—gray and uninviting and slightly damp.

And for his part, Jeremiah didn't feel particularly different. He pinched his forearm. It felt real enough. But it had

288

always felt that way—hadn't it? He took inventory of himself and found that—as far as he could tell—things were all very much in line with the old status quo.

After several minutes spent in such pursuits, Jeremiah reached the conclusion that—glass or no glass—he was going to have to come up with some plan of action, go somewhere, do something. He couldn't very well stand in this hallway for the rest of his Real Life, pinching his forearm. In Real Life, as in life, there were matters to attend to.

For example: Grubel had instructed Jeremiah, in no uncertain terms, to report back to him immediately after speaking with Mrs. Mayflower. But that was not a conversation Jeremiah was eager to have, and he reflected that there was as little point in reporting what had happened as in hiding it. Grubel would find out soon enough from Mrs. Mayflower's own mouth, and when he did, Jeremiah's stay on the Einstein IV would be extended for 2 or 20 years, depending on your preferred inertial frame of reference.

Further fast thinking and fast talking and desperate legerdemain was not necessary or even useful. The ax was no longer about to fall: it was falling, and was en route to his neck. At the very least, he supposed, it was falling in Real Life. And if he was now Really Alive, he might as well act accordingly.

Jeremiah decided to leave the office closed and check a few other items off the list of matters still unresolved. He set off to find Henry Chapin, who was dying, with the air of a man putting his own affairs in order.

"Nothing? You mean nothing interesting," said Mr. Chapin. His voice echoed in the abandoned pool room—Jeremiah had found him there taking his usual morning swim.

"I mean I found nothing at all," Jeremiah said. "The box was empty."

In response Mr. Chapin dried his arms with such vigor that Jeremiah was afraid even the plush towels of the E4 might damage his skin.

"You still won't tell me why you need to know?" said Jeremiah.

Mr. Chapin shook his head, spraying a little water in the process. He sighed and pushed his knuckles into his eyes.

"This is quite frustrating," he said.

"Mr. Chapin," said Jeremiah. "Henry. Does this have anything to do with your medical news from Earth?"

Mr. Chapin's head snapped up.

"How do you know about that? I haven't even told Sara yet."

"I saw one of your waves from Earth. I wasn't trying to snoop," said Jeremiah. "Not on you at least."

"I see. I suppose in a certain sense this makes things easier."

"Is there any hope?"

"It appears not. Funny, isn't it? Humanity has come so far: we can extract energy from empty space with the Quantum Caterpillar Drive, and block gravity with Inertial Dampers and build big, comfortable ships that push the speed of light. But when it comes to our own bodies, we're still the clumsiest of amateurs, futzing around.

"Do you know, Jeremiah, I didn't even want to come on this cruise? The world had already changed so much on me. I wanted to just take the two or three years the doctors could give me and get to know the place again before I left it. But Sara wouldn't consider it—she couldn't. She couldn't accept the idea that we wouldn't try every measure available to us. And I was touched, of course—that she loved me that much. So I agreed and we bought our tickets. But now things have turned out as I suspected they would, and I'm going home to die in a world even stranger to me than the one I left."

"I'm sorry," said Jeremiah. He wanted to say something else—something more—but what else was there to say, even in Real Life?

"That's not the worst part, though. The worst part is leaving Sara alone. We never had any children—which was my fault, entirely my fault. I spent our fertile years possessed with the self-righteous conviction that bringing a child into a world as broken as ours was the height of cruelty. Oh, I'd never lied to Sara about the fact that I didn't want children. The terms were all spelled out clearly in black and white when she signed up. That's how I thought of it. But marriage is a contract that's under constant renegotiation.

290

After enough years the whole 'party of the first part' and 'party of the second part' starts to blur—which I suppose is the whole point. Do you understand what I'm getting at, Jeremiah?"

"Not really."

"I mean that because I was principled and stubborn, I'll be leaving my wife all alone in this world, and she seems to have taken a shine to Roof, and I want to know whether to aid and abet that attachment or not."

"Wow," said Jeremiah. "That's—enlightened of you."

"Good God, Jeremiah, I don't mean right now. If he so much as holds her hand while I'm still drawing breath it will be pistols at dawn. I just mean arranging things for after I'm gone. Removing obstacles, paving the way. Inviting him out to the lake and things like that. But before I pave the way I need to make sure that he's a good man. By which I mean, a man who will treat Sara well. A man who's worthy of her—to some approximation."

"Isn't this really Sara's decision?"

"Well of course," roared Mr. Chapin, "I'm not talking about selling my wife into slavery. I'm talking about opening a few doors. If she wants to walk through them, she can. And if she doesn't, then she won't."

"All right, but doesn't Mr. Roof have something to say about it too?"

Mr. Chapin took a moment to catch his breath.

"Yes, and I know what you're going to say: he doesn't seem particularly enamored of her. Yet. Sara has a way of growing on you—a romantic nature that works on you while you don't know what's happening. You won't believe me— her passion is buried deep—but it's there."

"I believe you," said Jeremiah.

"Anyway, that will all take care of itself. Or if it doesn't, at least I tried. So."

"So?"

"So no one takes a two-year cruise through deep space in a tin can while 20 years pass on Earth just for fun. If Roof is not sick, what's he doing here? Running from legal trouble? Outliving someone he's wronged? Waiting for an investment to mature?"

"Surely at this point you've done everything you *can* do

except *ask* him? Isn't it time to bite the bullet?"

"We've been over this," said Mr. Chapin. "You know Roof—you know how he is about manners and customs. If I break the unwritten rule, not only won't he answer, but he'll be so offended that he'll never want anything to do with me again—or Sara. It's time to accept defeat."

He stood up from the deck chair. Jeremiah did not like to see his shoulders so stooped, his head so bowed.

"I'm going to finish my swim," said Mr. Chapin. He looked at his own arms, legs, hands. "There are many supposed pleasures I've tired of—things I won't miss when my life is over. But swimming I will miss."

He walked to the pool and dove into the water.

"Photos of *you*," said Jeremiah to Mrs. Abdurov. "Look."

He handed her the camera pen, which she paired with her PED. She took a few steps towards the back of her room and turned her back, as if to put up a privacy screen. When she turned back, her eyes were gleaming.

"He knew," she said. "*Vor* Drinkwater knew I would send you to open box, so he taunts me like this. He even digitally alters photos to make me look sour and angry."

"He's not taunting you—he's in *love* with you. He keeps these photos in his safe deposit box because nothing else is more precious to him."

"You are sweet, stupid boy, Jeremiah. You leave the thinking to me. I wanted to avenge my Marya Jana in front of her own cold eyes, but time is run out for me—we arrive on Earth tomorrow. Goodbye, Jeremiah. Thank you for inept help, but now this is job only I can do."

"What job are you planning to do, Mrs. Abdurov?"

"Is best you know nothing. This is a personal matter. A matter of *vory*."

"Are you planning to harm Mr. Drinkwater?"

"You go now. Don't worry, nothing comes back to you."

"You cannot harm Mr. Drinkwater," said Jeremiah.

"Oh?" Mrs. Abdurov said, drawing herself up to her full height and looking Jeremiah right in the nipples. "Who are you to tell me this?" She acceded to the height difference and glared upwards into his eyes.

"Mr. Drinkwater is under my protection. If you attempt to harm him, you'll have to go through me."

Slowly and sweetly, never breaking eye contact, Mrs. Abdurov reached up with both hands and placed one on each of Jeremiah's cheeks.

"Then this is goodbye, my sweet stupid boy. The next time we meet, is as enemies."

She took her hands back.

"You leave my room now," she said.

Jeremiah returned to the suite just in time to catch Katherine about to leave for lunch service. She had already changed into her uniform and was sitting on the sofa, putting on her shoes.

"I'll be out of your way in a second," she said.

"Katherine," said Jeremiah, "I have to tell you something."

"No you don't."

"It's a done deal. I'm going to have to stay on for a full cruise."

"I'm sorry," Katherine said.

"I'm not, because I sure as hell don't want to spend 20 years on Earth without you. Now I know I haven't—"

"Jeremiah—"

"Wait, I'm not finished. I know I haven't deserved you. I still don't. But I *have* changed. And I'll keep changing. I'll—"

"I'm leaving the E4," Katherine said. "This is my final 2/20. For the last however many years I've been putting all my savings and retirement funds into Golden Worldlines stock. Now that we're back in communication range I had a chance to check the quote, and think I've got enough to make a go of it. I won't be rich or anything, but I can start a life on Earth."

"But Katherine—"

"Don't make this harder than it already is, Jeremiah. I have to go to work now."

Which she did.

WORLD ENOUGH (AND TIME)

27

Without Further Ado

JEREMIAH had already visited the passenger dining room, where the talent show was to begin in three hours. The PA system was online. The refreshments were well in hand. Luis and crew were assembling the stage and hanging the curtain. There was nothing left for Jeremiah to do but wander and think about Katherine.

Real Life was turning out to be a bit of a mixed bag—the glass that had kept Jeremiah from it had also protected his heart from a depth of revelatory pain that dwarfed his other misfortunes and discomforts. If he made them Domenican lizards, Katherine was Godzilla. If he made them fire, Katherine was a supervolcano. If he made them swords and spears, she was a hydrogen bomb mushroom clouding in his heart.

The prospect of spending two years without her was excruciating. But the thought that those two years would mean 20 for her—that their worldlines would diverge forever, that they would number their hours and years differently, never again sharing so much as a calendar? Well that was intolerable, inconceivable, not to be considered.

As for Battle: Battle was nothing, a garnish of horseradish on a dish already so bitter that Jeremiah could not possibly swallow it.

But there was nothing else on the menu, and still three hours to kill, so Jeremiah walked, and walked, and walked.

The ship began to bestir itself as the dinner hour grew closer. Jeremiah fetched the bandora from Katherine's suite and returned to the dining room, where he hid behind stage left. It was hard to sit there with a musical instrument in his hands and not even strum it, and Jeremiah worried that his mind would drift and his fingers would repeat their recent rebellion, with disastrous results. After a while he set the bandora aside.

There in the wings of the stage, invisible himself, he commanded a clear view of the dining room. The chefs and servers arrived, and then the first few passengers. As dinner service began in earnest, it turned out Jeremiah had positioned himself with an excellent view of Katherine's tables in particular.

Jeremiah knew he should not be spying on Katherine like this, and not just because it was discourteous to her. This surveillance was no good for him either—these glimpses of her smiling and chatting were torture in the moment and were not destined to become happy memories. They burned his soul just as the fumes of the lacquer coming off the stage burned his lungs, with that deep pain that presages permanent damage. But he couldn't help himself, and as the dining room filled up and dinner entered its full swing, Jeremiah did not even want to blink for danger of missing a single glimpse.

Finally, when the desserts had been served and cleared, the last dregs of coffee and tea abandoned, the final sips of port swirled in the bottoms of the glasses and tossed back, Jeremiah stepped on the stage and up to the microphone. The suffering of his lungs and heart was eased for just a moment by the few gasps of genuine astonishment from the diners—who in that moment had become the audience.

"Ladies and gentlemen," he said, his voice booming over the PA system, "welcome to the First Ever—as far as we know—Golden Worldlines Passenger Talent Show."

Silence greeted his remarks, then a slow smattering of applause that built until most of the dining room was actually standing to deliver their ovation. The passengers seemed to harbor very little doubt about the level of talent they were about to witness. As the clapping died down, members of the crew filtered in through the doors at the back of the dining room. They lined up in rows starting against the back wall until they would have encroached on the guests and their tables if they went any further, at which point those who were passing through the doors remained in the doors, creating not just an obstructed view for those caught behind them, but a blatant violation of any sensible fire code.

"Some administrative details," said Jeremiah. "The list of acts is posted here." He pointed to the small table at the foot of the stage. "When your act is on deck, please set up backstage while the act before you is performing." He pointed left and behind the curtain. "And with that, please join me in welcoming our first act, Mrs.—"

Jeremiah paused. Mrs. Mayflower, at her own insistence, was slated to open the show, but she was nowhere to be seen. Had her lack of practice given her a change of heart? Was she still recovering from whatever shock Jeremiah had delivered by daring to play her banjo? Had she, at the moment of truth, decided that she did not in fact wish to display her talents for the benefit of these billionaires less fortunate than herself? Or was she arriving even now, parting the gasping crowd of crew and striding into the dining room, her gaze wandering neither left nor right and her chin held high, assisted in this exercise of focus by a huge circular ruff of stiff lace protruding from the collar of her deep purple dress, which looked as if she had excised it from an Elizabethan portrait? Was she furthermore proceeding towards the stage this very moment, hands clasped in front of her, as if walking up the aisle towards coronation, sleeves trimmed with ermine?

The evidence, sadly, pointed to this last possibility, for here she was arriving now in just the aforementioned dress and manner. Though she walked slowly and evenly, the ruff collar bounced a little at each step, which seemed to Jeremiah both ridiculous and the kind of thing one might get executed under penalty of some sumptuary law for attempting to satirize.

As she proceeded past the crew and through the ranks of passengers there was no more gasping but considerable confusion on many faces and many questioning looks exchanged between them. With great dignity, and disregard for the danger presented by her train, Mrs. Mayflower climbed the four steps to the stage, accepted the bandora from Jeremiah with one cold glance, and shooed him away with another. As Jeremiah went to bring her a chair, she wrinkled her nose at the strong chemical smell of fresh lacquer, then turned to address the crowd.

"My name," she said, "is Marianne Mayflower. For two years I have traveled with you, but not among you. We have broken no common bread and eaten no salt together."

"You shouldn't eat salt anyway," Sara Chapin whispered loudly to Henry Chapin. "Because of your blood pressure."

They were sitting at the table closest the stage, and Mrs. Mayflower glared down at them.

"But now," Mrs. Mayflower continued, "before our shared journey ends and we go our separate ways, I wish to share something of myself with you, my—" She struggled just a bit with the next word. "Peers. So, without further ado."

She sat on the chair that Jeremiah had brought on stage and set the bandora on one knee. Jeremiah could not watch— he turned away. Meanwhile Mrs. Mayflower, having decided that just a bit more ado was called for, was explaining the musical significance of the bandora in general and this specimen in particular.

"Jeremiah!" whispered Mr. Porter, approaching from Jeremiah's left. His shoulders were laden with bags of what appeared to be bowling pins, and he carried a large covered pail. "I'm next up. Where do I go?"

With whispers and signs, Jeremiah directed him to his place behind the curtains.

"Jeremiah!" said someone behind him. He turned to find Jack, eyes wide, looking relaxed and content and eminently mellow, and reeking profoundly of Aunt Mildred's Organic Iguana Treats. Suddenly Jack was not so much shaking Jeremiah's hand as pumping it vigorously with both of his own, as if a drought were stretching into its second month, and Jeremiah were an old well reluctant to give up its water.

"You're some kind of botanical wizard," Jack was saying, too loudly for Jeremiah's tastes. "I'm sorry I called you part of the System. I haven't been this mellow in years. Years! This is some of the best shit I have ever smoked." He dropped

his voice to add—as this part was apparently a secret: "Ever."
"I'm glad you're satisfied," whispered Jeremiah, emphasizing the last word in anticipation of any surveys Jack might fill out in the near future, and trying at the same time to extricate his hand.

Meanwhile Mrs. Mayflower had finished explaining the musical significance of the bandora in general and had moved on to rehearse the provenance of her particular instrument at an "Adam begat Seth" level of detail, unimpressed by the growing restlessness she was occasioning in her audience.

"You don't know what I saw," Jack said, clutching Jeremiah's hand tighter. "What visions were visited upon me. Castles, Jeremiah. Castles in the air. And princes and princesses and knights and dragons." His eyes grew even wider at the memory and his grip relented enough that Jeremiah could pull himself free. "I saw *dragons*, Jeremiah. Two of them. Great, green dragons, touched by fire."

Mrs. Mayflower's oral history was now deep into the 18th Century.

"That's great Jack," said Jeremiah. "Enjoy the show."

"*Dragons.*"

"And now," said Mrs. Mayflower, the bandora's lineage sufficiently specified, "without further ado."

She repositioned the bandora on her knee, which adjustment Jeremiah experienced as a sword heated in the fires of hell, quenched with ipecac, and thrust into his belly. But the bandora held.

"I spent a good deal of time and thought on the question of which madrigal would be most appropriate for this occasion," Mrs. Mayflower said. "*Come, sirrah Jack, ho!* by Thomas Weelkes, for its sense of raucous celebration? But that selection is long, and time is precious, and I wish to be brief. So perhaps *Thule, the Period of Cosmography*, by the same composer, for its stunning imagery? But the verse is so full of fire and brimstone, and I wish to entertain, not correct you. So in the end I have settled upon *See What a Maze of Error* by George Kirbye—whom I presume requires no gloss or introduction. So, without further ado."

She began to tune the bandora, plucking gently at the strings, and though Jeremiah cringed at each touch, the neck of the bandora miraculously held. He almost wished it would just break and end his torture.

"And now," said Mrs. Mayflower, when she was satisfied with the tuning, "*See What a Maze of Error.*"

She cleared her throat twice and hummed a tone.

"By the incomparable George Kirbye."

She brought her hand up high, ready to bring it down for an initial crashing strum of surpassing drama and violence, and it seemed to Jeremiah that the passage of time slowed to a crawl.

For example, he felt as if he had hours to decide exactly what flavor of terror was creeping onto Mr. Porter's face as he peeked out from behind the wing of the stage, his eyes widening as he beheld something at the back of the room. Was it mammalian horror? Primal shock? Existential dread?

Then, when Jeremiah had finished his leisurely speculation and turned to his left, en route to the object of Mr. Porter's gaze, he saw as if in slow motion Mrs. Abdurov approaching Mr. Drinkwater from behind, her face set in a mask of cold fury and her right hand reaching into her pocket, the very picture of an aspiring jailyard assassin. Jeremiah considered doing something about that, but there was still plenty of time—time enough to turn and see what Mr. Porter had seen: the ghost of Bernie Wendstrom—or perhaps Bernie Wendstrom sufficiently deprived of sleep and nourishment so as to resemble a ghost—standing at the back of the dining room, having just entered through the closest door, pointing towards the stage like a victim returned from beyond the grave to accuse his murderer.

Then there was time to turn back to the stage, his gaze passing Mrs. Abdurov again, who had hardly advanced upon Mr. Drinkwater in the meanwhile, and see that Mr. Porter's terror seemed to have spread to Mrs. Mayflower, whose own eyes were growing wide and whose mouth was making preparations for any screaming that might be called for in the near future. But no, it was not the ghost of Bernie Wendstrom that had spooked her thus—her eyes were focused on something else, something nearer to her, up and to the right, where Mr. Wendstrom was pointing, and where Jeremiah looked as well and found a figure hanging, like a green gargoyle, from the curtain of the stage.

"Carolus the Bold!" shouted Mr. Wendstrom or the ghost thereof from the back of the room, still pointing, his voice deepened by the slowing of time.

For it was he, Carolus the Bold, gripping the curtain with his long dextrous toes, still as a statue, regarding the stage and the human drama unfolding below with a noble and dispassionate countenance. Then his eyes shifted slightly and his expression became, if such a thing were possible for an iguana, amorous. Mrs. Mayflower followed the new line of his attention, and what she found there was enough to convert her latent scream to actual.

"Marya Jana!" Mrs. Abdurov slow-motion shouted from Jeremiah's left.

For it was she, gripping the opposite curtain and hanging like the mirror image of Carolus, as complementary as if they had been carved into a heraldic device for a house that had achieved nobility late in the age of kings, well after the wolves, bears, lions, and other more desirable animals had all been spoken for.

Mr. Drinkwater, hearing the harsh voice of his beloved so close behind, and ignorant of the harm she intended him, grinned and began to turn around.

Jack meanwhile looked pleased to be seeing the dragons again, though a tad alarmed to find that the others could see them too, leading him to wonder what exactly all these people were on.

Now Mr. Porter had stepped from behind the curtain and into Mrs. Mayflower's view. The lit torch that he carried in his hand attracted her attention to him, so she abandoned the object of Carolus' gaze and followed Mr. Porter's to the ghostly, pointing figure at the back of the dining room. Jeremiah followed her lead.

"Wendstrom!" cried Mr. Porter.

For it was—as previously established—he, looking either in excellent health for a dead man or atrocious health for a living one. Whichever was the actual case, his apparition represented the final straw for Mrs. Mayflower and her nerves. She kicked back in her chair and thrust her arms out in a vain attempt to keep from tipping, which sent the long-suffering bandora—still unstruck by her eager fingers—flying across the stage, where it landed and snapped in half once again, right at the base of the neck.

For what must have been no longer than a millisecond, even in this time warp, Jeremiah experienced a surge of hope—but no, the most cursory post-mortem of the bandora would reveal the age of the break, along with all the gluing and filing he had performed upon it.

The spectacle of Mrs. Mayflower screaming and tipping backwards, however, represented the last straw for Mr. Porter's own nerves, inspiring him to brandish the lit torch he had held—*had* held, because his grip failed and the torch skittered across the stage as well, stopping a few inches from where the pitiable bandora lay broken.

At this point time actually seemed not just to slow but to *stop* long enough for everyone in the entire dining room—human, iguana, and possible ghost—to turn their attention to the lit torch that was now lying on the thickly lacquered floor of the newly constructed stage and licking it with little tongues of flame. The shared second hand of their experience seemed to hold back just a bit longer, giving everyone time to admire the orange glow on the stage, the dancing flame, the shimmer of fresh lacquer transmuting under its influence.

Then time resumed its normal flow, or perhaps even ran a little faster than usual, as the stage went up like a Roman candle, the two iguanas scampered for the safe arms of their owners, Mr. Porter dragged Mrs. Mayflower from the stage, mass panic set in, and what little hell had, up to this point, remained tenuously chained, all broke loose.

28

The Glass Harp of Courage

Still Saturday (1 day until arrival)

EREMIAH would be the first to admit that he had been nowhere near Agincourt on St. Crispin's day, and had the lack of scars to prove it. Given the good fortune to be born in a country with a volunteer military, he had seized the opportunity, early and often, not to volunteer. Born into an age where the half-dozen simmering wars that the United States was half-heartedly waging around the globe at any given time were conducted mostly by remote control, Jeremiah's whole generation had not had a Trojan War, Vietnam, or even a decade-long Montreal Skirmish to define its relationship to armed conflict.

In short, Jeremiah had never been to war, at war, or anywhere near war, and had even, during his years in Detroit, mostly managed to avoid the areas of the city that most closely resembled combat zones—which was to say, most of Detroit. So although he had read about true bravery and coolness under fire in many a war novel, and watched its depiction in many a war wave, his opportunities to witness the real thing had been few and far between.

But now it seemed that, if he was about to go to a fiery grave—a possibility that appeared increasingly likely—Jeremiah would not leave this world without having witnessed true bravery at least once.

For while the rest of the dining room stood frozen in shock or ran in the grip of panic, Mrs. Biltmore had proven that, although her harp might be of glass, yet her heart was of steel.

She leapt forward and began tossing the contents of her instrument note by note towards the spreading inferno, barely disturbing her recent perm in the process.

Jeremiah saw her there, a black silhouette against the orange flames, undaunted and unflappable, a sight to thrill the heart and earn the respect of even the most grizzled volunteer fireman.

But this was a hungry and ambitious fire, and Mrs. Biltmore's well of courage was far deeper than her well of the crucial H2O. When she had at last gritted her teeth and shot her last, biggest arrow—the beer stein from which her rare talents could coax an impossible low C—the flames remained unaffected by the magnitude of either her bravery or musical sacrifice.

She turned, and her eyes met Jeremiah's, and it seemed to him that even in that moment, when all was lost and incineration imminent, this woman of astounding fortitude regretted only that she could not spend these last moments playing "Nearer My God to Thee" on partially filled assorted wine and other glasses to ease the passage of her moribund fellows, on account of her instrument being dry.

Jeremiah saluted her and prepared for the end, not just of Real Life but of every variety.

29

Soggy Bottoms and Loose Ends

Still Saturday (1 day until arrival)

THE designers of the Einstein Series had been handed
the unenviable task of designing a luxury cruise
ship that could survive the rigors of deep space.
Deep space was an unforgiving environment in the best of
circumstances—with its signature lack of air and its tem-
peratures even worse than Detroit in winter and its ample
opportunities for instant death by cosmic ray or random
asteroid—and a ship full of wealthy customers traveling at
near light-speed trillions of miles from the nearest roadside
assistance was far from the best circumstance. Hence the
invention of the Abdinoor shield, which could brush off a hit
from an asteroid that would have left a small moon reeling.
Hence the heavy airtight doors scattered throughout the
ship, never fully hidden by curtains and clever decorations,
to isolate any damage if the Abdinoor shields failed. And
hence the emergency spacesuits, distributed throughout the
ship behind panels activated by calmly labeled levers, in
case the Abdinoor shields failed *and* one found oneself on
the wrong side of one of those heavy doors. But asteroids
and cosmic rays were just the most obvious problems. What
about the enemies of sustained life aboard the Einstein IV
that were not foreign but domestic?

How those engineers must have debated about cap-
tains clutching their chests and keeling over. How many
man-months must have been spent poring over the various
malfunction modes of all the hardware and software that

kept the ship spinning at just the right rate to create artificial gravity—or the even more complex Inertial Dampers that prevented the ship's acceleration and deceleration from interfering with the same. Broken pipes must have been wargamed, and electrical shorts, and even mundane nuisances like ants and termites, which in space could represent a threat to rival the acid-drooling monsters of antique horror waves. And somewhere in those discussions there must have been a mention or two of how to handle the threat of fire, as the human species had proven quite adept, ever since Prometheus first bestowed his questionable gift, at lighting the most unlikely things on fire at the most inconvenient times.

Also present for these arguments must have been the inescapable bean-counters, laser-focused as ever on cost, and they must have voiced opinions. Counter-measures for fire in the kitchens? Of course, they must have said. In the various engineering spaces, where wires were likely to sit exposed and steadily dripping leaks were unlikely to be noticed and fixed? Without question. But in the dining room? Where the "candles" on the tables were weak, flickering bulbs? Where fondue was never on the menu and never would be? Any fires in the dining room were going to be small, local affairs, blown out as easily as a birthday cake, even by a population as emphysemic as that of the Einstein IV's. So why not throw a couple fire extinguishers on the walls and call it a day? And if that just so happened to save some credit in the process—well, all the better.

But in the crucial meeting with the bean counters, the engineer in charge of safety must have stood up and banged the table and said something like "Damn the cost—fire in the middle of space is nothing to fool around with. The dining room will have a sprinkler system powerful enough to drown a scuba-certified dolphin in 30 seconds, or we won't have a dining room at all, and then how many tickets will you sell, Mr. Bean Counter?"

Jeremiah would have liked to have bought that engineer a beer or ten.

Mere seconds after Jeremiah had saluted Mrs. Biltmore, the ceiling of the dining room had exploded like a tsunami, and for roughly the count of ten managed a passable imitation of Niagara. As the strength and pressure of the downpour ebbed it was downgraded to a mere monsoon lasting for another ten seconds, and finally a ten-second encore of cold spring rain—the kind that promised flowers in the dining room a month or so from now. To Jeremiah's knowledge there was not a dolphin on board—scuba-certified or otherwise—but if there had been, the sprinkler system would have left it floating like a drowned rat. The deluge had drenched the people in the dining room to the bone, the furniture to its joints, and left a good inch of standing water on the floor. It had also—almost as an afterthought—reduced the once promising career of the conflagration that had triggered it to a charred, partially collapsed stage and a sad plume or two of chemical smoke.

Now everyone was sitting—many still shaken, all still soggy—at the dining room tables, sipping the international coffees that Katherine and the rest of the wait staff were delivering, waiting for Battle or Specimen #2 to take their statements. Battle was occupied with Mrs. Mayflower, who was wringing water out of her ermine trim and holding her chin even higher to compensate for the fallen ruff of her collar. Specimen #2 was talking to Mrs. Abdurov, who was—unbcknownst to him—recording the conversation with a pen of her own.

As Jeremiah watched Mrs. Abdurov make faces at Specimen #2, Mr. Drinkwater came and sat beside him.

"Jeremiah," he said, "pinch me! I'm living in a dream. Mrs. Abdurov has invited me to her granddaughter's wedding!"

"Oh," said Jeremiah. It was the best he could manage in the circumstances, but it did not seem to dampen Mr. Drinkwater's enthusiasm at all. "How did that come about?"

"She was right behind me when the stage went up. I turned around and covered her with my own body, to protect her in case of explosion, but at first she fought me."

He paused, and a thoughtful look came over his face.

"She's very fit for a woman of her age and with her health issues. Anyway, I explained what I was doing, but I realized that with all the commotion—and her slight hearing problem, which I doubt you've even noticed—she probably couldn't understand me. So I mimed to her that she was in danger, and that she should follow me and allow me to shield her in the meantime, because I loved her and would gladly give my life for hers."

"You *mimed* all that?" asked Jeremiah.

Mr. Drinkwater nodded.

"And she understood you?"

"She understood me to the *soul*, Jeremiah. When I got her into the hall, and saw that the sprinklers had kicked on and everything was fine, I asked her if she was all right— with words this time—and she called me a mastermind. She said I was more cunning than a cobra and colder than a barracuda, and then she slapped me—and then—" Mr. Drinkwater's whole body melted at the memory. "—I shit you not— she *kissed* me."

Mrs. Abdurov, who was still being interrogated by Specimen #2, looked over at them. She smiled at Mr. Drinkwater, and then gave Jeremiah a deep, angry frown that became a smile attended by a wagging finger.

"Congratulations," said Jeremiah.

"I couldn't have done it without you," Mr. Drinkwater said, standing up and smacking Jeremiah on the shoulder. "I admit, there were moments I doubted you—when you told me to be cold, for example, or broke into my room and made me mime before I was truly ready. But you were right all along. I'm returning to Earth a satisfied man, Jeremiah. Oh, to *hell* with that, a *highly* satisfied man."

Mr. Drinkwater extended his hand, which Jeremiah shook, and then he was on his way, whistling, to wait for Mrs. Abdurov.

Even in his shell-shocked state, the mention of high satisfaction caught Jeremiah's attention. An hour ago his fate had seemed sealed, but now, when he enumerated the impossible duties he had been charged with, Ms. Domenico herself would have had to admit that Jeremiah had scored pretty well.

Mrs. Abdurov had been reunited with Marya Jana and, as a bonus, had found love of the blindest variety. Mr. Drinkwater had found Mrs. Abdurov, and had reason to believe that he had won her heart on the strength of his own mime. Carolus the Bold had found his way back to Mr. Wendstrom—who was not, it turned out, a ghost, but merely malnourished, dehydrated, sleep deprived, and auditorily overstimulated to the point of a psychotic break. Jack had gotten his hands on the elusive green item, and would arrive back to Earth with his anti-System nature intact and his precious mellow unharshed. The talent show had been organized, the stage procured, and—most unlikely and important of all—Mrs. Mayflower would never know what prior mishaps had befallen her bandora at Jeremiah's hands, since subsequent mishaps had reduced it to a piece of charcoal from which neither its own deformed cherubs or any evidence of Jeremiah's negligence could ever escape. If he had not committed the *faux pas* of playing her banjo, Jeremiah would have quite liked his chances.

In fact, he felt so emboldened by his recent string of successes that, when Mr. Roof walked by, Jeremiah accosted him.

"Can I ask you a very direct question?"

"How doubly American of you," said Mr. Roof. "To ask, and to ask if you might ask."

"How very British of you," Jeremiah said, "to pretend you've answered."

Mr. Roof laughed—a rare sight. His laugh consisted of a quick backward toss of the head and a widely open mouth from which no sound escaped, as if he were trying to bite an apple suspended above him as part of some seasonal game.

"May I sit to be interrogated?"

They sat down, Mr. Roof pulling his pants up a few inches first, just as always, and passing his hands along his pant legs to catch any lingering wrinkles afterwards, despite the fact that there were no wrinkles this time, because his thin wool suit was soaked through to his skin and smelled faintly of wet dog.

"Very well, Jeremiah, you may proceed to question me very directly."

"Why are you on the Einstein IV?" asked Jeremiah.

Mr. Roof looked nonplussed, as if this—rather than something about his political views, the balance in his bank account, or his sexual habits—were the one question he could never have predicted that Jeremiah would ask, and might not allow.

"Why shouldn't I be?"

"Are you sick, like most of the other passengers? Or do you want to make sure you live to see some book released, like Mr. Wendstrom? Or are there financial reasons?"

Mr. Roof drew himself up, running his fingers down his damp lapels.

"I am a gentleman, Jeremiah," he began.

"I didn't mean to imply—"

"I'm answering your impertinent question, not your impertinent implication. A gentleman leads a life of leisure. I have never, for example, worked a day in my life, nor do I plan to. But a life of gentlemanly leisure is not a life of total freedom—that is the life of a libertine. A gentleman is obliged to spend his time and credit in particular ways. A gentleman may become as wine-besotted as the next man, but he is *obliged* to besot himself with the finest vintages, or he has fallen short of his calling. Travel is another obligation. The gentleman must associate himself with the climates and peoples of the world. And when a gentleman has traveled the entire globe, not once but several times, having already sought out the unmapped roads and untouristed corners, what does he do then? Where does he travel when no deserts or jungles remain—when he has a favorite café in every city, and has even seen the view from the world's roof? When the very dimensions of *space* offer him no more opportunities?"

He stopped and looked at Jeremiah, waiting.

"So that's it?" said Jeremiah. "You're on this cruise to become a tourist of the future?"

"When you put it like that, Jeremiah," said Mr. Roof, "it quite sucks the romance right out of it."

"One more question, for my own curiosity. Did you have anything to do with Mr. Wendstrom's iguana going missing?"

Mr. Roof frowned.

"Iguanas are born free, and are everywhere in terrariums," he said.

"You mean terraria?" asked Jeremiah.

"I mean terrariums," said Mr. Roof, standing up. "And that is all I have to say on the matter, except that Bernard Wendstrom is a loud vulgarian who made his own credit and cheats abominably at backgammon."

With a snappy little bow, he took his leave.

310

A few minutes later, when Specimen #2 called Mrs. Chapin to be debriefed, Jeremiah wasted no time in reporting the contents of his conversation with Mr. Roof to Mr. Chapin.

He had hoped it would be a discreet operation, but Mr. Chapin was so enthused by Jeremiah's news, and so openly appreciative, that they drew looks from several in the room—including Mrs. Chapin, who was just finishing up her debrief, and whose attention Jeremiah had been especially eager to avoid.

And he did avoid it, by spinning on his heel while eye contact was still plausibly deniable, thereby nimbly escaping Scylla and finding himself face to face with Dr. Charybdis herself.

"Hello, Kimberly."

"Jeremiah," said Kimberly, her damp cheeks glowing and her hair still streaming rivulets, "can you ever possibly forgive me?"

"You know my motto, forgive and—I can never remember the second part."

"Oh Jeremiah, you were always so funny. I will miss that about you."

Which had a very promising ring to it.

"But still," Kimberly continued, "can you forgive me for leaving you to burn alive?"

"I'm not sure what you're talking about, but the good news is that I didn't burn—not alive or any other way."

"But I couldn't have known that. You're my fiancé. When the fire started, I should have rescued *you*. That would have been the Categorical Imperative. But instead—"

Kimberly paused to lower her head, wipe away a tear, and draw a shaky breath.

"—instead I tried to rescue Bradley."

"*Tried*? Is Bradley all right?"

"He's fine," said Kimberly. "He's just over there lying down—he hurt his back while I was carrying him to safety. I already gave him first aid. Oh, it's just like you to worry about *Bradley* after I left you to die. I'm so ashamed of my actions."

"Well, you can't—"

"But this experience also taught me something. I am a rational creature, Jeremiah—but *life* is not rational. It makes no sense. In a blink it can be stolen from you by a raging inferno at a talent show on a spaceship. Only the heart truly understands life. So if my head, citing the Categorical Imperative, tells me to be with you, but my *heart* is telling me to be with Bradley, can I really fight against *life* my whole life? Isn't it better to live with a disapproving head than an unsatisfied heart?"

Jeremiah could find no flaw in this logic.

"Pretend our engagement never even happened," he said. "I wish you and Bradley nothing but happiness."

"Oh, Jeremiah, I knew you'd understand. And I want you to know: Bradley might have my heart—but you will always have my head."

She kissed him on the cheek and started to leave.

"How about the necklace?" said Jeremiah.

"What?"

"If Bradley gets your heart, can I have the necklace back?"

By reflex Kimberly reached up to touch the rich gold and deep rubies, as if she could see them through her fingertips. She frowned—she seemed to think that Jeremiah was asking a lot.

"Of course," she said finally, though she spoke through a frozen smile. "I mean, if our engagement is over."

"Or never even happened," said Jeremiah.

Slowly and deliberately Kimberly reached behind her neck and unclasped the necklace, giving Jeremiah ample opportunity to consider how it looked on her and plenty of time to change his mind if he felt so moved. She could not even look him in the eyes as she handed it to him.

But then, once it was off her person, a weight incommensurate even with the generous amount of gold of which she had divested herself seemed to lift. She laughed—a pleasant sound.

"Take care of yourself, Jeremiah," she said. "Follow your heart."

She practically pranced away en route to administer second aid to the miserable Bradley.

For an instant Jeremiah felt a weight of his own lift as he tested the heft of the necklace in his hand, but he'd hardly had the chance to draw a relieved breath before he felt the crush of a still heavier dilemma. There were two distinct parties expecting delivery of this one necklace, and—as Jeremiah himself had once pointed out to Luis—necklaces were not as easy to split in half as, say, chocolate bars, family fortunes, or even (as recent history had demonstrated) bandoras.

With the benefit of his new clarity, however, Jeremiah realized he had seen tougher conundrums in the buffet line. There was no question where the necklace would be put to better use—the only *real* question was whether he could find Luis before Mrs. Chapin found him.

"Jeremiah," said someone behind him, imbuing his name with distinctive husk and musk.

In other words: no.

"Mrs. *Chapin?*" said Jeremiah, as if he had not even been aware that the two of them were on the same cruise. He turned to face her.

"Jeremiah," she said again, and reached out to take his hand—not, he was happy to see, the one with the necklace. "Oh, Jeremiah. You poor, poor boy. I know everything."

"You *do?*"

"I even know what you told Henry."

"Even *that?*"

"And I'm not upset."

"You're *not?*"

Mrs. Chapin winced—he seemed to be breaking the mood for her, and at this point Jeremiah himself could hardly stand the tonal pattern he had fallen into.

"Well," he said normally and with great effort, "I'm very glad to hear it."

"You gave the necklace to that doctor girl, didn't you?"

"I did," said Jeremiah. Truth—above all, truth. Truth was the only thing that separated us from the animals (though Jeremiah could not identify an occasion on which he had discovered an animal lying to him, he assumed that was an indication of just how good they were at it).

"Because you love her."

"That's—that's right," Jeremiah said. After all, there was not one sole truth in this shades-of-gray universe, but many.

"So Henry wasn't inventing anything when he told me that he'd seen her wearing a necklace similar to mine. He put that together with the hints I had been dropping about youthful passions reawakening, added one and one, and got twelve. Henry thought I was having an affair, didn't he?"

"He—yes," said Jeremiah. "He did." There were higher purposes than mere truth and slavish accuracy.

"With a woman, isn't that right? That doctor girl?"

"It is." Higher purposes than remote accuracy, even.

"Just like when I was back in college. And you told him about my revolutionary activities—breaking your vow of secrecy—because you couldn't stand to see him suffer so under that delusion."

At this Jeremiah could not bring himself to speak, but only to nod—it turned out he did have *some* standards.

"You're taking this very well," he said.

"How could I be angry with you, Jeremiah? Everything you did, you did for love. And—though I know it doesn't show—I am an incurable, dyed-in-the-wool romantic."

Mrs. Chapin leaned in as if to kiss Jeremiah on the cheek, but she blew right by his cheek and kept leaning closer, so close he could smell the perfume sizzling on her wet neck.

"*Viva la revolución*," she whispered. Her voice was like smoke in his ear. The impression was strengthened by the sudden guest appearance of fire. Jeremiah yelped and jumped back: Mrs. Chapin had bitten his earlobe.

As he reached up to check whether the entire earlobe—to which he had always been attached—was still present and accounted for, Jeremiah realized that his right hand was mysteriously freer than it should have been. The mystery did not last long, for he looked and saw that Mrs. Chapin had left his earlobe but come away with the necklace.

Before Jeremiah could make any noise about it, Luis walked up to join the party.

"Jeremiah," he said, "I feel so much all about—*this*."

He waved his arm in the general direction of the smoking, ruinous area that had once been the dining room of the Einstein IV. There was a wide tolerance for error.

"That was you?" said Mrs. Chapin before Jeremiah could reply.

"*Sí*," Luis admitted sadly.

"You're one of the Mexicans Jeremiah told me about. You were responsible for all this?"

"Yes, yes," said the miserable Luis. "Me, just me. No one help me. No one else involve."

"You are a great man," Mrs. Chapin said, pressing the necklace into Luis's hand, "and I know you will do great things with this."

While Luis was still too stunned to speak, Mrs. Chapin leaned in as if to kiss him on the cheek, just as she had with Jeremiah. Judging from Luis's yelp of pain, Jeremiah suspected that she had not settled on a kiss for Luis either.

And then, with a sly smile that could have been meant for either or neither of them, she was gone.

"Jeremiah?" said Luis when he had regained the power of speech.

"Yes, Luis?"

"Jeremiah, I liquored the *hell* out of that son a bitch."

Jeremiah wandered the ravaged dining room for a few minutes, looking in vain for some way to be useful.

"Everyone seems highly satisfied," said someone behind him. It was the one voice that could make him feel somewhat better about the developing trend of people sneaking up behind him and starting to talk, of which in general he was not a fan.

"Hello, Katherine."

"Cup of coffee?"

She walked around in front of him. Unlike Jeremiah and most of the others, Katherine was not soaked. She had been standing in the doorway to the kitchen when the sprinkler system had triggered, so only her shoes and the cuffs of her pants had taken on water. She was carrying two cups of coffee, which she put down at the table next to them. They sat, drying off the seats first with some napkins she produced from her pocket.

Jeremiah took a sip from one of the mugs and made a face.

"Strong?" Katherine said.

"Yes."

"Too strong?"

"Just about right for tonight."

"It has been a big night for you, hasn't it?" she said.

"It has."

315

"Good big or bad big?"

"Mostly good, I guess," said Jeremiah. "Or a bit of both. Or I don't know."

"Do you think now that the incriminating evidence has been destroyed, you've got a chance?"

"Maybe. Earlier today I took a priceless banjo down from Mrs. Mayflower's wall and played it without permission, which she didn't seem pleased about. But I guess I'll find out after the evaluations tomorrow morning."

"Do you think—if things go well tomorrow—that maybe you'd be willing to come visit us back on Earth sometimes? It would be nice to see a friendly face now and again."

"Us?"

"Me."

"Is 'us' you and Reynolds or you and Battle?"

"Does it matter?" asked Katherine. "Would you come?"

"I don't know."

Jeremiah genuinely didn't know. When he had been sure he was about to be stuck on the E4 for another tour, Jeremiah had been more than willing to suffer the vision of Katherine with Battle, as long as their timelines didn't drift apart. Now that there was some hopeful doubt about his own future, the idea seemed impossible to stomach. Emotions in Real Life, Jeremiah was learning, made as little sense as ever, but felt 100 times sharper.

"All right," Katherine said, standing up. "I guess I'll leave you to it. Anyway, congratulations on tying up all your loose ends."

"All but one," said Jeremiah.

"You mean Boyle? No one bats a thousand."

But Jeremiah had not meant Boyle. He had not meant Boyle even remotely.

30

When Biscuits Bite Back

"**G**OOD morning, Jeremiah," said Grubel. Have a seat."

Jeremiah did. Grubel's office felt colder than ever, as if the spirit of the place sensed the tyrannical power it wielded out here in the void waning, and was lashing out desperately in response. The feeling gave Jeremiah some hope.

"Quite a show last night," Grubel said. "Mr. Porter insists that he alone was responsible for what happened. In particular, he claims that you had no knowledge of his intention to use open flame. Is that true? Never mind—what's done is done. Occasions like last night are what insurance is for. And sprinkler systems. Let's take a look at your evaluations."

Mr. Grubel poked at the screen of his desk a few times, dragged something from left to right with his index finger, and examined the results.

"I have to hand it to you, Jeremiah, I was not expecting anything like this. Highly satisfied, highly satisfied, highly satisfied, highly satisfied. Here someone has added a note complaining that there was no option for 'Exquisitely Satisfied.'

"There are remarks about your talents at fostering romance, furthering the cause of social justice without bloodshed, and—ahem—procuring chemical refreshment of high potency. Presumably Jack did not realize that the survey on which he put his name was not anonymous."

"They were iguana treats," said Jeremiah.

"Even Mr. Wendstrom rates himself 'somewhat satisfied', and notes colorfully that—"

Mr. Grubel read from the screen.

"*While Jeremiah is not yet a winner, if Michael L. L. Gregory had half his work ethic, he would have managed to finish* Ultimate Battle Royale *in the last 20 years instead of being on life support, paralyzed, typing it out letter by goddamn letter with some contraption they've hooked up to his eyelids.*"

"Poor Mr. Wendstrom," said Jeremiah. "He's been waiting a long time to read that book."

"A long, unbroken string of satisfied passengers. And then we get to Mrs. Mayflower."

Jeremiah shifted in his seat.

"You have some sense of how important Mrs. Mayflower is to Golden Worldlines," said Grubel. "You have seen the ample residence she maintains here on the Einstein IV, and can imagine how well she pays to do so. So it will come as no surprise to you that I—and Golden Worldlines—take her happiness and satisfaction very, very seriously. But it may come as a surprise to you—it certainly came as one to me—to see her evaluation."

Mr. Grubel made a brushing motion with his left hand, as if waving off an overly eager waiter, and the evaluation leapt to the screen behind his desk.

Unconscionably slow servicing of antique musical instruments, read the evaluation, *but a young banjo player of considerable promise. Il miglior fabbro. Somewhat satisfied.*

Jeremiah's heart surged into his throat. His eyes locked with Grubel's.

"So that's it?" he said. "I'm done? I can go?"

"Not quite," said Grubel. He waved his hands again and another evaluation appeared on the wall behind him.

"Do you know, Jeremiah," he continued, "I'm actually excited. I'm not trying to gloat, or twist the knife. At the beginning I was sure you would flame out in a day or two, but you have—despite some obvious character flaws—latent but undeniable talents. I consider myself something of an expert at ironing out character flaws. With the benefit of my close personal supervision, I believe you could offer valuable service to Golden Worldlines, and I think you'll get something out of working with me, as well. When I look at you—I never thought I would say this—I see myself fifteen years ago. Searching for something that just isn't there. Completely deluded about real life, and what it does and doesn't offer. I learned to take life for what it is. I'm happier now, Jeremiah. Not *happy*. But happier. I think I can help you be happier too."

Jeremiah did not fully absorb this speech, because he was busy reading and re-reading Mrs. Idlewhile's evaluation, meanwhile cursing her, himself, and anyone else he could remotely bring to mind.

I'm not saying he stole my last package of chocolate biscuits, the evaluation read, *but since he fixed my Relaxation Station I haven't been able to find my last package of chocolate biscuits. Highly dissatisfied.*

"We'll have plenty of time to talk about deeper matters like this," Grubel said. "Some administrative details: you have one month Earth leave. No later than 30 days from now you are expected back on the Einstein IV to prepare for her next journey. The space elevator takes a week each way, so I suggest you plan accordingly."

The next shuttle is now boarding at bay ... **FOUR**.

The familiar pair of calm voices made the announcement over the PA, one taking the words and the other swooping in to finish up with the number.

"Not to worry," said Grubel. "The shuttles are for the passengers, then for their luggage, and only then for us. You still have plenty of time."

———————————

"Jeremiah!" said Mr. Chapin. "Come in! Sara is getting her hair done before we board the shuttle, she'll be sorry to have missed you. How did it go? Are you free?"

"Not quite," said Jeremiah. "In fact—in fact I'm here to see if your offer still stands. I could pay you back—at least I hope I could, it depends on the ferrets more than me. But either way, I'd work for you, or for Sara, for the rest of my life—for free. Revolutions, espionage, whatever you want. I'm sorry, it kills me to even ask you this, but—well, there's a girl."

It took Mr. Chapin a moment to understand what Jeremiah was asking for.

"Damn," he said when he had cottoned on. "Damn and double damn. Jeremiah, I wish you had asked me yesterday— we've just moved everything into a triple-blind trust. Given my prognosis, our money guy recommended it as a way to skirt some of the death tax. But there's a 90-day cooling off period, during which we can't touch the assets. I could ask him if we're allowed to sell one of the houses…"

"No," said Jeremiah. "Never mind—I'm sorry I even bothered you with this. It's no big deal. I'll work it out."

———————

Given that competence was one of Katherine's defining traits, Jeremiah figured that she would have been on one of the first shuttles available to the crew. Eager to avoid her, he went to the cafeteria and sat for a while over the saddest bowl of ham soup he had ever experienced. He had managed about a spoonful and a half when Luis and Heriberto joined him.

"There you are," said Luis. "I look all over for you." Out of courtesy, he translated for Heriberto, who nodded in agreement.

"Where are Manny, Carlos, Carlos, Héctor, Adelfo, Humberto, Jesús, and Carlos?" asked Jeremiah.

"They are already getting ready for the shuttles, but I want to find you and offer you a job in the garage I will start with the credit from the necklace. You not allowed anywhere near the veecars. But you can work the desk and keep the books, sí?"

"I would love to," said Jeremiah, "but I didn't pass my review. Maybe if you still need someone in 20 years."

"That sounds like—how you say?—a real banner. But at least you have Heriberto to keep you company." Heriberto, hearing his name, grinned.

"Heriberto's not going to work in the garage?"

"No, I already tell you, he want to stay on the E4. That way he get to read more physics papers. Heriberto is loco for the physics—every two years, he come back and gets 20 years of papers."

"Physics?" said Jeremiah. "I didn't know Heriberto liked physics."

"He don't *like* the physics. He *love* the physics. He is the one invented the—how you say?—inertial pampers?"

"Wait," said Jeremiah, "you mean the Inertial *Dampers*? Heriberto invented Inertial Dampers?"

"Dampers, that's it. Well, he say he no build them, but he the one discover how they should work, because he want to stay on the Einstein and read more papers and he no like making the turn when the cruise is half done, so he invents the Inertial Pampers. I tell you, he *loco* for the physics."

"Wow," said Jeremiah to Heriberto, "I suppose you secretly speak English, too."

He looked at Heriberto for a moment, who looked back at him cheerfully and with no visible comprehension.

"That don't make no sense," Luis said. "Of course Heriberto don't speak no English. If he speak English, why I am translating for him all the time?"

The next shuttle is now boarding at bay ... **NINE.**

"We going to take this one," said Luis. He clasped Jeremiah's hand. "Good luck, Jeremiah. If I continue alive in 20 years, and continue with the garage, and you continue need a job, you come find me on Earth. I wait for you there. And Heriberto sees you in a month."

Heriberto saluted, and the two of them took their leave.

Still hoping to avoid Katherine, Jeremiah did not board the next shuttle, or the next, waiting for the warning that anyone who didn't feel like hanging out on the E4 for the next couple days at least had better hurry on down and get a spot on this, the final shuttle, which he did. As luck would have it, that meant he ended up seated directly across from her.

As they detached from the Einstein IV, Jeremiah tried not to look at Katherine, tried not to notice how her hair began to float in a starburst around her face—tried not to think that this might well be his final memory of her. It was not the sudden desertion of artificial gravity that made his stomach lurch and turn.

Some 20 minutes later the shuttle docked at Tsiolkovsky Station, and as the landing clamps found their grip, Jeremiah felt his body fall back away from the restraint straps and into his seat. After a few minutes of the shuttle's crew radioing cryptic arrival procedures to each other, the airlock clanged and banged and the shuttle door opened. Jeremiah sat and waited while the others—including Katherine—filed through. He was the last one out.

As long as he did not look up, Jeremiah was not unbearably dizzy, but he could not stop looking up. There above him, framed perfectly in the glass ceiling of the concourse, was Earth. The blue marble was merely thousands of miles away now—a stone's throw compared to the light days and weeks tossed around over dinner on the Einstein IV. He was almost home, but he felt farther away than he ever had back on board the Einstein IV. Jeremiah was just managing to hold back the tears until he saw him.

Appleton was standing at the end of the concourse, huge arms folded over his massive chest. He had aged—he was finally old enough to look like the father he had always been to Jeremiah. But like a tree he had aged by becoming bigger and thicker, and now—in his mid 60s—he still looked like he could have lifted the rear of a pickup truck if mood or need struck him. His choice to go bald—which he had made as a young man, long before Jeremiah ever knew him—seemed wiser than ever. All the same there was no doubt that Appleton *was* older—that some of the weight he had added was not muscle but *weight* incurred by a slowing metabolism and 20 years of accumulated worry and trouble.

He stood, planted like an oak, at the end of the concourse, a full head above the next tallest friend or family busily greeting their loved ones, and as Jeremiah walked towards him, Appleton received him in his gigantic brown arms and gathered him in for a bear hug during which Jeremiah could not and did not wish to breathe. Appleton released him, and suddenly both were laughing and slapping each other on the shoulder, their eyes full of water. Appleton's slaps stung.

"I was starting to think I had the wrong Einstein," said Appleton.

"Your auto-responder said you were on vacation."

"Where did you think I was vacationing? Didn't you see my other response?"

"Other response?" said Jeremiah.

"When did you last check your waves? Never mind," Appleton continued after Jeremiah had considered inconclusively for a stretch, "you were always shit about staying in touch."

"I've been a little busy, you know."

"Yes, a life of service, wasn't it? The next elevator car doesn't arrive for a few hours. Buy me a drink and tell me about it."

"What's a beer go for these days?" Jeremiah asked as they started to walk.

"Good beer? 75 credits. The stuff I drink is 50. Here in the bar it's probably worse, with the space elevator prices. We're a week away from the nearest competition."

"Then you're buying, because I'm destitute. I *am* destitute—right?"

"That kind of talk," said Appleton, "is going to require beers safely in hand."

WORLD ENOUGH (AND TIME)

31

Arrivals and Departures

PPLETON drained his beer fully and put the empty mug back on the tray the waitress had just delivered it on.

"Another, please," he said.

"Right," said the waitress. "Just the one?"

"I'm still working on mine," said Jeremiah, by which he meant he had not yet started it.

"I meant for him."

"Let's take it as it goes," said Appleton. He wiped his chin with his napkin and smiled at the waitress as she left.

"Same old Appleton," said Jeremiah. "I thought maybe the eighteen years I gained on you would give me a shot at out-drinking you for once."

"Dream on, Bullfrog. At my funeral I'll drink you under my coffin."

"Tell me about your life. Tell me how you are, how you've been."

"Thriving," said Appleton.

"Details—I'm starved for details."

"Let's tackle the more pressing matters first. To your earlier question: yes, you are destitute."

"But employed—or about to be."

"Voluntarily?"

Jeremiah was taking a sip of beer, so he shook his head.

"On the ship?"

Jeremiah nodded.

"That's going to be a bitch," said Appleton. "The will isn't going to be easy to break in the best of circumstances, but if you're not in the same reference frame, it's not even worth trying."

"So what are my options?"

"Go back on board and work off your debt?"

"What are my options that are at least marginally more pleasant than a swift kick in the family jewels?"

"You *could* just refuse to leave Earth," said Appleton. "Slavery hasn't been legal for centuries, and I doubt Golden Worldlines is going to fly up in a veevan and put a bag over your head."

"Sounds like a great way to end up in jail."

"More like court. We're talking breach of contract, not murder. But you'd lose everything."

"Wait," said Jeremiah, brightening, "that has some promise. My everything is *nothing*."

"I don't mean the everything you have now—I mean everything you ever earn in your life. They'll garnish it till there's nothing left for you to live on."

"All right—option three?"

"You could throw yourself on the mercy of Golden Worldlines and beg them to let you stay on Earth while you contested the will."

"Do you think it would work?"

"No," said Appleton.

"Wait, which part do you think won't work," Jeremiah asked, "begging GW for mercy, or contesting the will?"

"Which part were you asking about?"

"Why did you answer if you didn't know which part I was asking about?"

"Exactly," said Appleton.

Low from Jeremiah's throat came the sound—impossible to represent in the Roman alphabet—of a point being taken but in no way enjoyed.

"Bad option four: you could just disappear. Like every big company, Golden Worldlines loves to litigate, but they're not likely to send mercenaries to hunt you down in a foreign country and bring you back. They'll write off the loss and nail you hard if you ever resurface."

"Just so I understand," said Jeremiah, "bad option four means fleeing creditless into the poorer regions of a world in which I already have no commercial prospects? Sweeping barroom floors for peanuts and sleeping in the park? That kind of thing?"

"It wouldn't quite be creditless—I could give you some pocket credit. Otherwise, yes, you've got it."

Appleton folded his arms, tucking his ham-hock hands beneath his boulder biceps. He looked miffed and slightly embarrassed with his inability to cut this knot. It was not an attitude Jeremiah had seen him strike often. He could remember only once, when Filibuster, Jeremiah's first and only dog, had been hit by a veecar. Jeremiah liked to see Appleton like this even less than he imagined the big man liked to feel this way. It was disquieting to be reminded that there were powers in the world greater even than Appleton—forces as cold and impersonal as he was warm. Jeremiah wanted so badly to make him feel better that he almost mentioned bad option number five—turn in Reynolds for suspicion of murdering Boyle and earn such massive PR credit that Golden Worldlines would be unable to sue him. But Katherine's decision to find a little lakeside cottage with John Battle could not change how Jeremiah felt about her, or how he wanted her to continue to feel about her adopted father.

"Stay on Earth and prepare myself for a lifetime of lawsuits it is, then," he said.

"I'm concerned you're still not clear on the drawbacks of that option," said Appleton. "Let me run the numbers for you: from every ten credits you earn in the remainder of your natural life, Golden Worldlines will take eleven."

"I get it, but I don't have a choice." Jeremiah took a sip of light liquid courage, sighed, and admitted the shocking truth. "There's a girl."

"Of course there's a girl. I know that."

"How could you possibly—"

"There's always a girl. Even during a two-year journey on a deep space old folk's home, you managed to find a girl. Just how old is this girl?"

"I think about 200," said Jeremiah, "give or take."

"A 200-year-old singer?" said Appleton.

"She's a waitress."

"Oh, Bullfrog, tell me you haven't forgotten the one useful piece of advice Leo gave you. Never fall in love with anyone—"

"Who works for tips. I know."

"Given any more thought to another beer, handsome?" asked the waitress, who had walked up to the table during this exchange.

Appleton inclined his head, as if to point out exhibit A.

"Bourbon," he said. "With a bourbon chaser." He turned back to Jeremiah. "Jeremiah, listen very carefully: forget the girl. She sounds wonderfully mature, but there's always another girl. If you go back on the Einstein IV, ten minutes later there'll be a new girl."

"Not like this one. This one is different."

"Because she's 200 years old?" asked Appleton.

"Because she's different."

"Is she 'different' because she hates credit? Otherwise I can't see her interest in you surviving very long. And I don't mean 'hates credit' as in 'believes that too much credit can be bad for you,' I mean 'hates credit' as in 'I've always wanted to try not having enough credit to buy food to put in my mouth and chew.' "

"She's going back to Earth to live in a lakeside house— possibly with my rival, who is basically the expression of genetic perfection. Or she thinks she is—she doesn't know how much lakeside property costs."

"Then what the hell are we even talking about?" said Appleton. "It's a raw deal, Bullfrog, and I'll miss the hell out of you, but there's only one real option: go back and do your time on the ship. And honestly, kid, maybe working for a living wouldn't be the worst thing in the world for you."

Jeremiah was about to suggest that, as the collective stewards of Jeremiah's future, they could perhaps set the bar a little higher than an option that could still be, by Appleton's own formulation, the *second* worst thing in the world for him, but while he was phrasing the thought he was interrupted by the arrival of Katherine, who walked up and stood at the side of their high table.

"I'm sorry to interrupt," she said. "I wanted to say goodbye."

As it seemed that Jeremiah's wits were not available for

immediate response, Appleton took matters in hand himself.

"Hello, I'm Appleton," he said, standing up and offering his hand.

"Appleton," said Katherine. She took the huge proffered hand in both of her own, leaving plenty of room to take it with two or three more hands if she'd had them. "It's so good to put a face to the name." She gave an odd smile, as if at the impersonal pleasure of finding a face that lived up to the stories that had preceded it.

By this time the desperate manhunt for Jeremiah's wits had yielded fruit.

"This is Katherine," said Jeremiah to Appleton. "She's the one I was telling you about."

"Katherine," Appleton said. "It's a pleasure. I see that Jeremiah was telling the truth: you *are* different."

Both Katherine and Appleton were now blushing slightly, equally aware that their non-traditional handshake had gone on too long, neither wanting to be the first to break contact. Jeremiah had seen such moments before, when two people of real quality encountered each other and, like two rare elements, underwent a reaction, as if in all the ways that mattered they had understood each other immediately and completely. Everything about this meeting seemed like it should have been taking place in the glow of a Christmas tree, with children running and chattering in the background, and the entire experience could not have thrilled Jeremiah more or made him more miserable.

Appleton finally took his hand back.

"Why don't I give the two of you a minute," he said.

"So," said Katherine. She sat down in the seat that Appleton had left.

"So."

"How did it go? Are you a free man or—"

Jeremiah shook his head.

"I'm sorry," said Katherine. "What are you going to do?"

"That mostly depends on your views regarding extreme poverty and / or running away with me."

"Jeremiah—"

"Wait, please, I need to say something."

In fact Jeremiah needed to tell her a great many things: about how he understood she had looked into the world's absurd heart and decided to be kind, about life and what it was and wasn't, about how he realized now that Real Life had always been there, trying to reach his heart, and the glass hadn't been *out there* somewhere but *inside himself*. But the words wouldn't come, and he could feel the clock ticking.

"Isn't there something between us, Katherine?" he said instead.

"Yes," she said. "And in the storybook, you're the right choice—the charming ne'er-do-well with the heart of gold. But the thing about ne'er-do-wells in real life is that they never do very well."

If Katherine and he had been engaged in a debate team competition, this would have been about the moment that Jeremiah waved a white flag and proposed post-debate drinks at a nearby bar, but too much was at stake here to let mere logic and force of argument carry the day. While he was still gathering his thoughts for the return salvo, however, Reynolds approached the table.

"Sorry to interrupt. It's nice to see you two young people together," he said. "Jeremiah, I owe you an apology. Two, actually. I left you to your own devices a bit in the office— no, I did, I did—and a bit in the dark about why. You see that little girl over there?"

Reynolds did his hands-free glasses swap, and Jeremiah looked out into the hallway where Reynolds was looking and saw what appeared to be a mother with her child. The mother was wearing loose, colorful robes that looked African to him, and holding the child—who must have been approaching two years of age—upright on a beautifully fashioned rocking horse of wood. The child was rocking. When the mother saw them looking at her, she urged the child to wave to Reynolds, and then did so herself.

"The mother is Marai. She was four months pregnant when she came on board," Reynolds said, "running from the troubles in Sierra Leone. Technically GW doesn't hire pregnant women, but they don't look too closely either, and once we were underway and Claudetta was born, what were they going to do, shoot her out of an airlock? Anyway, I just fell in love with the child. I became something of an unofficial grandpa. Now that we'll be going our separate ways—they're heading back to Sierra Leone since things

330

have had a couple decades to calm down a bit—I wanted her to have something to remember me by, so I dusted off my old woodworking skills and built that rocking horse. That's why I wasn't around much.

"And then I was rude to you in the storeroom, when you caught me flatfooted with the pesticide. The last pieces of wood I found for the rocking horse were lousy with termites, and I was worried someone would get upset if they found out I was using GW materials for a personal project. I should have just told you. But all's well that ends well. Good luck to you, young man."

Reynolds put his hand on Jeremiah's shoulder and shook him gently, as if testing a pylon he'd just driven.

"Anyway, Katherine," he said, "I'll see you on the elevator?"

"Of course, Dad. John and I will find you."

"Ah, excellent," said Reynolds, but he didn't sound too pleased at the prospect of making the journey back to ground level in Battle's company, and Jeremiah loved him for it.

"So if it wasn't him—" Jeremiah said to himself as Reynolds rejoined Marai and Claudetta in the hall.

"If what wasn't him?" Katherine asked.

"Nothing," said Jeremiah, too quickly, "just thinking out loud."

"You mean if it wasn't him who killed Boyle?" Katherine said. "Of *course* it wasn't him. What's wrong with you?"

"I just said it *wasn't* him."

"Which means that at some point you thought it *was*. Because of the pesticide he was talking about?"

"That, and his unexplained absences, and his cold manner when we examined the body. You have to admit, it was all suspicious. And then there was his access to the keycards."

"You thought Alfred Reynolds, who took me in when my grandmother died, and who builds rocking horses for refugees from Sierra Leone in his spare time, was a murderer because he had access to an encoder for our oh-so-reliable keycards? The same keycards that stopped working for the whole ship one morning?"

"I see now how foolish that was, but to be fair, not *everyone's* keycard stopped—wait," said Jeremiah. "Of course. How could I not have seen that before?"

"Seen what?"

Jeremiah looked around and immediately found the man he was looking for sitting across the bar.

"Follow me for a second," he said to Katherine.

Cornelius Werther was sitting alone, swirling a cloudy tumbler of scotch and staring so deeply into it that he did not even notice Jeremiah and Katherine approach.

"It was you," Jeremiah said to him. "Wasn't it?"

Mr. Werther jumped, and for a split second his face took on a look of panic, but almost immediately he smiled in the profoundest relief.

"Thank God," he said. "How did you know?"

"It was the keycard," said Jeremiah. "Everyone else's stopped working, while you 'lost' yours. But you didn't lose it at all, did you? You swapped it with Boyle's card, so he would think his had stopped working, instead of reporting it missing. But why did the all the other passengers have problems with their cards too? Coincidence?"

"I swapped theirs with each other. As many as I could get my hands on, to throw up a kind of smokescreen."

"But why did you do it?" asked Jeremiah. "I mean, why did you kill him?"

Werther closed his eyes for a few seconds, remembering.

"She's a lovely woman, Elizabeth. Physically, of course, but also in her spirit. The sweetest soul you could ever hope to meet. None of this," he added hastily, "was her idea. Make sure you tell them that."

"Them?" asked Katherine.

"The police. *He* wanted to divorce *her*, did you know that? The way he carried on, you would have thought she had been lying in wait to ambush him with divorce papers the moment she found out about the lottery ticket. But he'd already retained a lawyer before he even bought it."

He frowned at his drink.

"Do you think I could have a glass of water?" he asked.

Jeremiah and Katherine looked at each other. Both started to stand up at the same moment.

"No," Mr. Werther said, waving his hand, "I've changed my mind again."

He drained his scotch in one pull instead, made a face as it burned, and then continued.

"She came to my firm for advice when she found out he'd booked this trip. She had questions about what the time dilation would mean for their shared custody of the children, her right to sell the house, and so on.

"I knew right then, the first moment that I saw her, that I would do anything for her. Whatever the consequences, whatever the cost, I couldn't permit this creature in front of me to suffer any more.

"It was insane, of course—impossible. I was old enough to be her father—her grandfather, in some parts of the country. There was no way she could possibly think of me that way. But as I worked on her case—*pro bono*, of course—I began to hope against hope. She found excuses to stop by—she baked things. She touched her hair when she spoke.

"I know what you're thinking," said Mr. Werther, and he smiled ruefully. "That she was playing me. That she is still playing me. But you don't know Elizabeth—that would have been impossible for her. And there's no way she could have known, ahead of time, about the technicality."

He paused to wipe his forehead with a napkin. A smudge of green ink from the bar's logo stayed behind.

"I discovered that they weren't really divorced, you see. It was one of those idiotic procedural things, but it opened the door to a whole host of disasters if Boyle decided he wanted to cause trouble. He could say he'd changed his mind and refuse to sign the updated papers, or re-open negotiations. Worst of all, he was about to get on this ship for 20 years—from her point of view. And if she happened to die while he was on his cruise—which was the whole point of his taking the cruise, after all—her children might get nothing. He never cared about those children. Did you ever even hear him mention once that he had children?"

Jeremiah shook his head.

"He has three. Had. So I decided: I would tell everyone— Elizabeth included—that I had been diagnosed with something. As far as she knew, I was just another of the traveling sick, putting my hopes on the future. I would spend everything I had on a ticket, and I would go on the cruise with Boyle—but only one of us would return. In the meantime Albert Einstein would have allowed Elizabeth to gain eighteen years on me, and we would make a perfectly respectable October / December romance. Not an eyebrow would be raised.

"And that's all there is to it," said Mr. Werther. "There aren't many reasons to kill a man, and mine was love. You have no idea how hard it is to carry that around for two years—the intention to end a life. They say confession is good for the soul. That remains to be seen, but it is a relief. Now if you'll excuse me, I believe I need to visit the restroom."

"Wait," said Katherine. "Why did you wait so long to do it? You could have killed him at any time."

"I wanted to make sure that Elizabeth would still be alive when I returned, of course. It's not as if I were eager to commit murder, and a lot can happen to someone in 20 years."

"Photos from Beth's 65th birthday party," said Katherine, remembering. "The wave you received."

"Yes," Mr. Werther said. "How did you—never mind, it doesn't matter. Thank you—thank you both. It's not an easy thing, to kill a man, and harder to live with, even if it was the right thing to do. You have no idea what a relief it has been to tell the truth. I don't think I'll make it to the restroom. Remember to tell them that Elizabeth had nothing to do with it—and please tell her that when I fell asleep, I was thinking of her."

With that, he pitched forward on the table.

32

That's What You Do

Still Sunday (day of arrival)

KATHERINE, Appleton, and Jeremiah stood in the hallway, leaning against a stretch of wall next to the gray door of the space elevator's security office. Katherine had folded her arms first. A few minutes later—unconsciously, it seemed—Appleton had followed suit. Jeremiah had fought as long as he was able, but now he too had folded his arms, feeling like the three of them were posing for the cover of their latest album, which was not how Jeremiah wanted to be feeling after what he and Katherine had just witnessed.

Occasionally a muffled shout or soft thud made it through the door. Inside the office, the elevator's security officer was interviewing the bartender who had served Werther his fatal libation.

"*The next earthbound elevator departs in* TEN *minutes*," Jeremiah's favorite duo proclaimed over the station's PA. Appleton, Katherine, and Jeremiah all looked at each other.

"That's enough for me," she said, "I'm leaving. John and Alfred will be waiting for me at the elevator."

"I'd advise against it," Appleton said. "Wait it out, answer the questions the security guy asks you, and then be on your way."

"No," said Katherine, unfolding her arms and stepping away from the wall. "I've had enough. I just saw a man kill himself right in front of me, and I don't have any desire to answer that guy's pointed questions about it. He's not the police after all, just a squinty little security officer."

"He did squint a lot," Jeremiah agreed, "but Appleton has a point. The real police are bound to get involved once you're back on the ground, and you don't want any trouble."

"Just tell him I had to go," said Katherine. "Well, Jeremiah, I guess we solved the mystery after all. It didn't feel like I hoped."

"Me neither," he said.

She seemed to be considering a kiss on the cheek, and for his part Jeremiah was considering throwing himself at her feet and begging her not to leave like this, but before either of them could decide one way or another on either of these courses of action, they became aware of a crowd gathering around one of the screens mounted on the wall across from them. Someone turned up the volume.

Take 5 News, a man's deep voice announced over a thrumming bass line, *all the news from the last five minutes, brought to you in just 60 seconds. Because the news never takes five—and neither do we.*

"This just in," chirped the severe blonde anchorwoman. "Wall Street darling Golden Worldlines is filing for Chapter Eleven. Its share price plummeted in after-hour markets on the news."

"According to an unnamed source," continued the swarthy anchorman to her right, "the cruise line's difficulties began with the departure of one of their most frequent—and profitable—passengers, exposing what one financial analyst is calling an 'unsound business model that is 20 years out of date.' "

"You'll have more on this breaking story the minute we do," promised the anchorwoman, and both smiled in horrifying unison as the shot cut away.

"This segment sponsored by Barnaby's Wood Adhesive," a resonant baritone informed viewers. "Nothing adheres better to wood. Nothing."

Just at that moment, before the viewers who had assembled in the middle of the hall could even gasp collectively, another disturbance compelled them to abandon the center of the passageway and hug the walls. Moving through the concourse like a presidential motorcade, eleven surprisingly spry butlers in Edwardian tails jogged in formation around a courtesy cart piloted by what appeared to be a linebacker sporting sunglasses and a chauffeur cap. Perched exquisitely on the back of the cart, wearing a smart white pants suit with matching pillbox hat and holding a pink clutch on her bended knees, rode Mrs. Mayflower.

When she saw Jeremiah, she raised her hand, and the motorcade stopped short just in front of him. Two of the butlers slid aside to give her a clear line of sight.

"You were right," Mrs. Mayflower said to Jeremiah.

This was not a phrase Jeremiah had heard much in recent memory, and he required clarification.

"It was Uncle Dave *Macon*," said Mrs. Mayflower.

"You're going back to Earth," Jeremiah said, and Mrs. Mayflower pursed her lips in disappointment that he should have squandered the capital he had so recently acquired by spouting something so obvious. Her hand fluttered, as if she might signal her motorcade to drive on and end the conversation there. But it seemed she was in a celebratory mood.

"I am going to establish my museum," she said. "Through an intermediary I have acquired a swath of land near Montreal. He reports that the area is accessible, the climate sufficiently temperate, and the radiation levels low enough to allow for the preservation of the antiquities. The site inhabits a microclimate where the rain is unusually free of acid, so that the stones of the cloister that made up my courtyard may be exposed to the natural air. Construction will begin as soon as the stones can be transported from the Einstein IV, and if we do not welcome our first visitors sometime next year, I shall be greatly disappointed."

Her tone of voice suggested that for Mrs. Mayflower disappointment was not an unpleasant emotional state for her to occupy, but a state of *activity*, in which she planned to cause widespread and unpleasant emotional states in others.

"Perhaps it *is* selfish of me not to take the collection even further into the future," she said, as if Jeremiah had asked as much, "but recent, tragic events have made me realize that it is neither possible nor desirable to wrap these instruments in perfect safety. I want more than just to see them hang untouched in the perfect temperature and ideal humidity. I wish to hear them played. I believe I have earned that."

She frowned.

"I *hope* I have earned that. Roosevelt, what is the meaning of this?"

Roosevelt the butler had just arrived, staggering and panting as if he had once been the twelfth escort of the motorcade but, unable to maintain the pace set by the younger members of the cadre, had fallen off somewhere along the concourse. At the moment, despite Mrs. Mayflower's question, he did not appear able to explicate his exertion to any degree beyond what was already evident. He bowed shakily instead, and when he came back up his face was red.

"Do we have any Darjeeling?" Mrs. Mayflower asked him.

"No, milady," he said, with a pronounced breath in between the words.

"Bring me some. And for God's sake, don't run."

"But the elevator is about to depart, milady," Roosevelt said.

Mrs. Mayflower narrowed her eyes slightly as she responded.

"They will hold it."

Roosevelt bowed again and departed at a brisk but dignified pace.

"As for you, young man," said Mrs. Mayflower, turning back to Jeremiah, "the next time you are in the vicinity of Montreal, you are welcome to exercise the banjos."

She lifted her hand as if refusing a drink. With a fluid grace the detail of butlers slid back into formation and the courtesy cart started off with a jerk that did nothing to upset either Mrs. Mayflower's equanimity or her pillbox hat.

Eventually Jeremiah would have broken out of the daze caused by Mrs. Mayflower's visit and turned back around to face his friends, but without Appleton's timely clearing of the throat, he might have been too late to catch sight of Katherine walking quickly away from him down the hall.

"Wait!" he cried, but he did not wait himself to see if she would listen before running after her, which was just as well, as she did not stop until he had trotted up to her side.

"What do you want?"

"To see if you were all right," said Jeremiah.

"Why wouldn't I be? Because every credit I had in the world just went up in smoke with GW's stock, and any chance to return to my job along with them?"

"Now that you mention it, yes."

"I'm fine. Thanks for checking. Glad that things worked out for you—good luck with the ferrets. Goodbye."

She turned to leave again, but Jeremiah caught her hand.

"Wait. Things haven't worked out for me—not even remotely. Not if you turn around and walk out of my life."

"We have been over this, Jeremiah."

"Things are different now. We're both free, we can do whatever we want."

"What are you proposing? That I come live with you while Appleton wrests your uncle's credit from the ferrets, and then we live a life of travel and excitement, vowing to take in any stray iguanas or ferrets we happen upon in the meantime?"

"That sounds pretty good to me," said Jeremiah.

"No, Jeremiah," Katherine said, detaching her hand from his. "I don't need to be kept—I don't want to be kept."

"I'm not trying to keep you—I'm trying to keep myself *with* you."

"What am I supposed to do in the meantime? Pretend that you're not taking me in when I have just about enough credit to my name to buy a beer in that horrible bar?"

"So what are you planning to do?" said Jeremiah. "Go with Battle? Go with Reynolds? Fine. Just tell me where, so I can get in touch with you."

"I don't know where I'm going yet. Wherever I can find work. It's not like I can go back on the E4 and get my old job back."

"Wait a minute," said Jeremiah. "Maybe you can."

He looked through the crowd in the hall until he spotted his target standing not far away.

"Mr. Wendstrom!" he said. "Bernie!"

Wendstrom's general appearance had improved dramatically after some food, a night of chemically assisted slumber, and of course the joyous reunion with Carolus the Bold. Instead of a ghost he now looked like a man who had recovered from a grave illness just in time to barely survive being hit by a truck—and who was now beet-red with fury and biting his tongue.

"What ith it?" Mr. Wendstrom asked, apparently unable to release his tongue long enough for lispless speech.

"I know why you're angry," said Jeremiah. "Because Michael L. L. Gregory is still working on the last book, but since GW is bankrupt, you can't take another cruise while he finishes. Right?"

Hearing the tragedy of his situation summarized so succinctly was almost too much for Mr. Wendstrom. He nodded, but he was now biting down so hard that Jeremiah feared for the structural integrity of his tongue.

"I know what you can do," said Jeremiah. "Buy Golden Worldlines."

Slowly, slowly, like a dog releasing a favorite ball, Mr. Wendstrom eased his teeth from his tongue.

"Not a bad idea," he said. "If I've got the credit."

He whipped out a communicator and began to speak into it in low tones. There was a moment of tense silence as he waited for the person on the other end.

"Get it done," said Mr. Wendstrom, full voice. "And put it all in Carolus's name—just in case."

He hung up.

"It seems that while we've been away," he said, "my brand value has skyrocketed. A lot more winners up there than there used to be." He looked with fondness at the blue marble through the glass ceiling, which had been showering credit upon him in his absence. "And GW is a distressed asset, so I'm getting it on the cheap."

"Congratulations," said Jeremiah. "Now that you're about to own GW, can Katherine have her old job back?"

"Waiting tables?" said Wendstrom. "Wouldn't you rather run the dining room instead?"

"I—yes," said Katherine.

"What about me?" Jeremiah said. "Can I have my old job back too? Working in Guest Services?"

Bernie Wendstrom looked him up and down, narrowing his eyes skeptically.

"I don't know, Jeremiah. I have some questions about your methods. I have this nagging suspicion that you got lucky."

"I had some luck at the end," said Jeremiah, "but I had

340

to stay in the game long enough to get lucky—which wasn't easy. And I had the idea for you to buy GW. Anyway, I thought losers focus on methods. Winners see only results."

Wendstrom took a step back, as if to escape the explosion of his own faithless petard. Then he stopped and considered Jeremiah for a moment.

"All right," he said at last. "At the end of the day, you did smooth things over with Porter. Carolus the Bold is back where he belongs, and thanks to you he might still get to read *Final Battle Royale* before he dies. You've earned a shot—but just a shot. One chance to prove to me that you're actually a winner, Jeremiah. Don't blow it."

"I won't. Thank you, Mr. Wendstrom. Appleton, let the ferrets keep the credit. Oh, and there's a guy who I worked with on the E4—Luis—who was wrongly accused of stealing a veecar. He's got some credit now and wants to start a repair shop with some friends. Would you take him under your wing and make sure things work out for him?"

"Of course I will," said Appleton, "but are you sure about this?"

"Never surer."

"Never mind," said Katherine. "I mean, thank you for your offer, Mr. Wendstrom, but on second thought I've decided I'm not going back to the E4."

"Me neither," said Jeremiah. "But thank you, Mr. Wendstrom. Appleton, prepare yourself for battle—we're going to wrest my birthright from the clutches of those grubby little weasels. I still want you to help Luis, though."

"Actually, Mr. Wendstrom, on third thought, I'd love to run the dining room," said Katherine.

"In that case," said Jeremiah, "I would also—"

"Damn it," said Bernie Wendstrom, "would you two make up your minds? I have a business to run."

"Are you just going to go wherever I don't?" Jeremiah asked Katherine.

"Are you just going to go wherever I do?"

"Of course I am. That's what you do when you're in love with someone."

"So now you're in love with me?"

"Of course I'm in love with you."

"We've never even kissed," Katherine said.

"A shocking omission that we should remedy at the very first opportunity."

"What if I don't *want* you to be in love with me?"

"Finally we've found something that's none of *your* business," said Jeremiah. "What *is* your business is deciding if you love me. Or even if you *could*, maybe, someday. Because I can't possibly face a future where our worldlines diverge—not if there's any chance, the remotest snowflake's chance in hell, that maybe you might change your mind. It's not like I'm asking you, right now, to go live with me on a lake instead of John Battle. Just let me stay on the same side of Albert Einstein."

"Oh, for the love of God," said Katherine, "I'm not moving in with John Battle. We've been on a few dates. Don't grin so widely—you and I haven't even been on one."

"Maybe not, but we solved a murder, liberated an iguana, and breathed together with the stars—and I wouldn't trade that for anything. Look, Katherine, all I'm asking is for a chance, and I'm willing to fight for it, but if you really want me out of your life, tell me right now—say those words—and I'll never bother you again."

Jeremiah held his breath through the most anxious seconds in all of his life, Real or otherwise. But as five seconds became ten, and ten became 20, Katherine opened her mouth but did not say the fateful words.

"That's good enough for me," Jeremiah said finally. "I'm going where you're going. Which is?"

A crowd was slowly gathering around them in the concourse. Henry and Sara Chapin had stopped to watch, as had Luis, Manny, Héctor, Adelfo, Humberto, Jesús and Carloses one through three, one of whom was nodding and giving the thumbs up. The security officer and bartender had just emerged from the office as well, the latter looking shaky and the former warmed up.

"You," said the security officer, pointing to Jeremiah, "you're next."

"Just a minute," Jeremiah called back. Then, to Katherine: "Say the word and we'll stay here on Earth and make a go of this insane future that neither of us knows the first thing about."

"What if I'd rather go back to the E4?"

"Then we'll go back," said Jeremiah. "I'll help crazy rich people arrange romances and fix their PEDs and track down their missing iguanas, and you'll serve them venison that tastes like oysters and oysters that taste like venison and brighten their long empty days immeasurably. And every day I'll wake up and overflow with gratitude for whatever absurd chance in this cold universe brought me to you, while life on Earth gets weirder and weirder, and we fall further and further out of step with it, just an old-fashioned romance smeared in slow motion across the stars."

By now they were surrounded by spectators. Alistair Roof had taken a spot next to the Chapins. Porter was there, looking somewhat insane with tears in his eyes, above which both brows had been singed away. And there was Drinkwater, his arm linked with Mrs. Abdurov's, who was smiling. Kimberly was clapping her hands in delight at the romance playing out in front of her, and Bradley was managing to keep his jealous fury simmering at a brooding intensity. Appleton had folded his bulging arms, but was smiling broadly with the air of a father whose son was finally wobbling down the street free of training wheels. Beside him, Alfred Reynolds looked pleased as punch to see the receding possibility of drinking said punch with John Battle every Christmas. And there was Heriberto, grinning like the mad genius it turned out he was, and Jack, mellow as a fall day in New England, and even Grubel, looking as sentimental as it was possible to look while being a possibly jobless bureaucrat and wearing lensless glasses. Here and there, patches of turquoise wool peeked through the crowd.

"You," said the security officer to Jeremiah again, "my office, now."

"Well?" said Jeremiah to Katherine. "What do you say?"

"I need a minute to think," she said.

"She needs a minute to think," said Jeremiah to the security officer.

"60 seconds," countered the security officer, squinting to show he meant business.

Jeremiah waited in silence. It seemed the entire crowd was holding its breath.

"Katherine?"

"I *said* I need a *minute*."

"You've already had 20 seconds," said the security officer.
"Then I have 40 left."
Jeremiah started to count in his head.
"Come on, Katherine," he said precisely 40 Mississippis
later. "While we're still young."

A Word About Reviews

Dear Reader,

First of all, thank you for reading *World Enough (And Time)*. I imagine that, like most modern men and women, you have a lot going on and limited opportunity for leisure, and I deeply appreciate that you've invested a decent chunk of that leisure time in reading my book.

So I don't take it lightly when I ask if you'd be willing to spend a bit more of your time posting a review of the book you've just read.

Readers are generally wary of taking a risk on an author they haven't read before, and that goes doubly for independent authors. Nothing gives an independently published book the patina of respectability—and encourages new readers to take a chance—like honest reviews from real readers.

If you'd be willing to take a few minutes right now and post a review on Amazon or Goodreads, I'd be eternally grateful. The review doesn't have to be long, or fancy—just a few honest sentences saying what you liked (or didn't) about the story.

I've created some shortcuts so you don't have to search around on Amazon and Goodreads:

https://ewj.io/weat-amazon will take you to the right Amazon page.

https://ewj.io/weat-goodreads will take you to the right Goodreads page.

In any event, thank you again for reading *World Enough (And Time)*, and cheers.

Edmund

Acknowledgements

Jeff Ward created the excellent cover art. You can see more of his work, and hire him yourself, at stungeonstudios.com.

Moira Racich designed the excellent cover. She is also a very fine painter, whose art can be found at moiraracich.com.

I am grateful to the friends who read and responded to early drafts of this book: Kevin Crowe, Ben Johnson, Stephanie Nelson, Deirdre Ralston, and Eric Yablonowitz.

Annie Stone gave me invaluable advice about the position of the book in its genre and the broader market.

Brianna Duff and Ellie Redding both provided detailed feedback and suggestions that strengthened the story considerably.

In addition to his novel-length feedback email, which was instrumental in making this a better book, Dan Milstein was extremely generous with his scarce time when it came time to write marketing materials and the like.

Robin Jorgensen and Jessica Werner both read multiple drafts and responded with helpful commentary.

Brian Jorgensen read every page of every draft, or damn near it, and helped the book find its heart in the process.

From the bottom of *my* heart, thank you all.

Finally, my profoundest gratitude, and all my love, to Mónica and Patrick.

About the Author

Edmund Jorgensen is the author of the novels *Speculation* and *World Enough (And Time)*. He has also written a short story collection *Other Copenhagens (And Other Stories)*.

He lives in Stoneham, MA with his wife and empirically adorable son.

You can find out more about him on his website, http://www.inkwellandoften.com, and sign up for his email list at http://ewj.io/signup.

Edmund welcomes email at ewj@inkwellandoften.com.

About this Book

World Enough (And Time) was produced almost entirely using open-source software.

The manuscript was written using the Emacs text editor[1], primarily employing org mode[2] and markdown mode[3].

Pandoc[4] drove the conversion to e-book formats, with some custom filters written in Python[5] and the pandoc-filters library[6].

The printed edition was produced with Pandoc and LaTeX[7], using some custom scripts in the GNU version of Awk[8].

All the above was orchestrated with the venerable GNU Make[9].

I am deeply indebted to the men and women who develop, maintain, and document all this excellent software and make it freely available for general use.

---

[1] https://www.gnu.org/software/emacs
[2] https://orgmode.org
[3] https://jblevins.org/projects/markdown-mode
[4] https://pandoc.org
[5] https://www.python.org
[6] https://github.com/jgm/pandocfilters
[7] https://www.latex-project.org
[8] https://www.gnu.org/software/gawk
[9] https://www.gnu.org/software/make

Made in United States
North Haven, CT
30 November 2021

11743363R00214